SPY FOR A SPY

SPY FOR A SPY

SPY ANOTHER DAY series
Book Two

Jordan McCollum

DURHAM CREST BOOKS

Cover design by Steven Novak

SPY FOR A SPY © 2013 Jordan McCollum

This is a work of fiction. Names, characters, businesses, places, events and incidents are either the products of the author's imagination or used in a fictitious manner. Any resemblance to actual persons, living or dead, or actual events is purely coincidental.

First printing, 2013

Published by Durham Crest Books
Orem, Utah
Set in Linux Libertine

ISBN 978-1-940096-03-2

PRINTED IN THE UNITED STATES OF AMERICA

For Ben and Diana, my parents,
who appear nowhere in these pages,
other than the acknowledgments where they belong.

Thank you.

CHAPTER 1

I DON'T DO LACE. Or ruffles. Or frills. In fact, I don't do tulle, taffeta, satin, sequins, bows, beads, flowers or froof.

Then again, until a month ago, I didn't do marriage, either.

So I was wrong on one count. But the other things? I'm less than excited to spend my lunch break twirling for my sort-of friends in any of the above and acting like I love every second. Of course, none of the girls from church know I'm a spy.

I have another hour before I face them and the long hard look in the mirror—and first, I kinda have to finish that spy gig. With a breath to cool my climbing heart rate, I adjust the headset of my classified listening device. No noises from the next apartment, even over the sound of my partner's silenced drill (not loud) and the dress shopping anxieties still ringing through my brain (loud). If our "luck" holds, Justin and I will finish setting up surveillance on our new Russian friends in plenty of time for my stupid lunch date.

"You're cute when you're focused, Talia." Justin pauses his drilling and waits until I meet his eyes before he winks.

"Wish I could say the same, but I've never seen you fo-

1

cused. Or cute."

He grimaces and turns back to his silent drilling. "Is that acerbic wit how you finally landed a man?"

I scoff. "Yeah, you're the expert on man-catching." Justin's an incurable flirt (and straight), but he's not interested in me. He just thinks it's hilarious to make me squirm since I got engaged five weeks ago.

Or maybe Justin's about-face has more to do with the fact I always worked more closely with someone else who saw himself as a charmer. Elliott made a great buffer until he and Will transferred to the embassy a month ago. But I can handle Justin. With a pointed glance at my listening device, I remind him we've got work to do. Yeah, high tech gadgets really are part of a spy's repertoire, though I can't say much about this one unless I want to risk a gruesome fate at the hands of DS&T, our version of Bond's Q. So let's leave it at a twenty-first century glass against the wall.

The neighbors' apartment is quiet. Maybe too quiet, since somebody's supposed to be home. If not, our job's easier: we can place this contact mic and get out of here that much faster.

Faster would be good, even if it means I'll still make my dreaded dress shopping lunch date. I should've told them I had plans with my boyf—fiancé.

Something stirs in the next apartment. My lungs trap my breath. A chair scraping on the floor? I hold up a hand, and Justin backs off with the drill.

Footsteps. So one person's at home, at least. Pity there aren't more. If they discussed their intelligence connections, we could figure out if this bug is worth the time and risk.

No such luck. The footsteps fade. Guess we'll have to stick to assessing and infiltrating this potential sleeper cell the hard way. I nod for Justin to go back to work.

"Do anything fun over the weekend?" he asks. I don't need the distraction when my most important job is, you know, *listening,* but I'll take the bait.

"I'm getting married in a month, and I've got exactly nothing done. I don't have time for fun." Because wedding planning definitely isn't that.

"We're through," Justin announces. I almost tease that we were never a "we" to begin with until my brain catches up to his subject jump: the drill. We're through the sheetrock.

Justin sets his tools on the table and digs into our kit again, this time coming up with a minivac. (DS&T does DustBusters.) He cleans up the drywall dust, a telltale sign your walls have some sort of bug.

The exterminator won't go after these. I flip open the case for our contact mic, a disc the size of a dime. Applied to the neighbors' sheetrock, the mic transmits sound waves from their apartment to our receivers. Better than a fly on the wall. (We have those, too.)

I give him the mic. Justin pulls out the right tool for placing it through the hole—okay, it's basically a glorified stick—and I refocus on the sounds of silence.

A knock echoes through the apartment. I flinch and jerk to look at Justin. I could be wrong, but that sounded like it was—

The knock comes again. Justin turns wide eyes on me. Yep. Our door. My heart hits the dirt since the rest of me doesn't dare move. "You order pizza?" I murmur.

"Yeah, I always have takeout delivered to places I officially never was."

I'm guessing my expression matches his, like we've both been caught with our hands in the international cookie jar. In reality, mine is still frozen on the listening device; the contact mic and stick in Justin's hands hang in mid-air. Like whoever's at the door can hear us move.

"*Vy tam,*" calls the man in the hall. My stomach crawls down an inch. The language isn't surprising, given we're in the heart of Ottawa's Russian enclave, but his inflection is odd. I

3

can't quite interpret his meaning.

"Translation?" Justin whispers.

Tricky. The pitch pattern is supposed to make the difference, and he didn't use one I recognize. "It's either 'Are you there?' or 'You're there.'"

Either way, he's talking to us.

Of course, my last Russian mission might be why my blood pressure's somewhere in the stratosphere. That op was an anomaly. There's no way things can go that bad again. Right?

"Answer him." Justin holds out a hand for my listening device.

"And say what? *Zdes' nikto krome nas kury?* Nobody here but us chickens?" I translate before he can ask. "Don't mind us, we're just tapping the neighbors?"

"How about 'we gave at the office'?"

Another knock. This dude isn't giving up.

Justin throws me the toolkit with my disguise. I twist up my long hair and tuck my dark bangs under a blond wig. Thick glasses with '80s plastic frames complete the light disguise. Wouldn't hold up under close scrutiny, but I'm hoping to keep this guy at a distance.

I call through the door. "*Kto tam?*"

"*Domovladelez.*"

Great. Landlord. I mouth that to Justin. He stuffs our tools back into our kit, a little rougher than I'd like with that sensitive contact mic, and kicks the bag under the kitchen table.

We rented the furnished apartment earlier this week, though obviously no moving trucks have been by. The landlord has to have noticed. I crack the door and peer out. The dude on the other side is short, stout and very Russian.

Cold lightning lances through me, and I grip the doorknob tighter. For a split second, I'm back in the locks of the Rideau Canal, a prisoner facing her captor.

Logic takes over. That captor's in custody. His intel led us here, but he's not the man in front of me. For one thing, the landlord's walking free. For another, he's walking at all. One deep breath and my pulse is under control. "*Da?*"

The landlord launches into a long speech about some obscure document he wants filled out, and shoves a packet of bright orange paper at me. I scan the Russian. An apartment inspection. Now. The cover sheet's bold text leaves no room to argue. *Obyazatel'noi.* Mandatory.

If I fight, this guy will remember the whole emotionally charged episode. If I comply, we can get through this and he'll forget me tomorrow. I hope.

"*Vhodite.*" I step back from the door to let him in. He grabs the papers from me and marches past. What little I gathered from the pages had to do with assessing the condition of the apartment because we're new renters. The apartment we just christened with a 1.5" hole. Yeah.

I dare to look. Now in light disguise, too, with a new mole and a dark wig covering his fashionably mussed brown hair, Justin's leaning against the wall maybe a shade too nonchalant, blocking the view of the hole. The landlord scrutinizes him, and the blood slows in my veins.

The repair fee can't be that much, but getting caught? Alerting the neighbors? Disaster.

The landlord cuts his eyes my direction. "*Pochemu on ne na rabote?*"

Why isn't he at work? Good question. Careful to keep from betraying the lie, I shrug. "*Leniv.*" He's lazy.

"*Trud cheloveka kormit, a len'—portit.*"

I never want to play Russian proverb roulette again, but at least this one fits: work feeds the man, and laziness spoils him. Justin's certainly spoiled. I grin; the landlord doesn't. Justin starts to smile. Once the landlord's gaze leaves me, I make a cutting motion across my throat.

Justin's eyebrows twitch in the subtlest acknowledgment

possible, and the grin melts into a glower. Good recovery. Now we need to get rid of this landlord before he gets *too* nosy.

Isn't that kind of what "inspection" means?

Without a nod to either of us, the landlord marches back to the main bedroom. We—meaning the Agency—have only been in the apartment a couple days. No one's living here, so we haven't dressed the place with toothpaste smears and dirty laundry. Like ours, the apartment's disguise is thin, a veneer that anybody being thorough would see through.

So I follow him down the short hall to the room. He's already there, examining the cheap, pressed wood desk that comes with the apartment, as if it's worth anything. He doesn't seem to care the desktop is bowed or the door to its storage compartment always drifts open. We're not complaining, either, but we don't have to put up with it.

The landlord rounds the double bed to check out the night table. He stops short to inspect the hospital corners on the sheets. Worry tugs at my gut again. Too neat. We should've gone for more disheveled. We should've raided a thrift store for clothes to spread around.

The landlord barely glances at me. A hand lands on my shoulder and I jump before I realize it's Justin. I shoot him a glare to try to send him out. Too weird if he goes back to leaning against that random spot on the living room wall. We can't afford suspicion.

"I see he's lazy in other ways, too," the landlord mutters in Russian, like Justin's not there. Or like the landlord knows Justin can't understand him. I'm not sure I understand him either, until he adds a dirty joke to the jab. I scowl and shake off Justin's hand.

I've got to get this guy out before he figures out we're not living here. What's the best excuse? I size up the landlord. Is he a hard smoker or drinker?

He's Russian, so probably both, though he doesn't show

many outward signs. Wedding ring? Yep. I take a shot in the dark and in Russian: "Dmitri upset my mother."

The landlord's grunt speaks volumes. Who doesn't sympathize with mother-in-law problems? I'm not married yet and I do.

He turns for the door leading off this room. Trouble. We've gone far enough to toss two toothbrushes in a glass, but if he looks for something as deep as, say, the tooth*paste*? Big trouble.

Justin wasn't there when we set up. It was me and Robby, who'd come in handy now, since he does speak Russian. Justin has no idea what he's getting into when he starts for the door. Is he stopping the landlord? What's he going to say, when the guy can barely get out a Russian *hi*? I have to keep him from going into that bathroom.

Oblivious, Justin grips the knob. The landlord steps up to the plate. But it's my pulse rounding the bases.

We can't afford this attention. The neighbors hearing us is one thing; them knowing we don't really live here is a different ball game. The landlord just became the bigger threat.

It's time for a sacrifice play.

I yank out the dresser's second drawer. It falls apart if you touch it, as I found out the hard way two days ago. Now the front of the drawer comes off, pulling out the drawer bottom. The plywood clatters to the floor.

Odds are good the landlord already knew this was broken— he's probably here to pin this repair on us anyway—but it's the best I've got. It'll make him remember me, it'll mean I have to stay away from this apartment building, and it'll cost us the repair money. Still better than the neighbors hearing rumors about the fake couple next door.

The landlord swivels to face me. He gapes in horror like I beheaded his beagle instead of defacing his dresser. "You stupid cow," he growls. "Don't you know how to open a drawer?"

"It was broken when we moved in." The defenses in my

voice aren't totally an act, because that dresser drawer's empty. Another giveaway. My adrenaline level kicks up a notch.

Then the cover pops into my head. "We couldn't even put our clothes in here," I complain. "This entire apartment is defective."

"Defective? Defective?" He raises the decibel level, forcing the argument into the next gear. "Did you have such an apartment in Russia?"

"With roaches and broken furniture?" I snort in a condescending laugh. "Yes, we did."

"You inspected it before you signed the contract!"

Which we didn't. As long as he's angry, though, it doesn't matter what he says. I'll keep stoking that fire. "Now you're inspecting it again, like we've destroyed it the first week?"

"Obviously you have."

"Obviously we haven't had time to do the damage I can see from where I stand." I toss the drawer front onto the rest of the wreckage. "We're moving out." I turn away.

"You signed a contract. You can't just leave." The landlord latches onto my arm, hard.

The second he touches me, real heat flashes through my chest. "Watch us." I jerk out of his grasp and march down the hall. The landlord practically races me to the door.

I fling the front door open and let it slap the wall. The doorstop's defective, too. "What a surprise. Something else that's broken."

"You can't just walk out!"

"Don't make us drag lawyers into this."

The landlord curls his lip and pauses in the doorway to wheel back to Justin, emerging from the hall. "You know where she gets this attitude," the landlord sneers, as if my fake mother passed it down, a vicious family heirloom. "Good luck."

Like my "husband" is supposed to stand in solidarity with the guy who manhandled his "wife"? Justin's response is narrowed eyes. Good one.

The landlord flounces into the hall and I slam the door, appeasing a little of my anger.

"Going out on a limb here," Justin says softly. "I'm guessing we can pack up the apartment before we go?"

"Good guess." I don't bother taking off the wig or glasses. I move back to the hole in the wall—which, fortunately, the landlord never noticed. "Let's get this in and get ourselves out."

Justin grabs the microphone placing stick and carefully repositions the contact mic in the clip on the end. I take up my listening post again, immediately picking up chatter in the room closest to us. Two people.

Now my pulse is racing for a very different reason. I hold a finger to my lips. Justin freezes.

I'm missing about a quarter of what they're saying—exactly why we're trying to get that contact mic in; it's a lot better than my listening device—but the gist is clear. They're talking about us. What happened. If they've ever seen us.

Yeah, great time to be making noise against their wall, even if their talking *might* cover it. Every second that crawls past, my anger cools into apprehension, and my heart rate climbs.

"Pack up first," I barely whisper. The place's thin disguise is supposed to be packable in fifteen minutes or less. I check the time on my phone. I don't have fifteen minutes to spare, between our surveillance detection route when we're done here and the boutique's strict no-late-appointments policy. After I've texted Beth, Beth, Beth and Abby (we're all so disappointed) (except not), Justin and I get to work stripping off the apartment's façade of living.

As designed, fifteen minutes later, all "our" earthly possessions are heaped by the front door, and we're back to waiting for our neighbors to walk away from the wall so we can get this thing in. I focus on my breathing to keep my mind off the possibilities: they hear us place the mic, the landlord still spreads crazy rumors about us that make this potential sleeper cell pack up and leave, the landlord comes back with a posse.

All unlikely, but I'm paranoid for a living. Despite my fiancé Danny's attempts to convince me otherwise, I'm still not sure it's possible to be too paranoid.

Finally, the voices fade, and I give Justin the nod. Placing the mic is the shortest part of the mission, and as soon as we patch up the hole (you wouldn't believe our paint-matching kits) and pick up our gear, this apartment's behind us for good.

Sacrifice the deposit? For a chance to listen in on a nest of potential spies? The Agency can take the hit.

We sneak past the lobby office, where I assume the landlord's hanging out. Halfway through that surveillance detection route, Justin gets the text message we've all been dreading.

"Guess who's coming to the office," he chirps.

I level him with a scowl. Nobody's excited to meet Will's replacement and adjust to a new boss, but when Brett Dixon, the embassy's old CIA Chief of Station, had a heart attack three weeks ago, even personnel issues had to be fixed on the fly. Will took over for him, leaving an opening at our office. An opening that's about to be filled.

I try not to let my imagination get too crazy before we get back. Following protocol, we take the elevator a level higher than necessary and the stairs back down to our floor.

My heart is still going pretty good, though, and I doubt it's the landlord argument half an hour ago or a flight of stairs that's keyed me up. I pause in front of the wooden doors embossed with Keeler Tate & Associates, Barristers and Solicitors. (Canadian for "attorneys at law.")

When I walk through those doors, the new boss will be there. Will definitely won't be coming back. And he definitely won't be bringing back Elliott, my de facto partner.

Justin, oblivious, plows ahead, past reception and the security card swipe, into the bullpen. Will *is* there. And so is some-one else, someone new, his back to me as he shakes hands with Robby.

Will spots us at the door. "Just in time," he calls. "This is your new boss, Vince."

Is it bad if I don't like the guy based on his cover name alone? A couple of us—me, Elliott—use real names with real law degrees to lend real credibility to our fake law firm. But most operatives in the field use cover names, even in the office, to prevent a mole from compromising us. A constant fear in Canada. Not.

Once Will's introduced him, Vince turns around, and I swear he draws it out to make it slow and dramatic, like he's expecting love at first sight with the only girl in our tiny office.

His gaze hits me like an arctic shockwave. That is *not* insta-romance. My stomach does a double barrel roll, and I fall back a step, colliding with Justin.

His cover name here in the field might be Vince, but I already know who he is. Ice blue eyes. Impeccably groomed stubble. Sun-kissed, golden curls and perfect tan, though I know they're both from a salon. Because I know this guy. Brandon Copley. Brand, for short.

My ex-boyfriend.

CHAPTER 2

IN CASE YOU CAN'T TELL, let me spell it out for you: it didn't end well.

Brand's ogling eyes trail down my legs, like that's the only way he'll recognize me. "Surprised to see me?"

"Yes, actually." My mouth is working faster than my brain, trying to come up with something to show him I'm better off without him, something to put him in his place, something good. "Didn't realize you'd last this long."

His gaze take on a mischievous twinkle—the same twinkle he always got when he was about to deliver a blow of blatant innuendo he apparently considered clever or coy.

He goes for the quicker kill today. "Yeah, didn't think you were really CIA material, either."

I refuse to flinch, though my cheeks flare up faster than a burn bag full of sensitive documents. That slap is a paper cut to my soul. With salt. And lemon juice.

Will intercedes (thankyouthankyouthankyou). "Oh, you two know each other?"

"Worked together at Langley, years ago," Brand says. Those icy blue eyes never leave mine.

"Briefly," I add. Which is true. We didn't work together long, and dated for even less time. But long enough that I kind of hoped to never, ever, *ever* have to confront him again.

Will observes us both for a second, one hand headed for his silver-haired temple. He drops it and straightens his shoulders. "Since I'm here, Talia, we should talk about your plans."

I have plans? I nod like I know exactly what he means and follow him to a spare office.

"We dated," I blurt out as soon as the door shuts. "But you know I'm not so immature—"

"As long as you do your job, it doesn't matter to me." Will's all business, bringing back too many memories of meetings like this in his office a few feet away.

Now it belongs to Brand—*Vince*.

Will scrutinizes me another minute. If he's expecting me to spill the rest of the story, he'll be waiting a while. "Don't let it get to you," he says. "It was a long time ago, and I've never seen you let anything come between you and your work."

I read his body language like I can tease out another meaning until Will smiles. He means exactly what he said. And if that's not enough, he adds, "I doubt Vince will change that. You're one of our best."

Over the last four years, I've fought every day to make sure that the boys' club, my coworkers and my boss, see me as more than a tagalong little sister. I've proven myself an equal, I think, but to have Will say it flat out? That respect and the little phrase of praise make all the work worth it. I hold in a grin and savor the warmth building in my chest.

I kinda want to hug him, but . . . boys' club. So instead I say, "Thanks."

"All right, then." Will moves along in his agenda. "Haven't gotten your travel form yet. Coming up, right?"

"I filed the request for time off to go home," I say, though Ottawa's as close to a home as I've ever had.

"That'll be back soon. Honeymooning in the US, too?"

And now for the four words I've always hated to tell my boss: "I have no idea."

Will's stormy eyebrow creeps up an inch. "You don't know if you're staying in the country for your honeymoon?"

"Danny wants it to be a surprise." Despite my efforts to control my expression, the eye-roll comes out in my voice.

Will blinks, slow, uncomprehending. "The Agency isn't big on surprises."

"I appreciate that."

"Make sure he appreciates it, too."

Yeah, let's see, the man I dated for a year before telling him I was a spy? I'm sure he "appreciates" CIA surprises, too.

The form is sort of a formality—they'll probably approve it around the time we get home—but it truly is the thought that counts. If I don't at least *think* of obeying the CIA's regulations, they could make my life a lot more difficult.

Like, I don't know, making my ex-boyfriend my boss. Coincidence?

"I'll get you the form," I finally say. Somehow.

"Good." He pivots to leave, then stops. I'd almost fall for that if his casual act weren't one click too calculated. "Oh, the examiner flew in today. He's here till tomorrow afternoon."

I don't need any more clarification in this context: the polygraph man is visiting the embassy, and I have to meet with him. Except that I'm not the one getting "boxed."

Danny is.

And he has no idea.

I know this situation is beyond Will's control, and typical for this sort of thing, but still. "You know, my fiancé doesn't enjoy surprises any more than the Agency." I temper my tone with a tiny bit of titanium.

"Does he know what he's getting into?" Despite Will's murmur, the words hit like a slap. As if I haven't wondered that at least weekly. Yes, we've dated for a year, so he knows how demanding my job is, but he's only had a few weeks to get used to the idea of Talia, CIA operations officer, instead of Talia, barrister and solicitor. I mean, I just trained him that CIA employees are "officers," not agents. (Yes, contrary to what Hollywood would have you believe, CIA employees are *not* agents. Agents are the regular people we officers recruit as spies.)

Will turns for the door again, back to the room where Brand's meeting my guys. I take one little second for myself before I have to face the rest of our team sans Will and Elliott, plus Brand. Yep, there's an agency surprise. One none of us will appreciate.

Once Will's gone, I manage to fill my afternoon with reports, follow-ups, and rescheduling my dress appointment with all the interested parties for tomorrow at lunchtime. Anything rather than interact with Brand.

Even the thought makes my heart dive.

I hate that he still has this effect on me. It's been years—what, almost four? Though it didn't end on an up note, it's not like I've spent the last half-decade living on pure hatred. I can't remember the last time he wandered through my memory. If he had, I think I would've hoped he'd forgotten me, never wondered where I was or looked me up on Facebook (I'm not there).

And I still want him to know as little about me as possible. He's my boss. That's it. Not a friend, not a confidant, not as close as Will—someone I could trust. Brand? Yeah, no.

I'm wrapping up for the day when my luck runs out. Will's—no, *Brand's* door swings open. He leans out to scan the room. I duck my head and hold my breath. Not me. Not me. Not me.

"Talia? Can I talk to you?"

A sucker punch of revulsion lands in my gut, and the fingers of one hand tie themselves in worry knots. I trudge into his office and narrowly avoid plopping into the seat.

He sits in his nice, cushy leather throne, several inches higher than my cheap office chair opposite his desk, like he wasn't already tall enough. The power imbalance rockets home. To have an ex hold this much power over you chafes like a cheap wig. (Believe me, I'd know.) I mean, if he wanted to, he could kill my career.

I really hope he doesn't want to.

"So, how goes the Great Game?" He grins.

I've always hated that nickname for the spy business, and even more coming from him. "Fine."

"Anything big to report?"

I tuck my hand under my leg. "You've read what I've sent to Langley."

"Yep. And I have something for you."

Against my will, I angle forward an inch. Curiosity probably never killed a cat, but the perennial plague of the spy has definitely done in one or two operatives. "What?"

"Direction." His eyes are practically dancing with self-delight.

So that's how it's going to be. "I'm fully capable of directing myself, thanks."

"Not what I'm trying to say." Brand laughs softly. Even his reassurances are condescending. "I'm just saying you've been working on a high-value asset."

Right. I know who he means without glancing at my mental docket.

If I had any doubt, Brand launches into a case description. "Samir Farooqi is Pakistani, so obviously we're left with you to target him."

"Glad to be such a vital part of the team." Not only am I our only Urdu speaker, but I placed the bug—very close call; thanks again, Elliott—and dug into the intel to find Samir, and I've spent the last month steadily developing our friendship. Clearly that means a whole freaking lot to Brand.

"Farooqi's got a famous relative. Hassam-ud-Din Wasti? Terrorist behind the almost-attack on Flight 999, guy who got explosives into Granny's wheelchair and Junior's shoes?"

I cut him off. "They're cousins, I know. Spare me the case file. Pretty up-to-date."

"Then you know Wasti's planning something big." Brand interlaces his fingers, places his forearms on his desk and leans over them, wearing a smile I grew to despise. "Pitch Farooqi."

This time, I don't bother with restraint: I roll my eyes. "He isn't ready." We both know if I try to recruit him as an agent before I've developed our relationship well enough, the guy could easily bolt. Probably straight to his radical cousin.

"He'll go for it. Wasti's the black sheep. Everyone knows."

"'Everyone knows'? What, you have a Pakistani family gossip hotline?" I certainly don't. "Wasti holds his family sacred, according to the traces." Langley's profiles are exhaustive.

"Doesn't matter if it was in his traces." Annoyance flashes through his voice. Brand resettles in his chair. The casual gesture doesn't mask the irritation still lurking in his gaze. "It's updated intel. None of our other sources are any good. This is the only way we can get this guy."

"By banking on his alleged hatred of his family." It's not a moral judgment—we've all used worse to get in with targets—but I'm not about to pretend to be happy with this idiotic plan.

"Bank however you like," Brand says, like he's being incredibly magnanimous. Yeah, the guy thought every little morsel of attention he gave me was charity: charity I'd have to repay.

I shove aside my own irritation and lean forward, tilting my head at a let's-be-frank angle. I'm not the trainee he knew four years ago. "Are you trying to spook him?"

"Yeah, I am."

I glance heavenward at the terrible pun. ("Spook" is also slang for spy, though obviously I meant "scare.") "Worst case scenario, we'd put more people in danger."

"Talia." His tone is a neat little balancing act between condescension and level-with-me. "I can see you're not exactly jumping to pursue this. Is it because of where this is coming from?"

I don't like the sound of that. "Is it coming from Langley, or you?"

"You know what I mean. Is this because the orders are coming through me?"

I pull back. "That has nothing to do with anything."

"Doesn't it?" He paints on a sad little smile, like I'm the most pitiful thing since a one-legged puppy. "Look, I'm not picking on you because we went out a couple times."

Hey, he was the one who called me his girlfriend after two dates. I just went with it. I just went with everything, and he was great with it, until I stopped going along and he pitched a fit.

And I'd tell him all that, but I'm the bigger person. Right?

Brand plays on my generosity again. "Sometimes, you just have to take a risk."

I'm on my feet, though I stop short of throttling him. "I don't know where you've been the last few years, but where I work, we don't take *unnecessary* risks. Is there a reason we need Samir now? It can't wait a few weeks?"

"More of a hunch. You can imagine how well the F-entity keeps us informed on Wasti."

Fifty bucks says the FBI isn't the only agency at the party, and we've got our own carefully covert eyes on a radical Pakistani.

His shoulders move in a minuscule shrug. "Yeah, it's a little gamble. That's part of playing the Game."

This time, I can't let it slide. "What we do is way more than a game, and if I didn't believe that, I'd have quit a long time ago."

"Maybe you should have." Brand stands slowly, his jaw set. "This long in Canada would make anyone go soft."

Heat steals up my neck in the silent seconds. "Soft?"

He holds up his hands and backs off a step, like my one borrowed word is an attack. "I'm just saying. Easy to get used to playing it safe, and forget how things run elsewhere, how much officers risk."

"How ... much ... ?" I choke back the argument ready to spring out. He has no idea what I risked, how much I nearly lost, less than six weeks ago. For half a second, the Ottawa River is closing over me and I'm drowning.

"Wasti is worth the danger." Brand's voice drags me above the surface. I'd almost rather succumb to a watery grave. "Did that kind of thing all the time in Tajikistan."

I'm done. "You can rag on Canada all you want—but you're posted here, too. Remember I've been around this office a lot longer, and I might know a thing or two about how things are done."

"Doesn't mean they're being done right."

If this is how he operates with coworkers, I can only imagine how he treated his Tajik agents. No wonder he's being shunted off to Canada (no reflection on me, I hope). "I'll think about it." I turn for the door, as if my tone isn't final enough to close the argument.

"No reason to be upset." Brand lays on extra charm. "We're just talking. Part of my job to help you keep your priorities straight. Strategize your next move."

"You might want to get the lay of the land before you try to reset the whole 'Game.'" I march out to the empty bullpen. Everyone else has already left.

Brand follows. "Then help me get a handle on the baseline."

"Fine." As long as it doesn't involve staying in this empty office together any longer. I rush to finish my cleanup and set out for the stairs. I don't bother to hope I'll lose Brand. "First of all," I begin. My echo bounces off the walls, and I cringe. Very clandestine. But the stairwell's empty. "You have to remember Canada's a friendly. We play by their rules and work with them. I'm sure Will took you around?" I don't mention the name of our Canadian counterpart, CSIS.

Brand speeds up to match me, on the same stair. "Yes. Mack, etc., etc."

"They have policies on what we can do. They consult with us. They pull us in." I reach the floor below ours and exit the stairwell to switch to the elevator, my usual routine. Our conversation stays on pause until the elevator doors close behind us, and we're the only ones inside. "That cooperation is our top priority here, because we need them as much as they need us. We stay within the bounds they've set for us."

"Officially."

Not a secret I want to let my boss in on, so I remain silent past another floor. "Our biggest danger isn't from the natives."

"The biggest danger always comes from the place you least expect."

I don't want to admit how right he is. "Didn't know you cared. You're pushing me on this case because you're looking out for me?"

He doesn't respond to the derision in my voice. "Look out for yourself. Always."

We hit the ground floor and it takes a superhuman effort to not run from his veiled threat. Still, my strides are longer than normal, and I'm getting tunnel vision focusing on those front doors and the free air beyond.

Of course Brand catches up. Isn't hard for someone that tall to keep my pace. "All right," he says. "I've heard you out. Now will you at least consider what I said?"

"Fine." I stop at the doors and hope he'll go on. "I'll consider it."

This time, the final tone does work, and Brand swishes through the doors. Once he's out of range, my shoulders lower. My fidgeting hand unknots. My heartbeat slows. I don't have to be on the defensive.

Someone touches my waist. I leap right back on my guard and away from this guy, then spin around to find my attacker.

Tall, dark hair just long enough to flip out behind his ears, warm brown eyes: Danny, watching me with a bemused expression. "Um, surprise?"

"Apparently." I hope that lingering note of annoyance is all in my imagination. Just in case, I force a smile. "What are you doing here?"

"I take it you forgot?"

Great. "Forgot what?"

"Remember? 'I'll wait for you in the lobby'; 'I'll be the one with the hair and clothes'?"

My brain finally shifts out of get-away-from-Brand mode and back into the real world. Where I was supposed to meet Danny in my building's lobby after work.

"Oh, right," I say. What I mean is *oh, crap*. How much of that did he see? "Why didn't you say something sooner?"

Danny peers through the doors after Brand. "Looked all . . . Top Secret-y."

"Top Secret-y?" I repeat with a hint of a chuckle.

He folds his arms, though I can see the grin in his eyes. "Yes, Top Secret-y. It's a technical term."

I should keep joking. All I manage is a sigh. "Sorry. Stressful day."

"Apparently."

Any lurking hope that he missed what was going on suffers a silent, ignoble death. "What all did you see?"

"Enough to not like it. Do I need to go deck that guy?"

I love Danny, but I know he wouldn't resort to violence because my boss and I disagree. He's an engineer. He thinks. Of course, he can throw a punch when necessary—and he has. Pretty sure the circumstances are different now. "That's my new boss."

He offers a low whistle and open arms. "You win the who-had-the-worse-day award."

"Ooh, such a coveted prize." I hug him back. He knows better than to ask anything else, simply letting me breathe in strength from his presence: the one solid, constant, real thing in my life. He is who he is all the time—and right now, he's exactly what I need.

"I didn't even tell you what comes with the prize," Danny says. "You choose dinner."

I don't miss a beat. "BeaverTails."

"The restaurant or the food?"

"Both?"

Danny pulls back to mock-scowl at me. "That's not dinner."

I could get extra sympathy points—and double my intake of fried dough slathered in maple butter—if I mention my new boss is Brand. Because Danny knows exactly who he is and what he did and what that means. That one little word could buy me an infinite supply of slack.

But telling Danny's the last thing I want to do. Aside from the fact that he seriously might deck Brand, I want to pretend the annoying guy asking me to do something stupid is someone I don't know—for the office, for Danny.

For me.

Danny gives me a final squeeze before I pull away. "What should we really eat?" he asks.

I go for my secondary tactic: fake pouting. I thrust out my bottom lip and put on the puppy dog face. He meets my gaze with one that's perfectly, completely, I-cannot-be-swayed-by-your-tears level, and holds. I try not to count down the seconds until my façade slips.

At the last minute, Danny turns away in disgust. "Fine."

His deadpan's pretty good, though I catch the twinkle in his eyes, his tell. This time I don't hold back the laugh, and neither does he. But the release of relief in my rib cage is a little too . . . little. I seriously doubt either of us would be laughing if I'd told him the *other* reason Brand bugs me (the non-classified one).

For now, I get to enjoy my favorite view in the whole city: Danny's totally unrestrained, eye-crinkling, Talia-melting smile. Until he kisses me.

My day just got a whole lot better—especially since I don't have to think about Brand or anything else remotely related to work till tomorrow.

CHAPTER 3

THE NEXT MORNING, HOWEVER, I have no choice but to think about Brand. He might not be here, since his office door has been closed all day, but I'm doing my best to avoid the line of fire. I'm not a gambling woman.

At ten thirty, my phone rings. Danny. I swivel away from Brand's door. "What's up?" I answer.

"Nothing, just wondering if you got the same call I did."

I don't know what he's talking about, and I can't commit to an answer based on that little statement. I wait in silence.

"About the wedding?"

My stomach inches toward my shoes. I still don't say anything.

"And the embassy?"

Why would the embassy—oh. Oh. They called him for the polygraph. And they're lying.

This *is* the CIA, I guess.

I was supposed to tell him about the polygraph, but after my last encounter with Brand, I tried to put everything work related out of my mind. "Yeah," I say, "about that—"

"Did you want to drive together?"

Since we got engaged, we've jumped to a whole 'nother level on the "together time" scale. We don't work that far apart, and we're finally taking advantage of that to see each other almost as much as we'd like. But this might be—

Wait, the chance to go with him when he gets boxed? Um, that's a duh. "Sounds great."

He promises to pick me up in fifteen minutes, and I hurry to finish my report. Once I'm in Danny's passenger seat, I gather the courage to try the truth again. "So, Danny—"

"Hey, you never told me how your dress appointment went yesterday."

The one I rescheduled for today at lunch? Darn. "Oh, man, I gotta make some calls."

Danny doesn't comment while I call the shop and text Beth, Beth, Beth and Abby with regrets once again. The drive to the embassy is long enough to give him too much time to ask about it. And he does. "I thought that was yesterday."

"Yeah, something came up at work."

A frown flashes across his features. "Don't have a lot of time left."

"Believe me, I know."

His eyes stay pointed ahead, focused on the distance.

I don't like where he's going, and I don't mean the embassy. He's silent until we're cruising the neighborhood for an available spot. (The parking situation is ridiculous.) "Sorry," he finally says. "I think I interrupted you earlier."

Yeah, let's add insult to injury now. Not only is your fiancée pathologically incapable of making a decision about your wedding, but to get that far you'll have to be polygraphed?

I'd better start small. "There's one more form I'm supposed to fill out if I travel abroad."

"Even back to the States?" He nabs a space across from the National Gallery and gets out.

I wait until he opens my door. "I mean for our honeymoon."

Danny scoffs and helps me out. "That's a ploy to get me to tell you where we're going."

"No. Unless the real reason you won't tell me where is because you don't know yet."

He sweeps a hand in front of him, like he's imparting a vision of the future to me. "Scenic Aylmer. You'll love it."

The suburb where he already lives. "Uh, yeah. Featuring sightseeing tours of the nearest Tim Hortons and three other donut shops."

"Told you you'd love it." He grins with too much teasing to count as a real smile.

"You're just lucky I love you," I mutter, faking aggravation. We stop at a crosswalk. "Donuts, huh? So . . . Germany?"

"*Nein.*"

The light signals for us to cross and we obey. "Would you tell me if I guessed?"

"Nope. Is that all?"

We've got half a block to the embassy. I study Danny's smile again. I've finally reassured him that I'm not subconsciously sabotaging our wedding. Do I really want to tell him about the polygraph? The last hoop so the CIA can approve him? So we can get married? I try to squelch the taste of terror running through my system. It's okay. It's okay. I love Danny, and I want to be with him. Getting married isn't the end of the world.

Or the beginning of a divorce.

I curse my parental-induced PTSD and take Danny's hand. I'm not giving him up just because everyone else in my family is incapable of staying married. I will see this wedding through. I have to. "I've got a really good feeling about this dress shop."

"You have something in mind?"

I dig deep to muster my enthusiasm. "It'll blow you away."

As we reach the front gates, Danny's teasing grin grows

into that full smile, one that lights up my heart as much as his eyes. Until it hits me: now today's polygraph isn't my only lie.

To make him this happy? Worth it.

The embassy is the epitome of efficiency today. Much, much faster than I wanted to be, I'm face to face with Will again. Judging by his glare, he's not real happy to see me either. He escorts us both through the complex to a blank door. Dead end.

Appropriately leery, Danny looks at Will. "They said something about paperwork? For the wedding?" His tone, hopeful but cautious, makes it clear Danny wants to believe the lie.

I pity him. I envy him. Been a long time since I believed the deceptions I deal in every day.

Will's glower is back on me. "You said you were going to tell him."

"I forgot. Some things popped up at work." Or some *one*.

Danny and Will turn away with matching expressions of disgust, though that's the truth.

I only wish I had a better lie.

"You're here for a polygraph, Danny," I finally say. "Company rules." Even here, with nobody present except CIA employees and Danny, we can't say more than that.

"Rules." Danny presses his lips into a line, staring at the door between him and his doom. Then he turns that intense gaze on me. I try not to shrink back a step. Even if Will's not happy with me, I'm grateful he's here, or Danny would definitely be using more than his eyes to argue.

I clamp down on the groan tearing through my heart. I don't like putting him through this stuff, from being unavailable three nights a week at least to having to file a form if I want to go home, go abroad, or go to the bathroom. But I signed up for this—and Danny didn't.

"Sorry," I manage.

"They don't trust me already?" Danny says.

"Trust is earned." I hated hearing that as a teenager from my stepmom, and it sounds worse in this little hallway, with the man I've lied to way too many times.

He slowly draws in a breath, then puffs it out. Nods. Like *you're lucky I love you.*

Believe me: I know. And that anger is still not quite gone from his eyes. "You okay?" I venture.

I think he hears what I really mean: *are* we *okay?* His shoulders fall under the weight of resignation. "If I have to, I have to." He glances at me. "You'd better be worth this."

I hope he's kidding. "No promises."

"And this is the last hoop? No more surprises lurking in the CIA catacombs?"

I look away, searching my memory. Don't have to search hard. "Travel form."

"Oh. Right. So, that's it? No words of wisdom for beating the polygraph?"

"Why would you need to beat it?" Will cuts in.

I deliver a karate chop to Will's interrogation and look to Danny. "You're not lying or under investigation. No need to beat it." Besides, that isn't the hard part. "Be prepared for the pretest interview. Imagine the worst, most invasive, personal interview you've ever had with a bishop. Times ten."

Our church leaders are supposed to ask sensitive questions; polygraph examiners are supposed to ask for more details. And then more. And then more. And then maybe a little more.

Danny's eyebrows do a little dance of uncertainty. "If you're trying to make me feel better, you're failing."

I jerk my chin at the door, my eyes on Will. "Anybody we know?"

"Lloyd Lindell."

I turn up the wattage to my real smile. "Oh, good. He's nice." For a polygraph examiner.

Danny checks the door again. "Are you going to watch

me?"

"No. Is there any reason I shouldn't trust you?"

"No."

Will clears his throat, and I realize I slipped into a classic polygraph examiner question. But Danny gave the perfect answer, and his body language indicates he's telling the truth. And still a tiny bit ticked. "Is that your advice?" he asks.

"Just answer the questions. You don't have to try to make yourself sound extra good." Liars notoriously offer unsolicited proof of what good people they are. Good people seldom feel compelled to prove it. "They're looking for anything you've lied about, or something someone could use to blackmail you, or me. You're a Mormon, an Eagle Scout, and a returned missionary. The biggest risk you run in there is boring the polygraph examiner to death."

Can't blame him when he doesn't look reassured. "What can you do?" Danny mutters. He takes another breath and marches into the room, ready to confront his fate.

Once the door shuts behind Danny, Will doesn't stick around for chitchat. I'm sad to see him go and a little disappointed not to see Elliott around. Spying isn't the same without my unofficial partner backing me up.

But Danny's right. What can you do? The world keeps turning and the CIA keeps churning. Landing me with Brand once again.

The hallway isn't designed to accommodate visitors. Left without a chair, I fold my legs under me, kneel on the floor (not a lot of options in a skirt) and wait. And wait. And wait. As long as these polygraphs feel when you have to take them, it feels a lot longer when you're waiting for someone else. Someone you care about. Danny's the most upstanding guy I know—and I've sworn to that for his work security clearances—but polygraphs freak. People. Out. Even ones that are innocent.

Speaking of freaking out: footsteps carry down the hall. I

know we're supposed to be in a secured area. We're also supposed to be *alone*. I leap to my feet, my breathing accelerating faster than the newest spy drone Danny's designing at work. And being asked about right now.

Not many places to hide in the typical office building hall. Clearly they don't keep the CIA in the cushy penthouse. Probably not receiving too many visitors down here.

But *I'm* about to get one. I move toward Danny's doorway. I don't dare interrupt, and I can't hide in the doorframe, though that little symbolic safety lends me a crumb of courage. I brace for the new arrival.

As soon as I'm "ready" for company, a man rounds the corner. A man I know, who's got tall, dark and handsome down pat—and he knows it. But Danny has nothing to worry about. It's just Elliott.

"Hey, T," he says.

I sigh out the breath I was holding and relax. "Way to scare me half to death."

"What, afraid of falling for my stunning good looks after all this time apart?" He smirks. Yep. He might work for the embassy under "official" (State Department) cover, but that's the Elliott I know. "Will wanted to go over some traces, potential cases."

I glance at the door behind me.

"We'll get you back in time." He claps a hand on my shoulder and starts back down the hall. Might as well. Elliott leads me through a miniature maze. I think we passed through the same intersection at least three times. I'm so glad to see him, and to not be sitting around waiting anymore, that I decide not to mention it.

Plus, I've got something else on my mind. "Were they hard on Shanna when they 'boxed' her?"

"She lived." He shrugs, though his gaze takes on a distant cast. Remembering or something else? "Didn't say much about it afterward. One more hoop."

"Aren't there enough of those already?"

Elliott laughs as we pass that same potted plant for the fourth time. "Just wait. You'll turn into bridezilla any day."

"I've canceled two dress appointments, both our moms think receptions are the best way to manipulate us, and my wedding party is all my brothers. Who am I supposed to go bridezilla on? Danny?"

I catch the little sidelong scan of suspicion from Elliott. "To be honest, I'm surprised either of you are going through with it."

"Shut up." The sibling-like teasing that used to come so easily for us has an edge. He shouldn't have gone there, and I didn't ask his opinion.

But is he right? Am I cut out for this? I've spent so much of my life in unhappy families that I've barely seen a marriage that works. Half my brothers failed at marriage. Why should I think I'll be any different?

We end up in Elliott's office, though I'm too preoccupied to be much help on the traces. We divvy up the potential in the pile. By the time Elliott leads me back to the room where Danny's being polygraphed, the anxiety has taken root. And grown. Like a bamboo torture device.

Will and Danny are walking out when we get there. Danny looks a little tired, though not too much worse for the wear. In fact, he shoots a dull smile at Will to go along with the handshake. They generally don't tell you your results right away—another way to make you sweat—but I'm not too concerned about Danny making the cut.

I'm concerned about me.

"So you work at NRC Aerospace?" Will begins. I figured their conversation would be over, and we could go grab a burger and get back to work. Why is Will just getting started?

"Yep. Engineer."

"Sounds like every kid's dream come true."

Danny quirks one corner of his mouth. "No kid dreams about that level of red tape."

"Tell me about it." Will chuckles. "But I bet they treat you pretty good."

Danny nods. I can't help my ever-present worries taking up a new topic: what on earth is Will getting at? Doubt he chats up all potential Agency spouses. I check Elliott's reaction. He shoots me a wary glance back.

Elliott clears his throat when we're still a couple feet away. As the other (former) most important man in my life, Elliott's formed an uneasy truce with Danny. But there's no time for tension as I move to Danny's side and take his hand to tell Will we're ready to go.

Will's not done. "Familiar with Kelly Johnson's stuff?"

"Who isn't? P-38, F-104, U-2—classics. I think the alumni association makes an annual pilgrimage to his grave."

I love that Danny loves his job, but if they're throwing around this much plane jargon, I don't have a prayer of following. I squeeze his hand and take a couple steps, a silent *we need to be going*.

Will is staying. "That's right, you went to Michigan, too, didn't you?"

I suppose Danny should know Will's familiar with his profile, and his surprise is almost undetectable. "Yeah, but I opted out of the minor in Johnson worship."

"Then did you know the U-2 was originally classified?"

We all know what he means by "classified," and it's hardly a secret the U-2's development was funded by the CIA. If you get Danny started on planes and designs and aeronautics, he may never stop—but he's not engaging with Will.

Good. "We'd better get back to work," I interject.

"Oh sure." Will and Elliott start down the hall. Though I doubt we could find our way out even with a Company-issue

GPS, escorting us gives Will more chances to chat Danny up.

"I don't have a degree in aerospace engineering," Will starts in again, "so maybe I can't vouch for it, but I've heard the stuff coming out of the Department of Science and Technology these days is as cutting edge as the U-2 was."

"Oh yeah?" Danny keeps his tone friendly in an oh-that's-interesting-and-I-have-to-keep-making-small-talk-so-I'll-be-extra-polite way. He's got his own classified projects in conjunction with Canadian defense, so I'm not sure the bait is that intriguing. Unless, I guess, American drones are that much better than Canadian ones. I'd have to ask Danny if that's the case.

"Anyway, I'm sure you're not interested in rumors." Will waves away his own topic. "DS&T is hush hush, and we don't see much of it here in Canada. Hard to keep up with the latest developments, but what I hear from my friends in the Middle East?" He gives a low whistle.

"That good, huh?"

"Yep. I'm no expert, but sounds like the kind of thing you'd be interested in." Will deposits us at the front entrance. "Have you two eaten?"

"Why?" I ask. "Going to take us to the embassy cafeteria?"

Will laughs. Elliott doesn't. "Even the cooks order in."

Will spears him with a sarcastic expression. "I was about to suggest you try one of the restaurants at the National Gallery. You guys like good food, right?"

"Yeah, who doesn't?" I say quickly. "Bye." I drag Danny out the doors before Will and Elliott head to their offices. I know what I want to talk about as soon as we're out of range.

Once we're past the embassy, Danny beats me to the conversation starter. "If I fail that polygraph, will they tell us we can't get married?"

I nearly trip on my feet. "What do you mean, 'if I fail'? Why would you fail?"

"Have you ever been polygraphed?"

"Yes. More than once."

He pins me with a my-point-exactly look. "Then you know how nerve-racking that is. You could've given me time to prepare."

The accusation stings, but I keep walking like I can leave it behind us. "Sorry," I try after a minute. "I really did forget."

A battle of belief wages behind his brown eyes. "I know," he says at last.

"Besides, they know people are nervous about polygraphs. They take that into account."

"Can they tell us we couldn't get married—you couldn't marry me?"

I try to remember how much of my life I signed away when I joined the Agency. Four years ago, I wasn't planning on getting married. Ever. So those details didn't exactly stick out.

What's the worst they could do to me if I don't play by their matrimonial mandates? Fire me? As we reach the Gallery doors, I settle on, "They could try."

The set to Danny's mouth is once again anything but reassured.

Once we're at a table by Café L'Entrée's massive windows, I pick a new subject. "So apparently Will's an aerospace hobbyist."

"You think so?" The little twist to his voice isn't sarcasm. It's doubt.

Yeah, me too. I push my greens around in their maple dressing, digging for another maple candied walnut. Oblivious to my thoughts, Danny reaches across the table for my free hand. "You sure I'll pass?"

"I'm not worried about that." I have way too much else to occupy the already-overdeveloped Worry Region of my brain.

Calm settles over his face, as if my judgment will count with the Agency when it comes to his polygraph and background check. (Man, I hope he knows about that.) He starts on his smoked cod mousse, gazing out the windows at Nepean Point, the grassy hill jutting into the river. "Think that's a good place for engagement photos?"

Great, yet another to-do. "Yeah, but so did Campbell and, like, four others from church."

"Oh, right. Never mind then."

"Have they drained the locks yet?" The cascading water where he proposed would make the perfect backdrop.

"Not sure. Probably will soon."

I finish my salad and my ham and pineapple panini, ready for dessert. The butter tart filling with pecans and blueberries is singing my name in an angelic chorus.

"So," Danny says, pulling my mind back to our table. "You've got your dress figured out? Going to blow me away?"

"Well, we have something in mind." A lie? A white lie. (Literally?) "Lace, and the skirt is—" I cut off like I can't explain it (because it doesn't exist). I conclude, "You'll love it."

"I'm a guy. I'll love anything you wear."

I shoot him an obviously fake glare of *that had better not be your final answer.*

He readjusts his response. "I mean, I can't wait to see it! I'm sure it's perfect!"

Why is his fake enthusiasm funny and mine freaky?

"You really that excited about it?" he asks. Like he read my mind.

I grin, but bite my bottom lip, like I'm trying to rein it in. Danny watches me another minute, and I hold onto that mask like it's my cover, my life, my salvation.

I can't afford to mess this up. Danny is my rock, my anchor, my everything. I will do *anything* not to lose him. Even lie to him.

"Better get dessert if you're going to," he says at last.

Best. Fiancé. Ever. I lean across the table for a kiss. As long as we've been together, his lips against mine still take my breath away.

"I love you," he murmurs as I pull away. "And I am excited to see your dress."

"I love you too." That's all I can echo before guilt chokes off any other response.

Bridezilla? Doubtful. At the rate I'm racking up lies, I might be lucky to be a bride at all.

CHAPTER 4

ONCE I GET BACK, Brand calls me into his office within ten minutes. The door closes behind me, and my shoulder muscles immediately snap to attention. I scoot my cheap office chair away from the desk to keep a slightly-greater-than-professional distance.

Either he doesn't notice or he doesn't mind. He settles into his cushy throne and pretends to ruffle his curls, relaxed but ready. "Thanks for the 'tour' yesterday, Talia."

I'm almost ready to accept his gratitude when his gaze subconsciously flicks to my calves. (Why'd I wear a skirt?) My hands practically tie themselves in a square knot. I dig deep in my willpower to keep them still. Brand can sense no weakness. See no weakness. Use no weakness.

"You know, I could use a real tour. Know any good meeting spots? Restaurants?"

"No." I scowl. "I've been here three years and I've never held a meeting."

He frowns, and I rein in my attitude. Right context: he's my boss, and he isn't out of line yet. "Sorry. I know a few."

"Great. You can show me around. All set for meeting with

Farooqi? Tonight, right?"

I nod. Quick. Decisive.

"Pitching?"

One shoulder twitches in as much of a shrug as I'll allow. Brand knows these things don't always go according to plan. Not that I'm *planning* on pitching Samir tonight.

"Why don't I come with you? A little backup never hurts." His trademark cocky grin surfaces. "Might even be able to give you some pointers. You know, as payback."

I shoot him a death look. "Samir doesn't know I'm CIA yet. You'll freak him out."

His eyebrow inches skyward, a silent dare. *I'll follow you*, it says.

I mimic the gesture with an added sarcastic lip purse. *You can try.*

Before he can read too much into that challenge, I push forward—and remember the stinging words he used to rile me up yesterday. "Maybe you've been in DC too long."

Brand bristles. I hold back my smile and continue. "But here in the field, developing agents takes time. Not a whole lot of foreign nationals traipse into Keeler Tate & Associates volunteering to spy for the US. Convincing someone who hasn't even thought of betraying his family or his country—"

"Is he legal?"

"Don't ask, don't tell." Canadian immigration policy is one thing that's not covered in our traces, and CSIS wouldn't look too kindly on American officers recruiting agents on their turf (even if they're agents with more American interests at heart). They'd probably want to swoop in and snap him up. They'd share the intel, but I still feel better handling Samir ourselves.

Myself.

"You need to find out his immigration status." Brand surveys me across his desk, like he's the king of the Company, and his word is law. "If he's illegal, you can use that as leverage. Or we can talk to Citizenship and Immigration, maybe have them pull him in—"

"You've got to be kidding. Everyone knows blackmail isn't an effective recruitment method. How long before the stress of spying gets to the agent, and deportation becomes an acceptable risk? Then we're out of ammo."

"So what have you got? A relationship built on mutual trust and understanding?" The scorn in his voice makes his point of view clear, though those two characteristics are actually important in a long term agent-officer relationship.

Enough—no, too much. I stand. "I'm not used to being micromanaged."

"Who's micromanaging?"

I fold my arms. "Seriously?"

"Talia, Talia." He stands and moseys around his desk to regard me with contempt. "I see what's going on. Don't you think you're being a little oversensitive?"

"Excuse me?"

Brand pats my shoulders. I jerk out of reach. He presses on anyway. "I know things between us didn't end on the best note."

Does he not know that people called me "Mormon ice princess" to my face?

"That doesn't mean we can't work together now. Like adults."

I turn for the door. "The adults I work with give me the space I need to do my job." And they don't alienate me from all my friends or let a personal relationship screw up an entire team.

"Whoa, whoa, whoa. We're blowing this out of proportion. I was only offering to help."

I whirl back on him, only unclenching my teeth to retort, "'Help' means asking what I want you to do for support, not stepping on my agents' toes."

Brand moves in. I can't give up ground to him, even if it means letting him get close enough for me to smell his woodsy cologne. Never did like that scent.

"I don't know how Will did things," he says, his voice low. "But I know this: it doesn't matter now. Will isn't here, and I *am*—for a reason. Are you?"

I shoot him a look of *you're deliberately being obtuse.*

"Then prove it."

"I will." I lift my chin and meet his cold blue eyes. "By doing this the *right* way."

"Don't let our past cloud your judgment on this case."

That's it. "Don't forget, I'm not the one who resorted to a two-year-old's temper tantrum tactic when he didn't get what he wanted."

"Apparently, you're also not the one who's over it."

My annoyance level skyrockets, and my cheeks tingle. I want to thrust my engagement ring in his face and shout, *This is how over you I am.*

I'm not the two-year-old. I won't sink to his level. And no way am I letting him get anywhere near Danny.

I grab the knob and fling the door open. I manage to neither run nor slink back to my desk. Even if I can feel his gaze pawing at my back.

I lock on my screen, though I can't read the traces Elliott sent. All I can see is Brand's condescending smirk and I'm-so-not-laughing-*with*-you eyes. All I can hear is my short, huffing breaths. All I can think about are Brand's words, echoing. Hitting too close to home.

Am I over him? Yes. Of course. Within days—hours—I questioned what I ever saw in him, why I didn't immediately toss him on the "yeah, right" pile.

Am I over what he did to me? What he put me through personally and at the office?

That's not such an easy question to answer. He destroyed

the team I'd grown close to, convincing all my friends that I was the bad guy because I said no. It sucks to have someone reject you over a lie. It's worse when it's the truth.

With a lie, at least you have that little security blanket to cling to: they wouldn't hate me if only they'd believe the truth. When that truth is exactly why they hate you, you know, once and for all, that it's really *you* they hate.

He turned every single friend and coworker against me.

The old wound's still there, grating with every heartbeat. I spent months building up a reputation and a résumé inside the Agency, and a few weeks with a guy I knew I shouldn't have dated nearly ruined everything.

Nearly ruined a lot more than my job.

So maybe I'm a little bitter when it comes to him. But could that affect my judgment on my case? Could Brand actually . . . be right?

I try to shake off the thought. Even that comes out more as a shudder. I know what I'm doing with my case, with my agent. Don't I?

After Brand's I'll-follow-you eyebrow this afternoon, my surveillance detection run is longer than normal. I see no sign of him at BeaverTails (a *great* dinner twice a week—maybe three times), or the gas station or grocery store. My SDR's almost over when a too-familiar five o'clock shadow at the dry cleaner spikes my blood pressure.

I might be late for my meeting.

Brand knows I'm seeing an asset, so I can't bore him with more errands like I would another tail. I'm going to have to lose him, just like I told him I would. I could run to my car and peel out, but that's an amateur mistake. If I leave before him, I'll miss my best opportunity to confirm what he's driving. Miss that little detail, and I can't be sure if he's still pursuing me.

I slip into my seat and pretend to enter the charge in my check register. (Does anyone do that?) Behind my sunglasses, my gaze is glued to the guy who thinks he can pull off a fedora.

Okay, fine, he does make it work. All the more reason to hate him.

He moseys down a different row of cars. Great. I won't be able to find him without baiting him into tracking me. My pulse rate starts up with my engine. I leave my spot, barely taking my eyes off Brand.

He gets in a goofy-looking white Toyota hatchback. I fix my gaze straight ahead while I cruise down his aisle, definitely slow enough that he can see me. The Toyota pulls out behind me. Too close. He won't want to stay that close for long, or I'd notice him. (Too late.)

I reach the parking lot exit, a traffic light. Most people are relieved to find a traffic light when they need to make a left across six lanes of traffic. But I'm wishing for a stop sign, so I could go in the first break in the cars, timing it so Brand can't stalk me.

No such luck today. I'm first in line when the light changes to green. The five cars behind me would surely notice if I forced them to wait. I make my left turn, one eye on the rearview.

The white Toyota falls back a couple car lengths, letting one or two others pass him. If he thinks that's enough to hide from me, he doesn't know me at all.

I take the first left, at another stoplight, and end up in the middle of some boxy '70s townhouses (the Finnish word for them pops into my mind: *rivitalot*). My heart drops an inch. Residential areas might seem like a great way to lose a tail, but you're much more likely to encounter pedestrians, speed traps, dead ends—or just plain get lost.

Only one car follows me before Brand. The main road through the complex leads past the townhouses and a couple high-rise apartments. That gray car, the only barrier between me and Brand, pulls onto a side street before the road comes to an end at a T-intersection. I think a right would take us back to the dry cleaner, so I head left once again. Within a minute, the newer '90s townhomes give way to 2000s townhomes, and then another traffic artery.

Brand's still behind me. This time, left would take me back to the dry cleaner, so I go right, cutting in front of another car close enough even a Canadian would honk.

The road's familiar, though not enough that I know the speed limit. I push my Company Camry as hard as I can in post-rush hour traffic. Still, the white Toyota looms in my rearview like a comical ghost. My foot holds down the accelerator, but it's my adrenaline system revving.

Brand isn't going to hurt me—I think—but if I can't shake him, things will get really uncomfortable. And if I keep Samir waiting too long, we won't meet tonight at all.

Finally, the trees lining the street thin out and we hit more commercial developments. I scan the landmarks. Baseball field? Right. Salvation Army Citadel? A Mormon and a Muslim walk into the Salvation Army? Setup for a bad joke. Rec centre? We have a winner.

Two minutes later, I'm parked and striding into the rec centre, fake gym bag in tow. The rec centre looks like a high school in teal and royal blue. I'll need to get past the front desk, but as long as it's a City of Ottawa facility, I've got a membership pass.

A pass that Keeler Tate paid for. (Gyms can be great places to meet assets.) Has Brand already set up his membership? My stomach ties itself in three kinds of knots.

I'll find out. Fortunately, everything here is clearly labeled, and I march up to the OFFICE/BUREAU like I've been here a million times. They scan my card and I'm down the hall marked DRESSING ROOMS/VESTIAIRES when I notice the doors to the hockey rinks.

My knotted stomach dives. Everyone knows how Pakistanis love their ice skating, right?

I turn into the women's changing room. In my peripheral vision, I see Brand on approach to the office. I'm in a changing stall before I realize I'm panting.

If he believes I'm here to meet Samir, Brand will surely pay whatever it costs to get in and track me down. But if he hasn't fallen for the diversion, he'll just wait for me to come out.

Then he'll be waiting a long time. I grab Justin's curly wig from Monday and tuck my hair under it, throwing on a slouchy tuque to help my disguise. The only makeup I have on hand: my usual brown eyeliner. Aggressive blending makes my cheekbones appear way more prominent. I borrow a page from my stepmother's makeup book and use the eyeliner as lip liner and eye shadow, though a pair of blinged-out sunglasses will hide part of my makeover.

I start out of the stall and reach the changing room exit before it hits me: my legs. My skirt isn't all that distinguishing, but if Brand remembers one thing about me, it's my legs.

I examine the bank of lockers. With a glance around to make sure I'm not being watched, I slip one more thing out of my bag: a thin piece of metal designed to shim locks. It makes quick work of the nearest locker. And my luck for the afternoon holds: bad though not 100% terrible. The pants inside are three sizes too big. No way will Brand recognize me in stonewashed jeans.

A scarf from my kit makes a good enough belt, and my eyeliner gets one more use: scrawling a note of apology to the pants' owner, promising to return them tomorrow. One final touch, a jacket, and I could stroll past Brand without quite having a heart attack.

When I leave the dressing room, adrenaline singing in my veins, just keeping my pants up alters my gait enough that I have no problem sweeping right past that fedora. But I don't dare breathe till I reach the parking lot.

White Toyota hatchback, check. Its driver? Still inside the building.

Like I said, Brand could *try* to follow me. I puff out my relief and hop in my car.

Fifteen minutes later, I'm scrubbing off my disguise in the bathroom of the Ottawa Public Library, Alta Vista branch: my final destination. I find Samir waiting in the lobby, dark skin, wavy black hair and strangely un-creepy mustache. He offers me a little smile. We've met enough over the last month that we're officially becoming friends. I'm one of the only ones he has here.

Generally, meeting with an agent is, you know, *secret spy work*, but Samir isn't an agent—yet. For now, he's helping me improve my rusty Urdu, and I'm refining his English. We head to our windowless study room. Once we've caught up on our small talk, we review basic Urdu food vocabulary and obscure English grammar rules. Obviously, Samir's more help to me than I am to him.

I try to explain (and remember) the dependent clause in one of his example questions, but when I check, Samir's gaze is focused somewhere closer to Pakistan. Not the first time to-night I've caught him distracted.

"Are you all right?" I ask in Urdu.

Samir puffs out a breath. My scalp tingles, though I try to restrain the excitement. Could be nothing. Maybe his cat died. Maybe he's worried about English. Maybe he hates his job.

We'd give Fluffy the Dr. Frankenstein treatment, practice with him four hours a day, *and* double his income if he wanted to work for us.

People usually want to talk. They only need an audience, and I'm the best you've met. Samir retreats into silence for too long. "Do you have a family?" he finally asks.

45

"Sure." I nod, my mind racing through all the ways we can get him one. Immigration help for someone in Pakistan? Tickets to visit home? Mail order bride?

"Your family must have no problems."

I can't help the snort. "Yeah, no."

Samir furrows his brow. "Is this a yes or a no, 'yeah, no'?"

"It's a no. The 'yeah' part is sarcasm." I'm not ready to leave the topic yet. "What's bothering you about your family?"

He takes so long to think, fiddling with an index card with "force" ("*zor*") on it, that I don't think he'll continue. Did I push him too hard?

At least it's a start. I'm ready to change the subject when he speaks up. "What do you do when you hate what someone is doing, but you cannot stop him? When he is family, I mean. And you'll always be tied to him."

Oh, let this be Wasti. I don't even care if that would make Brand right about the black sheep thing. Let. Him. Mean. Wasti. "Is he hurting himself?"

"No." Samir's head makes a slow side-to-side sweep. "I am afraid he will hurt others, though." Sigh. Whisper: "Many others."

"And you don't think you can stop him?"

He drops the card and stares at his empty hands, feeble and powerless, like his emotions have drained his muscles.

If I can give him that power— "Someone has to be able to stop him, right?"

"Perhaps someone, but . . . someone more great than me."

"Greater," I suggest gently. Playing my cover to the end.

"Yes, greater."

This is an opening. I want this so badly the chorus of *pitch him pitch him pitch him* sings in my pulse. But wanting something too much can come back to hurt you. It makes you eager. It makes you reckless. It makes you weak.

I'm none of the above, and tonight I refuse to be vulnerable.

"I wish there were something I could do to help you," I murmur, letting my eyes take on a far-off cast. "We can't make other people's choices for them."

"No." Samir's shoulders fall another inch. "Sometimes we cannot spare the innocent."

I try to swallow, but my mouth is cotton dry. The innocent in the States? The innocent here? I need a date, a place, a context to pin this guy down. "Do you have a friend who might be able to reach out to your relative? Stop him?"

Samir's bowed head drops closer to the tabletop. "We do not share many friends."

"Well, if you think it's this drastic, have you thought about talking to the police?" Like they'd know what to do.

"The police? Why would they believe me? All they have to do is hear my accent or my name. Then he will still be making trouble, and I will be in it."

"You're probably right." I pick up the "force" card and practice my vocabulary. It's not over—not by a long shot. Despite the siren song of his mini-confession, I know there's a strong chance he could balk, walk away, even warn his cousin off. I don't want to risk lives, especially not American ones. Killing any possibility of working with him by pitching him too soon might be deadlier in the long run.

For all of us.

Samir's sadness seems sincere, but there's no such thing as a human lie detector. Even Danny has to face a polygraph. Samir will, too, if he's ready to help us. His first real intel on his cousin will be his good faith effort, and once he shares that, he'll be in too deep to back out.

After another dozen cards, Samir slows down on the vocabulary drills. Distracted. I wouldn't be a friend if I didn't at least offer to help. I use an elicitation tactic to get intel without asking, trying to make him correct me. "Your brother again?"

"My cousin."

Victory. "Must be really hard knowing something bad's coming, being so helpless."

"I am trapped in a bottle, and I cannot reach the cork. I can *almost* help, but . . ."

My palms go clammy. "Maybe you can."

"*I* can?" A pitying smile plays across his face. "You think you can do everything, no?"

His voice, his eyes—something isn't right here. I have to give him time to think it over, to figure out how badly he wants this, to see how much he needs it. "I just know if I felt that hopeless, I'd listen to any suggestion. Especially if I might be able to protect innocent people."

Samir's gaze tumbles to the table again. "Yes. You are right."

I lean a little closer, and I swear I can feel the heat creeping into my cheeks. This is the tricky part. To be followed by all the other tricky parts. "Listen, if you really want to help your cousin and protect all those people, I know someone who might be able to help. Something you could do to make a difference."

He studies the table's faux wood grain for far too long. Every breath I draw grows shorter, faster, louder, until Samir has to notice in this eerie silence.

"I would like to make a difference," he finally murmurs. "I think."

I don't like that addition. I can only hope he comes to our next meeting armed with a little more conviction. We set up that next meeting for tomorrow night, and turn back to our language study. Samir gains speed with each right answer.

The big right answer had better be taking root.

CHAPTER 5

I WASN'T PLANNING on going to Danny's house tonight, but even making such headway with Samir isn't enough to totally dispel the things Brand said to me this afternoon.

I hate, hate, hate that he can still crawl under my skin and set up a sick amusement park.

"Did you go dress shopping tonight?" Danny's attempt to distract me from my distractions instantly kicks up my frustration. Another front I've got to keep up with the last person I want to lie to.

"Uh, no. The next opening that worked for all of us was Saturday." I break a chocolate chip cookie with a satisfying snap.

A frown tugs at Danny's lips. He takes half of my cookie without a comment. "But you know what you're looking for?"

Absolutely not. "Absolutely." I snag my cookie back.

"Awesome." Instead of delivering my favorite eye-crinkling smile, Danny contemplates the cookie halves between my fingers.

Not. Good. I started this little charade to convince him everything's fine. I don't know how it could backfire so fast—

unless I'm sabotaging myself?

I've got to try harder. "So, I'm thinking of one of those fit-and-flare style gowns, and Brussels lace." (Never thought I'd be grateful my ex-sister-in-law forced me to watch seven straight hours of *Say Yes to the Dress* every time we got together.)

He meets my eyes, but the worry is still there. "Lace, huh?"

"Of course. Isn't that just . . . classic 'bride'?"

I'm about to enjoy my cookie when Danny takes both halves and eats them, nodding slowly. I try not to scowl as I take another from the package.

"Did you talk to your mom?" he asks.

This time, I do shoot him a glare. Every conversation Mom and I have attempted in three years has fallen victim to my insane schedule and my mom's inability to talk about anything except herself. By the time I was twelve, my mom's narcissism had brought her to her third divorce in four years. The last thing I need is Mom ruining yet another marriage. (Doing a great job of that myself.)

"You have to at least tell her we're getting married in Detroit. Unless we're uninviting her." Danny's joking, and he knows this is hard for me—it's not easy for him, either, since he almost married a certifiable psycho a couple years ago—but tonight I do not want to be pushed.

"I'm sorry, it's just that I came here to get my mind off work."

"So our wedding counts as work?"

I don't like that note of concern in his voice. I'm not sure how to take back what I said. "Counts as stress, right?"

"I guess so." He steals another cookie from me. As if the package isn't right here. "I just want to be sure you're okay with Detroit. I don't want to make it harder on anyone. Even your mom."

With our families so spread out, there's no good place to meet. At least we don't have to find a venue—as Mormons, we're getting married in a temple. Advantage? It's cheap. (Read: free.) Disadvantage? We could get married anywhere from Montréal to Manila.

I pluck the stolen cookie from his fingers. "My mom wants everything her way. I mean, Dad never asked us to consider Florida, but Mom's refusing to do a reception because we didn't choose Chicago."

"We can do Chicago. No big deal." He pulls up a stool next to me at his counter and takes the cookie again.

I hold out my now-empty hand to say *see what I mean?* Apparently he doesn't. "I don't do codependency, Danny." Heat builds in my chest and I draw a breath to cool it. I learned a long time ago how to handle my mom; no need to get upset about something she hasn't done yet. "She'll have to hit up the narcissistic supply store before she gets into town."

He watches me a long minute. "Okay then."

"So." I turn my tone to teasing and lean in as if to kiss him. "Detroit, Chicago—are we honeymooning near the Great Lakes?" Without taking my gaze from his, I yank the cookie away.

Or not. Danny doesn't let go, but tilts his head closer to mine, toying right back. "You'll never guess."

I inch toward him in slow motion, ready to distract him from my cookie for real. "I'll take that bet."

I wait for Danny to give in, close those last few millimeters and give me the prime cookie-snatching opportunity I've been waiting for. Because somewhere inside, I have to show him I can keep up, I can hold out, I'm strong enough to withstand even this temptation.

Danny's not budging either. All the flirtation in his eyes melts away, leaving behind the same steel I've been trying to cover with cuteness.

"Are you sure about this?"

His quiet question cuts our connection faster than a pair of wire nippers. A drop of solid ice sinks into my gut. I don't realize at first that I've turned away. "Why? You're not—"

"No, no. Don't be ridiculous."

"Don't *you* be ridiculous." I press my palms on the cool granite of the counter, then pick them up to twist my ring around my finger. "How could you think that?"

Danny sets the cookie aside—I only realize now that I surrendered it—to take one of my hands. "I don't mean anything, I just want to be sure. To know you're sure." He finally interlaces our fingers and pulls me closer to wrap his arms around my waist. I hate feeling like my arms are restrained behind my back, even if it's Danny, but I fight down the plans to panic and hold his gaze. "Don't go freaking out on me again," he says. "Or flaking out."

"Are you kidding?" I force out an incredulous laugh. It isn't funny at all. I won't let that happen again. I can't. I can't lose him, not again.

Though I've promised myself I'd never, never, never spy on Danny, I can't help tuning into the CIA's set of people-reading skills to reassure him. Focus on his eyes. Slide my hands out of his and into a loose hug. Keep my voice measured and steady and normal. "The past is over."

There was more, a whole speech, but the next words come shuddering to a halt in my brain. The past is over with Brand, too, no matter how much he hurt me. We should be able to work together like adults. Like he said. I'll have to find a way to trust him, like I trusted Will.

Danny picks up his half-full glass of milk. "To the future," he toasts.

I grab my glass to clink against his and we both take a sip.

I need to tap into my spy intuition with Brand, too. I need to be objective. If he's right, if I'm letting my personal feelings cloud my judgment, any decisions I make about Samir or any other agents could be compromised. Brand's a CIA officer, my boss, an experienced spy.

So why can't I make myself trust him?

Every agent recruitment is different, though it's not unusual to impress the prospective agent with your money, your influence, your clout. A penthouse reception—private, uninterrupted, and complete with room service and celebratory champagne—is fairly common.

But Samir isn't in this for the money. He wants to help his family, and even more so, the innocent people they're going to endanger. Plus, with the Mormon Word of Wisdom and Muslim halal health codes prohibiting alcohol, champagne's only a good way to fritter away fifty bucks.

We're still renting a room, though much lower key, in an anonymous motel chain, with coffee for him and hot chocolate for me, our scaled-waaay-down drinks of choice. Getting here was a trip: a clandestine meeting, winding routes through the city, watching for surveillance. We're black, agency-ese for clear, but I still have a long way to go. "So." I set my mug on the table and lean forward in my chair. "Heard anything from your cousin lately?"

"Oh, he loves to talk to me about his big plans."

That could mean anything from *he's told me everything, just ask me the right questions* to *he's always been this crazy.* "Oh." I shoot for sympathetic. "So is he local?"

"No."

Check off the first box. "Is he looking for your help?"

Samir compresses his lips, draining their color away. "He wants my support, at least."

"For what, exactly?"

He studies his mug, his knuckles growing whiter. I can't imagine the internal war he's fighting right now: betray his radical cousin, trust his new friend, protect innocent strangers.

I'll have to do what I can to tilt the battle. I move closer. "You said you don't agree with him, that he could hurt innocent people. What's he doing that's got you so anxious?"

He abruptly sets the mug down. "Can I pray?"

"Um, sure." The CIA's Urdu course touched on cultural aspects of the language group's major religions, though I can't say I'm super familiar with the call to prayer.

Samir ducks into the bathroom and emerges with a dingy white towel. He lays it on the floor, aligned with whatever he's supposed to use, the window, Mecca. Is it rude to watch while he proceeds through the standing, bowing, kneeling and prostrate positions, murmuring softly?

I'm not used to such rigidly prescribed prayer rituals, and I can't help my own anxieties. Where I come from religiously, asking to stop a conversation like this to pray would mean something was really, really wrong.

Is it?

Hardly a fair comparison, a religion that encourages silent prayer when necessary versus one that doesn't. (Maybe?) I think I'll be hitting up Wikipedia when I get home. For now, Samir's not the only one praying.

He finishes and puts the towel away, then takes a seat on the bed again.

"You all right?"

He draws a deep breath and nods. "Just worried."

You and me both, buddy. "About your cousin?"

"Yes. Do you really think there is something you can do to help?"

"More like something *you* can do. I just have the right connections to help you protect all those innocent people." I hope. I take his mug from the table and offer him his coffee.

Samir interlaces his fingers around the mug, pulls them apart, realigns them. "Who are the right people?"

"The ones who can stop your cousin, who can help you protect the innocents you're worried about."

He focuses on his fingernails, a determined study. "Will they hurt him?"

"Not their preferred methodology." I don't dare make any guarantees—who knows what his cousin might do if cornered? And we don't exactly have a perfect track record. "We both want to keep people safe. Right?"

"Yes, but—"

"And I can help you make that happen."

He rubs the chair arms hard enough that I can hear the sound. When he finally speaks, his voice is a strained whisper. "How?"

"All you have to do is tell me what he tells you. I can get that information into the right hands in time to protect those innocent people." Yes, I'm harping on the innocents. As far as I know, that's Samir's major motivation in betraying his own flesh and blood. It's going to be a recurring theme in our relationship.

"How?" he asks again. "How can you do that? The people he threatens are hundreds of miles from here. What will you do, write to your embassy?" He shakes his head, but the way his eyes slide to the side doesn't read as disbelief. More like fatalism. Accepting that he's powerless.

"I have a *very* good connection with the US government." I wait until he turns back to me before I scoot closer and add the last word with extra emphasis: "Direct."

The understanding kindles in his gaze. He sits in silence, surveying me. Studying me. Scrutinizing me.

Panic time. I try to keep my face as still as possible, though my brain revs into high gear. This is my most vulnerable moment. I've spent weeks learning his schedule, finding a way to approach him, initiating the subtle little contacts that form the groundwork of recruitment. Then more weeks building our acquaintance, our trust, our friendship. Yes, I would've waited a little longer, and yes, it's crossed my mind that Brand's ever-so-helpful blind assessment might've influenced me. But until this second, I haven't risked anything quite yet. Now Samir knows what I mean. He knows what I'm asking. He knows who I am.

I can't undo what I've done. I can't take back what I've said. I. Can't. Breathe.

"You are asking me to be a spy." Samir's pitch doesn't turn up in a question at the end of his statement.

"In a sense, yes." If by "a sense," you mean pretty much every single sense there is.

"On my own cousin?"

I tap into compassion, hoping my face conveys that I understand his pain and his dilemma. "I wouldn't ask you to do this, Samir, except we both want to make sure he doesn't hurt anyone. And you said yourself you don't agree with him. Right?"

"Yes." He draws out the word.

"If there's ever anything we can do to help you, we will." You don't want to know what the CIA would do for this guy, starting with the cash in the CIA's coffers, and ending somewhere past the edge of my imagination. "Just help us keep those innocent people safe."

Samir ponders his wringing hands. I contemplate my escape options if this ends badly. He doesn't know my real name or where I live. Could he have picked up enough personal details to, say, track down Danny?

You'd think Samir has to have a lot of trust in us to protect him and act on his intel, and he does. But we—no, I, personally, have to trust him to protect me, even in a country that isn't hostile territory (though they don't exactly endorse us recruiting agents on their soil).

He finally raises his gaze to mine. One little glimmer of hope shines in his dark eyes. "May I think about it?"

"Of course. It's a big commitment, and you need to be sure before we move forward." Rejection stings, I admit, though anything's better than a no. Or a violent no.

I try to steer the conversation into small talk for a bit, so we can end on a more positive note, but after a few minutes, it's clear Samir is done. I set our next appointment, drop him off in a neutral area and start on my surveillance detection run.

Now we've both got a lot to worry about.

CHAPTER 6

THE WHOLE NEXT MORNING, I wait for the other I-told-you-so shoe to fall. But Brand's door stays shut. I'm almost ready for that sigh of relief by the time I'm packing up to go to lunch with Danny. And then Brand's office door swings open. I focus on my desk.

Doesn't work. "Talia?"

I paint on a benign smile. "Yes, 'Vince'?"

Ridiculous, I know, but just like we've both pretended I didn't lose his tail Tuesday, I'm going to keep up this entire pretense as long as possible. Everyone else in the office is using an operational name, and I want to pretend I don't know Brand from Adam or Aldrich Ames.

Brand nods for me to join him in his office. My back muscles tighten. He uses that nod all the time, I know. My stupid brain plays a montage of him nodding to invite me to a lunch table, to his apartment, to his loveseat.

All my personal clip show needs is a Taylor Swift breakup song. (Gag. Me.)

Brand closes the door behind me, but doesn't move for his desk chair. In fact, he doesn't move at all, standing just inside my personal space, leaning forward.

If he's trying to intimidate me, it won't work. I square my shoulders and stand my ground, though I can't have more than a step or two for retreat.

"I saw your report," he begins.

"My report? Where I was totally honest about Samir's doubts and nervous behavior, and said I don't know what he'll decide? Not exactly President's Daily Brief material."

Brand ignores my sarcasm. "So your next meeting is Friday?"

Don't like where this is going. "Yes?"

"I'm coming."

"No. No way. He hasn't decided if he can do this yet. How can I show up with a stranger before he's committed that far?"

"You're going to have to pass him off sooner or later." His tone makes it sound like a threat. No, that's just a fact. Agents can get too attached to their officers, trying to please them, so we turn them over to other officers.

But not Brand. Anyone but Brand.

And then I see the little light in his eyes, the gleam of excitement. And hunger.

I've seen that face before. I never wanted to see it again. The invisible grip on my stomach tempers into steel. "You can wait."

"I've got nobody here, no sources, no agents, no contacts."

"We all start from the bottom up."

"And we all inherit contacts. Will's still using his." Brand tilts his head to the side half an inch, that cajoling cast returning to his expression. "Come on, like you aren't busy enough."

"We're all busy."

"Except me." Pleading flashes through his face, but then he warms into his trademark slow, sly smile. The smile of a con man.

"Don't you have the rest of your job to do?" I want it to

come out as cutting. Instead, it's almost a whine.

"That's what I'm trying to do." Brand pauses long enough to let that subject die. He places a hand on my shoulder. "I don't think I've told you this yet: you look good."

I know his next move—run that hand down my arm. Not this time, buddy. I sweep a forearm block and knock his grip loose. "Don't pull that with me."

He recovers fast enough to grab my wrist before I can snatch it back. "Wait a second." He unfists my hand and examines my fingers—and the band of channel-set diamonds. "Married?"

"Just about." I wrench my fingers free. "Not that it's any of your business."

Brand smirks. "Guess things do change."

"No, nothing's changed."

He gives this little glimpse of innuendo that's all I need to push me over the edge to nausea.

I have to get out of here, get away, get air. It takes all my will power not to fumble backward. With the way he's looming over me now, I don't have room to open the door. But I have to get out—what bait do I have to throw him to make my escape? "You know what? Come meet Samir if you want. I have to go."

"When and where?"

"Now, and lunch?"

Brand gets the joke, though he won't accept the answer. "When. And. Where."

I can't look at him. If I lie, he'll make work even more uncomfortable next week. "Motel du Chevalier, Gatineau. Eight-ish."

Danny's been helping me with my French, and the practice shows, but I doubt that's why Brand's con man smile dawns again. "It's a date."

"Right." I don't bother softening the sardonic bite. Brand retreats enough for me to open the door. Three feet into free air, it hits me: I committed a critical error.

There's a reason I didn't mention Danny to him and vice versa. There's a reason I didn't produce my living proof that I've moved on. There's a reason my hands—my *left* hand flew to fidgeting every time he cornered me.

I didn't want him to know about Danny. And now he does. If Brand wants to torment me, he can dig around and dig up more about him. Possibly find *him*. I could show up at his house one day to find Brand lounging in the living room, trying to convince Danny they're old friends so he can share notes on me. Danny isn't dumb, and he'd never fall for that, but the remotest possibility of those two meeting? No. No. Never.

"And the latest dumps from the Russians' bug are in," Brand calls from his door. He ducks back in his office. The detonation cord wrapped around my heart is still on a hair trigger.

I'm late to meet Danny, and I need him—now. I check the office. Robby's already packing up, but he's my only choice. "Robby, translate for me?"

"But—"

"You owe me."

He groans. "Fine."

I send him the files and pretty much run to the parking lot. I can barely wait until I'm in my car to call Danny.

"Sorry I'm running late. Big project." He launches into the conversation before I can apologize for the same thing. "Should we meet somewhere?"

And risk Brand tailing me and seeing Danny? I check my mirror. Coast is still clear. "No, if you're that busy, I should come eat there."

Pause. "You hate eating here."

He's got me. He knows the full list of reasons I hate it: you can't watch your food being prepared, weirdos (and enemies) have too much access in the buffet-style setting, and grownup cafeteria food is still cafeteria food.

And oh, yeah, because I'm insane. Danny doesn't usually list that reason. Not sure whether he's overlooking or trying to forget it. Or help me get over it. He tries to tolerate my paranoid quirks, and I've been trying to slowly rein them in for his sake.

But now, I want to disappear in the noise and bustle of a hundred other people jostling for their lunches. I want to rely on the real safety in numbers. I want to take advantage of the security that's good enough that I can't charm my way past (I've tried).

I want Danny.

"Hey," I say. "You're the one who wants me to dial down the paranoia."

"Yeah, but could you do it more slowly? Maybe less *Invasion of the Body Snatchers?*"

"Picky, picky. Be there in five." Already, the tension is leaching out of my shoulders. I check my mirror again: Brand isn't behind me today. He says he's over me. Yes, he's still a manipulative jerk (though let's be honest: a spy's job is based on manipulation, so you can't color me surprised here), and yeah, Brand's wormed his way onto my case like he wanted all along. But I can still mitigate the damage. Right?

I try to convince myself of that through the short drive to Danny's office and the long line in Danny's cafeteria. He must be able to tell something's wrong, because he asks if I'm okay three times. Finally he accepts that he's not the only one with a big project he shouldn't discuss for national security. If schemes to escape Brand long-term count.

I swear, no matter how smart or upscale or big the company, corporate cafeterias are all the same. We march our food that was probably palatable when they put it in the display fridges yesterday through a maze of the same nondescript tables and plastic chairs I've seen in a hundred settings like this until we find two seats available side by side. (Danny's idea.)

I hook my heels over Danny's crossed ankles, still trying to come up with a way to force Brand to leave me alone. That tension I thought I was escaping tugs my shoulders taut again. Halfway through my sad sweet and sour chicken balls, Danny leans close to my ear. "*Ma puce?*"

A term of endearment—but it means "my flea." Since everything sounds more romantic in a French accent, seems the French decided everything's a nickname for your sweetheart.

I return Danny's worried look and pick my own stupid-but-real-(in-France) endearment: duck. "*Mon canard?*"

"You're thinking."

My concerned expression is history, and I nail him with a sarcastic glare. "Thanks for noticing. Figured I'd give it a try. First time for everything."

He matches my sardonic look. "I've seen you think before, just not with your mouth closed."

"You're hilarious."

And my humor tactic bombs. His smirk dissolves into apprehension. "You okay?"

"Worried about work."

Danny peers into my eyes a minute longer. "That's all?"

I could tell him now. It'd be so easy. *My boss is my ex-boyfriend.* Danny would understand exactly what that means. He's *Danny.*

Telling him would also give him another reason for concern. We're putting together a wedding in under three months, and I can't finalize the dress or the location or anything but the groom. Now my last boyfriend before Danny shows up?

I'm better off handling the worry for both of us. "That's all."

Danny leans a little nearer to trace a fingertip along my jaw, drawing me even closer. Normally we're not much for

63

PDA, though I'm not sure I care as he moves in. His lips touch mine, and the cafeteria sounds fade into the background.

Kisses are supposed to make your heart race and your palms sweat and your temperature skyrocket. Not this kiss. Soft. Gentle. Slow. Like he doesn't care who's watching.

And neither do I. The irritation thrumming in my veins fades away. The lingering tension in my shoulders dissipates. The anger coiled around my chest disappears.

I drink in this moment, this love, this kiss, like cool water in an oasis.

Danny pulls back entirely too soon. "Hi," he whispers.

"Hi, yourself." I soak in his gaze, the soft smile—not the genuine, amazing, eye-crinkling version, but the one that says *I love you and I can't believe you're real*. "What was that for?"

"To take your mind off whatever it is."

My laugh is way closer to a giggle. "It worked."

A tray clatters onto the table across from Danny, but he doesn't jump away from me.

"Don't you have an office where you can do that?" A short, redheaded guy plops into the chair. I know him from a Christmas party or something. Roger, I think?

"Jealousy actually suits you." Danny offers Roger a grin with the good-natured teasing, and slides an arm around me—sorry, Rodge. Taken. "You'll have to get used to it."

Roger turns to me. "You know you don't have to put up with this guy, right? Not too late to back out. Plenty of other fish in Canada." He wiggles his eyebrows.

Right. "Took this guy a year to wear me down. Nobody else on the planet is that patient."

"Good thing," Danny murmurs.

Roger mentions ailerons, and Danny sits up straighter to tackle this new challenge. I doubt he minds if I tune them out, glancing up at the ubiquitous TVs tuned to CBC News. They're finishing up the world briefs. Nothing of any particular interest to me: an election upset in Chile (probably not our fault), political shifts in Morocco (possibly our fault), and—

And Hassam-ud-Din Wasti's latest video, promulgated from his secret hideout. Threatening jihad. Big. Close. Soon.

Definitely not our fault.

Definitely something Samir would have intel about.

Definitely my responsibility to find out.

CHAPTER 7

'M ON MY FEET before the newscaster can move on to the next segment. Yeah, that's not obvious. I check Danny's reaction. He and Roger are still bent over a serviette (napkin in Canadian), sketching a plane wing. Perfect timing.

I brush a quick kiss on Danny's cheek. "Gotta go."

"Hey, no—" He shoves the napkin aside. "We can talk about the design later—"

"It's not that. Just remembered something at the office. You keep working. Love you."

"You too." Danny waits until I have to look at him again to add, "Drive safe."

The real message hangs behind his eyes: *be safe. Don't get killed. Come back to me.*

"Always."

I escort myself out. I've got to get back, check in with Will to see what we know—wait, no. Brand.

If Wasti's unknown whereabouts and latest video are hitting the international newswire, we should already know about it, a fact Brand definitely didn't bother telling me. Isn't that something I should know to recruit his cousin? It would've at least buoyed up Brand's case for pitching him now instead of developing him a little more.

Something else is going on. It has to be. Can I trust Brand?

If I'm questioning that, I'm really not sure this work situation will work out. I mean, I didn't always agree with Will, but at least I knew he had my back.

I stop short at my car door. I don't know where to go—track down Samir at work (dangerous for him), go back to the office and pretend nothing happened (not helpful), head straight in to Brand (dangerous for me)?

At the thought of facing Brand again, a shudder runs through me. Though my mind plays reruns of today's all-too-close encounters, the gnawing at my stomach isn't only about being in tight quarters with the creep.

Is all this stay-away-from-Brand panic more about my personal feelings or my intuition as a spy? I've been so caught up in trying to avoid the guy and all my memories that I don't know if I've really worked to get an accurate read on him. If that's possible.

I've got to try. I'm back at our building in five minutes, but before I can state my objectives for the afternoon, a gray van rolls to a stop behind my car, trapping me. I suck in oxygen, steeling myself to start the car and jump the curb if necessary, and check the rearview.

The van's driver is perfectly shellacked and spray tanned (okay, probably not that): Brand.

I should feel relieved, but . . . nope. He nods for me to come along. Again, not so much. I get out of my car and start for the building, placing the row of cars between us like a shield.

The van glides backward, keeping pace with me. "*Davay.*"

I shoot him a glower. Though my Russian knowledge isn't *quite* classified, it's not something I broadcast, either. At all. Danny didn't even know until I had to tell him everything.

"*Vi ruskiye druz'ya,*" Brand tries again.

My Russian friends, huh? If that's the best he can do in Russian, he's going to need my help. (He said, "Y'all Russian friends." Should be "*Vashi ruskiye druz'ya*.") Maybe this is my chance to prove to him I'm CIA material, in Canada or anywhere else. I reroute like I was planning on intersecting their path all along and reach his window. "What's up?"

Justin leans forward to chime in from the passenger seat. "You translated the tapes from the Russians' contact mic, right?"

"No, Robby did."

"Well, the Russians joined a gun club, and we need to figure out which one."

I can think of a dozen ways to do that, from tailing them to phone surveys to checking their garbage. But what does Brand have in mind? "What's this, a ride-along?" I look back to the dude cajoling me in Russian. Is Brand trying to steal this case from me, too? "I got this." More steel creeps into my tone than I planned.

Doesn't faze Brand. "Do you? If it weren't for you, we'd still have the apartment next door, and we wouldn't have to resort to this op. You're lucky we're including you at all."

"Excuse me? I saved the day there." I look to Justin again for confirmation.

None comes. "Like I said," Brand concludes, "you're lucky we're including you."

New strategy. "Then why don't you ask somebody who isn't such a screw up?" I bite back an insult, but if Brand's such hot stuff and we Canadian officers are so crappy, why'd he get sent here?

"Number one, Robby's busy. Number two, we need someone they haven't met to join their club. Who did you think it'd be?" This time he's the one who lets the slight go unsaid, though I can practically see the condescending little chuckle of *You?* fighting to get out.

"I could. I could join the gun club—I could run this op."

The smirk finally sneaks free. "Sure."

Heat burns across my face. Fine. I *will* prove it. I stride around to the back of the van and hop in. Before Brand takes off, he exchanges a little fist bump with Justin.

Great. Him too. Brand will figure out I'm not a new hire anymore. He'll trust me, he'll tell me about stuff like Wasti's new video, and we can all get back to work. Let's do this.

Brand turns back to talk to me. "Justin says you were a blonde at Morozov's building?"

"Yeah?"

"Pity. I've got a thing for blondes."

Disgust and dread battle in my belly. I don't know what he means, and I don't want to find out. Within an hour, we're setting up downtown, and I find I was absolutely right. Justin's driving the van, staking out the street, while Brand's kitted out with an earpiece and micro-microphone, which he forced me to put on him. He paces the sidewalk by the Marriott, wheeling his carry-on suitcase, biding his time, watching for a very special taxicab.

And me? Exactly where I don't belong: by Brand's side. I twist the ring around my finger. At least I convinced him I should switch out my real ring for fake bling.

We—okay, Brand—decided work would be the best place to approach the guy. When you're targeting a cab driver, that's more variable, so we've been waiting along his route for a while once we got set up. I've passed the time maneuvering our suitcases between us so Brand isn't tempted to sell this "second honeymoon" cover too hard. (I might have to hit him too hard.)

Finally Brand steps up to the curb and hails a cab. Man, I hate not being on comms. I was too busy battling him over what ring to use to fight for an earpiece. The taxi slides in front of us. Brand tosses his suitcase in the trunk and hops in the back.

Sure, make your "wife" load her own luggage at the end of your romantic getaway. I try not to grumble while I throw my bag in the trunk. I check behind us. Justin's pulling into traffic.

At least one thing's going right. I slam the trunk and join Brand in the backseat. Shudder.

Brand slides an arm around my waist. He doesn't seem to notice I lean away while he drums up a totally one-sided conversation with the stocky blond driver about the songs playing on the radio (American pop), the weather (getting nippy), the economy (could always be better). Before we've made it through two traffic lights, he's established his salesman persona perfectly: gregarious, outgoing and loud.

Not that different from real-life Brand. Watching him work, I can see exactly why he'd do well in the Agency. He's the ultimate inside man: he can charm anyone, anytime, anywhere.

Worked on me, didn't it?

"Let the poor man do his job," I mutter. I pull away from him again.

He slides closer. "It's fine, honey. I'm sure driving all day is boring." He hesitates a second before he haltingly slaughters the next two words. "Yevgeniy Morozov, where are you from?"

"Nizhny," he says, even those two syllables clipped.

"Is that in Russia? I know a little Russian! *Izvinite, pozhalujsta . . . ya . . . ne govorete . . . russki.*" Grammatically, that's the equivalent of *Excuse me, please, I doesn't speak in Russian.* No wonder he needs my help.

"*Khorosho.*" *Fine.* Yeah, sort of.

Brand forges right ahead. "Been here long?"

"Since July."

Brand finally releases me to lean over the seat, lowering his voice like he's initiating a new BFF. "Corporate wants to transfer me here, but I don't know. You like it?"

I watch Morozov, but don't hear a response. I'm guessing it's not a no, since Brand continues that tack. "What I'm most worried about is the kids."

Ugh. I hate him even more for my begrudging admiration: his I'm-such-a-tortured-soul look is classic. Brand hangs on to the cover until Morozov's eyes flick to the mirror.

"We had a break-in a couple months ago. The kids have taken it hard." Brand's note of earnestness could even have me caring, concerned, convinced. Until he takes my hand. Then I'm only concerned about myself.

I have to play this role, too. Of course he'd force me into something like this. "Don't know if we'd feel safe without a gun in the house," I murmur.

"That would be difficult here."

A complete sentence? I hold back a smile. Either Brand knows we've reached the limits of that topic, or he doesn't want me to show him up, since he steers the conversation another direction. "Checked home prices in the area?"

Morozov's answers grow shorter and shorter. If the guy could respond with a single letter, he would. Each monosyllable weighs on my heart, squeezing out hope. Great job, Brand.

Plus we're in the final stretch. The airport's so far from downtown that traffic has thinned out. That "Château Laurier courtesy van" had better still have our back.

My hopes perk up when a phone rings, and Morozov answers, "*Da*?" But Morozov's monosyllables continue for the caller, too. Is he allowed to talk on the phone and drive?

Finally, as we slow down for the airport speed limit zone, Morozov hangs up and Brand circles back. "Moving here'd be tough. All that stuff—and what am I going to do, sell my guns?"

"Here we have club," Morozov says, more life in his voice than I've heard the whole trip. "Is very nice."

Two sentences? He's got him back on the hook. I join Brand leaning forward.

"Like a hunting club?" Naïveté. Once again, a classic elicit-tation technique, getting our target to spill his guts without ever asking a direct question.

Morozov waves away that error. "Gun club. For shooting. For practice."

"Oh yeah? You know of a good one?"

And there it is. I automatically hold my breath for the split second before Morozov answers, though he doesn't hesitate. "Esquimalt Gun and Rifle Club. You must join."

"Esquimalt," Brand repeats. "Thank you, sir. Thanks a lot." The cab rolls up to the terminal. Brand parlays the rest of his gratitude into a hearty handshake, and probably a hefty tip. He retrieves our bags from the trunk, and we stride off for the doors until the coast is clear.

By the time we return to the passenger pickup, the cab's long gone and Justin's waiting.

I have to admit, Brand pulled it off without a hitch, from design to execution. Justin loads our bags for us, and we duck into the back of the van. I yank off his ring and replace my real one before the doors are even shut.

Once Justin's in the driver's seat again, he and Brand exchange another fist bump, and, okay, it's deserved. Brand looks back to me, like the teacher's pet searching for approval.

"Nice job," I tell him. The smidgen of praise only needles me a little.

"Now, can we talk about Samir?"

I lower my gaze. If that's what bringing me along was really about—yep, once again, he's played the "Game," played *me* perfectly. Maybe keeping Wasti's video from me is another of his strategies. "Tomorrow night," I say. "See you there."

I spend all of Friday waiting for Brand to tell me about the video (he doesn't) and surreptitiously interviewing everyone in the office to see if this is all in my head. Even spies aren't immune to a little eliciting when someone they trust gets past their defenses.

Unfortunately, Brand's spent most of his time listening to their current cases and palling around instead of talking, so I can't dig one little bit of analysis out of any of the guys. Useless.

Once it's dark, I start on my SDR to the rendezvous with Samir. The routine stops are uneventful, as usual. No Bond scenes or gunplay or even incorrect change tonight.

Contrary to popular belief, as a spy I rarely carry a gun. Aside from running afoul of Canadian gun laws, real spies actually *don't* want action. If it comes to bang-bang shoot-'em-up, that's not covert: attention, possibly press, all kinds of trouble.

Again, less than covert.

For the most part, we're all about HUMINT: human intelligence. Which is why officers like me rely on agents like Samir (well, I hope, anyway)—they provide information and, more importantly, analysis and insight we could never get from a drone or a bug.

And *that's* exactly why tonight's meeting is so important. Brand had better not blow it.

I park at the end of the alley where Samir should be waiting and try to squelch the nagging anxiety. It isn't too late to make this into a car meeting.

No, after yesterday, I'm sure Brand will be fine. Maybe he's right, though I hate to think it. Maybe I'm sensitive because of our past. I can't erase those memories, but Samir won't have that problem, I remind myself as I pause at the curb to pick him up. I count to five, like we're both supposed to, to make sure we're clear. Half a second late, Samir emerges from the shadows.

Now I have a real reason to worry. I watch his posture, his hands, his face, his eyes, even his mustache for any sign of what he's been thinking the last few days. His eyes stay focused, his hands aren't fidgety, and he's as close to relaxed as I've seen him. His mustache is okay too.

"So." I finally break the silence after a good ten minutes, though I don't want to start on anything too serious until we reach our destination. "Nobody followed you, right?"

"No. Who would?"

I pretend to laugh, though the image of Wasti's video flashes through my mind. Something is coming. Soon. And Samir might be the only one who can help us stop it.

But first—I brace myself for the truth. "I need to tell you something. A friend of mine will be meeting us there."

"Friend," Samir repeats, like the word tastes stranger than maple curry. "Someone you trust?"

That's the question, isn't it. "Someone who can help us."

He falls quiet again. Thinking. Calm.

We pull into the Motel du Chevalier, and I give Samir a keycard and drop him off at the exterior stairs. We wouldn't dare march into a hotel room together. I circle around and keep a close watch from the parking lot until the room door shuts. I reach for the handle of my car door—and a sharp knock at my window jolts me back. My pulse rushes in my ears. I turn to look, grasping for anything to use as a weapon.

Brand.

Great. I get out of the car. "Ready?" he asks.

"Yeah," my voice says. My tone's more like *I guess*.

Brand doesn't notice or doesn't care. He leads me to the room. Apparently he watched Samir walk in, too. I may be professionally paranoid, but when somebody IDs you and your agent that easily, you don't feel very safe.

Fortunately, Brand has to wait for me and the keycard, which gives me the chance to edge past him and get in first. "Samir, this is my friend Vince," I say once the door is bolted.

Brand holds out a hand. Samir stays where he is, the double

bed forming a barrier between us. His eyes are wide, watchful. Can't say I blame him.

"I hear your cousin's giving you trouble," Brand starts.

Samir looks to me and back to Brand. Silence.

"I believe Tara was telling you how we could help."

Samir's chin dips half an inch.

Brand takes an armchair from the table and sits. No invitation for anyone to join him. "Tell me about the problem."

Though I try to silence my sigh, it sneaks out. Samir and Brand swivel to me. I can't *say* I don't like Brand's pitch style, but I don't. If he wants to set himself up as Samir's savior—not the method I'd pick here—he needs a lot more groundwork than labeling the guy with a problem.

I have to show solidarity for Samir's sake, so I pull up the other chair and motion for Samir to sit on the bed. He does.

"So, Samir." Brand doesn't give me a chance to smooth my slacks, let alone the situation. "We want to help you."

If his next words are "Help us help you," I will drag that jerk out of this room by the hair.

"Sounds like a good fit to me." Brand narrowly avoids my planned rebuttal. (Dang it.)

Logic isn't the right way to approach him, either. Samir's "problem" comes down to emotions, namely guilt. Intro to Public Speaking, lesson one: you approach the audience how they need to hear something, not how you want to say it. Though I'm hardly surprised Brand would make pitching an agent all about himself.

I finally tear my glare from Brand and soften for Samir. "We do want the same thing—protect innocent people from becoming his victims."

That last word is supposed to have time to resonate, but again, this meeting is apparently about Brand. "I know how hard it is to feel like you're betraying someone you care about."

Doubtful.

"But you have to think about what's best for everyone here. The US government would gladly make it worth your while." Brand waggles his eyebrows, though last I checked, that meant cash or immigration favors or that kind of thing. (Not quite the edge of my imagination.)

Samir's chin juts out and he looks away. Trouble, trouble, trouble.

"Obviously you're not doing this for the money." I shoot Brand another *SHUT. UP.* scowl before turning back to wait for Samir's eye contact. "And neither are we."

"Have you *seen* the government pay scale?" Brand mutters.

Samir's gaze wanders away again. I cross my legs, "accidentally" (on purpose) kicking Brand in the shin. Seriously, what's he trying to do? Sabotage this contact? Doesn't he watch the news? Doesn't he know what's on the line?

Brand leans toward Samir in that classic all-right-let's-cut-the-crap posture. "We know Wasti's planning something big, and they always like to make a show, leave a path of carnage."

Ah, so *we* know this? Except Samir has never told me who his cousin is. Except Brand has never told me anything about Wasti's plan. Except I never told Brand what I saw on the news. Samir's question from the car echoes back to me: *Someone you trust?*

Obviously Brand doesn't trust me, so why shouldn't I treat him the same way?

Oblivious, Samir merely nods.

"And you know about it, don't you?" Brand presses him again.

"Only a little."

Brand scoots forward in his chair until his knees are almost touching the bed by Samir's knees. "And you could find out more, couldn't you?"

"Who wants to know more about these things?"

"The people trying to stop them." And for once, Brand's

answer is perfect.

Samir clasps his hands, still wary, still wavering. My gut inches downward. You can't push someone into becoming a spy. You don't have a chance if you can't figure out their values and motivations. And clearly we haven't quite pinned down Samir's.

"We need your help." Brand's voice gains a cast of actual sincerity I don't know if I've ever heard from him. "We have to protect these people—together. We can't do it without you."

Samir slowly lifts his gaze to Brand's.

"We could save thousands of lives. Innocent women and children." Brand searches Samir's face, and for a minute even I forget I'm not sure I trust the guy. "Please."

Samir opens and closes his mouth, like he's taste-testing the words about to come. "What would I have to do?"

I allow a smile for my celebration, but my heart feels ready to burst. We got him. We got him. And now we can get Wasti.

We set up the first Brand/Samir solo meeting for tomorrow, then launch into full-blown Tradecraft 101 with Samir, though I doubt he'll come face-to-face with too many enemies.

Maybe Brand just forgot to mention the video. Maybe he thought I knew. Maybe it was buried in something I didn't read, like an email that began with his passive-aggressive ploys.

And maybe I should start pretending nothing ever happened with him.

CHAPTER 8

THE NEXT AFTERNOON, I take as deep a breath as this modern equivalent of a corset/torture device allows and sigh. I haven't even gotten out of the dressing room yet and I'm already so. Done. With wedding dress shopping.

Brand's success with two missions this week notwithstanding, *I* should be the one meeting with Samir today. *I* should be getting ready—planning to fill in the gaps in our tradecraft lessons, probing for more details, trying to figure out how best to approach Wasti without sounding suspicious.

Instead, Brand's prepping and I'm jamming into dresses I can't wear without major alteration. Mormon modesty standards raise the difficulty of almost any clothing purchase, and apparently sleeves and a high neckline don't shout "couture" or "wedding day" even in Canada. Where, by the way, it gets *cold*. (Canadians might tell you they have about the same winter temps as the US, but I guess they haven't heard of a little place I like to call *the South*.)

"Aren't you done yet?" says one of the girls from church waiting outside the door—and I know exactly which. Not Abby, not AB Beth (from Alberta), not BC Beth (from British Columbia). No, that'd be "Sassy" Beth who seems to forget her nickname comes from her home province, Saskatchewan. They're the closest I have to girlfriends, though that one? Not so much.

Helps that I'm marrying somebody she was pursuing pretty hard last year, I'm sure.

"One moment," the attendant, Marie, calls. I certainly hope so: she's been tying this dress together for ten minutes, like it's not only fashionable but also a DIY project. Just what every bride wants.

Marie tugs one last time, cinching my waist another five inches, and bolts the sash in place. "All ready."

Easy for her to say. I brace myself (like my rib cage needs any extra bracing) and signal for Marie to open the dressing room door.

I'm not sure what reaction to expect from my "friends," but their looks of consternation, even Abby's, weren't it. Before I can shut the door and undo this mess, Marie pushes me out of the dressing room and to the wall of mirrors angled to give me a three *thousand* and sixty degree view of exactly why this dress is wrong.

The skirt, made of seven hundred layers of tulle, probably individually imported by hand from Montréal or Milan or Mars, poofs out at my waist to form a shape more like a bell than a human. I'm not tall by any stretch—average is a good way to describe me—but this makes me completely stumpy. I'm not sure what's up with the back; either Marie had no idea what she was doing or kludge is the new black.

"Well," Abby says slowly. "That's interesting."

"Yeah, I guess that whole ballgown style doesn't work unless you're . . . not you," Sassy Beth simpers, shaking her perfectly waved hair. Behind her, AB Beth and BC Beth trade a here-she-goes-again eye roll.

I will myself not to snap back. I can hardly blame her for not wanting to be here. I should be prepping for a meeting with an agent. I should be thinking about my next stop on my surveillance detection route. I should be recruiting spies and stealing secrets.

I shouldn't be twirling in froof for people who aren't my friends. I shouldn't be staring at a wider, stumpier version of me stuffed into a cross between Yves Saint Laurent and IKEA. I shouldn't be in a bridal store, at all, ever.

"Why don't we try something else?" Even Marie's tone clearly shows how bad this dress is for me. As if she couldn't have kept the other girls from seeing this disaster.

I guess the next dress will be better by comparison, if nothing else.

Marie helps me out of that one and into the next, but not even the persistent poking of the corset keeps my focus in this room. Is Samir doing okay? Is Brand treating him right? Are they both following procedure? Because the fastest way to get in trouble is to slip on tradecraft—

"All right." Marie zips me up and I've ended up in another pile of froof that would make a marshmallow seem substantial and solid. Like I can pull this off. Breaking in and bugging an apartment? Yes. Convincing high value targets to double-cross their motherlands? Sure.

Light or airy or ethereal? Ha. Ha.

The mirror confirms what I need absolutely no reminder of. The satin sweeps out into a full skirt. It doesn't chop my body off at the waist, but . . .

This. Is. Not. Me.

AB Beth apparently wants to make up for her roommate's rudeness. "That one's nicer."

"Not saying much." Sassy Beth grabs a bridal magazine, like I'm not worth her attention.

And she isn't worth my time. I turn to the one person I know will be honest with me, Abby. Tugging on her long dark blond ponytail, she scrutinizes me, the dress, me again, like she's calculating what went wrong where.

"That cut only works on someone a lot taller than you," Sassy Beth mutters.

I'm done. I stride off the little viewing platform, straight for the dressing room. The dress is just for pictures anyway, and—

"Wait." Abby takes my elbow before I can dive into my dressing room. "Wait."

"Please just let me get out of this." My brain means the gown, but when the words come out, I mean the entire dress shopping fiasco.

"This isn't you," Abby continues. "I know you can see that."

I stare down at the white satin. Why isn't this me? Yeah, I get the proportion thing, but . . .

Abby pats my shoulder. "It's just not your style."

Getting married wasn't my style, either.

"Why don't we try somewhere else?" she makes one last attempt. My thoughts stray to the stranger in the mirror. What does it mean when I don't see a bride looking back?

Abby takes a breath and releases it slowly, modeling for me. Yeah, like I don't know how to rein in my emotions (and like I can actually breathe). "It'll work out," she says. "I know another place—more your taste, I think. My sister got her dress there."

I don't point out I'll have to pay double for the rush alterations, if they can manage a total bodice makeover in time. I just want to get changed and go somewhere I can help, somewhere I belong—somewhere my agent is meeting with his new case officer for the first time.

"Did you want to head over?" Abby asks, still on the subject of her dress store.

"Sorry, I have a work thing. Let's try again another time."

"Of course. Right?" Abby checks with the Beths. AB and BC Beth consult Sassy Beth, like they're asking permission to answer.

She gives an I-couldn't-care-less-no-really-I-couldn't shrug. "If our schedules work out."

Excuse me if I hope they don't. I keep from tearing the dress off me, thank Marie and change back into my sweater and jeans.

I have work to do.

I break my own personal paranoia rules and go straight from downtown to our office to pick up necessary supplies. Then I use my quickest surveillance detection route to the rendezvous. That was all the planning I was privy to last night. Now I'll have to tail a trained operative across town without getting caught, and hope they're not meeting in the moving car. Aiming a parabolic mic and steering is tough.

A car turns down the quiet street and I don't look or duck. I hold still, hoping this is Brand, hoping he doesn't notice me here, watching, waiting. The gray sedan pulls to the curb, and in the still of a Saturday afternoon, I can hear the motor idling at this distance.

Brand's chilling in the driver's seat. Now I can't stop myself from sliding down an inch, like that'd hide me. I keep scanning the street. What would it mean if Samir didn't show? What would change?

Samir rounds a corner, emerging onto our street between me and Brand. For half a second, I think he'll come to me instead, like he's choosing me as his case officer. But he never sees me, heads straight for Brand, gets in.

I don't breathe till Brand passes. He doesn't glance my direction. Caution to the wind, or Brand's smarmy cockiness? Either way, it's working in my favor. When they're down the block, I dare to start my car.

I find them two cars up on the first main street we reach.

Automatically, I reach for my phone and its radio app to signal that I've got the "RABBIT" in my sights. But nobody's there to hear. Wish I had backup. There's always Elliott, but I'm supposed to protect his official cover, so I'm on my own unless it's a true emergency.

We have rules to protect us, though sometimes it seems they're just protecting the CIA.

Brand makes a quick right without signaling. Way to not draw attention to yourself there, dude. If I follow, there won't be any cars between us. And that's bad.

Believe it or not, we practice memorizing the make, model and license plate of every car behind us. (Honda Accord, ♥M1LAB. Want to know the last three?)

I roll past the corner, watching Brand, then hit the gas. Next street: one way, wrong direction. My heart rate kicks up a notch with each second ticking by—three—four—five.

Finally, a cross street. I whip down the road. My shot of finding him drops with each passing meter. I hit the red light wrong and have to wait. A corset tightens around my rib cage again, just as effective as the one in the dress store.

Until Brand passes in front of me. I laugh to myself and flip on my signal. Somebody's luck is changing today, and it isn't his.

He doesn't see me three cars back, I guess, because he only takes two more rights before he flips a U-turn. (There's an off chance he let a disguised Samir out in the two-second blind spot created by a right turn, and is using one of our popup dummies to make it look like they're still together, but I bet he didn't.)

Brand drives to a run-down warehouse complex. I let him take a longer lead, since I doubt there's another escape. After a few minutes I find his empty car half-hidden behind one of the warehouses. I keep going and park out of sight from the building.

This is a little more public than I'd like, though Brand always did have weird habits about these things. (And if someone who does SDRs to and from church considers your habits "weird," that's saying a lot.) Then again, between the echoes and the corrugated metal exterior, maybe he's onto something, since this isn't helping the top-secret version of a parabolic mic.

I have to get closer. Probably close enough to see and be seen—more the goal of a socialite than a CIA operative.

On a Saturday afternoon, there's not much going on around here, which means I'll be able to hear them better, but I won't have the advantage of background noise to cover any sound I make. Double caution around the warehouse's echoing cavern.

I head across the street, walking with purpose, like I totally belong here, and I know exactly what I'll do when I get there. My mind, however, can't escape reality: not only do I not belong here, but I have no plan, no preparation, and no backup.

How could anything go wrong?

I reach the front—make that the back, complete with loading docks. Did they go in here? How does Brand have this place after a week in town, when I'm the one giving him the "tour"?

I guess the Agency could've kept this place a secret from us lowly operations officers, but it might've come in handy a couple times over the last three years. (Once again, thanks a lot, Chief of Station Dixon, may you rest in peace.)

Three large garage doors stretch across the back of the building, and a cement ramp leads up to a regular door. Even if these big rolling doors weren't operated with electric openers, Brand would get me on the sheer noise. Plus he's got to be watching these from inside, right? There could be a security camera on me now. And if so, the best thing is to keep walking, like I'm going somewhere else in this massive complex of metal buildings that are so quiet it's eerie.

Once I'm out of a reasonable range, I do a 180 and pull out my mini binocs. A camera is mounted under the roof corner, pointing across the loading docks and out to the street.

Good thing I parked down the block.

The other parts of the roof I can see from here are empty, so I round the building to a long side with a faded RoTech sign. I don't know if that's a real company. For all I know, we're unofficially "borrowing" the place, but I doubt it. Not Brand's style. Of course, the whole warehouse thing has less swagger than his style, so who knows?

I take my time circling around to the glass doors at the warehouse entrance. In the dark interior beyond, I can make out a nondescript reception area. Gotta have alarms here, whether the place is real or covert.

No doors on the fourth side. Time isn't on my side anymore. I'm left with either breaking and entering the front, where they (probably?) won't see me until I set off the alarm, or from the back, where they *will* see me, either on camera or once I'm in.

Dress shopping might *look* easier, but I'd rather tackle this challenge than frills and froof any day. The parabolic mic picks up nothing from the office windows and glass doors, so they've got to be deeper in the building, in the warehouse itself.

I double check my wardrobe: dark jeans, black sweater. It helps that I already dress to blend in with the shadows. A quick stop at my car finishes my disguise with large sunglasses and that long blond wig. Should be good enough to fool any passersby. Now to trick the camera.

This problem calls for one of the odder spy supplies I keep in my car: bubble gum. Within a minute, I'm ready. Grateful my brothers taught me to shinny up a drainpipe quietly (something that may or may not have come in handy while rebelling against our stepmom), I haul myself within range of the camera and apply the gum to the lens. I'm invisible.

On to the doors. No scrap metal around to act as a pry bar. If I can get my fingers under the rubber seal, I should have a line of sight good enough for my distance mic, the tool for this job. The strain's not good for the sensitive equipment, but a spy has to have priorities.

I crouch down by the microphone and pop in the portable earbud. Samir's voice is muffled but distinguishable. "Bigger than the airplane attack," he says. "Not just kill Americans. Embarrass the whole country. He wants to be the man in charge, who everyone can look to."

Where's Wasti now? Who's bankrolling this op? If I could join the conversation via telepathy, I would. Instead I wait, the silence screaming in my ears. Then a metallic clang.

I need eyes. I work my fingers under the rubber seal again, making room next to the mic. In the tiny square centimeter of visibility, I see the open cement floor, metal racks twenty feet from me. In the empty area, Samir and Brand are packing up metal folding chairs.

Yeah, good thing I didn't go for the direct entry route.

I'd better get out of here quick if I plan on keeping this eavesdropping exercise a secret. Samir and Brand are quiet a minute, and I dare to double check their position before I run away.

In that tiny gap, I see Brand holding a stack of bills, his back to Samir. That's the kind of payment we'd typically make for this information. (Sorry, your taxpayer dollars at work.)

Brand thumbs through the bills. He peels off one and turns around, sliding the rest of the stack into his pocket.

The skin on the back of my neck grows cold. We have broad discretion with funds for agents, but unless Brand got that money in thousand dollar bills, that whole pile should go to Samir. My grip slips, now clammy, and the little window of visibility disappears. Samir's voice continues over my mic: "This is everything?"

"Yep," Brand says. Do they mean the money? The money Brand pocketed?

Stole?

Impossible. Why would he? He's got to be a GS- . . . I don't know what level he'd be on the government pay scale, but he shouldn't be hurting for cash. There must be a reason, a legit reason he'd take it. I need to find out.

I extract the mic, cringing at the amplified static hiss in my earbud from the rubber seal. I have to get out of here before they come out.

Did I really see what I think I saw?

A chill crawls down my back like a hundred arctic insects. Could this possibly be from my personal feelings? What, hating Brand for ruining my social life is making me see things?

I have to find out if what I just saw is real. I have to follow Brand for their next meeting.

I have to stop this.

If there's anything to stop.

Though how could there not be? I replay the two seconds of mental footage: Brand flipping through the money. Putting it in his pocket.

I have to see what he does next.

CHAPTER 9

BRAND ISN'T NEARLY AS CAREFUL as I am. (But, then, who is?) Even taking time to retrieve my gum, it's hardly a challenge to discreetly follow him back to the rendezvous point, where he leaves Samir.

I'll deal with Samir later. I have to stay on Brand. He doesn't seem to catch me behind him all the way back to the office, where he only has to switch cars.

The office is somewhere he might expect to see me. I circle around and park illegally next to the building, out of sight of Brand in the regular lot. (If this works, it's worth the ticket.) Can I look like I'm just coming out of work?

I grab an all-purpose kit disguised as a purse from my trunk and slip through the side door—Justin shorted the emergency alarm two weeks ago and apparently hasn't reported it, the idiot. Brand's been out of my sight for maybe ninety seconds, but that's long enough to escape.

I run to the doors and slow to a walk as I exit, catching my breath fast so I won't look winded when I run into him. Brand's strolling through the lot, away from the building. I jog to catch up.

"Working through the weekend?" I call, still twenty feet behind him.

He turns around slowly, mistrustful, even after he recognizes me. "Same as you, eh?"

"Yep." I hope he doesn't mean tailing him. He could've seen me, but—duh, I'm leaving our building. Though if I say I was making a report and nothing shows up in my files? "Forgot my key card."

Blame the security swipe. Works every time, right?

Maybe not. Brand contemplates me an extra long time. "Better not've lost it."

"Of course not. I'm sure it's at home." Only natural for me to ask about the agent I just handed over to him. And I do. "Seen our friend lately?"

Brand cocks his favorite eyebrow. "Nope."

Yeah, okay, he wouldn't tell me either way.

He checks his watch. "Well, I'd better head out. Man, I hate errands."

That's not an invitation, of course, but I don't care. As soon as his teal Nissan's doors unlock, I open the passenger side and hop in.

I shoot him a totally innocuous, happy expression, like *aren't you glad to have company on those stinking errands?* Personally, I love errands. When every drive requires three or four stops, it's nice to feel like you're accomplishing something in all that time.

Brand settles in the driver's seat and stares at me. Not a good stare. (Is there a good stare?) He could totally tell me to get out if he's willing to seem like a jerk.

Sounds like a safe bet. I push that thought away, buckle my seatbelt and cross my legs, blissfully oblivious by all appearances.

Brand starts the car, and I fight down the fear. I do know how to escape a moving vehicle. Before that becomes necessary, I need to take advantage of this situation. What do I have in my kit? Got to be something useful. Flashlight. Mirror. Camera. Snack. Water bottle. UV trace set.

Bingo. Where do you run an errand with a couple hundred (embezzled?) bucks burning a hole in your pocket? The bank. Or, on a Saturday, the ATM. The trace set's perfect.

Instead of a pad, the tracing ink's on wipes you can get out without opening the rest of the kit. I yank a wipe free and swipe it over the water bottle and cap. Drawback to the wipe method: no way to avoid getting the ink on me. I'll take one for the team. I uncap the water bottle and take a long draw, waiting until Brand glances my direction before I lower it.

Once his gaze moves to me, I roll my eyes. "Fine." I hold out the bottle.

Obviously he didn't ask, and again I'm pushing the boundaries of our nonexistent friendship—but as long as it looks like I'm shooting for camaraderie, I'm good. I hope.

Wary, Brand doesn't take the bottle until the next light. "Were you reporting on Morozov?"

"Should be able to get to them next week. Different report."

Is it safe to tell him about my other cases? Or could I be overreacting?

Brand caps the water bottle. I'll pretend I didn't notice he never took a sip. He touched the bottle and the cap. Good enough to coat both of his hands with that invisible UV ink.

I keep the discussion of my other case carefully noncommittal, silently praying we're close to his destination. Every ATM jumps out at me. How long until the UV ink rubs off?

At last, he pulls around the corner from an ATM and parks.

"Is that supposed to be an SDR?" I ask.

Brand snorts. "Hardly worth it in Canada. Besides, I'm not hitting an active site now. Are you?" He leaves me in the idling car without another word.

I only have a minute, but I have to wait until he's out of

sight. The second he's around the corner, I get out the tiny black light and check the steering wheel, trying to block the setting sun with my fingers. Purple streaks at ten and two. At least I know he got it on his hands. Now to make sure I don't give myself away.

The kit comes with a cleaning wipe, too, and in seconds I've got myself, the bottle, the wheel and the light wiped down and all the paraphernalia put away. Just in time—Brand plops into the seat, crumpling the deposit slip.

I want that.

"So what are you really here for? A free meal?" Brand asks. "Because I'm not buying."

"Kinda have a standing date." I'll let that sound like I mean work, though it's a total lie.

He drops the slip in the cup holder and whips around in a U-turn. "Does anyone know you're with me?"

Not a threat. Not a threat. Not a threat. Because if I think it hard enough, it's true, right?

"You know me, blowing up the Twittersphere with my every move." I need to give him a reason I'm here—and what works better than the truth? "I know you were supposed to meet with Samir. I just want to know how it went."

Silence. He shifts on the steering wheel, rubbing his fingers against his thumb. Can he feel the soap? Ink residue?

Keep him distracted. "At least tell me he asks about me."

"Constantly. Feel better?"

"Much. Did they have you behind a desk in Tajikistan too?"

"Are you kidding? Everybody's on the street in Dushanbe." Brand launches into a long story about a recruitment. If this is a joke, the punch line cannot be worth this setup.

I almost don't find out, but after this much of the story, I have to keep up the cover a little longer to hear the end once we're at our building. Instead of a one-liner, the story ends with, "Except the whole op was pointless because Rastin lied

91

about his access."

Sad and all too often true. I reach across the center console to commiserate, but stop short of actually patting his arm. I let my hand hang there awkwardly for another second, blocking his view of my other hand snatching the deposit slip. Finally I finally give him a thumbs up. "We've all been there."

I make my exit clean, and within twenty minutes, I'm back at that ATM with the black light. A remote jammer distracts the security camera, and I memorize the numbers that pop under the black light: 2, 3, 7, 8, 9. With the last four digits on the deposit slip to narrow it down, I can come up with a few thousand possibilities for the account number.

The least efficient way to handle this? Maybe. They'd love it at Langley.

Monday morning, I know the odds exactly: three thousand. Using those five numbers from the keypad, and given the last four numbers of a nine-digit account number from the deposit slip, there are over three thousand possible combinations. And now I'm staring at three thousand names of people and companies that bank alongside Brand.

No idea what name he'd use at the bank: his current identity, his real one, another alias he has handy? I can't even be sure anything's wrong, but I have to find out. I have to sift through sixty pages of names and pray something pops out—without Brand seeing what I'm doing.

On cue, the guy strolls by my desk. My heart gets a shock, but I squint at a computer file on one of Morozov's roomies. "Good or bad?" he asks.

That *is* the question. "Not sure yet," I murmur. Once he's gone, I slide my list onto my lap. I can only take a page at a time—too many and my eyes glaze over—so I alternate with researching my Russians and stewing over Samir to stay sharp. Sharp enough to catch any little hint that might jog a memory: old covers, ID cards I might have seen, anything.

With Brand walking by every twenty minutes, I don't get a lot of time to search. By midafternoon, I've made it through a third of the list, and for all I know, I've passed him.

Brand makes yet another round and again, I pretend I'm *not* investigating him. This time, he drifts to a stop at my desk, and I have to look up. "Yeah?"

"You said you knew some good meeting sites. Got time now?"

I wish he'd ask his little friend Justin (the traitor). I wish I could guarantee Brand would go away if I said no—but I can't. "Sure. Give me ten minutes."

He backs off long enough for me to run through two more pages before I pack up.

We meet outside the office doors. "You driving?" he asks.

With one final breath to steel myself, I nod. We take the stairs down and in another minute, we're in my black Honda, cruising out of the parking lot. Face to face. Alone again.

"Have a place in mind?" He doesn't wait for me to answer. "Thought we could try the Aviation and Space Museum. Sounds quiet."

"Nope." I clip off the single syllable. No way am I giving up any clues about Danny. "You want quiet? I'll show you quiet."

I wish the Currency Museum of the Bank of Canada was open, but I'll settle for second boringest—I mean, second best. The Royal Canadian Mint. Biggest drawback: it's down the street from the US Embassy, but I'd hope the officers in there know better than to contact agents in their own neighborhood.

I narrate the drive with the Mint's schedule, and the best tour to slip in, like my intimate knowledge of this museum, which I acquired on my own, proves I'm as good a spy as he is.

Brand gets out a block away from the beige stone castle.

(Canada does royal right!) I circle around to park so we can test out my intel on slipping into the same tour. By the time I get in, the tour's underway, and Brand's wedged in with three other tourists. The guide finishes her spiel, and I approach Brand.

He stares at a (fake?) gold bar on display. "Definitely quiet," he murmurs.

"Hard to bug," I point out. "Well guarded."

"They let questionable types in here?"

I scrutinize him. "They let you in, didn't they?"

"Would you bring someone like Samir here?"

"Sure." I survey the lighting like it's anything worth noting. The security cameras, on the other hand . . . "Speaking of our friend, how's it looking long term?"

"Only been one meeting. Too early to tell." He moseys after the tour guide, keeping a polite enough distance to keep up our conversation. "Do you not have enough cases?"

"No—yes—"

"How are our Russian friends?"

I watch him for a second, gauging whether he's doing his job or trying to throw me off the trail. "Still working on contact. Should go smoothly. Is Samir handling things okay?"

Brand laughs, and for once it doesn't sound like he's mocking me. The tour guide lowers the lights and starts a video on an LED screen. Brand drops the conversation to a whisper way too close behind me. "Don't you trust me?"

Who wouldn't trust someone who acts so creeptastic? He steps even with me before I murmur back, "Trust is earned. Even here."

He nods like I'm imparting wisdom of the ages instead of echoing the words I hated to hear from my stepmom. "Guess I haven't always done so well in that department with you."

I shift back a step, out of whisper range, and the overhead lights flicker back to full power. He actually sounds . . . sorry. Like he regrets what he did to me.

"Guess not," I manage. The tour guide dismisses us.

"So." He starts strolling again, but it's the leading little note in his voice that tells me we're going a different direction in this conversation. He slows to a stop in front of the Olympic medal display. "You're getting married?"

"Yep." I guess the polite thing would be to ask if he's seeing anyone.

Pardon me; I'm not here to be polite. I start for the exit.

Brand follows. "When?"

"In a month."

Again, the eyebrow twitch. "Halloween. Popular for weddings, huh?"

I don't acknowledge him, just push through the doors and head for the street. As if sharing a car is that much better.

He saves his next question until we're in said car. "Having fun with planning?"

My silence passes for my answer.

Brand's expression converts to concern. "What, getting cold feet?"

Only every time I think about the actual wedding. "That's ridiculous."

"Nothing wrong with it. I hear most people have second thoughts."

"Do most people hate wedding planning?" I merge onto the Queensway.

Brand smiles, and it isn't one of his I'm-better-than-you-and-you'll-like-it smiles, or his you-know-you-want-me-more-than-you-hate-me smiles. Just an amused grin. "Yep. Universal."

His smile fades before I can mirror it, and he sits up, now serious. I don't like this turn. Not one bit.

After a second of silence, he leans closer. "Listen, Talia. I need to tell you something." He licks his lips, but again, nothing about him is the slightest bit wolfish.

He's nervous. Do I want to know what about?

95

He meets my gaze. "Look, I know I didn't . . . handle things so well between us and—I'm sorry."

That's the second apology he's given me in ten minutes. I monitor his body language. Earnest eyes, tense shoulders, pinched mouth. He means this. He's waiting for me to respond.

"Yeah, you were a jerk."

"And I haven't been the best with you since I've been here. I guess I was just surprised to see you. Didn't know how you'd react to me."

I manage to exit the Queensway, though I feel like car interior is starting to rotate. This doesn't make sense. This isn't the Brand I knew. This is too weird.

And I can't help but wonder. Could this all be engineered to get me to back away from Samir, so Brand can do what he wants? All a tactic?

"Well, you didn't help the situation," I say at last.

"No, I guess I didn't."

More bizarre by the minute. He's agreeing with me? I shift away from him in my seat.

"But—listen," he says again. We reach our parking lot and he bows his head toward me, urgency in his tone. "There's another reason I wanted that case. I have something else in mind for you."

My mouth works, but no sound comes out. I'm gonna bet whatever it is, it isn't a confession. Brand leans even closer and any curiosity about what he's got is trampled by fight-or-flight.

I need to get away. What am I going to do? Shove him out? I reach for my favorite shield with a friendly (sort of friendly? Too friendly?): humor. "If it isn't the Russians, I've got enough on my plate."

"Later, then." Not the answer I'm looking for.

We pull into a parking spot at our building. There's one more thing I need from him while we're alone. "Quick question," I say.

Brand looks to me with a *yeees?* expression.

"Did you ever figure out what we could do for Samir in return?"

"He decided on the cash."

He says it so calmly, but the words drop into my brain like incendiary bombs. I know what I saw. Samir got a token payment. Brand didn't deposit *nothing* in the bank. Right?

Numbness creeps over me. I have to act normal. "Guess we all have our weaknesses."

Brand opens his door. I can barely make out his response. "Guess we do."

Cold prickles inch down my back. I have nothing: no evidence, no confession, nothing more than one second of a meeting and a bad feeling.

Suddenly, I feel like the woman who knew too much.

CHAPTER 10

I WISH I COULD RUN AWAY, but I can't, and the gravitational pull of Brand's charisma isn't what draws me back into the office. I have my list. Within an hour, I've whittled that to the last four pages out of sixty. My hopes are dwindling faster than the battery on a first-generation smartphone.

I check the office and flip to the next page. And then the name vaults off the paper. A spy should be better at hiding in plain sight, but there he is: Brennan Mathers. A cover he used five years ago, featuring prominently in stories of his derring-do. Too much of a coincidence, right?

Before I can talk myself off the high, I put in a request for the full records of the account. I've barely tucked the list in my locked drawer when Brand comes by. "It's later," he says.

I glance around. Justin and César are still working. At least we aren't totally alone.

"What do you want?" I ask.

He nods toward the doors. "You're about done, right?"

I'm supposed to meet Danny after work, just outside the security swipe. Could he be waiting already? I swallow hard. My stupid brain can't get in the right gear. "Sure." I shut down my computer and follow him out.

My mind and my gut wage war over whether this is a good idea. The upper hand switches with every step.

He was actually a decent person to me this morning.

He said Samir took the money.

He apologized.

He lied.

At the door to the reception area, my lungs squeeze shut. If Danny's out there, he'll stop me. He'll meet Brand. Worst of all, Brand will meet him. The whole charade will come crashing down, and Brand will win this round of his little "Game."

But the reception area only holds our receptionist, a local who supposedly doesn't know she's working for anyone other than Keeler Tate & Associates (and we take client confidentiality *really* seriously). Linda's busy typing away at a fake file we've made up. I take the lead and hurry to the elevator, punching the button twice like it'll come faster.

What if Danny's on this car? My heart climbs into my throat.

The elevator dings at our floor, and I clench my fists. The doors slide open—empty.

So why is it still hard to breathe?

We board. He hits the Door Close button. It feels like he cut off this little box's oxygen.

He launches into his meeting halfway through the short ride. "I'll be straight with you."

I don't bother to hope he'll confess this easily. I haven't mentioned my suspicions, and Brand was never the type to volunteer the truth. Not with me.

"I told you I need Samir because I have something else in mind for you, right?"

"And apparently it isn't Morozov."

"No, it's bigger. A lot bigger." He grabs one thumb and rubs it. Nervous again. "You're the only one I can trust with this—

the only one up to this." He puffs out a breath, like he's prepping himself for the big reveal. One floor left.

And then he hits the STOP button. We come to an abrupt halt. My lunch revolts, and I hang onto the railing to keep my feet and my stomach in place. Trapped, trapped, trapped.

"Can you handle this?" he asks.

No. No. No. But that little undertone of doubt in his voice makes my decision for me. "Of course I can."

Brand nods, somewhere between agreeing and confirming what he already knew. "Then I'll cut to the chase. It's Will."

"What's—"

"Will's the problem."

I can't stop my eyebrows' slow climb, incredulous, or my gut's slow fall, ominous.

Will, who just gave me that one bit of validation I've always craved?

Will, who talked with me every day to help me cope with killing a man?

Will, who shared some of the awful things he's done in the line of duty, things no one else knows, to coach me through that dark time and come out the other side?

Will being a problem, Will being in trouble? Brand might as well be speaking Bantu.

"I know it's a shock, but we've been shuffling offices partially because Will's done such a good job covering his tracks."

"Tracks of what?" I snap back. "What is this, another move in your 'Game'?"

Brand laughs softly, like I'm a pitiful story. "Tell me he doesn't have you wrapped around his finger like the rest of them. Nice ring collection."

I set my jaw and wait for him to continue. No way am I letting anything slip.

He starts circling me, the vulture. "Like I said, there's a reason we're shuffling people."

"You're saying Dixon's heart attack wasn't an accident? You telling his widow?"

Brand rolls his eyes. "It was convenient. Not like we went all MKULTRA on him."

That top-secret CIA project from the '50s on poisons, truth serums and psychotropics failed as badly as Brand's tactic is now. I back up a step. "This is ridiculous—"

"This is for real, and I need your help. Will is colluding with somebody. We just have to figure out who and how."

I don't trust Brand. I do trust Will. How can I take this seriously?

I have to make Brand think I am. "I assume the Agency is building a case against him? Collecting evidence?"

"We need more. We're talking *big* trial. Familiar with a little thing called 'treason'?"

"Not personally, no." My tone curls that into an accusation poised to strike.

Brand doesn't take the bait. "That's why we need your help. We figured you'd be the one person who he wouldn't have reached—"

"Whoa, whoa, whoa. First you're asking me to believe Will's conspiring with the enemy; now you want me to believe he's been recruiting the rest of my office, too?"

"Not recruiting, not actively. Just carefully turning away. Carefully misleading. Carefully spying on the spies."

"Isn't that what you want me to do, spy on the spy?"

Brand points at me, like *you got it, sister.* "I need someone who wasn't tainted. Out of anybody, that had to be you."

I search through that casual stance, that expression, that voice. I know it's there; I know it. This is all coming back to the reason we broke up. I don't think he's trying to punish me for not sleeping with him four years after the fact, though isn't that exactly what he's saying all over again? *Hey, Mormon ice princess, nobody can touch you up in your high tower?*

The condescension has to be there. It has to be. Incredible. The guy was apologizing this morning. "You're unbelievable."

Brand sighs. "Yep, that was my one concern. The reason I haven't come to you sooner."

My hand's on the button, but some masochistic streak makes me stop, to wait, to listen for the final blow.

He leans away from me to deliver his sad conclusion: "You're too caught up in the past to be objective."

"I know what you're doing. Won't work." He's trying to make me doubt myself, my impartiality, my instincts. The same instincts saying Will's good and Brand's bad. Very bad.

"Take some time. Sleep on it. I think you'll see the light."

I choke back a scoff and hit the STOP button. We judder to motion. I don't have time to stress before the doors slide open. No Danny.

"Think about it," Brand tosses over his shoulder. I press the button to go back to our floor. I'm still marching by the time I hit our reception area again. Laughter smacks into me like a wave of cold water. Who can laugh when stuff like this goes on?

Not anybody—my friends. Linda and Danny. My Danny.

I have never even disliked Linda, and all of a sudden, I hate her. Hate her. Like I'm thirteen and Danny's my first boyfriend, and she's the BFF betraying me.

Misplaced aggression much?

I arrive at Linda's desk to cut off their banter. French. I pick up something about a photographer before Danny spots me. "*Te voilà, mon cœur.*"

"Let's go."

"*Allons-y.*"

I give him a don't-get-Frenchie-on-me-now scowl. Confusion flickers across his face. He bids Linda *bonne journée* and we leave. "*Longue journée?*" he asks me.

Long day? Um, yes. "How many French swear words do

you know?"

He examines me from the corner of his eye, since neither of us (are supposed to) swear. "More than I did ten years ago. The worst Québécois swear words are mostly Catholic stuff." He's silent until we reach the elevators. "Why?"

I glance back, but we're around the corner from my office and the surveillance cameras trained on our doors. "My boss is a jerk. I mean, I didn't EOD yesterday—"

"EOD?"

"Enter On Duty. Start working at the Company." That's oblique enough for our hallway.

Now Danny pivots toward our doors. "Want me to set him straight?"

He flashes a hint of that he-is-who-he-is-all-the-time grin, mixed with a dash of I'm-so-clever-and-you-love-me, and the tension in my chest releases one little notch. Danny taking on Brand—aside from a horrible nightmare, it's hardly a fair fight. I mean, Danny's no ninety-nine-pound weakling, and he has a couple inches on Brand, but Brand's got at least twenty pounds, ten years in the field as an operative, and CIA training behind him.

Not that I think Danny's a wimp—he's not—and I wouldn't put my money on Brand. I just wouldn't let Danny take him on alone.

Once the elevator doors close behind us, Danny rubs my shoulders. The muscles are so tight, his little gesture of comfort grates over taut fibers. "I can make dinner," he offers. "You like macaroni and cheese, right?"

I turn to him, pulling free from his neck rub. "I'll pick something up on the way home."

"Oh." He frowns. "And the dry cleaning, and those library books you never read, and seventeen PO boxes you have under various names. . . ."

Though his voice holds a spark of teasing, he can't hide the unease in his eyes. I've been better since I told him I'm CIA, and admitted to (most of) my routines. He's tried to help me, but honestly, I don't know if I want to shake all of my paranoia.

For Danny's sake? "It's only six PO boxes," I admit. "And I read some of the books. For research." Two shreds of truth.

Can I spare another?

He takes my hand in the lobby. "Sorry you had a rough day," he whispers. "Still need those swear words?"

I can't help the laugh. "We can save them for next time."

Of course I could tell Danny the truth about Brand. Of course he'd understand. Of course he'd sympathize. He knows who Brand is, everything he did to me.

And of course, my phone rings as soon as we're out of the building.

But I'm not expecting this caller. Will. I pull Danny to a stop halfway through the parking lot. "Hello?" My tone walks a fine line between curious and cautious. To preserve his new cover, Will is never, ever supposed to have contact with me, especially not over the phone.

"Talia, do you and Danny have plans for tonight?"

"Does mac 'n' cheese and a movie count?"

"Macaroni and cheese?" Will's disdain makes it obvious he hasn't totally degenerated, despite living alone for I don't know how long. "Let me treat you. Early wedding present."

No such thing as a free lunch, or a free dinner. But how could I say no—without looking suspicious, without offending Will, without at least trying to see if Brand's blowing smoke?

I have no choice. Tonight I have to have dinner with my fiancé, and a potential traitor.

I leave out that last part when I convey the message to Danny, though. He agrees, as long as he drives, so we don't feed my paranoia. (My paranoia is very healthy; skipping one "meal" won't hurt it. Might hurt *me*.)

We head in the general direction of the embassy, and I

spend half the drive researching the place Will chose. Once my GPS app has taken over, Danny starts the conversation. (His day was fine. I rest assured.) "You never told me how dress shopping went Saturday."

I pull my hand back from playing with his hair where it flips out behind his ears. His little note of trepidation had better be my imagination. "No, I told you about it yesterday."

He shoots me a *really?* look. "When you said, 'Beth, Beth and Beth hate me'?"

"Hey, you *were* listening." I can play this off, right? "Besides, you don't seriously want to hear about a shopping trip, do you?"

Danny doesn't say anything, and I know I've played the wrong card. Not like the guy likes shopping—who does?—but apparently he needs to know . . . something. "Abby had an idea for another store to try," I say.

"Didn't find what you wanted at this place? Or did they give you trouble?"

"No, just . . ." Just me. Danny's greatest fear is discovering he's married a psychopath. My greatest fear is that his is about to come true.

I'm insane I'm insane I'm insane. Sane people don't do this. They don't treat the people they love this way. They don't rack up guilt and doubts faster than wedding gifts and debts. They don't second-guess themselves this way. Do they?

They definitely don't make at least three stops on the shortest drive to be sure no one's following them. They definitely don't search their apartment every time they get home. They definitely don't avoid restaurants where they can't see their food being prepared.

Yep, insane.

No. I will not let those worries rule me. "Maybe I'm being too picky."

"Talia?" Danny's voice carries the same doubts that are

plaguing me.

I force extra eagerness into my tone. "It's just hard when you've got something in mind, you know? And I want this to be perfect."

"Talia."

"But I'm sure we'll find something at the next place and Abby's confident—"

"Talia." His tone has sharpened to an edge, slicing off my protests. In the sudden silence, my own words, my own voice register with me, and I can hear the false, tinny brightness.

I have to try harder. I know my dress isn't a bigger deal to him than it is to me. It's not about the dress. It's about how badly I'm already screwing this up. Because I'm insane.

How can I tell him I'm terrified? How can I tell him anything?

I've already had too many people turn on me because of the truth. What if Danny hates the real me, the truth, just like all my so-called friends in DC? I've let him into so many secrets, but what if this is one too many?

Suddenly this lie is more than a little fib. It's my only protection.

The GPS app announces our exit and Danny merges onto Nicholas Street. "Sorry."

"I know."

"I'm glad you're excited about your dress."

"I know."

"And I love you," he finally murmurs.

"Danny, I know. I love you too."

He scrutinizes me a second, like he's gauging whether to believe me. The GPS takes over the talking, winding us through ByWard Market. "Where are we going again?" Danny asks.

I pull up the restaurant website on my phone. "It's called Play. York Street."

That's when I notice the little flag in the corner of the page.

Play is a sister restaurant to Beckta, both owned by the same chef. And Beckta is where Danny took me to dinner the first time he kissed me, the first time he told me he loved me.

It's also at least $60 a head. Will's paying, right? And I assume he made reservations.

Something about this doesn't feel right. Will breaks protocol and calls me at the last minute to invite us to a $200 reservations-required dinner?

Brand. Is. Wrong. Right?

CHAPTER 11

I TRY TO TALK UP MY DRESS AGAIN, to reassure Danny one more time, but he kind of obviously cuts me off to hunt for parking. By the time we meet Will at the door, I can't tell if the pressure on my ribs is more about wedding planning or whatever Will's planning.

We walk in, and I size up Will. He seems the same: same graying temples, same worry furrows, same eyes you can't help but trust. I avoid them as we take a seat at the gleaming wood bar. I doubt most people would want to sit here, though I'm in heaven—the bar is next to the glowing kitchen, and I can watch them prepare everything.

Chalk one up to my paranoia.

On a date with my fiancé, I don't ask about Elliott, and Will doesn't tell. The server comes by with her spiel about playing with their flavors and their small plates and their suggested wine pairings. At least we'll be saving Will a few bucks there.

Will orders us the charcuterie mixed plate. I have no idea what that is, though I'm in no position to negotiate, especially not once Will discreetly tells the server he'll pick up the check.

Discreetly? Uh, yeah. Spy.

I let Will steer the conversation in Danny's direction and observe for a few minutes as they both deflect questions about the classified portions of their work. (It's weird that I find that endearing from Danny, huh?) Something's different about Will, definitely, but I can't imagine—

Doesn't matter what I can imagine. It only matters what I can see here, what he says without speaking. And while that's not sending the exact same message as when he was my boss, the change doesn't seem to be one for the worse. No way he could have fooled us all this long.

Then again, it's happened before. Not just Aldrich Ames. Double agents who've tricked officers and examiners for decades. False flags. Moles.

I have to forget everything I know about Will and watch him like an impartial hawk.

The plate of sausage, prosciutto, salami and sides arrives, and the conversation lags while we eat. I watch Danny smear part of the spoonful of brown I-don't-know-what onto a little piece of toast. I saw them prepare our food, but they don't exactly use a big bin labeled with the ingredients. "Tell me that isn't spreadable meat."

"Cretons." Danny offers me a bite. "Big in Quebec."

Apparently I'm as out of place with haute cuisine as haute couture. I decline; Danny pops the tiny crostini into his mouth with relish. (The metaphorical kind, not the maple-sour apple stuff on the plate. Now, *that* I'd eat with a spoon.) The waiter arrives to take our orders for the next round with perfect timing. Danny picks the pork belly with sweet potato, I settle on the roasted beets with quinoa and blueberries, and Will has the hanger steak and "fries." The menu says "frites," but it's hardly worth correcting him. He's survived this long in Canada without French.

We revert to small talk as we survey the kitchen. I've watched many chefs make my food; this is different. Yeah, the premise of the place is playing with food and flavors, but I've never observed this level of adeptly arranged anarchy in a kitchen. Everything placed just so. Everything presented just right. Everything pieced together just perfectly. Hard not to be in awe of the choreographed chaos.

I know a little about choreographed chaos.

Much as I'm enjoying the show, I have something else I need to watch. I excuse myself to run to the restroom before our plates come. When I return, Will and Danny are chatting. I hang back for a minute to eavesdrop on their candid conversation.

I do *not* spy on Danny—but it's not him I'm spying on.

However, he's the one doing all the talking, using his hands to represent an imaginary plane to demonstrate some aerospace principle.

Will gives him a yes-and-let-me-tell-you-more-about-this look and jumps in. "So all they have to do to avoid the missile is accelerate."

"Yep. When your cruising speed is Mach 3.2, not a whole lot can catch you." Danny turns back to the empty charcuterie platter and idly pushes the spoon that held the cretons away. "Except for the Concorde, of course."

"Oh yeah." Will leans forward eagerly. "There's some serious speed."

"Yep." Danny still stares at the plate, though his shoulders have shifted. Why's he uncomfortable?

Will presses on. "That might be what they've been working on in the drone my friend was telling me about. He said they had to redesign the airspeed indicator to get an accurate reading."

In profile, Danny's expression reads somewhere between intrigued and incredulous.

This doesn't feel right to me, though I can't pin down why. If it were anyone else—two anyone elses—I'd wait and see how this developed. But Danny isn't just anyone, and neither is Will. I slide back onto the stool between them and pick up the menu. "*Quelque chose te tracasse?*" I murmur to Danny. *Is something bothering you?* (See?)

"*Plus tard*," he mutters back. *Later.* I want to ask more, but our food arrives with a flourish, each plate the size of an appetizer at any other restaurant. Danny leans in to whisper to me: "Nobody touched your food."

I shoot him a smile before I attack my plate. My beets aren't just beets; they're sweet and they're earthy, with the quinoa popping in my mouth alongside the tart blueberries. I almost feel guilty enjoying all this on Will's tab. But it was his idea and we *are* saving the guy thirty bucks by skipping the suggested wines, so I try to swallow my guilt and savor the rest.

The waiter swoops in at the perfect second to take orders for the next round. Will goes for lamb and polenta, I order gnocchi in brown butter cream, and Danny asks for tuna tataki.

Once the waiter's gone, Will takes over the discussion. "You're a fan of the SR-71?"

I'm guessing he doesn't mean me. Danny shrugs. "Sure, though there's a lot to be said for its predecessor, the—"

"The A-12?" Will cuts him off.

Danny's lips twist like he was expecting Will to bring that up. (I wasn't. Totally lost.) "I think that's it, yeah," Danny says. "I've never kept up on Skunk Works stats."

Now I know what they're talking about: "Skunk Works" is the nickname for a secret aerospace R&D division, and its CIA-funded black projects.

Will fiddles with his wineglass. "Most of it isn't common knowledge. People today don't remember the Cold War. Don't want to hear their tax dollars went to paying off witnesses, or guards' six-figure salaries, or chefs on call twenty-four/seven for steak and lobster."

Danny merely watches him.

Will steeples his fingers on the bar. "I guess it makes them wonder what we're spending money on these days. Because the more things change . . ."

I know what the CIA spends money on, and, yeah, the taxpayers definitely wouldn't like it. We try to keep the steak and lobster to a minimum, and only for special occasions, though cash for information isn't any more palatable.

Danny's finally fully onboard with this conversation. "Speaking of the Cold War—heard of the Avro Arrow? Delta-wing interceptor from the fifties. Canadian, axed right after flight tests started."

I clamp down on a groan. He. Is. Obsessed. With that thing. "Not this again," I mutter.

Danny winks at me. "Did I tell you? There's a full prototype on display in Toronto. I'm thinking honeymoon."

I shoot him a glare. I expect him to get me out of Ontario at the very least. He ignores me and leans forward to make eye contact with Will again. "Would we need that travel form?"

"Better safe than sorry." Will draws an envelope from his jacket pocket—and draws the discussion back to his real topic. "The Arrow does sound familiar. I'm sure the real DS&T guys would love to talk all about it."

"They're not the ones I'm curious about." Danny stabs a straggling candied pecan. It shatters, flying in three different directions. "Rumor has it the Arrow got spooked."

Clever. The CIA's possible role in killing the Arrow is something I really don't want to know about. But Danny does. Will leans closer to me. Closer to Danny, passing the envelope over the bar. (I nab it before Danny can.) "Now *that* takes clearances." He leans back to let the waiter slide his lamb, extra rare, in front of him.

Wait. My gaze stays on the gnocchi in front of me, but my mind strays seven weeks away. My last big case involved aerospace—and Will didn't know word one on the subject. I had to become the subject matter expert, with Danny's help. The realization lands in my gut like rubble, and the CIA's gold-for-gossip policy isn't the only thing less than palatable.

I know exactly what Will is doing. I've done it myself, time and again.

He's setting Danny up. To recruit him to DS&T. To the CIA.

Would that be a terrible thing? Transferring back to Langley, a snug, safe desk job, working for the same "Company" as Danny?

As sweet as it sounds on the surface, underneath there's the dark, hulking truth: if Danny were induced to take the job, if he took it for my sake, if he were trying to please me . . .

I poke at the little potato pillows on my plate. Even the perfectly nutty butter balanced with the salty-tangy-sweet relish doesn't taste right. I finish, but when Will suggests dessert, I decline. Danny agrees and takes my hand under the bar.

That should reassure me.

It doesn't.

After profuse thanks, we're out of there as fast as possible. Danny keeps quiet through the hasty retreat, through the walk to his car, through half the drive back to pick up mine. "So what's the matter?"

"Nothing." I don't even have a twinge of guilt to ignore at the universal girl lie.

"You refused dessert. Obviously you're not okay."

I wave away his worry. "Too fancy. I just want to go home. Don't you have ice cream?"

"Cookies."

We stop at a red light and Danny turns to scrutinize me. "This doesn't have anything to do with Will, does it?"

"What?" I'm pretty good at feigning ignorance, but I'm not sure I'm really trying. "Why would you think that?"

"Has he always been into planes?"

How much should I say? "I dunno."

"Because anyone who knew the first thing about aerospace should've laughed in my face. The Concorde barely doubles the speed of sound. The SR-71 more than triples it."

"You—you just—you're tricky."

"It's a gift."

I toss off a smirk. "But would everyone know that?"

"We're talking about a really fast, really big passenger jet versus the fastest air-breathing manned aircraft ever flown."

I'm too preoccupied to point out I wouldn't put that together unless led down the path. The silence slowly grows stale.

Will's talking way over his own head—always a bad idea in recruitment. But that means he's recruiting Danny.

Recruiting him to the CIA. Not to an enemy he's supposedly working for. Right?

"Talia? Everything okay?"

I don't have to look at Danny—the worry in his voice hangs over the car like a shadow. He pulls onto the shoulder, and we sit in the silence.

How can I tell him? I pick the fastest, shortest way, like each syllable of the truth costs me a pound of flesh. "I think Will's trying to recruit you to DS&T."

"No, you think?" Danny's voice is laden with sarcasm.

"You could . . . tell?"

"Of course."

I watch him for a minute. "Do you *want* to join DS&T?"

"Do you want me to?" His voice is almost a whisper, like he barely dares to ask.

"I don't—I don't know. I mean, I'm just—I'm going nuts here. This thing with Will is freaking me out, and work, and planning and dress shopping—"

"Whoa, one thing at a time. When's your next shopping trip?"

"In a week." We only have four weeks until our wedding, and I'm supposed to be excited about this, so I rush to explain. "The store has these weird hours, and I've got meetings—"

"Stop." Danny reaches across the center console for my hand. "This isn't like you. And not in a 'trying to not be so paranoid and it's hard' way. In a . . . weird way. Bizarrely excited."

I sigh. "Don't you want me to be excited?"

"Excited is fine—great. But airheaded, giggly . . . lace? Have you *ever* worn lace?"

"I just want it to be perfect." I think he can hear the real message right through those words: I want *me* to be perfect.

Danny waits until I have the nerve to meet his gaze. "You do realize this wedding is only one day of our lives, right?"

I let an eyebrow sneak upward. "The most important day of our lives . . . ?"

"That's a load of crap," he says matter-of-factly. "It's a wedding, and we'll be lucky if half our own families make it." Danny leans over the console and focuses his warm brown eyes on mine. "This one dress, this one day is way less important than the actual marriage. *Our* marriage."

I keep watching him uncertainly.

"I don't care if you have a wedding dress. *You* are more important to me than what you wear or what temple we get married in or any of the other details. You, me, temple, I'm good."

I manage a weak laugh. "Why don't we elope?"

"Yeah, how long do you want to alienate both of our mothers for?" He pauses a second, glances at me, and adds, "Don't answer that." Then he looks—truly *looks* at me. "If you're really not okay, I need to know."

"No, I—" Can I tell him? I search his face a second, like that'll tell me how he'll react.

"Do you want to get married?" he asks.

This time I don't put up the front, don't put up the fight, don't put up the fake enthusiasm that's propelled me through our last four conversations about wedding planning. "No," I breathe.

Danny sits back in his seat. Stares straight ahead. Nods.

Crap, what did I just say? "It's not that. I mean, if I marry anyone, it'll be you."

He studies me from the corner of his eye, skeptical. "Uh, thanks?"

"I . . ." My voice hangs there in the moment. Danny needs me. He needs the truth.

And I need him. I need to tell him this. For us. "It's . . . the stuff with my parents."

"Okay," he says, with a tone of *I can work with that.* "Why did your parents get divorced?"

Are we playing stupid? (Yeah, I'll win this game.) "Didn't want to be married anymore?"

He blinks at me, waiting for me to take him serious. So I do. "Because . . . my mom's pathologically incapable of thinking of anyone except herself, and my dad couldn't save her."

"Are you your mom?"

I consider that one a minute. What's he trying to say?

"Here's a hint: are you telling me all this stuff because you're thinking about yourself?"

He has a point. "No," I admit.

"Then maybe you don't need to worry so much."

The idea takes a strange shape in my mind. It might be one I could get used to. "It *is* my favorite hobby."

Danny glances heavenward. "Yeah, I know. So are you going to be okay?"

"Still freaking me out a little, but . . . I think I can work on it."

He leans forward, studying me a minute longer. "You can tell me the truth."

I let that sink in a second. "I promise, I am." About this. I offer my final evidence: "But there's no dream dress—in fact, everything I tried was awful. Abby's doing all she can to keep hope alive."

He must see the truth there, because his Talia-melting smile dawns. He leans in the last few inches to kiss me, and I savor this moment.

I'm more important to him than anything else, and even if he hadn't told me that, this kiss proves it. He finishes with a quick peck on my nose before pulling back into traffic.

"Honeymoon in Toronto, huh?" I joke. I give him the travel form.

Danny takes the envelope and grins, back in teasing mode. "You can't resist the Canadian Air and Space Museum. Full replica of the Arrow."

"You know me too well." And sometimes, that's the truth.

CHAPTER 12

STARTING TO RESOLVE SOME OF MY ISSUES couldn't come at a better time, because now I need to focus on my most pressing problem. Parked outside Will's house three days later, I readjust my binoculars and slump a little lower in my car seat. It's dark, I'm in a car he won't recognize, and he should have no reason to worry, but I'm nothing if not careful.

Will's not nearly as cautious as I am. (Seriously, no one is.) No surveillance detection run on the way home, no meetings, no signals, no nothing. In fact, this has to be one of the most boring surveillance assignments I've ever done. Brand. Is. Wrong.

The garage door to Will's unremarkable stucco rambler rolls open and there's everyone's favorite CIA chief of station in a Mr. Rogers cardigan. Leaving for a meeting with an agent?

Will heads past his perfectly nondescript car: Canada's most common make, model, and even color—Honda, Civic, white. He's got a bag. I train my focus on that black garbage bag, less than half full. To anyone else, that's just trash. To me, it's something he doesn't want people to see. My pulse picks up a tick. This could be important.

Will reaches the passenger side of his car. Opens the door. Leans in. He'll stick the bag in there and drive off and betray everything he was ever supposed to stand for.

Or not. He straightens, pulls out a Tim Hortons sack and stuffs it in the trash bag. He deposits the garbage in the black plastic bin beside his house and goes back in.

No relief allowed yet. Could still be a drop off. A risky one, sure, but we're in Canada. How secretive would a double agent from a friendly foreign country have to be?

It's a long, long night until the lights go out at Will's. I wait until he has to be asleep, each minute ratcheting the muscles in my shoulders, my back, my legs tighter. Finally, I open the car door and prowl along the hedgerow to check the back. Lights off.

I move to the garbage can and ease the lid open. Of course the bag is way at the bottom. Grateful it's well after dark, I lower the can to the ground and crawl inside.

Yes, the real life of a spy puts James Bond movies to shame. Nonstop glamour. I drag the bag out and replace the trash can, hunkering down beside it to hide from the street. Normally, I'd take this and run (yes, I do this enough to have a "normally"), but I can't risk Will noticing. I hardly need my flashlight to see that this is an unremarkable, sadly lonely load of kitchen trash: microwave dinners, desserts for one, budget meals. I almost feel bad for our $150 tab this week, like he's been doing penance for his accounting gluttony.

Nothing incriminating here whatsoever. Okay, so Will's trying to recruit Danny to the CIA. Doesn't mean he's gone to the dark side.

Could I have fallen for Brand's strategy all along: put me on Will's trail to keep me off his? Everything he's been doing—all that talk about how I can't be impartial, the "apologies," those "genuine" gestures, siccing me on Will, if only for a few days—it's not just Brand being obnoxious. It's Brand being covert.

Yep, I'm an idiot. I reload the garbage bag, slip it back into the bin and head out.

I know what I have to do. I have to watch Brand, and I have to be extra careful to make sure he thinks everything's fine.

The next day on my way to the office, I take one of my lesser-used surveillance detection routes, running through downtown. Mostly SDRs are a habit for me—one I'll try to break after the wedding—but today I'm glad for the extra time to think, to hammer out my plan of attack.

On Brand.

So it's definitely not a good thing when I reach the card shop that holds one of my postal boxes (I really do have six) and nearly run into the man himself, walking out the doors, blocking my path. I freeze. His eyes flicker wider the second he recognizes me.

I wish I could elbow past him, but even in New York City that'd be rude. "Sorry," I say, throwing on my best Ottawan accent. "Didn't mean to give you a fright."

"No, I'm sorry." He pats my arm, like he's making sure I'm okay. "You just reminded me of somebody."

"Somebody that you used to know?" I force my lips to smile, but don't bother unclenching my teeth.

He watches me warily for another minute until I have to edge past him to get in. The sign registers when I pass underneath—I'd forgotten. The shop is named Between Friends.

Yeah, right.

Bizarre. In a metro area of over a million people, I've never run into anybody from work on a surveillance detection run. Of course he'd have to be the first.

I think I keep everything neutral at the office throughout the day, but when Brand calls me in again before I leave, my worry-meter pegs out. I march in and take a seat in front of his desk like nothing's wrong.

Nothing *is* wrong—because somewhere between filing reports and filling out paperwork, I came up with a plan. I'm taking control. I'm taking Brand on.

Brand settles behind the desk, and I ignore the obvious power play of positioning. He's got a nice chair. I've got a nice ball of anger building in my chest.

"You know, I got an email the other day."

"Only one?"

He casts me an indulgent smirk. "One in particular I want to talk to you about."

Seems unlikely Samir's shooting the guy an email, and Brand made sure any of our friends from before aren't so mutual anymore. It could still be work-related. Right?

"You pulled a trace on one of my bank accounts, didn't you?"

Caught. My mouth goes dry. "Checking up on you. You're the one who said Canada isn't a promotion."

He scrutinizes me. I try to swallow. No luck. "Being cautious?" he asks. "Or are you worried about little ol' me?"

"Constantly." I roll my eyes, and for once, that's actually okay.

"Have you been working on that special project?"

We wouldn't mention Will by name here. I dip my chin. "Last three nights."

"Bet your fiancé loves that."

I texted Danny Tuesday that I'd be booked solid. I search Brand's gaze for that innuendo, like he's probing to see if that one "little" thing we couldn't "see eye to eye on" is still an issue. The overtones are buried so deep Brand may not realize what he's saying. I wish I could put him in his place and put that outrageous question to rest—no, I'm not sleeping with Danny and yes, we take our religion's moral standards seriously. But I have to look like I'm cooperating with Brand. "He's very understanding."

"I guess anybody would have to be." He gets back to the subject. "Anything unusual?"

"Not yet."

Brand adjusts his position, leaning over the desk. "I'm sure I don't need to tell you this is all off the books. No official paperwork yet."

Right. Keep it off the books, keep it unofficial, so he can manipulate the situation however he wants. Yep. "I got it."

"So you'll be on surveillance tonight?"

"I've got other meetings. I'll have to get back to it."

"Right. Can't let your other cases drop." Brand, always so understanding. I refrain from rolling my eyes again, tie up this meeting as quickly as possible, and take to my desk to look busy. Not hard; perusing my email is close enough until Brand leaves without a glance at me.

Perfect. Time to put my plan in action. I snag my favorite reversible jacket for pursuing someone, keys for a Company car, and a disguise kit and walk out after him. In the hallway, I hear the elevator doors sliding shut. Stairs it is. Faster than waiting for another elevator anyway.

I kinda regret that choice several flights later when I reach the ground floor. The jog winded me a bit, but I'll definitely live. I ease the fire door open a crack.

As Hollywood as the tactic sounds, I use a little mirror to peek around the door jamb. The elevator arrives. Brand steps off, alone. More perfect.

I already know what Brand drives. If he gets in his teal Nissan, nothing might happen tonight. Though I've wasted the last three evenings watching Will lead a sad little lonely life, I'll follow Brand and *his* sad little loneliness until he finds a listening ear. I.E. Samir.

Brand reaches the front doors, and I finally slip out of the stairwell to tail him. My shoes—comfortable flats, of course—still echo over the lobby's marble floors, but Brand's already outside. I gather my hair into a low ponytail first, then double it into a floppy bun before pinning my bangs to the side. My disguise kit provides a wig, light brown and waist-length, and I think my spare sunglasses are safe enough. By the time I reach the doors, I'm not Talia anymore. I hope.

Brand's halfway through the parking lot. I time my feet to march with purpose (and a much springier step than my normal gait). On an SDR, you often ignore people with direction and an air of competence. They're not the ones watching you; they're too busy with their own lives. Or so I want Brand to think now.

I have to pass him getting into his Nissan on my way to a Company Civic (seriously, the most popular car in Canada for two decades). He doesn't turn back, and my ribs release their iron grip. He might just pick up dinner and go home. Or he might not.

It's not hard to stay behind Brand at a safe distance with the other people leaving our building now. And once he gets on the Queensway, traffic is heavy enough that he doesn't have much of an opportunity to get away, though I doubt it's crossed his mind. Yet.

Nope, nothing to fear from the little silver Civic. Keep driving, Brand. Keep driving.

I know a couple of the signal sites and rendezvous he and Samir set up in our one meeting. Our crash intro to tradecraft included simple lessons in signaling and dead drops. When I learned this stuff at the Farm, it felt like things I'd never use in the field, just part of the curriculum to satisfy any CIA trainee's cloak-and-dagger dreams.

I was wrong.

The first signal site Samir, Brand, and I discussed is almost uncomfortably close to my home. (A kilometer is uncomfortably close to someone as paranoid as I am.) So when Brand takes the exit before mine, I can't help but grip the steering wheel that much tighter.

He can't seriously be this dumb, right? He hasn't made a single surveillance-detecting stop. Totally against protocol to go straight from a CIA facility to any sort of active site, or a dead drop. You have to check for people tailing you. Every. Single. Time. Even if you're in a friendly country because you never know who else there *isn't* friendly.

I know every decent surveillance-detecting stop within five miles of my apartment. He hits a drive-through Tim Hortons for a donut—doesn't count, dude—and navigates the surface streets.

Past the signal site we discussed. A belt cinches around my heart.

Into my neighborhood. The belt squeezes tighter.

Onto my street. Tighter.

Each cross street winnows the traffic between us further, until it's just me behind Brand. Across the street from my building. Where he parks.

Tighter.

I continue down the block and park around the corner, so I can barely see him.

And then my phone rings. I snatch it up, hoping, hoping, hoping it's Danny.

It's Brand.

"Hello?" I answer.

"Hey, you still in the office?"

Oh crap. He knows. He knows. My phone has excellent noise canceling, but I can't take the chance he'll hear the car passing in the background and put it together with what he can see. I fill the silence. "Leaving now. Did you need something from inside?"

"Wouldn't want to trouble you. I'll call Justin."

And speaking of background noise, if there's anything loud right about now—a car horn, a dog, music—I'll lose any semblance of cover.

Yeah, I'm not troubled at all.

Better make it clear that breaking into my apartment would be a really stupid move. "Well, better go. Gotta stop by my place first, and I don't want to be late." I barely wait to bid him goodbye and hang up. I grab the mirror I used at the office and find his car. Hard to tell from here, but I swear he's got binocs out, staring up at my building.

For obvious reasons, I made sure I got a unit that doesn't face the street. Now I'm officially glad I did.

Another possibility hits me like a bullet. If Brand knows I won't be home for long, he might just wait until I leave to make an entry. And of course I already know exactly how difficult to breach my apartment *isn't* for a trained operative. I'm too paranoid to put my paranoia on display with multiple deadbolts, and though they just had to install new, more secure windows (and I'm a couple stories up), they're always a vulnerability.

Brand gets out of his car. It feels like a hand's closing around my throat. I don't keep anything particularly personal up there. There's no threat to any of my agents. No secret diary. No box of keepsakes from our short-but-sour relationship.

No, it's just my home. My life. And I can't let him go there. I won't.

He leans against his car and pulls out his phone. The hand on my throat presses tighter and I hold my breath, waiting for mine to ring. Could he have spotted me, even around the corner, even through my disguise?

Wish I'd thought to bring a wireless interceptor. The nicest "parabolic" mic we have (like that, but better and classified-er) could pick up both sides of the conversation, but can I settle—

My phone rings.

Breathe. Don't choke out the answer. Don't take your eyes off him.

"Hello?" I think I almost sound normal.

"Everything okay?"

Yeah, guess I'm failing on that "normal" thing. But I know this voice—and it isn't Brand's. "Sorry, Danny, I'm in the middle of something."

"Oh. Okay. Just figured you might like dinner if you were at the office."

At the—? Brand's second phone call. "Who told you I was at the office?"

"Isn't that where you work? I mean, your car's still here."

"Yeah, had to borrow a Company car."

"Ah," Danny says. "Well, if you're done any time soon, I've got pineapple chicken."

Yep, he knows me too well. The thought of my favorite Chinese dish makes my mouth water—but my focus is back to Brand, chatting on the phone, watching my home. Could he be calling my super?

"You there?" Danny asks.

"Sorry, busy." This is one reason we don't usually bring our phone with us on ops. "Better go."

"I'll stick your dinner in the fridge."

"Freezer." I didn't use to keep food at all, until that habit got to Danny. The tiniest little compromise, and it took us almost a month, but hey, I'm working on it.

Brand hangs up and gets back in his car. I can breathe again—though now I really don't have time to talk. "Love you," I tell Danny, and end the call.

I don't think Brand's noticed me here, but I can't take any chances. I slip the brown wig back into my surveillance bag and replace it with a blond one and a fashionable beret I couldn't pull off in real life. My jacket turns inside out from tan to dark green. With a little help from some magnets, I even change my license plates quickly.

When Brand pulls out and flips a U-turn, I'm ready to take up pursuit again.

I stay a good distance back during the perfunctory stops of his SDR (or actual errands he's running). Is he even trying to not be followed? That's the point of an SDR—identify your pursuers, then bore them to death so they think you don't have anything, give them the slip when their interest wanes—but you'd think a criminal mastermind would at least break the speed limit or something.

Nope. Every appearance of the perfect citizen.

Until he parks on a quiet street in the middle of downtown and walks into an alley. I know better than to slowly cruise past and put him off his quarry, so I park down the block—ironically, by Between Friends—and hit the pavement.

The best operatives know that if you're caught doing something you're not supposed to be doing, the worst reaction is to jump. We practice listening to our instincts and fighting our reflexes, going about business as smoothly as possible, even when we're doing something that looks totally weird. Yep, I mean to dig through that garbage can. Yep, I collect boring rocks. Yep, I want this bottle coated in motor oil. Yep, love me some dead pigeons.

Dead drops are another thing that's way more glamorous in the movies.

I can't stop to see if Brand's getting into one now, but I stroll by the alley as slowly as I can, holding a pretty compact mirror. Sometimes when you can't conceal something, the best place to hide it is in plain sight. Or on display.

I make a show of checking the lipstick I'm not wearing, while angling the mirror into the alley. Facing one of the blank walls, Brand's got an old-school, standard-issue dead drop spike, a hollow plastic tube designed to hold anything small the officer or agent wants to drop off.

I can see from here this drop-off isn't something small. Brand dips into the spike again—and draws out a wad of green paper.

Cash. American.

Maybe Samir or someone else left something Brand's already retrieved. Maybe Brand's giving him the rest of the money from Saturday. Not the securest way to pay, but maybe.

I pretend to stumble and lose my heel. Brand doesn't look up, and I take the chance to pause, lean down, replace my shoe.

He's pulling the money out. And he's not even careful about concealing his subterfuge.

Static steadily invades my hearing. I make it around the block and back to the car. It could be discretionary funds. But . . . why would he be taking that *out* of a dead drop?

No misconstruing that scene, no misinterpreting, no explaining it away. And it's anything but good.

I've got to do something. I've got to figure out what's going on here.

CHAPTER 13

WITH BRAND WATCHING ME, I have to be extra careful. Know what extra careful looks like when you're already the most paranoid spy in Canada?

Actually, it looks like nothing. It looks completely unnoticeable, untraceable—unremarkable. So basically my entire Saturday is an SDR designed to bore Brand to death while I'm catching up with Danny, who plays right into my plans. We've enlisted a friend from church, and we spend most of the day driving across town and posing for engagement pictures. (Turns out it's the last weekend they're running the locks on the canal, and they're great in photos.)

By the time I head home for the evening, I know I'm safe to go directly to my real destination: Elliott's. I park down the block and watch the cute little brick rambler in the suburbs. Quiet. Peaceful. Wife, baby and picket fence: the complete American dream package. Except in Canada. The perfect hideout for a spy.

Brand's already suspicious of me. He might have everyone in the office under the same scrutiny. Or he might've added them to *his* jewelry collection, like he accused Will.

He knows Will. He knows César, Justin, and Robby. He knows Mack & co. at CSIS, our Canadian equivalents.

I need a plan. I need help. I need someone Brand doesn't know.

I need Elliott.

With him under official cover and me not, he and I shouldn't have any contact outside the secured area of the embassy. And we haven't, not one phone call or email or text. Wouldn't want to start breaking those rules with something that easily traced anyway.

Which is why I'm here. Most people don't expect visitors three hours after dark (even if it's only ten), so I can't blame Elliott when he answers the door with a guarded expression. But it doesn't go away when he recognizes me. "What are you doing here?" he says instead of hello.

"Good to see you, too."

"You're not supposed to be here."

I watch him a minute, willing him to figure it out. Close as we are—were—I wouldn't show up to chat, and I've been to his house all of no times, so something must be wrong, right?

"Are you in trouble?" he asks.

"I think I'm about to be."

Elliott scrutinizes me, and suddenly I realize how tired he looks. Even backlit by his house, the shadows under his eyes, the patchy whiskers on his cheeks, the grim set to his mouth are evident. All except that last one seem typical for a father of a newborn. I think.

"Bad trouble?" he asks.

"Would I be here if it weren't?"

He glances over at the street, then his shoulder, but he isn't really scanning the room behind him. He steps onto the front porch with me. "Come on." He leads me around the side of the house, through a gate to the backyard. An old metal playset, like a leftover from my kindergarten days, slumps in the corner of the yard. Elliott plunks down in a kid-sized swing.

Uh, sure. I take the other swing. "Everything okay?" I ask. Like the answer isn't obvious.

He laughs, a humorless, halfhearted huff that devolves into a sigh.

"I'll take that as a no."

"Been a long month."

When Elliott doesn't continue, I push off the mud to start the swing.

"Did you ever tell Danny about that time we—" Elliott breaks off, and he doesn't have to finish. I know exactly what he means, though we were never supposed to talk about it. (In fact, it was so Top Secret, we never actually had to talk about never talking about it.)

"No. He hadn't even asked me out." That was, what, three days after Elliott kissed me?

It was a cover. It was a cover. It was—

Wasn't it? I turn to Elliott. He's not looking at me. "Why are you bringing this up?" Concern creeps into my voice.

"Shanna found out."

"You mean you told her." I don't have to tell him how stupid that was, though they weren't married—no, they weren't even dating at the time. On a break, her decision.

"It came out."

My swing slows to a stop. "Elliott, don't tell me—this isn't about me—"

He cuts me off with a laugh. "I was trying to prove how much I've changed. Not like I'd throw away my marriage over you."

"Throw away—what happened?"

"She took the baby. Went to her mom's."

Because he kissed me over a year ago, when she was pushing him away? Sounds like things have improved (not). Now I hate to bring up why I came, like he needs more bad news.

"Wait," I say. "We aren't inside because . . . ?"

"How does that look? Shanna leaves and two days later, you're in my house?"

Once again, that's something he'd have to tell her. Or maybe he wouldn't. Sometimes it's the things we say that hurt people; sometimes, it's the things we don't say that hurt most.

"Do you think you can fall in love with the wrong person?" Elliott asks.

"Let's see. My dad did. My mom did three times. My only brother who's still married has a husband."

"Appreciate the suggestion, but I don't think that's gonna work for me." No humor hangs behind his words. His expression—I can't understand. Is he trying to warn me off marriage?

Maybe this distraction is just what he needs. "I need your help, E."

He doesn't respond at first. "Can't you ask Justin or someone?"

"Not this time."

Elliott kicks at the mud. And says nothing.

Okay, the guy's hurting, but this isn't like him. "Elliott?"

He grunts in response. Fortunately, I have four brothers, so I'm completely fluent in grunt. And that's a *what?*

"Will's replacement is trying to set Will up—possibly me too—as a cover."

Now I've got his attention. He slowly swivels to me. "Cover for what?"

"He's taking money. Something to do with an agent he pushed me to recruit."

Low whistle. "That's big. Told Will?"

"I can't ask him for help. It'd look like he's trying to protect himself. I need somebody who seems impartial. Somebody I can trust."

"Nobody else springs to mind for this suicide mission? I'm flattered."

I give him a fake elbow-nudge, even though I'm a foot too far away. "Come on, who else would I turn to in the face of certain death?"

"Yeah, again, flattered." He rubs his forehead with the flat of his palm, then slowly stops until he's just holding his head.

I know I'm asking a lot, but this isn't the response I was expecting from Elliott. "I can give you a little time to think. Not sure how long we have."

Elliott kicks at the mud again. Okay, it's a lot, yes, but we risk our lives every day (sort of). Catching a traitor is part of our job. Isn't it?

Finally, he meets my gaze, and he doesn't have to say it. I can see it—the slump in his shoulders, the pain in his eyes, the agony of holding my gaze. "T . . ."

I have to pretend he's not stomping on my heart, pretend it's not collapsing like an empty dead drop spike. And I have to get far, far away. I'm on my feet before Elliott finds the rest of the words to drop the guillotine. Jacket buttoned up, though it's not even below freezing. Hands in my pockets. Walking away. "I understand," I say over my shoulder. "No worries."

"T, wait."

Nope. I stride across his backyard, avoiding the mud, making a beeline for that gate.

Elliott catches up, catches my arm, whirls me around. "Don't think this is easy for me."

"I can see that. Can't say I blame you."

He studies me again. "I . . . I'm so sorry."

His face tells an entire epic that his mouth can't. He wants to help me. He really does. But right now he is so broken that he doesn't have enough shards left to give to anyone else.

"Focus on your family. Go get her back." I can use the courageous voice. I can put on the fearless expression. I can't stand here and watch Elliott's response. Not really that brave.

His quiet words reach me at the gate. "Good luck."

133

"You too." I don't turn around. Whether he's breaking a bit more or (gag) inspired by my "noble sacrifice" or I don't know what—if I have to see Elliott, this heroic façade will break, too, and I'll have to admit I'm totally alone.

I knew things would change when Will left and Elliott went with him. But I never guessed things would change this much.

I don't remember walking back to my car or driving away. Somehow it's half an hour later and I'm across town, going through the motions of yet another surveillance detection run, without actually watching for surveillance. I should. I need to. I just can't.

My phone rings. At nearly ten o'clock, I know it's got to be Danny, but that stupid little bloom of hope shoots up in my chest anyway. Has Elliott changed his mind?

It's Danny. And I'm not disappointed. I'm not. After all, this might be just what I need. I can head back to his place to drown my sorrows for an hour in his favorite comfort food, milk and cookies. "Hey."

"Hi." His voice, unnaturally bright, hits like an LED flashlight to the eyes. "Are you busy?"

Oh, this is bad. Bad, bad, bad. "What's the matter?"

"Nothing, nothing. But guess who just waltzed in to save our wedding and our marriage?"

"As long as it isn't a certain ex-girlfriend, I think we're good."

Danny laughs, forced, thin. "*Détrompe-toi.*"

I don't know what that means, but I do know who it has to be if he's this *un*excited. I'm not thrilled either. I do not need to heal from the Elliott-sucker-punch with my soon-to-be mother-in-law. Who happens to wish Danny was marrying his psychotic ex instead of me.

"All right, well, do I need to stay away for a couple days?" I ask.

The hollow sound of a door closing carries over the line.

"You need to get over here." Danny's tone is back to normal. "Can you?"

I check what neighborhood I'm in. "Do you need backup that bad?"

"She wants to take you wedding dress shopping. Monday, right after work."

How can I say no? Seriously, how can I say no?

"She's spent the last hour telling me that because you don't have a dress, you must not *really* want to marry me."

"And I suppose the fact you don't have a wedding ring means you should be her sweet little baby forever?"

Danny groans. He's actually the oldest, but he's the last of his siblings who's still single, and therefore, still available for total manipulation on demand.

Probably shouldn't talk that way about my STB MIL, but . . . no, I can't pretend to apologize.

"You know she'll harangue me until you agree to this."

I pinch the bridge of my nose. Any night except tonight.

"Don't you perform all the time?" Danny asks, the closest he can get to referring to my job with his mom in the province. "*Act* like she's being nice to you."

"Even I'm not that good an actress."

"What did you tell me? 'You have to *be* the part'?"

True. But again, even I can't be that part. "I won't save you from your mother forever."

"Isn't that the point of getting married?" This time, the light note in his voice is genuine.

"It'd better not be." At least one of us will get a happy ending tonight. I start my car and pull out. "Go ahead and warm up that pineapple chicken from last night."

How do I get myself into this much trouble?

CHAPTER 14

STARE UP AT THE STARS painted on the vaulted ceiling of Notre-Dame Cathedral Basilica Monday afternoon. Normally, I like visiting Ottawa's oldest church, but with the present company, even a house of worship can't be peaceful.

That cocky, well-coiffed company slides into the wooden pew next to me. "So a Mormon and an agnostic walk into a Catholic church . . ."

I don't bother to look at Brand. "Didn't know you were agnostic."

"I dunno." He shrugs one shoulder. "All seems the same to me."

I look past the parishioners filing in, to the ornate altar, the wood paneled choir loft, the light streaming through stained glass windows. Looks pretty different from my church (part of the reason I like it—reminds me of Russian Orthodox cathedrals, minus the icons).

Why am I here? Because Brand wanted a tour of good meeting places? Didn't he have the same training I did? I stand and edge past Brand. "Well, you've seen it," I say. "The next Mass starts soon." And we have just enough time to get back to the office for me to meet Kathi. I resist the urge to plant myself here and text my regrets because I'm "tied up in a meeting," and we head out.

Brand waits until we're on the sidewalk to ask, "Anything else you're hiding?"

My heartbeat slows down, though he can't know what I saw. He can't. I'm still safe. I have to be. And what's *he* hiding? What was with that dead drop spike? The fake investigation on Will? The money from Samir?

Brand continues before I can ask any of those. "Or did you show me all the good sights?" He might actually mean "sites," as in meeting sites. I've spent the afternoon giving him a tour of "prime" spots downtown—ones I no longer use for one reason or another. The Cathedral? Too weird contacting spies in any house of God.

I point across the street. "National Gallery. But now we're pretty close to the Embassy."

Also an awkward place to meet spies. As we reach the church parking lot, a text message comes in. Finally, one bit of good news: Abby's in for reinforcements tonight with Kathi.

If only I had backup with Brand.

He opens my door for me the second I hit the clicker. "Getting a lot done with your wedding planning?" he asks.

"Always more to do." I try not to let my tone sound as curt as my words. (And I fail.) I get in and yank the door from his grasp.

He takes the passenger seat. "Let me know if I can help. I'm always around."

An image of him staring up at my building last week leaps to the forefront of my brain. He's watching me, watching what I do. Even watching my wedding planning.

Much as that makes me want to fight back, follow him, freak *him* out a little, reality weighs down that prospect. Kathi's waiting, Abby's on her way to the boutique, and Brand could have someone watching me to make sure I'm actually planning a wedding and not orchestrating some huge plot against him.

Not yet.

We're halfway to the office when Brand tries small talk again. "When do I get to meet this guy?"

I grip the steering wheel tighter. "Never, I hope."

Yes. I did say that out loud. I'm not sure I regret it, either. I've managed to keep him from even learning Danny's name so far, and I'm not letting anything slip.

Brand waves it off, though everyone in the office usually works hard to keep their personal lives at home. No Bring Your Daughter to Work Day in this branch of the Company.

It feels like traffic's running at half speed, but we get back to our building way too soon. I don't know what's worse: braving Brand or Kathi.

Okay, she isn't that bad. Once we're parked at our building, I leave Brand behind with the briefest possible wave.

And Kathi's waiting in the lobby, like we agreed. Could've been worse. How many people need to chat up Linda? Kathi's not supposed to know I work for the CIA either. Now I have to keep my guard up. Brand's just primed the pump.

I grit my teeth for an embrace from Kathi that's over-compensating for not liking me by trying to squeeze the living daylights out of me. Like we didn't spend the last two evenings together, planning out today's excursion in excruciating detail.

We barely get past our hellos before another voice breaks in. "Aren't you going to introduce me, Talia?"

My stomach clenches, and it's not Kathi's arm-vise that's got me. That's Brand, smarmy as ever. I jam my brain's gears to ultra-secret mode. "This is my mother-in-law-to-be, Kathi."

"No. No way. This has to be the maid of honor. Maybe your sister?"

We both have dark hair, but that's where the resemblance ends. Kathi, tall, tanned and normally together, blushes. "Flattery will get you nowhere—though you can certainly try."

That was my strategy for the evening, but now it seems to be taken. Maybe my usual backup will work: average, plain, disappearing into the shadows.

Seems to be working already. Brand offers a hand. As soon as Kathi shakes it, he lifts her knuckles to his lips. "I'm Talia's boss. Vince Tate."

Is it me, or is even his cover name obnoxious?

"So, you're a partner in the firm," Kathi practically purrs.

No. No. We're not delving into our covers or getting friendly (or mentioning Danny's name!). At. All. I break up the lovefest. "Well, we have an appointment."

Have I mentioned Kathi is still happily married to Danny's dad? Yeah, let's not mess that up. They're kind of my only hope for my own marriage staying together.

That's really sad.

I usher Kathi out of the building and to my car. She ogles Brand until he' out of sight behind us. "Your boss is quite the charmer."

He knows that all too well. I steer the conversation from "Vince" to my other favorite topic lately: wedding dresses. Kathi hides a secret in her eyes instead of giving actual answers.

My hopes sink like a star-crossed Soviet submarine. Joy.

As bad as parking can be downtown, the real reason I snag a spot a couple blocks from the dress shop is to give me the chance to check for teal Nissans. "You know," Kathi says on the walk, "you're shaped so differently from Kendra that I'm not sure where to begin."

How about we begin with the fact that Danny hasn't seen or spoken to Kendra in nearly two years? Or that the last time they did speak, she was throwing plates and punches?

Not to mention the fact that Kathi's obviously insulting me. Stupid, well-endowed Kendra. Like I need any more insecureities.

"She had the perfect gown." Kathi sighs.

Yeah, I want to sigh already too. I knew Kendra had colors picked out, but a dress, too? "I didn't realize she'd had a gown."

"Well, of course she did. She wanted to marry Danny, after all."

Uh . . . yeah. No comment.

We reach the store and Abby waiting on the sidewalk. She shoots me an unspoken question and I wave her off, applying what's fast becoming my I-have-to-remember-I-love-Danny-so-I-don't-kill-you smile for Kathi. "I can say one thing for her: she's got great taste in men."

"Yes, she does," comes a voice from behind us. A voice I'm not expecting. A voice that trails ice down my spine.

How did I miss that teal Nissan? I wheel around slowly. "Checking up on us, Vince?"

"Just happened to be going to dinner downtown." He leers at Abby.

"This is my friend Abby. My boss." Not clenching my teeth through their introduction takes serious effort. "Well, don't want to be late."

"Nice running into you." Brand beams at Kathi, who bats her eyelashes at him.

Suddenly dress shopping is looking a whole lot better.

"Enjoy your dinner," I call, then drag Kathi into the dress shop. Abby follows us, and I remember to introduce Kathi and Abby. Despite what I told her about Kathi, Abby's really nice.

I've never made friends with those way-too-nice-and-sweet-to-be-real girls before. Maybe I've been missing out. (I could at least use the good influence, right?)

Abby asks about my day. I tell her what I can between checking the windows for Brand. Kathi takes advantage of the split-second distraction to swoop in on the sales clerk. By the time I get back to her, Kathi has shoved a three-inch thick scrapbook in the clerk's face. "Obviously everything will be different on *her*."

Ouch.

"But I think some of these ideas are still salvageable."

I don't like how that sounds. Abby squeezes my arm. Forgive me if I'm not reassured. I round Kathi to see the scrapbook, and sure enough, my worst fears are confirmed. I've only seen a couple snapshots of her, but enough to confirm that every picture is Kendra in a wedding dress.

Kendra is as blond and beautiful as any catalog model. And how much do you want to bet Kathi's forcing this scrapbook on Danny whenever I'm not around?

I'm really not this insecure. I know Danny loves me. And he'd rather lop off his own limb than ever talk to Kendra. But whoa. Not okay, Kathi. Not. Okay.

Kathi points at one dress: broad collar, tiny waist, full skirt. "I'm thinking we might be able to make vintage Dior work. You know, late '40s, New Look?"

"I'm right here," I mutter.

Michelle, the clerk, flashes a sympathetic smile. "It'd be great on you. Very flattering."

I frown. My resolve threatens to roll out the door. But that's where Brand was.

Submitting to Kathi's hostile takeover won't kill me. Famous last words. Within minutes, I'm squeezing into gowns made for women without ribs, internal organs, or self-respect.

All right, maybe that's a little melodramatic, though the top of the dress needs major reconstruction to wear in an LDS temple. Or in public.

The stiff neckline is something out of a Disney movie— Sleeping Beauty, I think: off-the-shoulder and too low for me. This is all to humor Kathi, who knows exactly what I can and can't wear, so I march out for the requisite twirling and ooh-ing and ahh-ing. Which usually ends up more as oh-ing and uhhing.

I step onto the pedestal before I bother checking the mirrors—and I stop. This actually does look pretty. Still way more froofy than anything I've ever worn in my life, even undercover. The only thing wrong in the mirror is my stunned expression.

"That's gorgeous," Kathi comments, again like I'm not there. "Almost an Audrey Hepburn effect."

Yeah, except for the person in the dress. I can pull off a clandestine meeting with a high value target. I can pull off a sensitive break-in-and-bug, "black bag" op with minimal support. I can pull off being a concert pianist, a ballroom dancer, or even a bus driver.

Even I can't pull off this dress.

"It *is* pretty, but I don't think it's really your style, Talia." Abby's tone smoothes over any objections. Kathi orders another vintage special, a tumble of Audrey Hepburn/*Sabrina*/ Givenchy/detachable train/without embroidery escaping her mouth so fast I can't catch up. Better to face her than Brand, so I stop worrying about catching up and just play dress up for her.

Michelle suits me up in a dress that's sleek, strapless, and still poofy before she turns me loose. I barely consult the mirrors because, yep, still can't do froof.

"This train's detachable?" Kathi asks.

Michelle unhooks the extra poof of fabric running around the back from hip to hip, leaving me in the straight, sleek version of the skirt swooping gently to the floor.

"Oh." Abby can't hold in her reaction. But that isn't disappointment. That's surprise, and it's all over my face in the mirror, too.

I wasn't doing this for my sake. This was for Kathi and Brand, but here I am, staring at my reflection. And liking it: I actually look like me. As a bride.

Even Kathi doesn't object. In fact, I think she's almost happy.

Michelle sees her opening and begins talking price, discounts, and financing, while Abby tries to move to alterations, fitting, and rush orders. Once Abby gets through, Michelle stops short. "You're talking about a total bodice reconstruction. How fast of a rush?"

"I'm getting married in three weeks," I say.

Michelle's eyes practically fall out of her head. "That kind of work would take three months! Why didn't you come in then?"

"I wasn't engaged then." Or planning on ever getting married.

She stands there, stunned for a minute, and it hits me how much I was starting to like this dress in the 2.47 seconds I've spent in it. Or maybe it's less the dress itself and more that for 2.47 seconds, I could actually imagine this whole wedding thing working out.

"What about if we didn't use the train at all?" Kathi asks. If she's on board with this, I know it's the best option, and maybe my last chance. "Could we get the dress faster without it?"

"No, I don't think that will help. I think it's quite lovely the way it is—"

"No." Kathi, Abby and I cut her off in unison. Our reasons tumble over one another: "I need sleeves"/"The back is too low"/"The bodice is too big." (Guess which is Kathi's?)

"What about a jacket?" Michelle offers. "We should be able to find something—"

"The neckline needs to be two inches higher, at least." Kathi scoffs. "What's she supposed to do, wear a T-shirt over it?"

Much as I hate to admit it, she's right. A jacket won't cut it. The defeat I've been waiting for rolls in.

Kathi leans over Michelle, using her height to its full, intimidating advantage. "Is there absolutely *any* way you could have the dress ready in time? No matter what the cost?"

"I'm sorry," Michelle murmurs, falling back a step. "I don't think there is."

"Is there a manager we could talk to?"

Michelle hurries away to fetch that manager. As soon as she's out of earshot, Kathi snorts. "A total bodice reconstruction doesn't take three straight months of work. You can always pay to get to the front of the line."

"Maybe *you* can," I mutter.

"If money's an issue, Terry and I would be happy to help." Without waiting for my response, Kathi bustles off to hunt down a manager herself.

Their "help" always comes complete with coordinating strings. Like how Danny's belated "graduation gift" had to be used on a house that met their expectations.

Money is a great manipulator. It's manipulating Brand, isn't it?

Can I be bought so easily? I glance back at the mirror, at the dress that even money can't buy. "Do you think she'll be able to convince them?" I murmur to Abby.

"No idea."

Man. I want this to be over. "Come help me get out of this thing."

Abby helps with my buttons, but there's something odd about her silence. She leaves so I can change back into my sweater and slacks. Before I exit the dressing room, I check my phone. A text from Danny: *Everything going okay?*

Sort of. I catch one last glimpse of the dress before I shut the door. I flop into one of the armchairs by Abby. "So close," I murmur.

She studies her crossed knees. "Pretty disappointing."

That's an understatement.

"Is that the only thing bugging you?" she asks. "You seem . . . stressed."

"I'm always stressed." That's true, but before I change the subject, I catch myself checking the windows again—watching, waiting, worrying over Brand.

I'm driving myself nuts. I have to talk to somebody. Michelle, the manager and, most of all, Kathi are nowhere in sight. Safe enough. "A situation at work," I admit. "Extra stressful."

"Anything to do with your boss?"

I flinch and turn on her. How—? Then the rest of the pieces fit into place: the boss I introduced her to thirty minutes ago (none too happily, either). Way to give yourself away, Talia.

But is it the end of the world if I tell one person, vent to one friend, pretend to be normal for five seconds? "Actually, it *is* him. We dated a long time ago. It was bad."

The whole relationship replays in a mental flash. The accidental kiss in his office that started everything. Innuendo that I pretended to ignore. The final, disastrous date that, until this year, was the closest I've ever come to real trouble.

The aftermath was the worst. "After we broke up, he made it . . . impossible to work with him. Made my friends hate me because I'd 'led him on.'" There's more—so much more—and I don't realize I'm telling her until I hear my voice. "Like, in a meeting, he'd make sure to stand by me, no matter how hard I tried to stay away. The second people were distracted, he'd do something like slap my butt, and I couldn't react without getting a bunch of attention. I'd have to explain, and he'd deny it, and—" The words have tumbled out and I only stop to breathe. I've never told this to anyone but Danny. I finish for Abby, "I was . . . trapped."

He lived up to his stupid nickname: he branded me, and if I'm honest, it still burns.

Abby casts me a concerned frown. "Is he doing that again? Harassing you?"

"No." I shake my head quickly. "Hasn't touched me at all."

And yet I still feel worthless. Used. Filthy.

"And now you have to work with him."

"Yeah, and it's like . . ." I slow to a stop when the weight of what I'm about to say hits me. "It's like I'm back in those days, a new hire who still has to prove herself. Because I'm nothing but a plaything to him. In his Great Game."

I was, and I am. I'm falling right back into those same patterns, those same behaviors, like three years in the field have proven nothing. Brand walks into our office, and I'm back in trainee mode.

Abby throws an arm around my shoulders. "I think somebody needs dinner, and then Timmy's? Rideau Centre?"

"Sounds great, except the part where we get donuts second."

Abby laughs, and I can't help but join in. Our laughter quickly fades when Kathi and the manager appear, wending their way through the racks of bridesmaid dresses. The set to Kathi's jaw says enough, even without the manager's half-bowed apologetic posture.

"Oh, man," Abby nearly shouts. "I'm so hungry. I haven't had a bite since lunch. Should we go down to the mall?"

I manage not to quirk an eyebrow at her antics. "Sure. Ready, Kathi?"

Kathi nods, though her frown doesn't soften the whole way to the Rideau Centre. (It's only a block, but still.) Once we're seated with our souvlaki and gyros pitas, I text Danny to join us. Abby strikes up a conversation mostly with herself about her day, and the insanity of the local Fabricland. (Fabricland!) (Sorry, that's how the classic commercial goes.)

"You work at a fabric store?" Kathi asks. "Do you sew?"

Oh good, I can show off how gloriously undomestic I am. I try to follow the conversation for what feels like forever, long after I've finished dinner, until finally that trademark dark red box drops on the table in front of me. Brand wouldn't know to go to Timmy's, right? I look up, dread and hope battling in my chest.

Hope wins out: Danny's standing there, wearing my favorite smile—and he brought donuts! "I've been looking all over for you guys."

I tap the Tim Hortons box. "Your first guess?"

"Figured I shouldn't let all that time standing in front of them go to waste." He drags the extra chair around to sit next to me instead of across from me. Out of habit, I cross one ankle over his. Also out of habit, he takes out a maple pecan Danish and gives it to me. "Didn't you get my texts?" he asks.

While Danny catches up with Abby and his mom, I furrow my brow and grab my phone. Three texts from Danny, asking where we are, and what donuts I want, like he needs to ask. I take another bite of my sweet maple goodness. What else have I missed? I check my email and take a quick glance at the headlines in my news app. I'm not stupid enough to have alerts on my phone for headlines related to my cases, and I make sure to check out two stories that have nothing to do with work to fill my browser history.

But when I see "Wasti Calls for Jihad in the US" in my news app, my Danish isn't so appetizing. Even the sinking feeling in my stomach can't keep me from clicking through.

Though the article doesn't have many details, all this is news to me. What did Samir tell Brand? A big attack?

The article info is coming out of DC, and they've traced the latest video to that area. All. Out. War. From inside the US.

Either Samir isn't as close to his cousin as he let on, or Samir lied to us. I know where I'm putting my money. I like the guy, but something's been off about him lately.

The only question is whether Brand knows the intel he's passing on is bad.

Is that even a question? He's funneling bad intel up the pipeline and pocketing the funds. Twice now I've found out about Wasti's next move way later than I should've. Brand doesn't trust me with the stuff he should.

And I can't trust Brand. I have to do something. Now.

"Talia?" Kathi's voice and my name snap me back to the present. Danny, Kathi and Abby are waiting for me to answer. Kathi's face is don't-you-think-so? insistent, while Abby's chewing her lower lip.

I've got to get out of here without making waves. "Sorry, problem at work. What did you say?"

"Abby here is an excellent seamstress."

I have to wonder how Kathi can vouch for the sewing skills of a woman she just met.

"And I was saying the only way to get your gown done in time now is to buy a sample off the rack that a hundred other girls have tried on, or to have someone sew one for you. And that might be easier, since your tastes are so plain."

I'll pretend that wasn't an insult. "So what's the question?"

"Do you want Abby to make your dress for you?"

"I couldn't ask her to do that." I turn to her. "It's too much."

Abby shrugs. "If we're sticking with that basic style without the train, I might already have a pattern. But we'd have to get started right away."

Speaking of right away—I hold up my phone. "Got a text. They need me at the office ASAP. Major crisis."

Kathi brushes aside my concerns. "You can work tomorrow. You only have one wedding, I hope." The last two words slice into my heart. Like she thinks our marriage is bound to fail and it'll be my fault.

Danny runs to the rescue. "Why, you want to throw us another one? Change your mind about hosting a reception?"

Kathi turns to Abby. "Isn't it traditional that the groom's family hosts the *luncheon*?"

Abby's eyes grow wide, but Danny steps in to help us both. "Save yourself the trouble and write us a check." He's still smiling, but there's steel under his tone. He's daring his mom to come at me again.

"Oh, Danny, I only mean that, given her family history—"

"Stop before I put you on a bus home." And this time he isn't smiling. No one is, especially not me.

But then Kathi smirks at him. "To Aylmer?"

"To Grand Rapids."

Abby and I glance at one another. I can't really object to Danny sticking up for me, but . . . awkward. I twist my ring around my finger. "I really need to go."

"Okay." Danny packs up the donuts. He offers me the box; I push it back to him. He nods. "You need a ride, Abby?"

"No, thanks, I'm a block away."

Ever resilient, Kathi leaps in. I brace for another blow. It doesn't come. "You wouldn't happen to have a measuring tape in your car, would you, Abby?"

Abby shrugs again. "Part of the uniform."

Kathi holds out a there-you-go hand. "You can get started tonight. Give me your number so we can discuss options."

I'm glad enough to get away I almost don't care what kind of "options." At least I know she's pushy with everyone. I kiss Danny goodbye (and say it to Kathi), and Abby and I leave.

As soon as we're on the street, Abby apologizes. "If you don't want me to sew your dress, I won't be offended. I know how personal these things are."

"No, Abby, I'd love it, if it's not too much trouble. And of course we'd pay for it."

"Sorry, I can only let you cover the fabric." She grins. "Guess I know what to get you."

"At least let Kathi pay you." I'm only half joking.

"Well . . . okay."

Abby hurries through my measurements, then bids me good luck at work.

I'll need it.

CHAPTER 15

I DON'T THINK I'VE EVER felt like I was infiltrating my own office, though that's exactly what runs through my mind as I park in the shadows. At least entry will be easy.

I can't make myself look at the nondescript stucco-and-glass office building. What hasn't changed about work lately? Will's gone, Elliott's gone—Elliott can't back me up—and I'm facing my ex-boyfriend-turned-CIA-mole. Alone.

Instead of going upstairs to do that, I dig through my glove box for an operational burner phone. I don't need to look up the number to send the message: *Could use you on my side, HAM.*

I doubt the comical nickname for Elliott's code name is enough to convince him. Stupid of me, especially using real codes over open comms, but I need the guy. I need somebody.

Before I get out of the car, the operational phone vibrates. *I'm on your side, FOX. Just don't know if I can be on your team.*

"Don't know"? That's an improvement over last night.

Think about it, I text back. I pull up the classified bells-and-whistles app to clear the phone's data. (Better than a factory reset, but that's all I know about the "nuclear option.")

A sick little beam of hope practically carries me up the

stairs. I don't risk switching on the lights. With only the glow seeping under the heavy wooden doors, our reception area's eerie.

Practically by feel, I approach the security swipe: the real barrier between anybody who walks in off the street and the classified, Top Secret intelligence we collect, process and send on. All I have to do to get through is slide my card, the card I use every day.

The card that will register my afterhours visit.

Only if someone checks the logs. Only if someone cares about a coworker running back into the office. Only if someone's trying to cover their tracks.

I have to make this quick. Once I'm inside, I head straight for our supplies. I'm not sure what I'll do and I'm not sure Elliott will change his mind, but I *will* be ready. I stock a disguise purse with earpieces/comms, two operational phones—although anything wireless could be intercepted. Though our texts were oblique enough that I think we're safe, it might be better to stick to a classic.

Low tech, developed a century ago, and the only truly unbreakable code: the one-time pad. I grab a pair of codebooks on mini-SD cards, and quick-dissolving paper, in case either of us gets caught without a lighter. (Not the tastiest thing in the world, but eating paper doesn't rank high on the list of the job's hardships.)

I'm past my desk on my way out when I hear the soft *swick* of the security card swipe again. I freeze, right down to my pulse. Somebody *is* watching our logs—in real time, from nearby.

Only one person has that level of access. And that could only mean—

"Oh, Talia." Brand doesn't bother to flip on the light, and the oblique shadows from the exit sign cast his face in ghoulish green. "What are you doing here?"

151

Excuse. Excuse. Excuse. "I had to come back for my phone."

He ponders that. "Maybe we should institute a hard line here, like at Langley."

Technically we're not supposed to have our phones with us in the office, but operations in the field are always different than what Langley expects. Before I call him out or leave, my phone chimes to announce a text message. From inside my purse. My breath catches.

"Already find your phone?" Brand crosses the distance between us. Slow. Casual. Stalking his prey. "In the dark?"

"Guess it was in my purse the whole time." I dig through the spy gear I just packed and finally come up with my real phone. "Man, I gotta clean that out."

The joke misfires. The spy moves in. The fear ramps up. I swallow against a dry throat.

I can't give up ground to him; I won't. But I also can't meet his eyes with him this close. I can smell that aftershave, that woodsy smell I know he thinks drives women wild.

Wrong kind of wild tonight. My adrenaline's high, though not from excitement. This is bringing back memories I thought buried so deep even the Agency doesn't know about them. (Not a whole lot they don't know about either of us.)

"I want you to know," he says, his voice soft. All calculated to draw me closer.

"I'm sorry, what?"

He starts over, a little louder. "I want you to know, I meant what I said the other day."

"Which time?"

"That I'm sorry about how I treated you. How I ended things."

Yeah, well, he should be. But I have to seem like I'm okay with this.

"I manipulated you," he says. "That was wrong. And I'm sorry. I know I was a jerk."

He moves slightly, and though he can't possibly know this, the one emergency light in the hall hits his highlighted hair at an angle, lighting him from behind like he's a medieval saint or angel.

Then it hits me. The whole reason he's apologizing. It's. So. Obvious. Something we're trained to look past. And I fell for it. Again.

To see the truth, sometimes you have to ignore the things they're saying that are true. The apology might be sincere. Doesn't matter. He's saying it to make me believe him, everything about him, the halo effect from the apology spreading over our relationship. Then he'll feed me whatever lies he wants about him and Samir and Wasti and the entire operation.

He's trying to convince me instead of convey information.

He's still manipulating me.

And I know how to manipulate him right back. "Thank you. Good to have closure."

Brand shifts his weight a millimeter in my direction.

Too far. "Have you seen the news tonight?" I hold up the question like a shield. "Wasti's in DC, calling for jihad."

Even through the shadows, I can make out his eyebrow tic, his tell. "Really?"

The surprise might be genuine. "Is there any reason they'd be running around like chickens with their heads cut off at Langley?" I ask.

It's a classic strike, a bold thing for one officer to pull on another: a bait question. Sometimes that alone is enough to shake out a confession.

Not today. "Doubt it. A terrorist on American soil? The F-entity might be freaking out."

"We have to say something, don't we?" If anyone finds out we just recruited Wasti's cousin and had no idea this was coming? Yeah, that'll hurt—and it could hurt a lot more than our pride.

I hope all that goes through Brand's brain, too, as he's for-mulating the lie. It's been too long now to judge whether any of his reactions to my question are deceptive.

My phone chimes again. Brand nods at the phone.

Danny. *So sorry about Mom*, says the first text. Then: *Should I really put her on a bus?*

"You going to take that?" Brand asks.

I hit the button to dial Danny. Brand brushes past me, as always way closer than a casual contact. At the proximity, a cold wave washes over me, but I stand my ground.

"You okay?" Danny answers the call.

"Fine," I murmur, keeping my back to Brand. "No busses necessary."

"We had a nice, long discussion on the way home. It'd bet-ter not happen again." His tone is pointed, as if his mom's right next to him.

"Why? You going to ground her?"

I'm way too aware of Brand's eyes on my back to join Danny's laughter.

Time to do something. I start for the exit. Ironically, to face down Brand, I have to get out of here. "Well," I wind up the call, "thanks for helping me find my phone."

Somehow I can tell exactly what kind of silence this is from Danny: knowing. He knows I had my cell at dinner—and he *knows* what I'm really saying. "Will you be over later?" he asks. "I'll muzzle her if I have to."

"Probably won't be necessary. A lot of planning to do."

I think he mutters, "You're not the only one," but I can't be sure. He still says I love you, so we should be good. Good-ish.

I let the bullpen door swing shut behind me before it hits me: Brand came in almost as soon as I did. Coincidence?

The door opens again, and Brand steps into the reception area. "So did you find a dress?"

"No."

"Time's running out." If that's supposed to be helpful advice, he shouldn't couch it in the voice and vocabulary of a threat.

"That really isn't your concern, is it?" The bullpen door latches behind Brand and the security swipe engages. I have to change the subject—and I have to check if he's really monitoring this. "Did you see if I shut my computer down?"

"Nope. Sorry." Brand strides for the main exit.

I swipe my card. Brand opens the door, but can't escape before an unfamiliar belltone dings. He freezes in the doorway. Silence stretches between us, thick with tension.

The bullpen latch clicks again, indicating it's locked. I swipe again—and the same now-not-so unfamiliar bell sounds. From the doorway. From Brand's phone.

Frost shoots down to my nerve endings. There's an app for spying on the spies?

I leap into the bullpen, counting one hundred too-quick heartbeats until I dare to peek out. No Brand. Where am I supposed to feel safe now?

I'm out of here. Though the operational phone I snagged has a triangulation-obfuscation app that's way beyond my understanding (not Q, here), I still want to be well clear of our office before I try this scheme.

I head into the heart of suburbanville, far from anywhere sensitive: work, Danny's place, mine, Elliott's. I pull out my operational phone, plug in Brand's number and twiddle my thumbs over the virtual keyboard. I have to get this message right. Might be my only shot.

You're not as safe as you think. I know what you're doing. We need to talk.

I second-guess the vague approach until the phone vibrates. *Really, Mr. Anonymous & Kinda Threatening? Sorry if I'm not quaking in my boots.*

Though normally it's not cool to be addressed as "mister,"

I'm actually glad he thinks I'm a guy. I'm that much safer.

Now I drop the vague act. My reply is a single word: *Farooqi.*

You've got my attention.

Understatement of the year. I allow myself one little smile. *Meet under the Plaza Bridge. Tomorrow, 1830.*

Let me guess. You'll be the one in dark glasses.

Blue jacket. Come alone. I add the last bit mostly for theatrics. Not sure who he'd use as backup. Not sure I want to find out.

Bring all the help you can get, he replies.

Cute—but all the help I can get might be sitting in this car.

If you're man enough to face me, that is, Brand adds.

I could have let him twist in the wind, but now I know I'll be there. Less than twenty-four hours to figure out how to fight.

CHAPTER 16

'M USED TO MAINTAINING COVER IDENTITIES. Just not at the office. But if I change my habits, if I don't show up, I'll tip my cards faster than anything else.

By three o'clock, I can only pretend to work, despite a good morning tracking Morozov's buddy. At quarter past, Brand's office door swings open. I flinch. I hope he doesn't notice—but if he didn't see the reaction the first fourteen times he marched through the bullpen, I doubt he'll start now.

He thinks he's meeting with a guy, I remind myself. He has zero reason to suspect me. I'm safe. Right?

"Talia," Brand calls. My gut takes a tiny dive. "Where's the report on the Russians from this morning?"

"Working on it." I keep my gaze on my monitor, like the two-paragraph addition to the Russians' file requires my complete concentration.

Brand's door closes, and my lungs function properly. My adrenal system shifts down through the gears until we're back in the normal range. No need to get worked up. Yet.

After one last proofread, I save the report and pack up. Why pretend anymore? I have prep work to do. I'm amazed

Brand's here at all—he should be reconnoitering too. He can't possibly intend to walk into this blind.

Unless he doesn't intend to walk into it at all. I need to find out. Instead of leaving, I go to Brand's office for one last little check. "Yeah?" he calls through the door.

"Got a minute?"

"Come in."

I've spent so long trying to avoid his office, it's strange to be relieved to make it inside. But I have to know if he's planning to show. My mind races through options, each less appealing than the last: invite him to catch up. Ask if he's seeing anyone so we can double. See if he wants to get together with Danny.

Yep, in the face of those options, I'll have to go fishing. With Danny as the bait. (Sort of—he's nowhere near danger.)

I shut the door behind me and place my hands on the back of the chair facing his desk. After a second, his attention shifts from his computer to me. "I think we got interrupted while we were talking last night," I say.

"Oh yeah, your phone."

"So I didn't get a chance to tell you—thanks. For the apology."

"Sure." His eyes reveal a current of caution, I hope because he doesn't know where this is going.

"Anyway, do you have any plans tonight?" Smooth. Yeah. "My fiancé and I want to have you over for dinner."

The eyebrow twitches. "Really?'

"Kind of a policy. New bosses get dinners."

"Thought I was never going to meet him. And isn't Danny's mom in town? Kathi, right?"

A cold chill buzzes down my spine. He's got me. He's got Danny's name. Crap. Crap crap crap.

Fortunately, the spy part of my brain is two steps ahead of the rest of me. "Okay, you caught me. She's the one who wants to see you."

Brand laughs, like he's hardly surprised ladies love Cool B.

And this might be the best way to sneak past his defenses. "She also wants to know if you're single."

He chuckles again. "A curse, you know."

"I bet." A sickening tide slowly rises in me. This is too much like flirting with him. Focus. "So, are you free tonight? Kathi needs to know how many to cook for."

"You can tell her I'm sorry to disappoint, but I have other plans."

A little flash of triumph jumpstarts my lungs. The completely ambiguous confirmation is the best I'm going to get, and I will take it.

"I'll relay your regrets," I promise. And it's totally natural for me to make my escape now. I wait until I'm out of the building and past my first stop to give Elliott a last chance. I text him again. *Meeting at 1830 under canal bridge at Rideau St. Wear blue jacket if you come.*

I'm almost done with the SDR when he writes back. *Jacket? Who wears a jacket when it's like 50 degrees? I'd look like an idiot.*

So . . . like normal? (And the guy isn't on centigrade yet?)

He doesn't respond. If that's a no, I'll kill him. But I don't have time to put him through the wringer. I've got work to do.

I survey the scene in front of me, both sides of the sidewalk flanking the emptied canal, beneath the bridge. As if I haven't already identified the best tactical position for me, Elliott, and our imaginary backup team. It's only 6:15, but I've nearly convinced myself neither Elliott nor Brand will show. Elliott should've been here an hour in advance to go over recon, lookouts, and game plans. Though we're familiar with the area, you can never be too prepared.

And if you can, it's not a bad state to die in.

I can't cover both sides of the bridge alone, and I don't dare text Brand to change the plans. Seems disorganized. Incompetent. Lost.

I'm none of those things.

The only contingency I haven't planned for is Brand not showing. Then what? Call him out as a coward? Clearly he cares so much about the opinion of an anonymous texter.

"What've we got?" comes a familiar voice behind me.

I jump. People are not supposed to creep up on me. At least this time I don't have to panic—I whirl on Elliott. "Thanks for the heads-up. You should've been here an hour ago."

"Hey, I've got work, too."

"Could've at least called." I'm glad enough to see him that I'm just teasing. How could I muster real irritation when he shows up, blue jacket and all?

I should ask about Shanna, and tell him how much I hope they're doing better, but I think that goes without saying. "Should I ask what changed your mind?" I ask.

"You really think I could leave you hanging if this is as big as you say?" He shakes his head like he can't believe I'd ever think that even though that's pretty much what he said. "What's my position? And what does this guy look like?"

Fortunately, I do have a picture of Brand, though I had to dig through years of digital photos and way more memories than I wanted to. I show Elliott the picture, brief him on the details, from Wasti to Samir, from Brand's meeting to his "dead drop."

Once Elliott's kitted out with information, an earpiece, and a recorder, I assign him to the west side arch. I slip into a blond wig, jog up to the street to cross the Plaza Bridge and take up my position on the east side, by the bike rental shop (which Danny and I used on our first date). Portals slice through the thick cement bridge support, arched windows with railings to hold us back from the empty canal. I can see Elliott in the middle portal, reading a newspaper.

"Snap your paper if you're ready," I murmur. Elliott does.

Not a minute too soon. 6:25.

The crowds flow and the minutes inch by until the rendez-vous time arrives. And passes. And keeps going.

Is he trying to take the upper hand by freezing us out? Or just not going to show?

The last rays of the sunset filter down from above. Elliott's maintained radio silence in his position, on the stairs to the street, perusing his newspaper. But after twenty minutes, he can't keep it up. "How long do we wait?"

"Why, you have other plans tonight?" I wince inwardly. Elliott gives the verbal equivalent of a smirk and flips to the next page.

A shadow passes over him, slows, crosses back. "Done with the first section, buddy?"

My breath snags in my chest. The voice we've been waiting for. Brand.

Does Elliott recognize him?

Nobody's nearby, but I barely dare to breathe the message to Elliott. "That's our target."

Elliott's already folding the first section and giving it to him. A rope wraps around my rib cage. I can only hope Elliott heard me.

Brand stands by him, flipping through the pages until he finishes the section. "Newspaper's always the last to know."

"Yep." Elliott stands, and suddenly I remember how good he used to be at this job. He's got the tall, dark and handsome spy part down, and tonight he acts it. "We've got a few things to talk about that won't make it in here." He folds his half of the paper.

Brand merely nods. "How about we walk and talk?"

Not part of the plan. "Go south," I tell Elliott. "Away from the river." I can't track with them if they go the other way.

Brand starts northward before Elliott can direct him. Crap. I've got to get over there. I press two fingers against my earpiece and jog to the steps. My thighs are burning by the time I hit the top of the double flight on my side of the bridge, but I can't stop.

"So," Brand's saying, "we have a mutual friend."

Please don't let him mean me. Luckily Elliott cuts off at least that route. "Seems like he's more than a friend to you."

Brand scoffs. "All business, isn't it? Once they're not useful anymore, it's over."

"Maybe. The question is, 'Who's being useful to who?'"

Good. Stay on point. I reach the stairs down to the west arch and practically fly.

"Where I work, there's only one way these relationships go," Brand says. I scan the sidewalk ahead for them, but I can't see anything. The disembodied voices over the earpiece create a spooky soundtrack to my searching. I concentrate on the sound filtering through my rapid-fire pulse.

"And where do you work?" Elliott asks. "Because I'm pretty sure you're on more than one payroll."

"Right." Yep, Brand, flip and dismissive as ever. "Shouldn't I ask where *you* work?"

"I think you know. At least you know someone I work with."

There's an echo—are they still under the arch somewhere? I scan the shadows, the part of the arch protected by the rock ruins of the old bridges from a hundred years ago. Nobody.

"That so?" Brand asks.

"Don't you know Will?"

I think I can hear their footsteps through the earpiece. Still echoing. I duck down to the portals where Elliott waited for Brand not five minutes ago.

"Doesn't everyone?" Brand continues. "Will sent you, then?"

"I'm hoping we can resolve this problem without involving him," Elliott sidesteps.

Thank you. If I'm not the one confronting Brand, I'm glad it's Elliott. I peer through the shadows, but I still can't see them. Nowhere to hide here. An uneasy sensation slips down my back, the smallest shiver.

"I hope you haven't wasted your time sending your paperwork on this straight to the top." Brand neatly avoids any reference to Langley. But what does that overconfidence mean? Does he have someone in DC to fix everything for him?

"Wasted my time?" Elliott snorts. "No."

The footsteps stop. "Good move," Brand says. "For you."

A deafening crack rips through my earpiece and the air. Another.

My body, my heart, my breath jar to a stop. I know that sound. Gunshots. Close.

All the oxygen feels like it's been sucked out of this tunnel. I force my fiery legs to follow the sound. I fight back the howling urge to run—too suspicious. Too much attention. A few other gawkers start in the direction of the sound, but more are hustling away from the shots for safety.

I catch a glimpse of a guy with that gratingly perfect tousle of curls headed the opposite direction before I hit the real commotion. A woman screaming, a crowd gathering, three or four people pointing into the drained canal. Dread sinks in my stomach and closes my throat.

I know what I'll find, but panic makes me elbow my way through the onlookers to the edge, to look into the canal, to see what I don't want to imagine.

Elliott on the bricks. Broken. Bleeding. Because of me.

CHAPTER 17

MY CAREFULLY CONSTRUCTED SEMBLANCE OF CALM SHATTERS. People crowd in behind me, bending over the canal, too. A cry builds in my lungs.

No. No. I can't panic. I have to act. I swallow the shriek and retreat through the crowd. Run to the nearest ladder and half-climb/half-slide down. It's a jump from the bottom rung to the cement-lined canal floor. The shock lances up my legs; pain hasn't stopped me yet.

How far is the fall? How did he land? Is he okay?

I manage not to call his real name. I don't know his cover, if he has one. When I hit my knees beside him and another quick-thinking guy, that's the first question I ask, and then, "What happened?"

"Josh Lee." Elliott grunts and gasps for air. The other guy attending to him tries to calm him down, applying direct pressure to the bloody wound below his collarbone.

Please don't let that be his heart.

Elliott tries to knock him away. "Mugging," he groans.

Ottawa's really safe for an international capital—DC has eight times as many robberies per capita—but that may be a good enough cover. "Do you have somebody we need to call?"

"How about 9-1-1?" He coughs and grimaces at his own attempt at humor.

The helpful guy rocks back on his heels to survey the growing crowd above us. "Somebody call 9-1-1!"

While the guy canvasses the onlookers for someone who isn't too traumatized to dial, I lean over Elliott to block the crowd's view. I snag his earpiece, then empty his jacket pockets. His wallet holds $20. I grab it and any ID with his real name on it. Next, his phone: the nuclear option app. Clears out everything but a couple designated contacts.

I stuff Elliott's stuff in his pockets before the other guy turns back to him. "How's his breathing?"

"Still breathing," Elliott groans.

The guy relays that information to the crowd above, whoever dialed 9-1-1.

Elliott's hand clamps onto my wrist. "You need to go."

I know. I nod. I stay.

A couple other civilians crowd in, elevating his shoulders, making him more comfortable, edging me out. Elliott finds a break in the cloud of helpers to catch my eye. "Go," he mouths.

I back away a few more steps, numb, stumbling, lost.

The last thing I hear before I leave the echoes of the canal is Elliott's choking cough.

And I walk away.

I jolt awake in the dark, the image of Elliott bleeding still imprinted on my eyelids. It was a dream? It wasn't real?

It was a dream. A nightmare. I draw one sweet breath of relief and sigh, willing the cold sweat away. Elliott's fine. I imagined the whole thing. We're still safe.

Then something—some*one* next to me shifts, a weight

pressing on my ribs that's more than just the residual fear from seeing dream-Elliott shot.

Adrenaline spikes in my system, panic screeching in my ears again. I try to back away, but something soft behind me blocks my escape.

I have to save myself. I do what any sensible person would and shove whoever this is off me. He tumbles to the floor with a sharp little gasp that I recognize.

Danny.

What is going on?

"Ouch." His tone is flat.

In the moonlight through the blinds, I pick up enough setting cues: the familiar TV and love seat. That means I'm on his couch. We both were, until I freaked.

I dare to peer over the cushions' edge. Danny simply stares at me. "Sorry," I murmur.

"Just . . . don't wake me up like that when we're married."

The pieces fall into place. The crazy long SDR, hours of trying to outrun the memory. Parking half a mile from Danny's. Sneaking through the woods to his back door. Danny jumped when I crawled in after twelve, while he was putting away his late night snack. His mom had made cookies. I couldn't even touch one.

Because it wasn't a dream. Elliott really was shot. And Brand did it.

And it's my fault.

A weight hits my chest, heavier than even Danny: guilt. Desperation. Fear.

Danny sits up and squints through the dark at me. "Are you okay?"

I try to respond. There aren't any words. I can't form the letters that would make this make sense, make this okay, make this not real.

"You're starting to scare me here." He checks his I'm-an-engineer-so-I-need-a-freaking-graphing-calculator-on-my-wrist watch. "You came in five hours ago and started bawling."

That doesn't sound like me. But I know it is without checking my face to see if I'm puffy and blotchy.

"You turned down chocolate chip cookies," Danny continues.

"And we fell asleep on the couch?" I pat the black cushions beneath me.

"Yeah. Is this something I'm not supposed to know about?"

"I don't know." I don't realize how true those words are until I hear them. Can I tell him anything that happened tonight, or would that put him in too much danger?

Still sitting on the floor, Danny studies me for a long minute. Even in the shadows, the I-wish-I-could-fix-this-for-you in his face is all too evident. At last, he tucks my hair behind my ear. "I know you're the international superspy here—"

We both glance at the stairs, though his mother's surely fast asleep. Neither of us have any plans to tell her I'm not a lawyer.

Danny continues. "But if you ever need me, for anything, I will be there."

The image of Elliott lying at the bottom of the canal flashes through my mind. This time it's not Elliott broken and bleeding on the cement. It's Danny.

I shake my head, hard and fast. Elliott's life was in my hands and I let him down. I will *not* let the same thing happen to Danny. Not even metaphorically.

"Okay," he says slowly. "But the offer stands."

"Only one person could've helped me." And now he can't. I barely hear my own whisper, and I'm not sure the last part is out loud. Danny touches my arm. I try to make my shoulder pat as comforting (and non-condescending) as possible. All I can see is Elliott/Danny/Elliott there, gasping for air, sending me away for my own sake.

He could be dead.

He probably isn't. Even with a chest wound, you have a good chance of surviving one or possibly two gunshots.

Still. If it weren't for me, he wouldn't have been shot.

I won't put Danny in that position. "I'm so sorry," I say. I can't bear to look at him, burying my face in my arms. "I have to do this. I'm the only one left." My voice breaks, squeaking out the hysteria growing wild in my mind. I'm the only one left that I'm willing to sacrifice.

"Talia?" Danny's murmur breaks through the mounting guilt/panic attack. "I love you."

"I love you, too." And that's exactly why he gets to stay right here in his safe little suburb where the closest he comes to danger is working on his defense contracts.

But he's not done. Danny's gaze is so intense that I have to avert my eyes till he speaks. "Please."

That single syllable plea is self-explanatory: please let me help. Please let me be there. Please let me in.

I can't. I can't. I have to protect him.

The seconds of silence squeeze between us, the chasm growing every second, pushing us apart. I need him almost as much as I need him to be safe.

And then I see the concern—the fear in Danny's expression. He doesn't understand what's going on, and for him, *that's* the scariest part of all.

He doesn't know what *I* do. "He shot him, Danny. He shot him and it's my fault."

Danny's eyes widen to the size of satellite dishes, and the fear doesn't dim. "What? Who shot who?"

"Elliott."

"Elliott shot—?"

"No, Elliott *got* shot, and it's my fault."

Apparently this is bigger than he was expecting. But also note: I walked in and immediately broke down, so he should've been tipped off already. "It's not your fault," he says.

"I asked Elliott to back me up and he got shot. My fault."

"Do you know who shot him?"

I've been striding into the surf, and suddenly the sandbar beneath me shifts and gives out. I squeeze out the answer before my head sinks below the surface of terror: "My boss."

Danny eases me to sitting up and joins me on the couch, one arm clamped around my shoulders as if he already knows I need the extra support to stay upright. "Why would your boss shoot Elliott?"

I shift to study him. This is something I shouldn't tell him, something that's too classified and way too dangerous.

I have to. I have to let someone know, don't I? "I think he's skimming CIA payouts. They're supposed to go to an agent."

"Elliott's skimming?"

"No."

Danny bows his head, half an inch closer to mine. "Are you saying—?"

"Yeah."

"Are you in danger?"

I wish I could tell Danny no, but my brain flashes to Brand peering up at my building, trying to get a visual on my apartment.

The biggest betrayals within the Agency aren't upending ops. They're selling out officers to the enemy.

I might be in even more danger than I thought. Backed into a corner. Betrayed.

"I have to go away." I'm on my feet before Danny can react. I'm pacing, wringing my hands, my mind flying in a thousand directions, and my feet running in circles. "I have to . . ."

Danny stands, catches my hands, pulls me in. "It's okay, it's okay. We'll figure it out."

I'm supposed to be the one calm under fire. But when you're confronting literal fire—

"You need something to eat." Danny tows me to the kitchen and leaves me by the counter to dig through the pantry.

Okay, eating might be a decent start, but I need to brainstorm beyond breakfast. I'll have to think three, four, five steps ahead to make it through alive.

Danny sets about making oatmeal the way I like it—actually, he doesn't particularly care for oatmeal, so the fact he has any in stock is sweet. While he works, I put my over-taxed, under-rested brain to work on the next step—

"Montréal," he breaks in.

I doubt a city two hours away has much to do with oatmeal. "Why would—?" And then the other meaning hits me. Montréal has the closest LDS temple. He's talking about eloping.

Yesterday, I probably would have taken him up on the offer. But today, something scarier hangs over our pending marriage than my persistent fear of dress shopping and divorce.

In our church, we don't say "till death do you part" or "as long as you both shall live." The ceremony says "for time and all eternity." Marriages sealed in the temple can last beyond death.

And what Danny's really saying isn't *Let's forget all this stupid wedding planning*. He's saying, *I'm afraid you're going to die.*

"Don't." My words are a tense whisper, my feet are around the counter in an instant and my insistent finger is in his face. "Don't you do that to me."

"What? You're the one who wanted to elope."

"I need somebody—I need *you* to believe I'm coming back alive."

Danny leans closer. "Then do."

I nod, moving less than a centimeter, as near as I can get to a promise. Danny watches me another minute, like I might renege at the last second, before he finally turns away to pop my bowl in the microwave.

The hum starts up and the seconds count down, and *now* I put my over-taxed, under-rested brain to work on every possible choose-your-own-misadventure scenario. Brand hunts me down here. Brand hunts me down at home. I'm stupid enough to come into the office—

The office.

"Wait a minute." I hear myself say it before I realize I'm talking.

Danny presents me with a raised eyebrow and my apple juice oatmeal with brown sugar and maple syrup. Exactly how I make it—but that's not what's so perfect.

"He doesn't know." The relief, the excitement in my voice are just the beginning of my mental celebration. This is a way out. It has to be.

"Who doesn't know what?"

"My boss doesn't know I was there. He doesn't know it's me. He doesn't even know it was Elliott." I wander a few feet from the counter. Much as I want to take Brand down, fast and hard, this means not only am I (sort of) safe, but I have time to bide my time. I can wait until I have everything I need. I don't want to—I want to make him bleed like he made Elliott bleed—but I have to. Because if I don't, Brand will know exactly what I've done.

Danny slides the bowl in my direction again, and I drift back to take a bite. "I know I'm no Elliott," he says, "but if I can do anything, please tell me."

I almost choke on my oatmeal, and my rejoicing cuts off as abruptly as a needle scratching a record. (What? I'm old enough to remember those. You know, kinda.) I would—will—*do* risk my life every day so that Danny will never, ever be in that same danger.

I won't lose him. I can't.

Apparently my reaction speaks for me. "Hey." He offers his hands like he can't understand my objection. "I'd hope I've proven myself."

"Yes, you were great." I mean it, I really do. We've fought for our lives together—he might have been fighting harder for me than for himself. But staring at my oatmeal probably isn't convincing Danny. Even if I'm only doing it to keep fear from spiraling out of control.

That hypothetical of him and Brand squaring off against one another? Cue the repeat loop in my brain. I've already lived that nightmare, or close enough for a thousand lifetimes.

Danny isn't done. "I won't pretend like I'm James Bond here, or that I've taken up MMA—"

I can't help an incredulous look at that one.

He holds up his index finger and thumb an inch apart. "Eh, just some cage fighting."

"Ah."

"The point is, I want to be there for you."

I can feel my shoulders fall. How could I ask that? I concentrate on eating. With each second of stillness that slides by, the oatmeal, the conversation and the kitchen grow colder.

At last, I push away my bowl. "Listen. I already asked someone for help. Someone who, no offense, is a lot better prepared for this kind of thing."

"Elliott isn't the only one—"

"Yes, he is," I cut him off with a hiss. Elliott may not be the only person who can help me, but he *is* the only one: the only one I can risk. "And see where it got him?"

Silence slams down on us. After a long second, I dare to meet his gaze. Danny isn't looking at me. His eyes focus in the middle distance. He nods. Even in the light from the pantry, I can see the set to his jaw. He isn't agreeing. He isn't giving in. He's just ending the conversation.

"Elliott's out. I have to depend on me." What's left to say? "Sorry. I have to go to work."

"Are you crazy? You can't go in there with this guy—"

"I have to. If I don't, he'll know something's up." I shove in a final mouthful of oatmeal and start out. Before I reach the back door, I practically trip over a bag there. My bag. With all my supplies for last night.

I look back to Danny. He wants to help. He wants in. He's been there and he knows what he's risking. I wouldn't ask it of Danny over any other alternative, but if Brand's half as careful as I am, he'll be watching my every move. And Danny's the one person Brand would expect me to contact. Which makes any contact I have with Danny that much less suspicious.

I could get away with calling or texting him, unlike Will or anyone else. And it's not like Danny would have to be the back-up himself. He can just call in my cavalry.

I dump out the bag on Danny's counter, then shove the operational phone and memory card at him. "This phone should be clean. Nobody else should call. If I need backup, I'll send you an encrypted message. The memory card has a one-time code pad with the app."

"Is that supposed to mean something to me?"

"Wikipedia explains it well."

He takes the phone, though his expression doesn't change from *I can't believe you don't trust me*. "Wikipedia? Sounds really secure."

Probably a bad time to tell him about Intellipedia, the country's intelligence wiki, huh? "One-time pads are the only unbreakable code. They use a random set of numbers as a key to encrypt the message, and we have the only copies of that key. Just run the app to decrypt it. Don't forget to destroy it after."

He purses his lips and takes the card. I can see what he's thinking: *the things I do for you*.

I know.

"I love you," I say.

"Prove it."

I flinch. Not the response I expected. I hold up my left hand, wiggling my ring finger.

"Live to make good on that promise."

He knows I can't swear to that. I mean, geez, I could fall asleep at the wheel and drive off the Champlain Bridge. Get maimed in a wreck. Be attacked by a rogue bear in the woods.

Okay, all those are a lot less likely to bring me harm than Brand. The CIA's life insurance policy can't actually ensure the "life" part.

"I'll do everything I can," I say. "Not like I'm running around with a death wish."

"You're seriously going into work with this guy?"

I nod.

"Close enough."

"I told you, I have to. If I don't, he'll suspect me. Trust me, okay?"

His gaze hits mine and we have target lock. "Trust. Me."

I gesture to the phone and things I'm leaving with him— which, hello, are government property—and, yes, a scoff escapes me. How much more does the guy want?

"I don't want your stuff," he answers my unvoiced question, firmer than even with his mom. At the last second, he softens enough to break my heart, adding, "I want *you.*"

And I don't want you to die, I manage not to shout back. "I'm sorry."

"Yeah, I got it. Depend on yourself. And Elliott, when he isn't hurt." Danny turns away. I'm not sure whether he can't bear to watch me go, or I'm being dismissed.

I hesitate at the door. We have to say *I love you.* It's not like I've forgotten, and demanding I come back and marry him is a pretty clear message, but the silence still hurts.

I slip onto the back porch, letting the door swing shut behind me. By the time I reach the stairs down to the yard, the door still hasn't latched. I retreat to get it. Danny's a couple steps behind me, and my about-face doesn't stop him. He slides one hand around my waist and cradles my head with the other.

Now *this* is target lock. Everything he didn't or couldn't put into words comes through in this kiss. I love you. I need you to come back. And I am so, so scared.

Those feelings and fears, raw and vulnerable, echo through me. Finally I have to withdraw to wipe my tears.

I can't afford fear now. I definitely can't face his. Play it off. "You going to see me off that way every day?"

"Every day you're taking on the guy who shot your co-worker, yep."

Danny draws me close before he could've seen my sarcastic look. He rests his chin on my head, wrapping me in a full-body hug. "I just worry, okay?" he admits in a whisper.

"Hey, I should be the worried one if you didn't care that much, right?"

I feel more than hear his laugh, and then his sigh. "I know it's hard for you, so thank you. For telling me the truth. About Vince."

The realization hits like a cold splash. I've told Danny the terrifying truth, all of it—except who "Vince" really is. And if I did . . . what would he say? Especially when he thinks I've sac-rificed so much to let him in? He has no idea.

"I love you," I murmur. Maybe it's me, but the words sound hollow.

"I love you too—that's why I'm going nuts here."

I hug him tighter. "I know."

"For the record, I'm still opposed to this," he says.

"I know."

He pulls back to meet my eyes. "And if you ever need any-thing—"

"Danny," I cut him off. "I know."

And we both know I will never, ever take him up on that offer. Not when I'm facing off with a would-be killer.

CHAPTER 18

MY BUILDING IS SUPPOSED TO BE one of my only refuges, but now I want to run away from it. I've already called the hospital to get a status update on Elliott. Pretending to be Shanna backfired—she was in his room. Good on two counts: she cares, and he's well enough for visitors. But it also means I'm out of stalling tactics.

All I have to do is act like it's any other Wednesday at the office. Pretend I wasn't there when Brand tried to blow Elliott away. Fake like I know nothing. Because if I don't, Brand will know right away. And right away the first test comes: as soon as I pass the security swipe, I find Brand standing at my desk. Watching me. My stomach drops and gives me twenty lurches.

Looking at the man who shot Elliott, my mind starts fabricating memories of them walking down the sidewalk. Brand drawing the gun. His finger pulling the trigger.

My brain reels backward, but my feet keep carrying me closer. Brand waits until I'm in range to speak. "We need to talk."

He leads the way to his office, and I draw in as much air as I can. Why couldn't I have woken up in time to hit my best gun cache while no one was around?

Sure, firearms are the opposite of covert in a developed country with strict gun laws, and a "lawyer" would know that all too well, but I want the comfort of knowing for sure I'm not alone with a guy who's packing.

No, I don't have a gun on me, and yep, believe it or not, guns aren't nearly as useful to spies on a daily basis as you'd think, especially not spies in Canada.

Except for maybe one. Brand holds the door open for me, then locks it behind us. He might as well grab me by the neck, my throat closes so fast.

No. I have to be reasonable. It's a little early, but we're not alone in the office. Even a suppressed gunshot would attract too much attention.

Didn't make a difference to him last night.

I walk a couple feet into the office, like I can't let myself get too far from my (locked) escape route. Brand stands a yard away, studying me. No way will I let him see the truth. I shoot for a wary, but wondering expression—not too hard, considering I'm both wary and wondering.

"There's no easy way to say this." He edges closer. I'm not sure whether I should stand my ground or obey the instinct to flee.

"Say what?" I curse my voice for being no stronger than a whisper.

"Nobody else knows."

Fear creeps down my spine on cold, clawed feet. I steel the muscles in my face to keep the same confusion there. "What are you talking about?"

"You know Josh Lee?"

I have to shuffle back to keep my balance. To keep him at a distance. He knows. He knows that's Elliott. Brand knows I was there.

I'm dead.

Brand watches me for an eternity. "You know he's CIA?"

It takes two full seconds to register: he's not talking about yesterday. "Yeah, we worked a case with a Finnish contact together, years ago. Why?"

"Were you watching Will last night?"

"No. Dinner with my fiancé and his mom, remember?"

He moseys over to cut off my escape route. "Bad night to take off. Lee was shot. Seems Will's the shooter."

Fortunately, I'm shocked enough at the cover story that my relief stays hidden. (He doesn't know it was Elliott! He can't trace it back to me!) "Is Lee okay?"

"Hospitalized."

"Why would Will do something like that?"

Brand sighs, like he's sorry to be the bearer of bad news to someone so sweet and innocent. "My theory is Lee was getting too close to the truth."

"And where's Will now?" I have to probe how far Brand's willing to take this cover story—and how far he's already taken it to cover his tracks.

"Embassy legat." *Legal attaché*, the FBI presence in the embassy. He's in custody.

Yep, Brand's taking it pretty far. He could've planted the gun at Will's by now, and that's just the beginning.

I've got to stay safe. I've got to stay afloat. I've got to stay useful to him.

If I'm the only one he told about Will, he needs me around, right? He needs me to "establish" his suspicions. My "reports" on Will's nonexistent activities were off the books. Never expected that to fall in my favor, but Brand needs me. I just have to remind him of that, make him think I'm on his side. Sick. Twisted. Wrong on every imaginable level. And my only choice.

"All right." Like I can compartmentalize my colleague being critically injured (and it secretly being my fault). "What do you need from me to make this happen?"

His eyebrows make their little surprised leap, though he doesn't betray any other response, not even to shift his weight. "What do you mean?"

I'm careful not to let the triumph show, but I have the upper hand. "I'm the one who's been watching Will. If anybody can help you hang him—and believe me, if he did this, we all want that—it's got to be me."

"Yeah." The gears of Brand's brain obviously churn to catch up. "Start cataloguing what you've seen. Don't use any established code names."

"Right." Maybe if I can work this, I can turn it all back on Brand.

Or maybe it'll all come crashing down on me.

A risk I have to take. To save Will. To pay Brand back for Elliott. To keep my promise to Danny.

"I'll get to work." I move for the door. Brand doesn't move, and suddenly I'm close enough I can practically feel him breathing.

Close enough to kill the man who could've killed Elliott.

Realistically, Brand has every physical advantage. But for once, I'm not afraid to be close to him. No, this time, it takes all my strength to rein in the rage running rampant in my veins.

But I will wait for my advantage. I will watch for my chance. I will outwit him. I maneuver past him. Because I *will* catch him. Somehow. Soon.

I spend all morning crafting a narrative of Will's espionage adventures (based on a true story, though not his) until Brand leaves for lunch. Ten minutes later, I'm out the door.

There's one resource I haven't tried yet, one last backup who might actually be able to back me up: our Canadian spy counterparts, CSIS. Normally, we work together quite a bit, though obviously my schedule's been a little full lately.

I park outside an office complex. I have no reason to have Mack's cell number, but hello? Spy. Of course I do. Not exactly surprising when he answers with "Royal Canadian Mint."

"Mack, it's Talia." I don't bother with the formalities and spy stunts we'd usually go through to make triple sure we're both clear to speak and not under duress. "We need to talk."

"We have rules about these calls, you know. Protocols? For our safety?"

"Speaking of safety, Will's in trouble. He's being set up."

Mack's quiet a long minute. Maybe too long. "By whom?"

The grammar shows it: he's choosing his words carefully. Is that good or bad?

"By his replacement here." And, also, me. I omit that part.

Again, two beats too long a silence. I tap my knuckles on the steering wheel until he answers. "Sorry, Talia. I'd like to help, but we can't step in the middle of a CIA turf war."

"A CIA war on *your* turf?"

"That may be, but this seems like an internal affair. Sorry."

I stammer for a reply. I can't come up with anything more convincing than *I really, really want you to.* (Couldn't blame him for saying no to that argument.)

"That everything?" He wants to hang up on me, I know, but his Canadian conscience won't let him. Yet.

"You're my last hope. This guy is willing to kill for this, and he nearly has."

That gives Mack pause. "You're talking about here?"

"Yes."

"And he's working with foreign intelligence? Selling Canadian information?"

Oh. Crap. I have no evidence of selling out anybody, though shooting Elliott isn't exactly playing nicey-nice—

"Talia?" Mack says slowly. "Can you give me any proof?"

"Only my word. I'd hope that's good enough." We've worked together for years.

Apparently that's a couple years too long. "I want to help you," he says again. The unspoken *but . . .* hangs in the air.

Defeat steals my breath before Mack can finish.

"I understand," I say.

"It's just that . . . you have a reputation."

"Wait, what?" My seat belt seems to transform into a lead vest. Did Brand get to Mack, turn him against me? My old—okay, friend is a little strong—

"Come on." Mack's voice trails into I'm-breaking-this-to-you-gently territory. "We all know how you watch your food and your back and your . . . life. I'm sorry, Talia. It really is possible to take it too far."

Yeah, I'm paranoid, I know, but #1, I'm working on it, and #2, the whole reason for my cultivated paranoia was to make sure I—*we*—never, ever got hurt.

I guess I already learned that was a pipe dream, at least in my personal life. Now it's coming back to bite me at work, too.

And what do you want to bet I'd get all this resistance and more if I called Langley? With my luck lately, I'd end up on a direct line to whoever Brand's got there to fix all his problems.

"Mack, please." I sound too close to begging, but CSIS might be my last hope.

"Look." Mack's tone turns more to *I'm trying to find a way to help*. "Maybe if you brought me some proof, something I could show to the higher-ups?"

"Yeah." Level. Flat. Zero emotion. I understand where he's coming from, but I definitely don't have to like it.

"And it'd be best if you could point out the threat to Canada, too. Wouldn't want it to come off as you guys' office politics."

Uh, *ouch*?

"Call me the minute you have it, okay? I want to help."

Suuure. "Okay," I say, my tone still firmly in neutral. I start the car and end the call before Mack apologizes again. (Canadians sometimes.)

Believe me, nobody's sorrier than me.

This time, it isn't terror that keeps me from going back to the office. Nope. I have somewhere else I need to be, and someone else I need to see.

Takes two to tango—and no, I don't mean Danny. (He doesn't dance. Don't ask him.) If Brand is betraying us, I have to go after the person who very well could have recruited him.

I hate to think Samir set me up, too, but I can't rule out that possibility until I talk to him.

I kill half an hour sitting in a brick-lined alley next to a Chinese restaurant. Not just any chain or chop suey shop in Chinatown. This one's special. And after thirty-seven minutes, the exact reason it's special comes waltzing out the side door to the dumpster.

I push off the wall and stroll down the alley toward him. I wish it were darker, lending me at least the element of surprise. I'll take what little surprise I can get from the setting sun at my back, and I start the conversation before he notices me. "Hello, Samir."

He jumps. The lid of the dumpster clatters shut, the metallic boom echoing through the narrow street. "Tara?"

I'd almost forgotten the cover name I used with him. "How are you doing?"

"I very much need to get back to work." He focuses on opening the dumpster again, tossing the garbage bag in, shutting it carefully.

"How are things with Vince?"

"You should ask him." He heads for the door.

I give a mocking chuckle. "If I could ask him, don't you think I would?"

Samir pauses, then pivots to me. "What is going on? Is Vince all right?"

"Vince is in more trouble than he knows." Or he will be. I hope.

I have to move quickly here. Samir will be missed inside. Normally I'd build to this, but I need to hurry to set the bait, infect his mind with a virus of mistrust, create the expectation Vince has already betrayed him. And why not? He betrayed the last people who paid him (us), didn't he? "Is there any reason he'd tell us something that could hurt you?"

My observation skills jump into overdrive for five agonizing seconds, soaking in the fire hose of Samir's feedback. His eyes, his hands, his posture, his words: I have to watch everything. Even a polygraph is only as good as the examiner.

For one second, two, three, he makes no deceptive moves. But he isn't answering my question, either. Finally, before those crucial seconds are up, his Adam's apple bobs. Swallowing before he answers. "I cannot think of a reason, no."

That *might* be a deceptive indicator. I need to dig deeper, get into the meat of the issue.

I amble over to stand between Samir and his target, the restaurant door. "Pity, Vince can recall a lot more of what you've said and done. Didn't take long to come to this, did it?"

"As I said, I cannot think of a reason Vince would do . . . whatever you are talking about." He shifts his weight, and his voice is even less certain than his balance.

"Do you feel like you know Vince well?"

"Not really. I have only seen him a few times."

I start the vulture's death-spiral gyre around him, keeping him moving to track with me, off his game, unable to concentrate on the lie he's surely concocted in case this ever happened. "I've known Vince for a long time. Years, in fact."

"And do you trust him?"

"I'm sorry, do I look brain-dead?"

Samir's moustache twitches. Uncertain. I may have introduced Brand as somebody I trusted, but if Brand's not just skimming the cash, Samir could be as guilty as he is. Guiltier.

Still circling, I run through the parts of the short speech before a question like this, and hope I hit them all. "Samir, I have to ask you something, because it's important we know. We understand nobody's perfect, and we won't blow anything out of proportion. The real problem here is obviously on our end, but I have to ask you: why did you offer Vince the money?"

He flinches. "Did he say that?"

I'm supposed to be the one asking questions *he*'s not prepared for, but that's not the response I was anticipating. Even I can't read something deceptive into his genuine surprise. And now it's my chance to turn liar. "He didn't have to. Did you think we wouldn't find out?"

"Vince told you I offered him money?" Samir runs the tips of his fingers through his wavy hair, like that will muss it less and still soothe his mind. "Tell me I misunderstand you."

The pity in my frown is genuine (almost). "Oh, no. I think we both understand what's happening here." I move to rapid-fire questioning, giving him little time to construct new lies. "Then you did give money to Vince?"

"I do not under—"

"Is it possible you left something for him in a dead drop?"

It's hard to deny such a broad prospect. Yet Samir shakes his head—but that's not denial. It's confusion. (I was there when we taught him what a dead drop was, so I know it's not a language barrier.) "There must be some mistake."

"Yes, I think you did make a mistake. One that has very, very serious consequences."

"But—"

I cut off Samir's counterargument. "It comes down to one simple thing."

"What is that?"

Abruptly, I halt my orbit, and Samir's rotation grinds to a stop, too. "What did he say when you offered him the money?"

"I did not—"

I break in before he gets out the whole denial. "Then how did it go?"

"You do not understand." Samir's posture, position, even his pupils change from persuading to pleading. "Please. That is not how it happened."

I infuse my tone with the same level of earnestness. "Help me to understand."

Samir glances down. Fear that I've lost him flash-freezes my lungs. Then he looks up, levels my gaze and gives a little must-be-subconscious headshake. "I did not ask him to do what you say."

"Then . . . ?"

It's time for the big admission, and this time, Samir doesn't hesitate or waver. He states it right out. "Vince told me he had all he needed. He said I am finished."

Then they haven't been meeting? He isn't even going through the motions, just taking money and ignoring the best way to stop a deadly terrorist on American soil?

A block of ice sinks in my middle. The betrayal cuts even deeper than I'd imagined. Not because I thought I knew Brand— I was disabused of that notion years ago—but because I never believed one of us could do this, this sort of double cross.

And if he's using someone I recruited as the pawn in this Great Game, and he's setting up Will, and he's tasking me with keeping tabs on Will—I've played directly into his hands.

Me going after Will seems like I'm a rogue officer working for a foreign power. Brand's power play with Samir could be construed as damage control, separating me from a valuable asset, or he might claim Samir tipped him off about me.

He isn't framing Will. Brand's setting up one person to take the fall: me.

Frost cascades down my spine one bone at a time.

I've been the perfect patsy.

CHAPTER 19

I LOOK TO SAMIR AGAIN. "Did Vince say why this was a good idea?"

"He said my cousin might find out. But Vince has a plan to help us all, he says. Protect people, keep my cousin safe, help us." He groans. "I knew to believe I must be a fool."

I know exactly how he feels. I turn away. This time Samir circles around with me to keep in my line of sight. His eyes add the silent *please.* "He told me it was the only way to help. You must believe me."

My expression must be grim enough to make Samir think I don't. I do. He's not exhibiting any deceptive behavior clusters, just a normal level of nerves. But I've already assumed too much, given the benefit of too many doubts. I can't afford to take Brand's word—or Samir's yet. I can't afford to be taken in again. I still have to be careful. "What kind of punishment would be appropriate for someone who's done what I think you've done?"

His shoulders stiffen. It's a big leap, and "punishment" is the last thing anybody wants to hear from a CIA officer. The images that jump to mind aren't pretty.

But it's an important question, too. You'd be amazed the revealing things people say when they're asked to mete out their own hypothetical judgment.

"I . . . I cannot imagine," Samir barely manages. "I have only tried to help, but if this is as serious as you say . . ." His face grows as pale as possible with his dark complexion. "You would be lucky to go to jail."

All right, not a bad answer, although a harsh punishment doesn't tell me whether he's being deceptive.

I move on. "What does Vince do with the money?"

"I do not know."

"What have you done with the money he gave you?" Another CIA questioning tactic, presuming guilt to get them to admit it.

"Food. I can give it back—I will be paid again next week." He gestures to the restaurant.

I shift into observational overdrive again, watching for hand-to-face activity, feet movement, grooming gestures.

Nothing. All I read on this page is honesty. And not the *like I told you before, I swear on a dozen Qurans, I'm not that type of guy, it doesn't make sense for me to do that* "honesty." The real kind, the kind where he doesn't have anything to hide. I run through my mental catalog of the conversation, but his body language confirms it: he's telling the truth.

Which makes things a lot more complicated. I scan the alley once again. "Is there anything—*anything*—else you can think of that might explain this? Anything else you need to tell me?"

Samir pauses long enough to reflect. "I have told you all. Please, I only wanted to help."

"I believe you. I'm just trying to figure out what to do next." It's not quite true until after the words are out of my mouth. Because that's when it hits me.

I don't have nearly enough resources to figure this out on my own. Brand is definitely far gone off the Farm, but how can

I be sure this ends with him? Is someone else pulling his strings? Someone on our side?

Brand has already cast suspicion on Will, but I doubt Will could be involved—too big a risk for Brand to turn the investigation on his accomplice. Never know whether the conspirator you're framing might roll on you, and poor strategy is one sin I can't accuse Brand of.

The side door of the restaurant swings open next to me. I jump to my left, narrowly escaping the door's metallic slap against the bricks. The owner, a surprisingly tall Chinese man, doesn't notice. He's too busy immediately launching into a tirade aimed at Samir, who's appropriately cowed. I edge behind the still-reverberating door and count my quick heartbeats.

We do *not* need to be seen together, not here, not like this, not in a clearly covert meeting.

The owner pulls the door to a 90° angle and stomps inside, waiting for Samir to follow. He casts me the quickest glance. I hold one finger to my lips and nod to say sit tight, say nothing to Brand. Samir's done all he can. I'll take care of this. I'll figure it out. I'll handle it.

I'd better.

The door closes after him, and I sag against the bricks behind me. I thought things were deep when I was fighting the Ottawa River for my life. Now I'm really in over my head.

My usual level of caution seems like a joke as I watch for surveillance at a ridiculous number of stops on the way home. Anybody who knows me wouldn't be fooled by my side trip to Fabricland (Fabricland!), but there's nobody tailing me (and Abby's not working tonight). I'm trying to shake the feeling, the feeling I'm not only being watched, but set up. Chased. Hunted.

I'm falling into something far more sinister than I expected, the consequences a lot worse than one rogue officer in Ottawa.

By dusk, I'm done. I trudge up to my apartment, that dread weighing on my feet way more than the doubled errands of my route. I'll check my tiny studio apartment twice, as if the packing boxes I now room with could hide an extra bad guy.

I round the corner to my hall. A figure in a black jacket and wool cap loiters by my door.

My ribs freeze before I can even gasp.

Set up.

Chased.

Hunted.

I don't dare pivot or run. As silently as possible, I slide back around the corner. A mirror. I'd use that compact to see past the angle, but I don't know if I can take even that small a risk.

And, crap, it's in the car.

With a deep breath locked in my chest, I edge back to peer around the corner. The person—a woman, or a guy with a slight build and really long brown hair—bends over in front of my apartment, drops something, tucks it under the door as if to keep it in place.

Oh no, you don't. I duck back behind the corner before my "mystery date" can see me. But I'll definitely be seeing more of her.

The hallway carpet muffles her retreating footsteps enough that I can't be sure whether that's my pulse in my ears. I force myself to wait, to breathe, to think this through. I'm so hyper-cautious I wouldn't live somewhere without multiple escape routes, but there aren't that many places to go in a hallway: toward me and away. Nobody rounds my corner by the time I've finished my meaningless, self-imposed countdown.

I risk a glimpse of the hall—no one in sight. Not for long. I dig deep, down past CIA training and hit that year of ballet I took at twelve, and the one skill I retained: dance running. (It's quiet, okay? Noisy ballerinas get ridiculed and kicked out of class. Even if they were freaking hilarious, Madame Willikers.)

As I pass my door, I swoop down to collect the brown paper packet. The contents feel soft and the paper crinkles under my fingers. I can't risk a deeper investigation now. I run down the hall to the corner. Hasn't been long enough for her to completely disappear, has it?

Who is this girl and how did Brand recruit her? I check the package again. Anthrax is overkill, even for Brand, right?

I still my panting and try to listen, but my pulse is still too fast, too loud, too harsh. I'll have to take another look. I crane my neck—somebody there—snap back behind the corner.

Subtle. Nice.

Definitely no time to open the package. A door down the hall slams, and my adrenaline level spikes. Did this girl bring backup? Do I have any I could call in?

The door's exact resonance finally registers: metal. Fire door. The stairs. On her way out.

Then so am I. Taking a gamble that this soft packet isn't a bomb (not a safe bet), I tuck it in my waistband and dash to the stairs. I'm quieter than my quarry with the door, holding onto the crash bar so the latch doesn't clang shut, echoing through the concrete stairwell. But that takes extra seconds I don't have, and before I let go of the bar, a second clatter rises from below. Ground level door.

I hustle down the stairs. Not quite in enough of a hurry to slide down the railings, and with my luck lately, I can hardly take one more neck-breaking chance. I reach the ground floor and ease the door open.

And run right into someone. A woman, staring back at me in shock. A freezing bolt takes hold of my system and I can't move.

"Talia?" the woman asks.

She knows me. Panic beats that into my brain until the rest

of the pieces fall into place. She's wearing a red cardigan. No hat. And, hello? She lives on the third floor. Florence Parsons.

Cover, cover— "Did a woman come from the stairs? My friend left her cell at my place."

Thank you, subconscious fears of leaving my phone somewhere stupid.

Ms. Parsons wrinkles her nose, thinking. "Don't believe so."

"Thanks anyway." I maneuver around her. The back way out is less accessible, and if you don't live here (and study the building plans like a borderline psychotic), you wouldn't guess it exists at all. The front doors have got to be her route.

I think she's far enough ahead that I'm safe running through the front doors, but I won't risk it. I can't. But I also can't go skulking around without getting more attention than I want. The best way to slide under the radar? Use that purposeful walk again. Stay focused on the goal.

And I'm definitely focusing on mine. If I can find her. Out on the street, the sun is setting way faster than I'd like and my mystery date is missing, invisible, or very, very lucky.

She can't have gotten that far that fast, right? I scan the sidewalks again, the seconds ticking by in my brain like a steady drum, like her footsteps, like my heartbeat.

There. Black jacket, black wool cap. Way too warm for that. Across the street and halfway down the block.

Jaywalking is too much of a gamble—not the risk of getting caught, but the risk of attracting notice. I follow my target (generic code name: RABBIT) from across the street until I reach the red hand/Don't Walk signal at the next corner. Waiting for the light, I take care not to watch her too obviously, without taking my eyes off her. Most people can get away with watching the signal, browsing their phones or staring into space at a stoplight, and I pick door #3. Whatever gets me closer to bachelorette #1, who's quickly becoming very eligible for payback.

Finally the signal changes. I manage not to launch myself

across the street, maintaining my purposeful pace. The RABBIT's nearly a block ahead, but not walking as quickly as I am. How far before she reaches her car? Parking can be tough around here, but we're far enough from my place that it's starting to get a little ridiculous.

Halfway through the next block, I'm close enough to see she's on the phone. I close to eavesdropping range, then slow down like I'm thinking about something really important.

"I'm sure she'll get it," the RABBIT says. Her voice is familiar, I realize with a jolt. Brand's attacking me on a personal level. Recruiting someone I know. "No," she continues, "I think she'll understand."

A sheet of ice crystallizes in my stomach, brittle and sharp. They're talking about me. They have to be. I have to find out who she is, figure out how Brand got to her, how anybody could hate me this much.

The RABBIT reaches the corner and takes the right, bowed over her phone as she ends the call. My opportunity. I break character, break into a run, and break around the corner in time to grab her. In one flash of anger and heat, I shove her against the nearest building, my forearm pinning her shoulders in place. She screams and struggles against me. I push her harder, then whip out the brown paper packet and shove it at her. "What are you trying to—"

And then the streetlight hits her face, and I see exactly how stupid I am.

Abby. Her jaw falls, too, recognizing me at the same time. "Talia?"

I drop her, drop back, drop the bravado. Once again, I'm scrambling for a cover. "Abby, you can't go skulking around people's apartments."

"I'm sorry. You weren't home, so I thought I'd leave it for you. Sorry."

I glance down at the packet in my hands. The paper's

ripped beneath my fingers, showing a glimpse of white. I tear back the paper farther. White fabric. I survey Abby again.

"Samples for your dress. Since I know you're busy."

Oh, wow. I underestimated my stupidity. Here she is, trying to do something kind for me, and I attack her. No wonder I have so many friends.

"Thanks, Abby. That's really nice of you." But . . . what she was saying on the phone—she met Brand two days ago. Suspicion creeps into my words. "Who were you talking to?"

"Danny's mom? Kathi?"

"Right."

Her smile's uneasy. I can hardly blame her. She's still trying to be nice, though. "Is work getting to you still? Is it Vince?"

For a split second, cold ripples shoot down my back—but then I remember. Brand didn't get to her. *I* told her about him. "Yeah. That."

"We could look at the sketches now, if you want. Pick up some Timmy's? BeaverTails?"

A girl after my own heart (and sweet tooth). The possibilities are calling to me: I could have a break. I could have fried dough and maple syrup. I could have a few minutes to pretend my biggest concern is my wedding dress instead of staying alive.

Even after how I treated her tonight, I could have a *friend*.

Abby self-consciously rubs the back of her head where I slammed her into the stucco. Yes, the most unbelievable part of this whole sneaking around over satin scenario is that anyone would be nice to me after the fantastic friend I've been: standing her up, taking advantage of her sewing, throwing her against a wall.

Because I thought Brand got to her. If he did, I don't want to imagine what he'd do to her—

My erratic manners aren't the biggest reason it's best for me to not have friends. Spies live and die by their secrets, and so do the people closest to them.

I like Abby a lot, but she's better off staying one step above an acquaintance.

"I wish I could, but I have casework to catch up on tonight, or I'll get it in the morning."

Abby winces for my sake. "Okay, just let me know what you like best. There are a couple pattern sketches in there. Nothing too fancy—I know you."

No. No, you don't. But that's how it's supposed to be, and how it has to be. "Thanks," I repeat, like that'd be enough to repay this gesture.

"It's nothing. Sorry to scare you."

"Sorry to beat you up."

She doesn't quite laugh, one hand drifting up to the bruise on the back of her head again before she bids me goodbye and we go our separate ways.

After my little chase, and knowing what I know about Samir and Brand, I don't want to go back to my empty apartment to cower by myself. But right now, I can't deny it's safest for me to be utterly, completely alone.

CHAPTER 20

I DEVOTE THE NIGHT to packing more of my stuff until I get a text from Danny: *At least tell me if you're still alive.*

I'm an idiot. How could I have not checked in? *Texting from beyond the grave*, I reply.

Not funny. And he includes the period. Very. Serious.

I type an apology, but another text comes in first: *Would this be easier if I worked for DS&T?*

My heart crawls downward. The truth is yes, of course, some of this situation—some of my *life*—would be easier if we both worked for the Agency.

This is one time I think Danny deserves a lie.

The CIA may have all kinds of listening devices, and Brand could eavesdrop on my conversation, but Danny is more important than feeding my paranoia, so I hit the button to call him.

"Am I interrupting anything?" I ask when he answers.

"Please, please do."

I don't even want to know what his mom's making him sit through—please not the scrapbook—but I guess I see how he learned to be so patient with me.

I'm not brave enough to broach the topic that made me call

yet. Instead, I relate the story of stalking Abby framed in a less threatening light. We segue into small talk about her samples. Not that I'm much help; I know nothing about fabric or sewing, despite Abby's handy labels.

"So satin is smooth and shiny, and crepe de Chine is bumpier and . . . not shiny," I explain. "Chiffon is kinda like a see-through version of crepe de Chine."

"*Crêpe de* . . . what?"

I take a stab at the French pronunciation, moving the nasal part of the word into the vowel. "*Crêpe de* . . . shi-en?"

"Spell it?"

I do, and that seems to make it click for Danny. "*Crêpe de Chine*," he corrects my pronunciation: more like *sheen*. "Chinese crepe."

I wrack my brain for the translation of my mispronunciation. "I said *chien*, huh?"

"Yeah, and I was wondering why dog crepe was one of the options."

"Cute. No, just satin, crepe, chiffon, silk taffeta and charmeuse. If I weren't looking at these, I'd have to ask if they were fabrics or desserts."

"You'd like them better as desserts, huh?"

"Probably." I fold them up and pull the sketches from the packet. If Abby drew these, she's really good. And if she drew these, why's she working at Fabricland? (Fabricland!) They all have the same silhouette we liked with different details and fabrics, if that's what the notes in the corner mean. Now I just have to figure out which one is me.

I thumb through the sketches, eliminating #2 (Too . . . flowy? I don't know.) until Danny breaks in again. "Did you get to talk to Abby at all?"

"Not really."

He pauses. "Hm."

I don't like that.

Danny presses on, delving into a work personnel problem. I think he'd actually be happy to take a demotion if it meant he didn't have to manage people anymore. He usually figures out the best thing to do by talking through it, so I'm here as a sounding board. Not that I mind. The verbal equivalent of an SDR is the safest route if someone's listening to our conversation.

As if Danny hits the end of an invisible three-minute timer, he abruptly drops the topic of his job and the idiots there. "How was work today?" Either he's been dating me too long, or he's gotten way too good at that fake-innocent tone.

"Stressful." I close my eyes to the sketches. Is this how we're going to talk about DS&T? We have to be careful on an open line any time we talk about work, but especially now.

"Heard anything from Elliott?"

"No." I silently pray we can keep up the cover in case Brand's listening somewhere. "He's probably shook up. I think he knows Josh Lee."

"Who?"

There's no nice, non-suspicious way to say *shut up this instant.* I set aside the sketches. "That guy who was shot downtown yesterday? He works for the embassy, too."

"Uh . . . huh. How was your boss?" Danny won't let it go.

"Fine." Suspiciously fine, or at least I hope Danny can read between the lines to hear the real answer.

"So, any news?"

None that I can share over the phone, thanks. "Nope."

Danny falls silent, and this time I *know* it. The fake innocence, the repeated questions, the little hesitations: this pause is really bad news. I brace for the topic of DS&T.

But when he speaks, it's even worse than I feared. "So were you ever going to tell me?"

I sit up straighter at my table, searching around like I've got a life jacket stowed around here. "Tell you what?"

"About your boss?"

"What about him?" My stomach turns sour with dread.

"He's Brand."

The worst part—the worst part is *how* he says it. If he were mad, if he'd shout at me, if he'd accuse me, lose his temper, anything—I would know how to react.

I have no defense against the pain in his voice.

"Why would you tell me his name was Vince?"

More stuff I shouldn't share over the phone. I drop my volume and try to think of a neutral way to explain the operational name. "Because I have to. I wouldn't even know his first name if I hadn't known him back in DC—wait, how do you know this?"

"Abby called. She's worried sick, convinced you flipped out on her because he's stalking you. She said you used to date. You've only got one ex-boyfriend at work, and he isn't named Vince."

Suddenly I don't feel so bad for banging her head into a wall. She wasn't supposed to tell—but she didn't know. Now Danny's engineer brain has fit all the pieces together, including the things I've told him about Brand that I've never told anyone, above and beyond the little Abby knows. Not only the backstabbing at work and the psychopathic punishment he meted out for not putting out, but the stuff that even now I'm too spooked to repeat. Taunting, pinches. Middle of the night calls. "Accidentally" brushing against me. Threatening "gifts."

Uh, yeah, Danny should be deeply displeased. And not just with Brand. "Is there *any* reason you wouldn't tell me?"

"Of course. I—" All those good reasons, whatever they were, immediately abandon me. All I can think of is why I never once used Danny's name in front of Brand. To protect Danny.

Now I'm so glad I didn't, even if Brand figured out who he was anyway, even if Brand might be listening now or reading a transcript of the conversation tomorrow. But that logic doesn't work both ways.

And Danny waits for an answer. An awesomely effective tactic to get the info you need, since this is one awkward silence I really want to fill.

But I have no idea what to fill it with. No idea what to give him. No idea what I could do to explain. "Danny, I'm sorry."

"Are you covering for him?"

I scoff. "Of course not."

I'm covering for me. And somehow, that's worse.

"Is this fun for you, lying to me?" The words are accusatory, but the tone's a lot closer to heartbreakingly hurt.

"That's not fair—"

He laughs without humor. "Not 'fair'? You're kidding, right?"

"Of course not."

"And how's it fair that I'm supposed to settle for whatever scraps you're willing to throw me? Do you have to be so stingy with the truth?" Now the anger's starting to come through. "Or are you pathologically incapable of thinking of anyone but yourself?"

That blow hits hardest of all. Am I my mother?

Danny sighs, away from the phone, like he's trying to hide his annoyance (too late). He's always been crazy patient with my job, even before he knew I was a spy, but there are limits to everything. Even Danny.

"I'm sorry," I try again, like the two weak little words are both a peace offering and a heat shield. "I'm trying—I'm trying to think of you. To protect you."

Another exasperated exhale. "Nice job."

The heat's gone out of his anger, though the hurt hasn't. And that cuts right through me.

I'm trying to protect him. I am. But now I can't remember how exactly my paranoia and keeping the truth from him was supposed to keep me safe—*him* safe. That was always the plan: keeping him in the dark about my job, keeping him away from danger, keeping up the façade. This is obviously not the first time the plan has utterly, miserably failed.

I can imagine his expression: jaw set, mouth pressed into the bare outline of a frown, gaze conspicuously avoiding mine. I can't make this better. Even the truth feels like a small consolation after keeping up the lie for so long.

Danny breaks the tense silence. "Knew I should've decked the guy the first time I saw him."

The veneer of humor only lowers the tension a notch. Because he's right. I had a good reason for keeping Brand away from Danny, and I have a better one now. Despite the promises I made to myself when we started dating, and despite finally telling him the truth about my job and my secrets, I'm still playing the Great Game with Danny.

And I can't pretend I was doing it all for Danny's sake. Are you kidding? This is for me.

"Next thing you'll tell me you and Elliott dated, too." Danny's trying to be funny, though my sinking feeling says it's going to backfire. Big time. We didn't date—not even close—but this is hardly the time to tell—

"Talia, why aren't you saying anything?" His voice is filled with uneasy suspicion.

"We didn't date." My rush to reassure him is too rushed.

"But . . . ?"

I smother a moan. "He kissed me. Once. Before we started dating."

"I thought you said you and Elliott didn't date."

"I mean before you and I started dating. It was just a cover." To me. But holding back even that sliver of the truth hurts, so I tell him that part, too. "It was nothing."

"If it was nothing, why didn't you tell me?"

"Um, because it would upset you?"

"But it's the truth." Once again, he has a point. Before I can begin to figure out how to make up for my mistakes, Danny groans. "*Si je ne vais pas divertir elle, ma mère va piquer une crise.*"

He has to go entertain his mom, or she'll . . . "*Crise?*"

"Fit."

What do you want to bet that's the bad kind? Neither of us has to stipulate that this discussion is far from over. Until I retire from the spy business, we might have this conversation every month about something I kept from him when I didn't have to, another time I played the Game when I shouldn't have.

What if you can take the spy out of the CIA but you can't take the CIA out of the spy?

With these prospects, it's a wonder Danny hasn't asked for the ring back.

"I love you." I hope that note of *please, please love me back* is all in my imagination.

"I love you too." And his tone is way too close to resignation.

I stare at Danny's smile on my phone's screen until it goes dark. We never even talked about DS&T, and I still hurt the last person I wanted to alienate.

What was I just thinking about being completely alone?

I won't let Brand win like that, stealing everyone I have. I. Will. Fight. I've started writing up "Will's" activities, but that's not enough. By the time I get to work Thursday, I have the full report—the real one—in the one place I can keep something that sensitive. My pocket.

I don't beat Brand in even this early, but he's in his office, so I don't have to face him. I fire up my email, trying to figure out the next step to take Brand down—until a message from

Elliott catches my attention. Even if it's just a status update, that's the first thing I want to read.

Released from hospital, reads the first line. I allow myself one silent sigh of relief, though that's it for the personal message. The rest of the email is a link. I click. The CTV News Channel page takes forever to load. My shoulders tense every second, and my eyes flick between eyeing Brand's closed door to make sure it stays that way and searching the screen to make sure there isn't a video loading that'll automatically begin playing (the minute Brand walks by, I'm sure).

Finally, the page finishes and I can scroll past the oversized photo of police tape around a suburban rambler. The dateline is Falls Church, Virginia, and already the chills do a cha-cha down my spine. It's a small town outside of DC, and yeah, they have crime like everywhere else. But this particular suburb happens to be fifteen minutes from Langley. And this particular crime happens to have made the world news.

That doesn't mean anything, right?

Of course. Totally a coincidence. Sure. Like it's a coincidence I couldn't peel my eyeballs away from this article if I tried.

But it's not until I hit on the name of the victim that the time-for-total-freak-out switch flips in my brain: Ali Muhammad Wasti. Brother of Hassam-ud-Din Wasti, who allegedly holds family sacred.

As far as I know, we had no clue Ali Muhammad was anywhere near the US, let alone fifteen minutes from Langley. Not that a dead brother will do Hassam-ud-Din much good—but the unwritten message here is clear. The "execution-style murder" is actually an execution.

We might have figured out where Hassam-ud-Din has been hiding.

I'm the first to admit I don't use Intellipedia like I'm supposed to (though it's mostly geared toward analysts anyway), but you'd better believe that's the first place I'm checking. It was established a few years after 9/11 to make sure the various agencies in the US intelligence community would never again fail to connect the dots. With any luck, the FBI's playing nice and we'll be able to start making those connections.

As a developing story, Ali Muhammad Wasti's article is changing by the second. My first skim confirms my theory: we didn't know he was in the country, but official reports (partially leaked to the press?) cite the apparent execution by beheading, and speculate at the tensions between the brothers. And that's all we've got, speculation and more speculation: differences over an op. Maybe Ali Muhammad was more of a pacifist.

I reload the page. Another theory. According to one report, Hassam-ud-Din allegedly stole one of his brother's wives. No real foundation to back up that accusation.

And this is the problem of an agency of analysts. When there's no concrete, actionable information out there, analysis can only go so far before it starts to go crazy.

We're going to need some help. We're going to need more intelligence. We're going to need another dot.

And I know exactly where to find him.

CHAPTER 21

NEED TO GET TO SAMIR, but I think someone (named Brand) will notice if I disappear without any explanation or excuse two days in a row. So I go through the routines of a day at the office: filing reports, coordinating with coworkers, catching up on reading, biding my time. By mid-afternoon, I'm running out of things to do when I hear the footsteps over the office carpet. I freeze, pretending not to hear, pretending to read the Intellipedia article on an old case with a Turkmen scientist, pretending not to know exactly who's slinking up behind me.

The security swipe in the reception area is a physical defense against a brute force attack. But now I feel less safe here than I do in the hall or on the street. A lot less safe.

I sense Brand so close behind me that the flashbacks I've worked so hard to hold back resurface with a vengeance. The heat of embarrassment rises in my cheeks and my chest, though my skin prickles with cold.

I make myself not move, not give in that much, not show that kind of weakness. Not to Brand.

"What are you reading?" he asks.

I fight the urge to whirl around. "Checking up on old cases.

Looking for new developments."

I hope Brand doesn't want to page through my tabs. I have half a dozen Intellipedia articles open, including one on the execution of Ali Muhammad Wasti. Not a huge deal for me to keep up on Samir's case, but I can't raise Brand's suspicions.

Brand leans over my shoulder, places his hand over mine on the mouse. My heart constricts like he's gripping that instead.

He hasn't done anything—not a single thing—beyond words here. Nothing in front of the guys. Nothing in his office. Nothing in years. So why am I breaking out in a cold sweat because he's close?

He guides my hand an inch to the right and clicks the mouse button. "Work much with the Lebanese?"

"He was Elliott's contact. Colleague of my contact."

"Elliott?"

I can't move. What have I done? I've given away—

No. No. He doesn't know who Elliott is. "Old officer here."

Brand releases my mouse to squeeze my shoulder. Exactly the thing you'd do to an employee who's doing a decent job, exactly what Will would've done, exactly what I don't want. "Any new insight on the case?" he asks.

"Both our contacts went home a year ago, and nobody's been able to get up with them."

"You recruited them while they were here?"

Brand's as trustworthy as a faulty grenade, and I am *not* about to pull that pin. I can't think of a reason Turkmenistan's or Lebanon's energy technology has anything to do with Wasti and his ilk. Despite the logic, my paranoid gut says this is a piece of truth I should be stingy with.

One piece? When it comes to Brand, I should be a freaking truth-Scrooge.

"No," I say, finally rotating my chair to see him. "We just started on them. They didn't seem to catch the drift quickly enough."

"Ah." Brand heads away. It's like he's stepped off my chest.

And then he turns back. "So did you hear about the latest in the Wasti case?"

I watch his face, and not just to monitor for deception signs. I won't look back to my computer. I won't look away like I'm remembering something. I. Won't. Give. Him. Anything. "What happened?"

"Apparently his brother came into the country—America—and got himself killed."

"We're still in America."

Brand smirks. "You know what I mean."

Oh, I think I do. Like he's trying to drive that point home, he circles back around my desk to stand over me. I have more disadvantages than the sitting vs. standing question. When we need to examine someone for deception, we stick him in a swivel chair like mine. No table. No anchor. Let him twist in the wind—almost literally—and watch the subconscious lie indicators add up. The best-trained operative can't control every muscle of his body every second. Even Brand couldn't hide every little gesture of deception.

And neither can I.

I try to slow my racing adrenaline and lean back in my chair, the perfect picture of composure. "The FBI figured it out yet?"

Brand regards me in silence. Oh crap. I tipped my hand, or at least one card. The FBI wouldn't get involved in just any old murder. Even the brother of an international terrorist hiding in the US isn't enough to get their attention sometimes. (Usually not much help tracking the living terrorists. You know, the whole "dead men tell no tales" thing.)

They'd at least want to get on the scene, right? "Or don't their crime scene techs want to talk to the spooks?" I finally add.

I can only imagine the subconscious twitches Brand must be seeing now. But he laughs. "You know the F-entity."

That's his cue to leave, check up on someone else, go do whatever he does behind closed doors in his office all day. He doesn't. He settles against my desk and folds his arms, his expression somewhere between curiosity and suspicion.

Please don't let him question me.

"Tell me what you know about the Ali Muhammad Wasti case," he says.

Great. I pivot to my computer like following up on year-old cold contacts is way more pressing than this line of questioning. "First I've heard of it." I bite back the natural "I just told you that." That type of referral statement is another deception indicator.

"Ah." The single syllable doesn't betray whether he believes me or not. "Not hunting for a connection between your Lebanese guy and Wasti?"

I check my computer. "Should I be?"

"Just an idea. We've got to get a line of sight on this."

Not exactly. We don't need an angle; we need the facts—but when it comes to me and Brand, there is no "we." Especially not since he elbowed me out of the only case we were sharing, however briefly. I should be relieved not to work with him shoulder to shoulder, but my *spy*-dey sense is tingling.

I don't want to say anything, though if I don't, it's an even bigger giveaway. "Don't you mean *you* need to talk to Samir?"

That should be his first thought, not bugging me. He has the best access to the best asset.

"Yeah, but last time we talked he had no clue something like this was coming."

Right. "He knew Ali Muhammad was here, right?" I lay out the pieces of the trap.

Brand's eyes narrow a split second. "Uh, yeah, he did."

"So how has Samir been taking all this drama?"

Brand clears his throat, switches feet. Not a good sign for whatever he says next. "Hard on him. Family 'trauma,' you know. Always sucks."

A dysfunctional family isn't a résumé requirement for the Agency, but a lack of deep family ties isn't exactly a drawback when your work keeps you away and impossible to contact for years at a time. Brand and I are both among those "lucky" people unencumbered by a happy family, so his discomfort with "family stuff" alone doesn't make it a lie.

It's all the rest of his behavior that makes it obvious he's lying.

And I'll make this as bad for him as I possibly can. "Did he have any intel on Ali Muhammad?"

"I didn't know Ali Muhammad was in the country, and I'm guessing Samir wouldn't keep that from me."

I resist the urge to rock back in my chair. "Seeing a lot of him?"

"Of course." Brand slaps on that trademark smirk. I know it's only a cover, but it still creeps me out, and not just a little bit. He shoves off my desk and starts away.

Oh, no. I'm not letting him off that easy. Until I figure out exactly how to get him, I want him to suffer as much as possible. So I swivel in my chair, tracking with him. "What does Samir say Wasti's next move is? Regroup? Change locations again?"

"Kind of obvious. What other choice does he have?"

I squeeze my lips together like I'm thinking, not suspicious (or sarcastic). "How long before he contacts Samir next?"

"Not like they have a set meeting schedule. Wasti calls when he wants something."

"And what does he want from Samir?" I shoot for a tone of innocent, speculative questioning, not laying a trap.

Brand's eyes slide away, his brow furrowing. I can't tell if that's concentration or fabrication. "All we've come up with so far is he's hoping Samir will support him. Validation. At the outside, he might want Samir to come help him directly. Maybe head up a Canadian op."

"Right." My worst possible move: that one little sarcastic syllable slips out, the challenge and the disbelief plain.

Brand's gaze locks on mine. I can't read his face, but my built-in alarm system sounds a warning. Those blue eyes go beyond *don't you want me?* right into *don't you look tasty?*

Can he turn this back on me? Of course he can. It's Brand.

Each second that ticks by ratchets my ribs another notch tighter, and he just stares at me. I won't be stared down, no matter how the goose bumps creep up my back.

Then Brand stalks around my desk. Stops at my feet. Leans closer, closer, closer, until his eyes are level with mine, his face inches away, his hands on my armrests—trapping me. "Talia, listen to me. I know we've got . . . a history." His gaze takes a round-trip circuit of my body. Checking my body language, I tell myself. Not checking me out. I clamp down on the shudder that threatens despite my logic.

He doesn't move from there, but I can feel his hands moving over me, fear closing my throat, hopeless, helpless—

No. It's nothing. It's nothing. It's nothing. He's not doing anything.

It's everything.

Maybe this is the real reason I didn't tell Danny the truth about Brand sooner, because if I let myself think about the past, the things I've managed to hold back would break the surface.

If that's the case, I was right.

Brand's eyes snap back to mine. "But if we can't work together, if we can't trust one another, we've got bigger problems than Wasti."

He closes another inch on me. "I need you with me."

I swallow, or try to. I hate the way that sounds, but I make my reply convincing. "Of course." Like all of this goes without saying. Like he's the one weirding out right now.

And believe me, he is.

Brand gets another centimeter closer. "Good." His voice is a hair above a whisper, and I can feel his breath on my lips.

In the split second before he pulls away, I relive the stupid slip that brought us together. The flirting never would've gone anywhere—not if it'd been up to me—until the minute we were alone in his cubicle, and he took it to this level, to this contact.

Then he closed the last three inches. Or maybe I did. I've never been sure, though it was easier to blame him. To pretend like this was never my idea. Definitely not my intention. But suddenly that day back at Langley, we were kissing.

I knew better than to go there then. Now awful experience has proved me right. I've kept that locked deep in my memory, alongside the fear that flooded my veins that day, the same frigid sludge pumping through them now. My palms sweat; my stomach pitches. I swallow against the nausea.

I have to get out. "I got it." I don't bother hiding the tension in my tone, digging deep into my resolve reservoir to shoot him an unmistakable back-off-now signal.

Brand releases me, off to his office like nothing happened. It's a lot more than nothing. My hands are shaking, and somebody's going to notice this hyperventilating if I don't get it under control. I glance around. We always have an audience here, but César's coming back from the bathroom, Robby's absorbed in his computer, and Justin conspicuously avoids my eyes.

I'm on my own. I challenged Brand; nobody said a word as he escalated like shock and awe was the best defense. And I cowered like it was working. Just like I always have with him.

Am I not enough to take him on?

CHAPTER 22

I DON'T CARE HOW IT LOOKS. I'm getting out of here. I pack up before anybody can say a word about Brand's behavior and head out on a surveillance detection route.

Intimidating me might be his game again, but it's a lot more than my irritation level on the line. Though I try my hardest to fight back the memories, I can't help but relive every second of the nightmare.

Four years gone, and the memories still make me feel every bit as trapped as I was in my chair this afternoon with Brand in my face, holding my armrests, pinning me down.

The images and feelings I'd banished from my memory rush in between my boring, routine stops. My perennial professional paranoia and communicating with cashiers and clerks aren't enough to pull me all the way out of the past.

I've already endured that idiotic mistake that started the whole thing. Now I feel his hands on my hands, my arm, my waist. I feel him dragging me a lot closer than I ever intended. I feel him pressuring me, the little innuendo that I stupidly chose to ignore, the caresses that weren't accidental, the romantic setup that blew up when he found out I was really, really serious about the whole no-sex-outside-of-marriage thing.

And then having to work with him. Dreading every day of my "dream job" until I was almost physically ill. Holding out until the Farm, hoping and praying and begging that things would be different there. Working alone. Eating alone. Suffering alone.

Shame, embarrassment, anger all vie for top billing in my emotional train wreck. I hate that I didn't do anything about it. I hate that I didn't tell anyone, regardless of whether they'd believe me. I hate that I let him make me into a victim.

I. Hate. Brandon Copley. I hate him for every minute he made my existence miserable. I hate him for ever coming back. I hate him for what he's doing now.

But hate isn't enough. Like I said, wanting something too much can come back to hurt you, make you reckless, make you weak.

I can't let this be personal. I have to be deliberate. Cool. Calculating.

Like Brand.

Finally finished with my last SDR stop, I drive a block past my destination, a lamppost by a blind alley, and park around the corner. I pull a stick from the box of chalk under my seat.

Back at the Farm, aside from being reminded that not *every* man in the CIA is a villain out to ruin my life, I learned the art of signaling, another of the cloak-and-dagger, we're-teaching-you-this-to-make-you-feel-cool elements of the course. Though we have less of an occasion to use it in Canada than in hostile territory, sometimes we get to do our trainers proud.

Tonight is one of those times. I hold the chalk hidden in my fist and walk down the street like a woman with a purpose: to blend in among the rest of the pedestrians, slip through their short-term memories, disappear.

Not a lot of foot traffic to weave through, but I make sure to barely outpace the general speed and maneuver to the sidewalk's edge, toward one particular light pole. I check the plate glass window as I come even with my target. Nobody behind me. At least nobody suspicious.

I twist my hand with the hidden chalk outward and let it brush the light pole, pocketing the chalk before I'm five feet away.

To be honest, this isn't completely safe—it's one of the signals Brand and I taught Samir together—but unless I want to track him down at work again (can we say "fired"?), this sign is the best I can do to let Samir know it's time for a meeting.

It's well past time for a meeting.

I have hours to kill before Samir is supposed to follow through on that little chalk signal. I don't dare go home or to Danny's—not that he wants to see me anyway. I drift through another SDR until I roll to a stop in a cute little suburb filled with happy little people living happy little lives, happily oblivious.

Meanwhile, the equilibrium of my whole life is shifting like the mix of ice and water and mud that takes over the Ottawa River during the spring break-up season, changing so quickly I hardly have time to think about thinking ahead. Every path seems equally dangerous.

I need help. I need that one place I can always go when things are uncertain. For the second night in a row, I'm drowning in my memories and my paranoia. I need my anchor. I need Danny. *How was your day?* I text.

Long.

I do not need to overanalyze that (though I will anyway).

Danny texts again before I can keep up the pretense of small talk. *I can't sit around here worrying about you every day.*

You could go to work. Lame attempt at a joke, I know.

He ignores it. *For all I know, there's more you aren't telling me.*

Only the stuff I can't.

So, if I were with DS&T, you would've told me that part?

About Brand? Yeah, no. But Danny texts before I reply: *If I were Elliott?*

I flinch, the jab is so unexpected—and if I'm honest, close to home. I don't respond fast enough, because Danny texts yet again: *You told him, didn't you.*

I don't even get the benefit of a question mark? Rather than prolong the miscommunication (if that's what it is), I hit the icon to call him.

"You *did* tell him, didn't you?" he answers.

"Some of it. Only what I had to."

"Of course—that's why he's the one out there getting shot for you."

His mother had better not be in hearing range. "Did you want to trade places? I think he'd jump on that."

"At least I'd be doing something."

I rest my forehead on the steering wheel. "Sitting around recuperating from a gunshot wound wouldn't help me. At least this way you can keep your mom at bay, right?"

"Starting to think I'd rather have the gunshot wound."

"Very funny. Be grateful you haven't had to endure the scrapbook—"

"Oh, no, I've been subjected to the scrapbook."

Not the one she had at the dress shop. "Her scrapbook of Kendra?"

"Trying to avoid it, believe me."

"Who's being stingy with the truth now?" I strive to drain the sarcasm from my voice.

"Don't—I didn't—" Danny pauses. "Okay, I didn't tell you something. *One* thing. I figured telling you would just hurt you."

Bingo. I give his engineer brain half a second to put that together.

He sighs. "Fine. Point taken."

"I love you too," I chirp.

"Yeah, you're just lucky I love you."

I totally am. "Danny . . . I didn't tell you about Elliott because I never wanted him to kiss me. It was a cover—I mean, you and I had already started talking, and that prospect alone was better than . . ." The truth: "He reminded me of how Brand was at first, okay? But I didn't tell Elliott who Brand is, or what happened in DC. Just about what's going on now."

This time, the radio silence has a totally different timbre. I hope it means Danny's engineer brain is working that piece into the puzzle, realizing the implications, understanding that Elliott might be the one I need, but Danny's the one I trust.

"Thank you," he finally says.

"I love you too," I chirp again.

He laughs. "You planning on coming by tonight?"

"Nice segue. Wish I could." I really do. And I tell him that. He seems to appreciate it, but the sentiment kinda kills the conversation when it's obviously code for *I have to go out and do more stupidly dangerous things tonight, and you're definitely not invited (because you're not Elliott) (who's also not invited because I got him shot).*

After a few minutes, I have to let Danny go run interference with his mom, and I start the car. Almost subconsciously, I end up at the one place I know I shouldn't look for help: Elliott's. I don't dare knock—because seriously, how much help is a guy recovering from a gunshot wound? Instead, I park down the street, staring at his windows as the sun's last rays abandon the sky. His living room light switches on, and it occurs to me: I've never been in his home.

We've been so close, been through so much together. Yet in so many ways, we hardly know each other.

The blinds are open, revealing the perfectly decorated living room. Shanna's already put up an artsy black and white portrait of their newborn. Now who knows what'll happen for his family? I keep thinking that's my fault, though I know it's not.

But him being shot? 100% my fault.

I get my phone and type in his number. He answers on the third ring. And that's when I realize I don't have anything to say to him beyond, "How are you?"

He grunts. "Have to say I've been better."

"I'll bet." And we fall into silence.

I've spent a lot of time not talking with Elliott—twelve hours of surveillance together, and you run out of things to talk about pretty quick—but this silence is different. It isn't a lull or a pause or a break.

We've run out of things to say to each other. Maybe forever.

"Busy night ahead of you?" Elliott asks.

"Yeah." That's not him offering to help. He'd better be on a leave of absence until he's fully recovered, but Elliott will jump back into work as soon as the doctors clear him. And he'll shop around until he finds an MD to do exactly that.

I watch his window, and Elliott strolls through living room. At least he's up and around, healing faster. Not fast enough that I could (or would) ask anything of him. I wish we could run through options and scenarios, and I could ask for help. But I can't. I just can't.

"Feeling okay?" I ask. "Taking care of yourself?"

"Yep."

"Good."

It's too quiet on the line, leaving the thoughts to echo through my mind: I have nothing to say to him.

Then it finally hits me, why I really wanted to call.

To say goodbye.

The air turns cold. He stands with his back to the window, to me. Because it's over. We don't work together anymore, and it probably won't be long before he's shipped off to his next station. Even if we both stay in Ottawa, we'll hardly see one another. We're not partners, not coworkers. Just old friends.

And yet I can't look away. I sit there, watching another minute. Then Shanna, very tall and very blonde, walks in. She comes over to him, eyeing his injury, her head tilted like she's asking a question. He turns, and even in this light, I can see the reassuring smile he flashes her.

She's back. They're back.

The release in my chest might mean I'm losing the guilt game. Apparently I did Elliott a favor. All I had to do was get him shot.

"Stay safe out there," Elliott says.

"You too." I start the car. I don't have anywhere else to be, but this isn't where I belong anymore. I can't quite let myself hang up as I pull past his house.

"Hey, T?" His voice is quiet. Hesitant. Like we haven't been through the wringer and crawled back together.

"Yeah?"

"People will call the cops on you if you drive around here without your lights on."

Of course he's there. Of course he saw me. Of course he has my back, as much as he can. I can't ask any more than that.

I'm on my own.

It's time. Samir's in position. I'm sure he's expecting Brand, and when I roll up to the sidewalk where he's waiting in the dark, his black eyebrows gather. But he gets in.

I don't bother with a greeting as I drive away. "We've got work to do. A lot of it."

"What has happened?"

I huff out a syllable of a sarcastic laugh. What hasn't happened? I'm freaking Danny out, Elliott's out of the game, and oh yeah, my boss is selling out our country.

Worse still, there's a terrorist loose on American soil and for all I know, Brand knows exactly where the guy is. He might actually be helping Wasti.

I'm in over my head, and I can feel the water closing over me. Brand's setting me up. He's targeting Americans. And I have no proof.

Samir leans forward to examine my face. "You need my help?"

We were supposed to be helping him. Now I'm the one who needs help. The river's mud and water and ice mix of spring break-up flashes through my mind again, with all my options equally treacherous.

This is big, big trouble, and I have no one left to turn to for help: not Mack, not Will, not Elliott. Especially not Danny.

I look to Samir. He's studying me, waiting for my next response, and I can't help it—a slow smile.

Spring break-up on the Ottawa River is tricky, but the city makes it easier to get ice out of the smaller Rideau River when temperatures rise. All it takes is 10,000 sticks of dynamite.

I know exactly who'll help wield that kind of firepower (you know, metaphorically). Because he's sitting right next to me.

CHAPTER 23

FOR A WOMAN ABOUT TO GET MARRIED, I spend way too much time in hotel rooms with strange men. I bolt the door behind Samir and gesture for him to sit at the desk.

"What are we doing?"

I pat the back of the chair. Samir complies, his face watchful. "Have I done something?"

"No." And that's our first problem. With Brand cutting him off, Samir has pretty much done nothing. That's about to change. "I need you to call your cousin."

"Now?"

I make my nod as firm as possible. "You told me you wanted to stop him, to keep him from hurting people. Be honest: has Vince done a thing to make that happen?"

His eyes slide away. He knows the answer, and he's afraid to admit it.

"Tonight that's going to change."

"How?"

I come to stand over him. "You're going to call Hassam-ud-Din and find out what we need to know to stop him. Now," I add before he can ask again.

Samir's focus stays on the threadbare carpet. He grips the phone in two hands like he's praying. (Not sure that's how it works in Islam.) With each passing second, the air in the room grows heavier. At last, he shakes his head and pushes the phone across the desk. "He will know."

"He won't." I place the phone back in his possession. "And here's why." I drop to my knees in front of him and fasten my gaze to his. "You. Are. Samir. Right?"

"Who else would I be?" I've never seen this sarcasm from the man—I thought that was a cultural thing.

"You're his cousin. That's all I'm asking you to be. Be yourself. Don't pretend. Don't lie. Just *be you*."

Samir contemplates the phone, though before I ready my second salvo of shoring up, he's already dialing. I hide my face so he can't see my flash of panic. I was kind of depending on having one more minute to coach him on what to say, what to dig for, what to do next, but I'll have to roll with this.

"Hassam-ud-Din?"

I might be the local Urdu specialist, but it takes every scrap of my concentration to keep up with Samir's side of the conversation. He's on his feet, pacing, before he gets past the pleasantries. (Wasti's wife is fine, if you're wondering.)

I grab the hotel notepad and write a cue for Samir. *You're worried about him.* He stops long enough to read it. I follow up with another stage direction. *You saw the news about Ali Muhammad.*

The flicker of a flinch around his mouth tells me Samir *did* see the news. Because Ali Muhammad was his cousin, too. But neither of us have the luxury of sensitivity. Samir moves on to my cues before the pain passes from his face. "I saw the news about Ali Muhammad," he says. "Is everything all right with you?"

Samir's eyes move back and forth like he's reading the faded watercolor in front of him. I wave to get his attention, point at my ear to remind him to reflect the conversation back to me, but he turns away. "I want to help," he says (I think). "But it is not so easy to cross the border."

Um, not so much. Why is he lying?

"Are you safe? Not in trouble, are you?"

Good thing Samir isn't looking at me, because if his cousin isn't in trouble now, he's about to be. His cover depends on *being* the part. Never smart to remind yourself you're not.

Samir's pacing halts abruptly, and his spine straightens. He's frozen there for an interminable moment. "I will be there," he says at last. He ends the call, his back still to me.

And I have no idea if we got what we needed. "Well?"

He keeps his back to me, staring at his phone. My blood runs chill. When Samir said he'd be there, he didn't mean it, did he?

"The UN."

I startle out of the worry. "What?"

"The UN. They are targeting the UN. Monday."

"But . . . they were outside DC. Ali Muhammad—"

Samir turns around. "No, it was a ruse. Two birds with one rock. Ali Muhammad was always a problem. Hassam-ud-Din has been in New York the whole time."

Tension mounts behind the floodgates of my mind. This is big. Very big. A terrorist on American soil. Targeting the UN. Soon. And sacrificing his brother to help with a set up? The situation gets darker every second. I have to get organized, to plan, to act. "Did you get his exact location? At least enough to find him?"

"I think so."

As soon as I can get a secure line, I'm calling the highest-ranking person I know at Langley, no matter who Brand might have on his side. But if they arrest Wasti, we lose our chance to stop someone who's selling out our country. Someone who might do it again.

Time to start setting that dynamite.

"This is all that you need?" Samir breaks into my thoughts. He keeps his tone level, though there's no mistaking the hope in his eyes. Hope that we'll be able to stop Wasti, hope that he's done his part, hope that he's finished.

No such luck. "There's another problem here. Hassam-ud-Din isn't the only threat."

"He is the only one I know—"

"Vince."

The silence in the room freezes solid, a palpable presence of its own. Finally Samir swallows hard. "I cannot."

"You have to."

"No." He cuts off the argument, wheeling away. "You can do this. You can talk to him."

I'm on my feet, circling around to face him. "Are you kidding? Do you have any idea what he'll do if I confront him without evidence?"

"Are you not a witness?"

"All I have is my testimony against his." Not enough to take a big risk. I doubt Brand's interested in polling a jury of his peers. If I'm the only one who can bring him to trial, it doesn't bode well for me.

"Well, he must have this money, yes?"

I give an exaggerated shrug. "I tried going after his financial records. He found out, and he'll do it again. Either a report will come back to him, or someone will call to check up, or he'll hunt it down."

Hunt me down. If I don't truss Brand up and serve him on a silver platter, if I don't have absolutely everything we need to put him in custody when I contact Langley, he *will* find out and he *will* make sure I don't get the chance to finish.

My life depends on bringing Brand in before anyone knows I'm targeting him.

Because I'm not the first who's tried. I turn to him. "I've

done all I can think of. When I had another friend help . . . Vince shot him."

"How can I . . . ? A man like me?" Samir wipes his forehead. "You believe I can stop him."

"You're the only one who can."

He ponders the floral bedspread. "What must I do?"

"Just keep doing what you've been doing. Playing along."

"Playing along with what? I have not seen him in days."

The beginning of the relationship is crucial—even without a bomb scheduled for the UN. And Brand isn't meeting with Samir, just pocketing the money.

It'd be one thing if it were only embezzlement. Internal investigation, criminal charges, sure. But feeding us false info to cover and not even pretending to collect the intelligence we need so desperately? That goes way beyond skimming your agent's cash. That's treason.

I need the details. I need an audit of Brand's finances and reports. I need a complete account from Samir telling when they met, what they said, what he got. Probably his bank records and a thorough search of everything he owns to prove he wasn't getting the money.

Or we confront Brand and hope he says something to incriminate himself, show our cards to make him show his.

I don't want to do this alone, but the last time I brought someone with me, he got shot. Yeah, I think I'm gonna err on the side of caution. Because no matter how I play it, big, big risk.

I paint on a self-assured smile for Samir. He's my dynamite, after all. Now I have to wire in the blasting cap.

I hold out my hand for Samir's phone. He furrows his brow, but gives it to me. I type in the phone number and return it to him without hitting *Send.* "Tell Vince what just happened."

"Did you not say he was betraying your country? Why would I want to do that?"

224

"I need evidence." Okay, shooting Elliott is pretty dang obvious, but I have to collect the hard evidence of exactly how Brand's double-crossed our country if, as Mack so helpfully pointed out, he isn't selling information or colluding with foreign intelligence. "I have to see what he does when we tell him something he needs to pass up the chain."

And if he doesn't—sometimes it's the things you *don't* say that hurt the most, right?

"We have to do this carefully," I say. "Normally you wouldn't have this phone number."

Samir glances at his phone, his mouth set in that same uncertain line. If he really knew what we were tackling, he'd run like I offered him a ticket to Guantánamo.

We're not taking on some random, unsuspecting target. We're working against a trained CIA operative who knows he's violating that trust. He has to be five times as cautious as the typical officer.

Fortunately, that would make him about half as paranoid as me. I have to bet on the weakness that brought Brand here in the first place: his overconfidence.

"Vince will be suspicious." I stand to square off against Samir. "Why are you calling?" I challenge him, prepping him for the coming confrontation. "How'd you get this number?"

His eyes frantically search the room. "Telephone directory?"

I shake my head, dropping the façade. "Cell number. Blame me; tell him I gave it to you for an emergency. The night we all met the first time—but don't volunteer that. Only if he asks."

Now his eyebrows mimic that grim line. "Tara gave it to me," he says, testing out the words in his own voice. "In case there was an emergency."

I'd never, *ever* give an agent a contact like that. If Brand knew me better, he'd see through that first line like he was wearing our real-life X-ray glasses (not as cool as they sound).

I'd like to think if Brand knew me better, he'd know not to turn traitor.

Samir tilts his head, silently asking if he's doing his job all right.

"That's great. You'll get him." I slide into interrogation mode. "Why are you calling?"

"It could not wait. It is urgent." A little stilted, maybe, though the earnestness shows in his eyes. Maybe a hint of worry in his tone, though that adds to the effect.

Of course, it *is* true. Like I told Samir, I'm not asking him to do anything but what he was supposed to do all along: report to Brand. It's what Brand does next that I'm interested in.

Even now, I'm willing to give the guy one last chance. If he does a 180, runs out and calls Langley—if he files a report—heck, if he updates Intellipedia, I'll ease up a little. I can't unsee what I've seen, I can't unshoot Elliott, but as long as Brand's willing to protect the US by delivering that intel, I can take things more slowly. Cautiously. Deliberately.

Yeah, a big part of me wants to do that. I think it's the paranoid side.

Another part of me is already relishing taking Brand down.

It's not personal. It's not personal. I won't let this get personal. This is about doing our job, defending our country, keeping our vows.

Not vengeance.

Before I can psychoanalyze myself any more, Samir holds up the phone. "And then I just tell him what my cousin said?"

"Yep. Just leave out the parts about me, and you initiating contact with Hassam-ud-Din."

Samir contemplates his screen. His dark skin grows pale, and his cheeks look hollower.

I give him the go-ahead-you-got-this nod. Let's be honest: does Samir understand American gesture nuance? Unlikely. He gets the message, though, and he hits send.

"Hello?" Brand answers on speakerphone. (That Samir. Sharp.)

"Vince," Samir says on a hiss.

"Why are you calling?" Brand demands. He's going for harsh, and he's definitely that, but underneath that façade I hear the fear.

Hear it? I relish it like the first taste of dessert. Just deserts. This is what he deserves.

I resist the urge to tell Samir to draw this out as long as possible. Plus I doubt he knows that hand signal.

"Tara gave it to me, in case of an emergency. Before we met the first time."

Now I'm resisting the urge to slap my forehead. (Or Samir's.) His answer isn't what we rehearsed. Avoiding Brand's question and answering one he didn't ask both look suspicious.

"Why are you calling?" Brand asks again. This time, the fear has frosted over, as cold and hard as ice.

"Hassam-ud-Din has called. You must hear this."

Way too long of a pause. "What's going on?" Mistrust rings through Brand's every syllable. It only makes sense for him to be wary but, yeah, it's feeding my paranoia.

My neuroses don't need the Miracle-Gro.

Samir relates the real, true story of the phone call—this time, following instructions and omitting the little fact he initiated the call—right down how he's supposed to get to Hassam-ud-Din. Every last detail.

Everything Brand should run and report.

I don't hear any jogging. "Hm," Brand says. "You're sure about this?"

"Yes. Of course." Something in his tone isn't even close to sure.

I brace myself against the sinking feeling. All isn't lost, though. Brand should report this despite any doubts.

"Hm." The little syllable is incredulous. "Thanks for letting me know."

No. The right choice is to keep asking questions, trying to trip Samir up if Brand doesn't believe him. If he does believe him, he should squeeze out every ounce of information, interpretation and intelligence.

No further questions.

"Can we meet?" Samir asks.

My fingernails dig into my palm. That's too much to hope—and freaking brilliant.

"Sure. Let me know when." And he ends the call.

Not ideal, but enough. Now I have to figure out whether Brand is reporting it. I should be able to waltz into work tomorrow and . . . break into his office to check.

Great.

CHAPTER 24

THE NEXT MORNING, I'm ready to take him on. Almost.

I stop at our heavy wooden doors, staring at the gold-lettered Keeler Tate & Associates. Ten steps and I'll be in the bullpen. Ten steps and I'll be in the same room as Brand (probably). Ten steps and I'll begin the grand finale of the charade.

One final deep breath before I grab the handle. Once I'm inside, there'll be no second for hesitation, no second-guessing, no second chance. In the next instant my equilibrium will tip. I'll commit to the dive, commending my future to the hands of gravity and momentum.

Danny would probably remind me of the definition of inertia. Paraphrasing: something to do with a failure to move.

Yeah, that would be me now.

Let's do this. I suit up in my mental Kevlar—pray, adjust my ring, take hold of my cover with both hands—before I sweep into the reception area. Linda barely looks up from whatever occupies her time before I swipe my card into the secured area.

I'm on.

I take in the bullpen in an instant: Robby and César on their phones, and Justin and Brand doing their favorite little buddy-

buddy thing, laughing like obnoxious frat boys. (I know, are there any other kind?) (Okay, I'm going off Hollywood here; there are no fraternities at BYU–I.)

The two of them swap stories and jokes nearly every day. Brand's even taking this, my coworkers, my guys, like he did in DC. My resolve drains away so fast I'm almost dizzy. I sink behind my desk stacked with files. Before this happened, these other cases and agents seemed important. Now my work, my life—Brand's taking over everything. Nothing on my docket is more urgent than trapping a mole.

Especially when that mole is Brand. I watch him and Justin. My hand instinctively moves to my pocket where the USB drive waits, the only copy of my real reports, my real observations, my real case. It's not leaving my person until after Brand's in jail.

At this rate, that'll be a while. I need more evidence. If he's written his own report telling Langley where Hassam-ud-Din is and what he's targeting, I may never be able to pin this on him. He can still come back from what he's done, turn in the money, do things properly with Samir, and generally straighten up and fly the metaphorical spy drone right.

Would that be a bad thing?

I don't know. And I won't know whether he'll correct the drone's course unless Brand wants to CC me on his reports. It ain't just his door and passwords standing in my way. I've got to get Brand out of his office and me in without drawing anyone's suspicions.

I need to play to Brand's weaknesses. I would say that I am, or used to be, one of those weaknesses. But let's be honest: little about our relationship, now or then, has anything to do with *me*. It has everything to do with him, my reactions to him, making him feel powerful.

I've spent the last few weeks (last few years) fighting that dominance, keeping him from lording it over me. But to work him like any other asset, I need to play to his need for power.

If I make a U-turn, he'll know something is up, so I can't go traipsing in to fawn over him. I still have to bide my time, and I spend my morning covertly surveilling that closed door.

"Case going well?" That voice next to my desk makes me jump, a shock landing in my gut. Hours of trying to hide my neck swiveling like I'm watching a ping pong match, and he manages a sneak attack.

I shove the annoyance aside and spin my chair to simper at Brand. "Could be the biggest of my career."

His eyebrows make a little that's-impressive jump, then he checks the office. "That one assignment after all?"

"Yep." Perfect. Let him think I mean Will.

"We should touch base." Another check of the office. If anyone is paying attention, he's already acting suspicious. "Are you free for lunch?"

The emotional side of my brain screeches, "NO!!!!" on an endless loop. The logical side sees this as an opportunity. I glance at my desk, my ring, all the things that should make me say no. Then I turn back to Brand, biting my lip, like he's the temptation I can't refuse, even against my better judgment. "I guess."

A slow, satisfied smile spreads across his face. He must think he's finally got me where he wants me. But that was always going to be the easy part. The tough part is next: getting myself back in here with leeway to snoop. Snag his phone and pretend to go fetch it for him? Too likely he'll want to come along. And what do you want to bet his office is locked?

I have to get his keys—without him picking up on it. (Yes, keys. You think we have the budget for biometric locks in Canada?) I check my desk one more time before I stand to try the first and only lame tactic that comes to mind. "I'll drive."

"I got it." He dangles his keys from his fingers.

Bingo. Now to get those away from him. I'd better be better

than him at sleight of hand. I open my desk drawer and hold out two more sets of keys. "Company car. Black or red?"

Aldrich Ames famously bought a red sports car with the proceeds from his betrayal. I almost want Brand to choose the red sedan, like that's enough evidence to convict.

"Black, I guess." He shrugs like this is all sooo immaterial. Of course it is. The point isn't what car we drive. The point is that I'm giving him the choice. The power.

And, of course, to get his keys. I snag a prestocked brown leather purse from my desk before I toss Brand the keys to the red sedan. He slides them into his pocket. Step one: get him out of the office. Check. Now to get those keys. I go through the motions of small talk until we're in the elevator. The second those silver doors slide shut, foreboding clenches my throat.

I have no time to deal with this stuff today. I force myself to swallow the fear, the memories. "Oh, wait," I say, injecting a note of obviously fake apology into my voice. "You said black?" This time, I'm the one dangling keys to the black sedan from my fingers, taunting him.

Brand pulls out the chain I gave him to the red sedan, and his regular keys. He offers the red car set.

I yank the black car's key ring out of reach. "I said I'd drive."

He smirks, like he's enjoying this game enough to humor me, and holds out his free hand.

I want to draw this out a more, make it more convincing, but we'll be on the ground floor any second. "Fine," I sigh. I toss the black car keys at him, in front of the hand holding the other keys. Brand has to scramble to go for my set with his empty hand. That plan fails faster than one at a certain porcine bay and Brand dives sideways, dropping all the sets.

I'm there in half a second, gathering up all three fallen keys.

"You throw like a girl," Brand grumbles.

Not even close to true, and any one of my brothers would gladly beat him up for saying so (and other reasons), especially since they beat me up to make sure I did no such thing. The elevator chimes for the ground floor, cutting off the clever retort that I haven't come up with yet. Brand strides out first, like I've damaged his pride.

I stay on the elevator until he turns around with impatient arms folded. But I'm already busily pretending to dig through my bag. "Dang, left my phone on my desk." I silently pray it doesn't ring before I can get the doors closed. "Better grab it."

Brand joins me on the elevator again. Time to make my move. I release his keys, letting them slide inside my bag, then toss both sets of company car keys at Brand. "Bring the car around, would you, Jeeves?"

He catches one chain; the other deflects off his chest and clatters to the lobby floor. I hit the button to close the door before Brand recovers. The silver doors slide between us, changing his face into my dull reflection. "You catch like a drunk sloth," I murmur.

It's not a perfect plan. He could easily race up the stairs if he wants his keys back. But I can just as easily pretend it was an accident.

My phone rings. Good thing that wasn't ten seconds earlier. I glance at the display. Could always be Brand checking my story. (Not too hard to backstop the cover now: don't answer.)

Danny smiles up at me from the screen. I want to answer, but if Brand's waiting for me at our floor and I'm chatting on the phone I "forgot," it's a lot harder to pretend nothing's up. I pick the icon to ignore the call, and send one of the preset apologies as a text. The elevator dings at our floor, and I drop my phone in my bag. At the last second, I glimpse the message I sent to Danny: *I am in meeting.* Who wrote that message? Right, like he won't text back to that halfway-human response.

My reflection disappears as the doors slide open, and I hold my breath. No Brand on the other side. I step off, my lungs still trapping that air like it's my last. But Brand doesn't jump out from the shadows.

Okay. He bought it so far. He might know I have his keys, but it looks like an accident. Checking my desk should only take a minute or two, so I don't have long. Linda hardly notices my return so soon, and I swipe my access card to get into the bullpen again, my other hand clenched around his keys.

Justin's the last one working—lunches are a prime time for a spy. Contact you're trying to recruit? Take him out. Pay for a nice meal. Butter him up. Move in for the kill.

And speaking of moving in for the kill, I beeline for Brand's office. I have to hurry; I don't have long before Brand gets impatient. And suspicious. Plus, when you act like you know where you're going, people trust you do.

People who aren't spies.

"Didn't you just leave?" Justin asks when I pass his desk. I stop short and turn back to him. His grin says he's sort of flirting. My paranoia says he's sort of digging.

I almost call Brand by his real name before I tighten my grip on both our covers. "Vince forgot his phone."

Odds are low that they've been chitchatting in the last thirty seconds, but the tingle at the back of my neck makes me think Justin will call my bluff.

He sits there, staring at me, watching me. Do I seem suspicious? Or is it just him?

I give him a business-nod goodbye and resume my straight course for Brand's office. Behind me, Justin's chair squeaks. Again, I stop short, and that tingle at the base of my neck becomes antennae for my Justin radar.

Crap. He's following me. I pull out Brand's keys and jam them in the door.

Justin's hand lands on mine and the tingle zings down my spine.

"Let me help you look," he says.

Crap. Crap crap crap. The last thing I want is "help," when I need to be hacking into Brand's computer. "Thanks, but I'm sure you're busy. I got it."

"C'mon." He twists the knob and pushes the door open. "We'll find it faster together."

No, no we won't. I press on a smile to convey my thanks until I turn away.

Justin starts around me, going for Brand's desk. No way am I letting him back there first. He'll check the desktop and desk drawers and dismiss the whole area—meaning I have no excuse to get back there and at the computer.

I can't maneuver around Justin without being really, *really* obvious, and he beats me back there. I try to appear busy moving around the files—Brand's personal bills, actually—on his cabinet while Justin tries the drawers (locked) and scours the desktop, shuffling around papers we're probably not supposed to see.

Justin's searching slows to a stop. "He sent you up here with his keys?"

Play it off, play it off, play—I heave a sigh. "I know, right?"

He doesn't take my meaning, narrowing his eyes. That's bad. He rounds the desk, strolling up to me. Like a wolf on the hunt. Like Brand would. Bad, bad, bad.

I steel my shoulders, don't let my feet slip back in the step I'm dying to take. I can play this bluff. This is *Justin*. No matter how tight he is with Brand, Justin wouldn't turn on me.

Would he?

Justin reaches conversational distance, but doesn't stop there, closing in on me, stealing a page from Brand's predatory playbook. His gaze drills into me, intense and serious. One of my feet does slide back, but my heel hits the filing cabinet. My throat tightens.

Cornered.

CHAPTER 25

OBLIVIOUS TO MY RISING PANIC, Justin bows closer. "Is something going on?"

I shake my head, then realize I should've spoken. Less suspicious.

Justin frowns. He knows, he knows—oh, no, *he knows.* "Look," he says. "I'm not blind. I can see what you're doing."

And then the indignation hits, hard and hot. Unbelievable. I'm up here trying to catch Brand red-handed, and Justin— *Justin*—thinks he's catching *me*?

I sidestep him and march back to the desk. "I don't know what you think you're seeing, but whatever it is, you're imagining things."

I pretend to focus on pulling out Brand's keys and finding the one for this drawer, like I can't see Justin still frowning. He approaches again. This time I have the desk between us.

And no escape.

"Talia."

I expect his voice to be made of steel, not silk. That alone makes me pause and meet his eyes.

"I know why he's treating you this way."

I highly doubt that. "What do you mean?"

Justin licks his lips. "Calling you into his office all the time? Sending you on these little errands? Hovering over your desk?"

Now I really don't know what he's talking about. No way does Justin know our history, and this has absolutely nothing to do with what Brand's actually up to.

Unless Justin does suspect something. Maybe I'm not facing Brand alone after all.

My expression must betray my ignorance or indecision, because Justin's frown gets deeper. "Not exactly a secret that you're the only woman allowed past reception. Doesn't make you his personal slave."

"Oh, yeah, that." I try to ignore a needle of disappointment and check the drawers again.

"You don't have to jump every time he says."

"I know." I don't dare look up. For a second, I let the scenario play out in my mind: what if I told Justin? Would he believe me?

Right. Even Elliott called me the princess of paranoia. Once.

My phone rings. Good thing I didn't give that excuse to Justin. I dig through my bag for my cell. But it isn't Danny calling back. It's Brand. I pick my greeting and my tone to carefully skirt the line between my lies. "Found it."

"Well, then, come on."

And there goes my time to raid Brand's office. Frustration knots like a fist in my chest. I need another chance.

Later. I nod for Justin to walk out with me. Have I been jumping every time Brand says? Maybe. It's only to lull him into that false sense of security. I think.

Justin follows me into the elevator. I have one minute to assess him. He might have misinterpreted Brand's sexism— maybe not—but could he believe Brand's a traitor?

"Do you really think Vince is singling me out?" I amp up the sympathy factor, making my eyes round and innocent.

237

"Probably not intentionally." He's already apologizing for the guy. Men. "Some guys do it subconsciously."

"Oh." My real disappointment shows in that single note. Fine. I can do this alone. Besides, how many people do I have to jeopardize? Isn't one shot friend enough?

The elevator reaches the ground floor once again, and once again I'm holding my breath, expecting Brand to appear when those dull silver doors part.

And once again, he doesn't. The tension in my ribs releases. I dig through my bag. The purse is only a cover—a miracle nobody's noticed yet—but I have to have something I can use. I track behind Justin, partially on purpose and partially to give myself that tiny window of opportunity.

It's all I need. I finally find exactly what I'm hunting for: a key impression kit. On the outside, it looks like a mini Altoids tin. I flip open the hinged lid, but the only thing curious about the interior is that it's filled with our specially formulated, moldable yet not meltable putty, a thin sheet of plastic separating the top and bottom layers. I can't let Justin see what I'm up to. Drifting to a stop in the middle of the lobby, I grab the key—I hope it's the right one; impossible to tell without looking—and position it over the divot in the tin's side.

"You coming?" Justin's at the front doors, waiting.

"One sec. Can't find anything in this bag."

"Why are you even carrying it?"

A chill races over my skin, but my fingers keep working, snapping the tin lid shut tight, forcing the putty around each groove and tooth. The better this impression is, the better the resulting key will work. It's not the easiest method, but it has definite advantages in a situation where I can't pick the lock.

Justin's still watching me from the door. I need to explain why I have the purse. I let the key, inside the molding tin, slide in the bag. Fortunately, here in the open, I can't go into too much detail. "I have a thing later tonight" is all the reasoning I offer.

Justin accepts that answer. He holds the lobby door open for me. A black sedan idles at the curb, Brand in the driver's seat. Justin trails me to the sidewalk and opens the door to the sedan for me. "My Lady," he says with a mock-bow.

"Your ladyship wouldn't sit next to the chauffeur," I murmur. Gone is Justin's show of solidarity, as if, like so many others that we have every day, that conversation never took place.

I sit in the front seat, navigating between the current reality and the memory of the first time I sat in a car with Brand. A simple date. Just a dinner.

And today is just a lunch.

"So," Brand starts as soon as we're out of our parking lot. "What do you have on Will?"

"Actually, we need to talk about the Russians."

"Sure." He draws out the syllable, sounding less sure, more suspicious.

Now would be a good time for me to come up with something to say about the Russians. "How *is* your Russian, anyway?"

"Rusty. Mostly spoke Tajik Persian. Related to Dari and Farsi, so I'm better in those. Got any Tajiks for me?"

"Dang, you know, just the other day we used up our last Tajik contact."

"More's the pity." Brand's enjoying this word play. Glad one of us is.

Lunch is one more thing I have to get through. Before I can make a cast from that impression. Before I can get him out of his office. Before I can get in there myself.

Unless a direct question would work better. I focus on my bag, like I'm looking for something, instead of covering for removing his key from the mold. "How's Samir doing?"

"Farooqi's all right. Not as in-the-know as I'd like."

The words sink straight into my stomach. I still try to hold my hand steady to twist the key imperceptibly. Just enough to free it from the putty. I have to do this carefully or I'll ruin the mold entirely.

But the key lifts easily. I think it even comes off clean. Unlike Brand. Samir has very, very good intel—that's very, very sensitive—and very, very far from "not in the know."

I'm not overly inclined to trust the guy, but there's always the possibility that Brand's downplaying it for me. I need the proof. I need to make sure there are no reports. And I need something to happen to get him out of that office.

Correction: I need to *make* something happen.

But before I formulate a plan, Brand's phone rings. He checks the Caller ID, furrows his brow, answers. "Yeah?" Two beats of the man on the other end talking, and Brand whips around in a U-turn on the road just outside our building. I brace against the door. "On my way." He ends the call.

I will *not* let this scare me. Could be anything. "Bad news?"

"Hm?" Brand breaks his stern concentration to glance at me, like he's forgotten I'm here at all. "Oh, no—good news, actually. Robby just pulled priority. Rain check on lunch?"

"Sure." As in *sure hope not.*

Brand parks and heads back into the office while I loiter in the lot like I'm leaving to pick up my meal without him.

This doesn't happen to me too often, so take note: I'd rather not eat. Nope, now is my chance to begin the attack. From my car. Weird, I know, but it's a lot less conspicuous than ducking into an extra office and running the risk of setting off the fire alarm.

Even the CIA impression kit, the best available in the world (as far as we know), usually takes one or two tries to make a good key. The kit includes the calibrated candle to go with the specially designed alloy: melts fast, cools at the right speed, won't liquefy the molding putty. Once the candle burns down to the first mark, hold the little crucible over the flame until the candle hits the second mark, then pour into your mold. Tap out the air bubbles, wait two minutes, and you've got a key. Well, sort of. The teeth portion and half the handle. Works in a pinch.

The two minutes are up and I pull out the key, but one of the individual divots is too wide. I check the mold. It's good. An air bubble must've blurred the bitting. Again, lather, rinse, repeat until you get a good impression.

See? Hard. I can't fill in a missing tooth. I take a scalpel tool to the mold, drawing the tiniest line out from that one messed up divot so the air has another way to escape. Any metal that gets in there will file off. I relight the candle, reclamp the mold and restart the process.

If that sounds tedious, try actually doing it. It's 2 PM before I have a cast that will work.

Holding that lukewarm key feels like I'm taking control of my destiny. I am. I'm moving forward with Brand in my sights.

There are so many directions I could—should—go now: break into his office, call Langley, file the reports on Samir's intel myself—if I wanted to give myself away. We can't collect the evidence we need of Brand's betrayal if we bring in Wasti first. Plus, to make the arrest, we'll have to go to our favorite domestic buddies, the FBI. (If you detect sarcasm, DING DING DING!) The coordination effort will make everything twice as slow. Realistically, I need to have told them to bring Wasti in yesterday if we don't want our hands doused in blood.

The CIA's classified calculus has a patented formula for weighing out potential lives lost vs. potential sources revealed, extrapolating the lives any betrayed officers might save.

I don't have that. All I've got left is my key. And all I need is the opportunity to use it. I slip the key into my pocket and go to the office. I wish I could wait for a covert entry, but with Brand watching the logs and time running out, I have to get in the office and get Brand back out.

The bullpen is bright. Bustling. Booming. With Brand at the helm. I stand in the door staring for a minute, stunned by the mass of people on a Friday afternoon. The full staff is here, plus a couple people I kinda know from the embassy, everyone busily working and conferring over stacks of paper and schematics and photographs. (Always kind of disorienting to see other women in an office where I'm usually alone.)

Robby and Justin are mapping something on the whiteboard, and Brand's circulating, checking up on each group's progress. If I wanted to avoid him, I'm out of luck. He's the first to spot me.

"Oh good," he says. I think he might mean it. "You got my text."

Obviously I didn't. I walk in the room. Brand points for me to join Robby and Justin.

I start that way, sliding my phone out of my pocket to check my text messages. Sure enough, I missed one while I was casting that key. *Mtg w big client tomorrow. Strategizing today.* I'm not sure I'd understand they wanted my help. Frankly, he probably doesn't.

I scan the whiteboard. "What've we got?"

"Robby's made headway with one of the Russians."

I glance at the photographs propped up on the marker tray. One of *my* Russians, he means. I didn't even know Brand had doubled up our assignments. Haven't put in a ton of time on the case, so I try not to be too upset. (Something else occupied my schedule; I forget what.)

The team brings me up to speed: Robby made friends with Morozov at his gun club. Since then, they've done lunch a couple times. Robby even found the guy a better job.

Good setup, honestly. Robby would be fine meeting without us tomorrow, like I did with Samir, if it weren't for a couple statements the guy's made that raised a red flag or two, and, of course, he's got access to a gun.

I contribute what I've learned about these guys and their habits and schedules, but I'm watching Brand. When can I get in his office? He's being way too attentive and involved. Like a good manager. Like Will.

Will, who's in custody because of Brand. And Elliott would be here helping with setup and surveillance if it weren't for Brand. And, oh yeah, in two days hundreds of people could die.

Unless Brand's reported that threat. I need to get in that office. And that won't happen with him lurking around here, watching.

What now?

CHAPTER 26

NINETY MINUTES LATER, I'm still waiting and plotting, but I'm trying to look like I'm working on the same scheme as the rest of the team.

Robby comes over to confer on the map. "So where's Elliott?" he asks, way louder than he needs to if he's talking to just me. "Figured he'd jump at the chance to get in on this case with Kozyrev's intel."

Elliott isn't the only embassy CIA employee missing—thank goodness—but I know he'd be here if he hadn't been shot. (Nothing like tracking down foreign operatives from the intel of a spy you helped catch.)

"Yeah," Justin chimes in. "Or is he too good for us?"

"Who's too good for us?" Brand catches wind of our conversation and saunters over to join in. "You holding out on us, Talia?"

I open a folder and fix my eyes on the photos of the meeting site, gold onion-domed Protection of the Holy Virgin Memorial Church. Brand isn't baiting me, using "holding out" as a double entendre. Though he totally is.

I have to act like nothing's wrong. If Brand had an inkling

of where Elliott is—*who* Elliott is—how long would it take to trace the entire meet-me-under-the-bridge op back to me?

"Elliott Monteith," Justin supplies. "Used to work here. Placed at the Embassy temporarily to help with the transition."

"Hey." Robby smacks Justin's arm with the back of his hand. "Remember when Elliott talked his way onto that helicopter with that Kyrgyz general?"

"Are you kidding?" Justin laughs. "Only the greatest thing I've ever witnessed."

Brand doesn't try to cover up a condescending little chortle. (I know, what kind of jerk chortles?) "What, a helicopter ride? Things are slower here than I feared."

"No, no." Now Justin's the patronizing one. "All about the dismount."

I snap the folder shut to fan myself. Did it get hot in here all of a sudden? And do we have to keep talking Elliott up?

Before Brand can ask the question written in his eyebrows, I slap the folder into his chest. "Followed the general," I provide, my tone flat, like it's this totally boring office legend and the next schematic, the plumbing under the church, is far more interesting. Elliott's escapade was all Justin says and more, but does Brand need to know that?

"Out of the helicopter," Robby adds.

"Without a parachute," Justin finishes.

"The general had one." I sit on the nearest desk, still going for the casual, why-do-you-guys-still-tell-this-dumb-story? attitude. I don't know how else to downplay Elliott without looking really weird to the other guys.

The only reason this is a good story is because Elliott did catch up with him and did live. (And, in the end, did recruit him to spy for us. Triple win.) If that stupid ploy hadn't panned out so well, now he'd be a star on the wall at Langley and a cautionary tale.

He came close to that fate again this week. But Brand

doesn't know that. I hope.

Brand checks the room, ending with me. "Then yeah, where is he?" He comes to stand by me, leaning against the desk I'm sitting on, casually brushing his hip on my leg.

That's a big NO. Still staring at the schematic, I hop off the desk. "Elliott's good in a pinch because he has to be," I toss over my shoulder on my way to the whiteboard. "Because he's bad at planning ahead." I squint at the marker strokes like I'm trying to match something I'm seeing with their plans.

Robby takes the subject-changing bait and comes up to join me. "What have you got?"

"Nothing." I toss the schematic on the desk. "Won't work."

"So have you heard from him?" Robby asks.

I indicate a photo on the marker tray. "Who, Morozov?"

"No, Elliott. He should be here."

Great. On the spot. I need a story. And what's better than the truth? "Heard he was having trouble at home," I murmur.

Justin instantly shifts, rubbing a knuckle with his thumb. Robby finds his file absorbing.

"Well." Brand taps on a stack of files. "Better go check on those traces." And he retreats into his office. Exactly where I need to be.

Now to get him back out of there. Especially if he's about to ring up the embassy to ask for Elliott.

I wish I had a sacrifice play today: a Russian I could call in to bring Brand running, or better yet a Tajik or Persian or . . . anybody. But I can't exactly call Spy-busters.

I pull out my phone, like I can page through my contacts and find somebody to take Brand down. No assassins on my list. I return the phone to my pocket.

Wait. I don't have anybody to help on that phone, but I have something else. I take out my cell again and pop open the cover, and then the case. A quick raid on my desk drawer produces the phone I used to text Brand. With one eye on the rest of the office, I remove the battery pack to switch out the SIM cards. Battery back in place, and I'm ready to attack.

Brand must think he's solved his one little problem. I've been avoiding news stories about "Josh Lee," so I don't know if he realizes the guy isn't dead and is still a threat. Either way, Brand's about to get bad news.

Last time, I was compelled to drive as far away as I could. Today, there's no time. I need Brand out of his office now.

I type that text as fast as possible. *It'll take more than that to stop me. Honestly, I was expecting you to at least offer me a bribe.*

I wait, but no reply comes. I'm not stupid. If Brand responds, I can't leave the ringer on so he can put two + spy together. My phone on vibrate, I slide it back in my pocket. The same one with my key to Brand's office.

Brand's door swings open. My gasp of surprise—triumph—slips out. He's taking the bait.

But . . . taking it where?

Straight to—Justin. Within seconds, they pick up their buddy-buddying, their obnoxious laughter loud enough to drown out the rest of the office. And don't think I don't notice the way Justin keeps casting glances of *Seriously? Her?* my way. (Yeah, thanks, dude.) Did Brand not get the text? Do I dare check the number?

No. I consult my computer and the latest info dumps from our Russian friends' contact mic. Right off, I can see there's some useful stuff here—especially Morozov mentioning his meeting with Robby—but my gaze jumps to where Brand's working, or pretending to work.

He's looking at me. Not mocking, not threatening, not even lusting. Just looking. I turn back to my actually-important-for-once files. If we can be useful to the Russians, solve one more problem for them, that will get us in that much faster—

My gaze wanders back to Brand. He's checking his phone.

A harness cinches around my middle tighter than a parachute's. My message? Can he triangulate my phone from here? Does he have the app for that?

I try not to chew my lip. Show no weakness. Show no weakness. Show—

My phone. I didn't put the case back on, and Brand could be here any second. It'll be faster to put on the cover, and at least it'll *look* complete. I snap the cover in place and slip my phone back in my pocket.

"Trouble?" Brand. He's right next to me.

That harness hitches a notch tighter, but I repeat my mental chant to hide my vulnerabilities until I glance up at him. He's squinting at my desk. "Problems with your phone?"

The back of the cover's still on my desk. So much for hiding. "No problem. Just froze."

"Fun. Got anything good?"

"Yeah, we definitely have the Russians' interest, at least. Searching for one more thing we can do for them to seal the deal."

Before he says anything else, my phone vibrates in my pocket. His reply. We can both hear it. I don't dare lower my gaze or move for it or breathe.

Brand's eyes stray to my lap, then back. "That yours?"

"Guess so."

"You going to get it?"

Lie. "I just texted Danny about our plans for tonight."

He leans against my desk. "That new-boss-free-meal policy still in place? Kathi around?"

My palms break out in a sweat, as if to balance out the dry mouth. "Tonight's not good. He's working." My brain jogs to correlate my lies. "I'm trying to figure out what to bring him."

"Better not keep him waiting."

I'm not falling for that. "I think we can figure it out in time." I give my computer a meaningful look, reminding Brand

I'm working on something, you know, important.

Right. Because Brand so has those priorities straight.

He peers over my shoulder. Awesome. "Got to be something we can do to be useful to them. Immigration problems? DUI?"

"So far these guys are smart enough to fly under the radar." And legal troubles are the exact opposite. (Man, I wish I knew somebody with the Mounties or the Ottawa Police who could make Brand's life hard.)

"Can we *give* them problems?"

Oh. Right. Creating trouble so we can swoop in and save the day, and recruit some spies along the way. "Not my favorite MO."

"Oh, not how we do things here?" His voice oozes derision.

I'm not backing down a single step. "Excuse me? Are you going to run every case like this?"

"Are you?" He won't budge either.

"Worked well enough for the last few years here."

Brand snorts. "Canada. Right. Do you need to be reminded how it is in the real world?"

"Back. Off. Let me do my job, and you do yours."

He straightens slowly, like that simple movement is a threat. "One slip, Talia. That's all it takes."

What brought this on? I watch him walk away, only allowing my eyes to follow him until his office door shuts behind him. I grab my phone to read Brand's text. *This again?*

Not promising, but . . . I glance at his door again. Could be bravado, and he really is feeling threatened. His little show just now would make more sense if he's doing it because he needs to feel powerful.

Which means my tactic is succeeding. I text back: *Meet me at the Rideau Centre, in front of Jimmy the Greek.*

And if I don't?

I watch Brand's door. What can I say to make him concerned enough to get him out of here? *If you want to shut someone up, next time aim for the head.*

Or the wallet?

I have to give Brand hope without appearing too easy, saying, "Yeah, sure, I can be bought like you." Maybe . . . *If the price is right. And you get here in ten minutes.*

That's hardly enough time for a straight drive, let alone a proper surveillance detection route, and Brand should definitely be extra cautious.

Thirty minutes, Brand texts back.

I dump my phone in my drawer before he can leave his office. After thirty-two seconds (Who's counting? ME.), his door swings open. I release the breath I didn't know I was holding.

And Brand looks straight at me. Frost flash-freezes my heart.

He can't know. No way does he know. I school my features into an expression of *I'm totally normal; what are you up to, weirdo?* and hope that's enough of a defense.

Brand gives me an all-business nod and goes to Robby's whiteboard. Robby's face lights up, like he's thrilled to have the attention. The little fanboy.

As a cover, I skim Intellipedia's entry on Ali Muhammad Wasti as if we've discovered something new in a case that's growing colder by the minute, and as if the best source isn't being totally neglected. Oblivious, Brand moves on to chat with the president of his fan club, Justin. Will Brand ask someone to go with him?

After a minute, Brand double-taps the top of Justin's desk, a little good-job-soldier dismissal. My gaze snaps to the Past Known Residences section of the Intellipedia article until the door to the reception area closes behind Brand. And then the article's words finally register.

Dushanbe, Tajikistan.

A cold-bellied snake slithers over my shoulders. That's where Brand was stationed. The capital. It's got to be a huge city, but . . . could this possibly be a coincidence?

I check the door to the reception area, the office, the spies I work with every day. I feel like everyone can see that I know, what I know. Exposed.

Hundreds of thousands of people might live in Dushanbe, but how many of them are the brother of a terrorist targeting the US, and how many of them are CIA case officers hunting for that exact kind of asset?

Somewhere on the way, something went wrong, something reversed, something broke in Brand's brain. No coincidence that the first case he targeted when he got here was the only case with any relation to Wasti. The last piece of the puzzle. But is it the last piece of evidence I need before I can bring him in?

The CIA is not law enforcement, though they did finance my law degree (those real credentials we need for our firm to look real). You can convict with circumstantial evidence, if there's enough. In fact, you're lucky to have more than that, even in this day of CSI and DNA. But high crimes and treason have a bit higher standard of evidence, something with a better paper trail than cash deposits and late reports—

Reports. I need to see if Brand's filed about Samir, and now's my chance.

CHAPTER 27

WITH THIS MANY PEOPLE IN THE BULLPEN, there's no way I can hide what I'm doing. Unless I hide in plain sight. I need to make this seem legit.

Having a key is half the battle. I switch to my SIM card to text Danny: *Call me now.* I fix my eyes on "Dushanbe" on Ali Muhammad's Intellipedia page until my phone rings. "Hello?"

"You okay?" Danny says.

"Yeah."

"What's up?"

The call's a cover, so I can't explain anything else. I glance around at Justin and Robby, etc. "Sure, I guess."

"Um . . . what?"

"Yeah, I still have your key."

Danny's quiet half a second. "Do I want to know what you're doing?"

Probably not, but I can't answer yet. I get my key and head for Brand's office. "Where do you think you left it?"

Danny's obviously figured out I'm not calling to chat with him, and he sits in silence. (Okay, he could be standing. Lying down for a nap. Whatever.)

I say a silent prayer the key works, that I filed off all the excess. It jams against the lock instead of sliding in. My stomach twists; the key doesn't. The disappointment sinks into my gut.

"Dang," I tell Danny. I can maintain my bluff. I have to. "Looks like it's the wrong key. Sorry about that."

He sighs. "Are we not going to talk about this?"

Doubt he means my breaking and entering escapades. "Yeah," I say. "Later."

"We're running out of laters."

"I know. I'll work on it."

I'm running through my options for a neutral way to exfiltrate myself from this phone call when César appears at my elbow. He points at the phone. "Can you let him know we've about got the cathedral scenarios locked down?"

I mouth, "Sure," and inform Danny of our progress.

"Uh, yeah. Love you."

Definitely not saying that while on the phone with "Brand." "Yeah," I say. "See you."

"I'm going to pretend that's code for I love you too."

Awesome. I don't even have to make up the code. I end the call and rush to switch the SIM card back to the one I used with Brand. Still have time before he's supposed to meet me. Elliott. Josh Lee. Whoever.

Obviously, nobody will be there to greet him. Not sure what Brand's reaction will be. Text back? Assume the danger has passed?

He's no me, no princess of paranoia, but he isn't stupid, either. He isn't safe as long as someone knows what he's really doing. He needs to eliminate that threat.

And I need extra insurance. Time to backup that USB drive.

But not here, not now, not with all his little fanboys surrounding me. How long would that take to get back to Brand? Seconds.

I occupy myself with researching Ali Muhammad Wasti in Dushanbe while looking like I'm still working on the intel from the Russians' bug. Seems that Ali Muhammad was nearly invisible in Tajikistan. The falling feeling in my middle seems to indicate he had some help. I'm no closer to figuring out that angle by the time Brand returns at five, sullen and silent.

Focusing on my monitor, I avoid his eyes and pray nobody mentions the key incident. I fish the offending casting from my pocket and reexamine it. The cast itself is good. So what do I have a key to?

I turn the key to view it from the tip—and I recognize this. I recognize the pattern of grooves there. Because I've seen it before. Because I have one just like it.

Because it's the same as my deadbolt key.

The disappointment of two hours ago isn't even a distant memory now. It's a different life. And this key might be a ticket to a whole new one.

Robby's op is well planned (yay for my support role yet again), so I think I'm safe to stock up on supplies and slip out. In fact, I'm safest making an exit now, giving me time to plan away from Brand's cronies. Because I'm totally back on the breaking and entering track.

Just as I reach my car, I finally take out my phone to see the text message—message*s* from Danny at lunchtime (i.e., before I had him call me). *English much?*

I scroll up to see what he means. Right, the *I am in meeting* from this afternoon. But that isn't his last message. *Dinner much?*

And then *Talk much?*

I have to get to Samir ASAP, but yeah, I definitely need to talk with Danny. I check the time. After six. He might still be at work, and it'll only take a minute to check. I drive over to his office complex. I'm almost to his corner when I spot his silver Mazda headed the opposite direction. So much for the element of surprise. I'm on the phone in half a second.

"Hey," he answers.

"Pull over." Oncoming traffic clears enough for me to flip a U-turn.

"Pull—why?"

I don't respond until I see him on the shoulder. I park behind him and wait for another break in traffic before I get out. The passing cars aren't a lot safer than the drop-off on the other side of the shoulder. I choose the lesser danger to go knock on Danny's passenger window.

He jumps, but recovers quickly to unlock the door. I take a seat. There's something between us a lot bigger than the center console.

"Fancy meeting you here," he says, putting away his phone.

"I was in the neighborhood. Welcome to your first car meeting." I subconsciously check my window. CSIS headquarters are right here, though I can only see the trees in the fading sunlight. They were supposed to be my backup. Now who's left?

"Listen—" Danny starts.

"I'm sorry." The words tumble out before I lose my nerve.

Danny watches me in contemplative silence, waiting for me to go on. Yeah, I got nothing. "I'm just sorry," I finish.

"Me too." He offers his hand on the center console. I stop twisting my ring around my finger and grab on, though I try not to squeeze like he's my last lifeline.

That contact isn't enough to dissipate the tension between us. "I was being selfish," I try.

He watches the sky turn orange. "Yeah, you were. But I don't think you're pathologically incapable of thinking of anyone except yourself," he says softly. "I . . . it was below the belt."

"You think?" The relief loosening my ribs is enough to make me forgive him.

"I know you're trying to protect me—I just hate that you think the only way to do that is to push me away."

Did I say relief? Yeah, I meant guilt. And instead of loosening my ribs, how about crushing them? I focus on our interlaced fingers, and we slip back into silence for a minute.

"Once upon a time," he starts at last, "there was a beautiful girl."

I clear my throat. If he means me—

He checks my reaction. "A hot girl?"

I give him a slow, semi-teasing, choose-your-next-words-carefully blink.

"Woman—I mean woman."

I squeeze his hand. "Good boy."

Now Danny clears his throat.

"Good . . . man."

He fends off a smile as long as he can. "Anyway, there was a beautiful woman. And there was this guy—"

"Hot? Brilliant? Ridiculously patient?"

"Oh, you've met him?"

I reward him with an I'm-humoring-you expression and gesture for him to go on.

"Nah, he was just a guy—and she was the puzzle nobody else could solve. Nobody knew anything about her, not even where she was from. Whenever he tried to talk to her, he could see it in her eyes: shields up, all the time."

After dating a year, of course we've rehashed the story of how we met and got together. But I've never heard it like this.

"Until he made this stupid joke and she smiled. Those heat shields finally came down, and he was a goner."

"Poor guy," I murmur.

"I know, right?" Danny turns to the windshield again. Getting darker. "I don't have to know everything. I know I can't. I'm not asking you to share secrets, I just want to feel like . . . I know you. Not the sanitized, censored, redacted version of you—the real you, all of you." His gaze falls to our hands. "That's all I've ever wanted."

The silence settles again. I have to give him something. And all I have is a story. A story like his, one I've never told quite like this. "Once upon a time," I start, my voice soft and shaky. I try again. "Once upon a time, there was a girl--woman." I tilt my head toward Danny to whisper, "She was a spy."

He lifts our hands to press his finger to his lips, promising to keep my secret all over again except his eyes are joking. Our fingers still intertwined, he maneuvers both our elbows onto the console so he can rest his chin in his palm. Ready to listen.

"So her job—her whole life—revolved around manipulating people. Not trusting them. It was too hard to talk to normal people when her whole life was built from layer after layer of secrets. So she tried to not be seen. Kept everyone at arm's length. Kept anyone from knowing her, even the people she considered friends."

He's fighting a squint like he's not sure where this is going but he's willing to find out.

Which is awesome, because the next part is my favorite. "And then one day this hot, brilliant, ridiculously patient guy was totally checking her out—"

"You will never let me live that down, will you?"

"Nope." I grin. "And you like it."

"*You* liked it."

"I liked you." It'd be so easy to let it pass, flirt more, pretend like things are hunky-dory, but there's more to my side of this story. "Once this guy stopped looking at her legs and started looking at her, it was like . . . someone could *see* her. He could see *her*. Not the self she put out there, the front. She couldn't tell him all the truth all the time, but he knew her, through and through. And he was the only one who did."

Danny moves an inch to kiss my finger. "Is that your story's happy ending?"

"Eh, well, they both had all this baggage, and there was this meddling roommate—"

He laughs, though that fades faster than the light, and he ends with a sigh.

"You were right," I say. "I did have those shields. And I guess I must be crazy to ever put them up again. Maybe just crazy, period."

He gives this little eyebrow-shrug, like he's telling me *you're not wrong.*

"Those shields were to protect me. Once you got past them, I only needed to protect myself from losing you."

"Point of order: I'm not the one with a high-risk job."

"My job isn't normally that high-risk."

Danny's already seen the ugly side of my job firsthand. But he doesn't understand how dark this is. I take a deep breath. "Brand has taken *everyone* away from me, one way or another: my friends in DC, making it harder for me to trust people here, Elliott. . . . I will not let him take you. I won't."

Danny lowers our hands to lean across the center console. "That won't happen. You can trust me. Maybe not with all the Top Secret-y stuff, but the regular stuff."

"I don't know where the Top Secret-y stuff ends and the regular stuff begins sometimes. Not when it comes to Brand."

"Are you sure you don't want me to deck him?"

"Ask me on Monday." I glance up at the twilight advancing across the sky. I need to go.

I can't. I settle back into my seat. "Speaking of secrets, are you at least going to tell me what to pack for our honeymoon?"

"Clothes would be good."

"Antigua clothes or Antarctica clothes?"

Danny mock-frowns at me. "In between."

"You're useless."

He lets go of my hand. Before I can panic that I've offended him, he reaches across the car to open the glove box. He pulls out a standard white envelope, and fishes out a small piece of paper, business card sized, then gives me the envelope. I pop up an eyebrow at the card; Danny flips it between his fingers to show me the front. Just a name and phone number: Will's.

"So what's this?" I hold up the envelope. "Your résumé? You ready to join up?"

He takes that more seriously than I meant. "Do you want me to?"

The whole truth, the real truth, is ready in an instant. "I want you to be happy."

"Then I don't want to work for the CIA. Your hours suck." He taps the envelope. "That's your travel form."

I turn it over, eyeballing the open flap. I could take out that sheet and know exactly where we're going. Even if it were sealed, I can get in there without being detected, but still—

Trust is earned. Apparently I've done something right over the last year because if this isn't his trust, I don't know what is. I lick the adhesive and press the envelope flap shut. "I'll hand this in," I murmur. "I better get going."

Danny watches me. We both know what that means. He leans across the center console to kiss me, relief and fear running through us like a current. He pulls back to kiss my forehead.

"I love you," I tell him.

"I love you too."

"I need to go." I check his eyes, and I can already see the disappointment forming.

The question screams to get out: *Where?*

No matter how much I trust him, this isn't his job. I kiss him goodbye, and I'm halfway out of the car before it hits me. "I didn't ask. Does your story have a happy ending?"

"Not exactly." He squints pensively. "More of a happy beginning. I hope."

Me too.

CHAPTER 28

A QUICK STOP TO DIG UP A CACHE and retrieve a gun chews through even more time. It's fully dark by the time Samir and I roll into the right part of town a little later than I wanted to be. I park to let Samir out half a block from our destination: Brand's building.

We've got a lot to do tonight.

But first? I swivel to Samir, serious in the reflected glow of the streetlight. He's watching me, waiting for a last bit of wisdom, I guess.

If I had any of that, I wouldn't be sitting in this car. "Here." I fish something from my pocket and offer it to him: a stack of bills. "We do try to take care of our friends."

Samir fixates on the money. "I cannot."

I keep holding it out. "We would've given this to you no matter what."

"No matter what?" He ponders his hands. "No matter what," he murmurs again.

"Is there something else you need? I mean, this is the least we could do, after all you've risked for us. You name it—"

He turns back to me. "Your friend was shot, you said?"

I keep my gaze level despite the images in my mind, Elliott in that canal. "Yes, he was."

"And Ali Muhammad? And the people Hassam-ud-Din will kill?" Samir looks away. "It is blood money."

I swallow my own guilt and take back the cash before I offend him further. "Thank you. For your help."

"Stop him from killing again, and that will be thanks enough." He gets out of the car.

I hope and pray we can deliver. Before I drive off, he bends down with the same trepidation that's hung behind his eyes all night. I roll down the passenger window. My brave bluff had better fool him. "You can do this."

He nods, then straightens. Man, I hope he can do this.

Of course, he has the easy part. I roll away from Samir, still watching him in the rearview. He's already asked Brand to see him, but we need to get more specific. We need to signal for this meeting. Time to drop off our engraved invitation.

All Samir has to do is find Brand's car and stick a message under the windshield wiper. Simple. Samir finally veers for the parking garage.

Now it's my turn. I park around the corner from Brand's building and get out a disguise kit. The CIA turned to Hollywood decades ago and nearly poached an Oscar-winning makeup artist (he decided he'd rather consult). Our effects pass close examination and change our appearance enough our own mothers-in-law couldn't recognize us. (I. Wish.)

Oh, did I mention they're designed to be applied in under a minute, while walking through a crowd? Seriously. Four years with the Agency and I'm still in awe.

I apply my prosthetic: a new nose to change my profile. With a wavy blond wig and glasses, I'm ready to fool even Kathi. Brand might be a different story—and I'm about to find out.

I check my supplies (real keys, fake keys, apartment key,

clicker, micro jammer, disguise and bag) until Samir texts with the go-ahead and the number three. I climb out of the car, leaving a pair of binoculars on the passenger seat. Halfway down the block, I cross paths with Samir. I execute a classic brush pass, invisibly passing my keys to him without a hint of a pause. He does pretty well, considering he wasn't expecting it. I stay on course.

Hooray, yet another purposeful walk situation.

I keep up my march into the parking garage until I find that teal Nissan on level three. Sure enough, Chinese takeout menus are tucked under the wipers of the whole row. (You're welcome for the free advertising, Chez Szechuan.) Without slowing, I check the walls for cameras: three, all with good views.

I got this. I draw my hand from my pocket and "accidentally" slide my fake keys out too. They clang against the cement, and it takes me two paces to stop.

I sigh, making a show of turning around, and gathering my jacket and my skirt around my legs to bend down. If you've got it, flaunt it, right? And Elliott, Brand, and every other man I know has made it clear that I've got it: legs that drive guys to distraction.

Not that I want to objectify myself, but, hey, any diversion is a bonus for a spy.

The next bit requires crucial coordination. I make sure the magnetic micro signal jammer is stuck on my thumb before I place my left hand on Brand's trunk, close to the license plate, like I need help to balance while bending over in these heels. With my right, I scoop up my keys, grabbing them by the DS&T-issue fob. I hit the special "pandemonium" button. Brand's car alarm shrieks to life.

I curve my thumb to attach the magnetic signal jammer to the trunk above the license plate half a second before I stumble away from the screeching. Pretending to glance around for the owner, I hurry away.

Now Brand's got a problem. The jammer will block the signal from his real clicker. He'll have to come all the way in here and unlock the car with the key, or maybe start the ignition to switch off the alarm. Meaning that not only will he get the message on that menu, but he'll also have to leave his apartment as soon as the garage attendants let him know he's the one disturbing the peace. (Oh, wait, that's me.)

Step one: check. On to step two. In the stairwell, I reverse my jacket, switch out my skirt for slacks and sling on the sneakers in my huge purse. I trade my blond wig for light brown. Before I hit the street, I've added two scars and a spritz/dab of freckle paint. Sorry, the application technique's classified.

I check the windows of Brand's building. About half the lights are on. Happy Friday night. Then I spot what I need: lights off, flashing blue. Somebody watching TV. Fourth floor.

Though the next part might not be strictly necessary, I want to make this to look as believable as possible. I'm sure when you live in a building with a buzzer, you get lots of calls for your neighbors. But I'm also sure when you design a building like this, you make the buzzers loud—loud enough to be heard from anywhere in the apartment. Louder than a standard movie night.

The pandemonium button has more than one application tonight.

I count three cars past the garage exit and hit the button. Not sure how it works, though it's just as effective as with Brand's car—the nearest vehicle starts up its obnoxious wail.

Even in Canada, land of little crime, car alarms are no cause for alarm (except to grab your keys to make your car shut up). But doing this once also isn't enough to pull off my plan. I count out three more cars and hit the button again. Lather, rinse, repeat until the people in the movie apartment are hitting the button to shut up the car or turn up the television. Or both.

Samir's been using the binocs. He times his arrival at Brand's building for when I reach the corner of the block. Now to tackle the so-called obstacle of the buzzer.

Man, I hate those things. I know, you'd think someone as paranoid as me would want a building guarded by that extra level of security. As I obviously already know too well, you can't trust your security to random strangers trying to be helpful.

I text Samir a single digit: *4.* He knows what to do with the intel. He heads up to the buzzers and hits one. When they answer, he's supposed to explain his plight: those neighbors can't hear the buzzer over their movie. From my vantage point crossing the street, I can see him holding up a Chez Szechuan takeout bag, like the microphone is transmitting his image, too.

I'm at the end of the block when I hear the door buzz. My sneakers slap the cement as I sprint down the sidewalk. Samir holds the door for me. I hand off my bag and jog in.

I don't have time to catch my breath—but I don't have any breath to catch, either. Brand will be walking down these halls any second, and I have to march past him. Are purposeful walking and prosthetics enough to fool a trained operative who's watching his back?

My adrenaline level picks up with the mounting worries. A loose edge on my cheek scars will show. My nose is *too* crooked. My eyebrows don't match my wig—crap, they don't match.

No. It's fine. Lots of people dye their hair. I skip the elevators and hustle up two flights of stairs. By the third, my pace is closer to a trudge, but still faster than waiting around.

I reach Brand's floor. My cover is dating one of his neighbors (though I'm hoping not to explain that), so I have no reason to slink around. I stroll down the hall like I belong here.

Until I round the corner and nearly smack into someone. I stop short: Brand.

My system hits the deep freeze. I fake a nervous giggle that I hope's more annoying than my real laugh. Brand barely notices me. "Sorry about that," he says, Canadian accent in place.

"No problem," I murmur. He's already down the hall, his keys in hand.

I drag in a deep breath, thawing my heart and restarting my pulse—but that's only the beginning of my job tonight. Once the elevator around the corner has chimed, I zip to Brand's door. My would-be office key slides into the lock and turns.

I'm in. No time to celebrate. I shut the door behind me and scan the apartment for a laptop. Nice place, new gray couches, hardwood floors, neutral walls, but not many places to hide in the same style of décor I have now: mid-century moving boxes. (He always did have great taste.)

The card table in the messy kitchenette holds my quarry. I open the laptop case. The power button starts automatically and the screen flips on, revealing a picture of a city at night.

No icons for programs. No menu bar, if this computer has one. No password box.

Did I break it? Great way to betray myself.

Now what?

CHAPTER 29

I DON'T HAVE TIME TO MESS AROUND. Setting my key aside for a minute, I'm on the phone to my personal tech support hotline in ten seconds—and no, nobody at Langley.

"I take it you're still alive," Danny answers.

"I'll keep you posted on that front. How much do you know about hacking?" I know, I make conversation an art.

He pauses, though I doubt he's ignoring me. "Do I dare ask what you're doing?"

I shouldn't say, but keeping secrets from Danny has blown up in my face lately. He's got the background on the case, knows the danger—he even has clearances. All Danny wants is to know me. I just have to let him. "I'm hacking Brand's computer to see if he's reporting intelligence from that one source."

"And if he is?"

If he is, the UN isn't in danger in two days. But that falls on the Top Secret-y side of the line. "I have more time to build the case. So, how much do you know about hacking?"

"Not enough to talk you through it."

Dang. I check Brand's keyboard, like he's worn out the letters used in his password. My eyes travel back to the skyline on his monitor.

His touch-screen monitor.

For once a stupid, frivolous business expense might work in my favor. "How about hacking a touch screen?"

"Sure," Danny says. "Tilt the screen in the light to see the fingerprints."

Duh. I push the screen back to catch the light at a raking angle. My thumb brushes the bottom of the screen, and the cityscape rolls up to reveal a password pane next to a picture of Brand skiing across his monitor.

Fingerprints slash across the surface in all directions, but a couple streaks are more pronounced, like they've been repeated more: tracing Brand's skis and a circle around his face.

Narcissist.

"Sometimes you can set up a touch password," Danny provides. "The right motions in the right order unlock it."

"And let me guess: too many mistakes lock it down completely."

"Depends on the computer."

Great. That wouldn't be a dead giveaway.

My phone vibrates and I pull it away. Text from Samir: *On his way back.*

My stomach plummets to the ground floor. No time to mess around. All right, if the guy's so self-centered, maybe his face is first. The fingerprint streak runs clockwise and lifts off at the top. My breath stops of its own accord as I follow the pattern, then trace his right ski and left ski.

The picture password is incorrect. Please try again. The little defeat lands in my gut like a punch.

"How many attempts do you get?" I ask.

"Dunno. Typically three. It can be pretty tricky—personally, I hate them."

I try again, ignoring the tension stealing into my shoulders: face, left ski, right ski.

And once again, I'm in. I have to hide the mental party. "Got it."

"And where's your boss now?"

"You don't want to know." I fall silent to focus on checking his email—crap. The mail client downloads his new messages. I glance over them. Nothing seems relevant. A quick search for Samir's code name in the outbox queue yields no results. I skim each of the sent messages from yesterday, in case he's changed Samir's code name. Today's messages.

Nothing.

No. No. He had to have reported at least once. At least that he was taking over the case. I search the sent messages. Before the results come up, keys jingle outside the door. My heart lodges in my throat.

Yep, just what I need. Brand's back. "Gotta go," I whisper to Danny. "Love you."

I pocket my phone. Three of Brand's emails pop up for my search. I click the last and scan it. A key slides into the lock. My fingers are already hitting the keys to kill the program when the words hit my brain. *TARMAC determined unreliable, limited access. Relationship terminated.*

The doorknob twists. I slap the laptop shut and scurry into the bedroom. By law, there has to be another way out, right?

Behind me, I hear the front door click closed. Brand sighs and either throws something big and heavy onto the couch, or he's plopped down. "Stupid car," he moans under his breath.

Nice that he still has the freedom to breathe. That makes one of us. I slide my feet over the carpet to reach the window and peer out. Fire escape.

I have no idea how well the window works—it could scrape, it could squeak, it could be painted shut—but I have to at least try. My heart clenches as I work my fingers under the sash and give it a tentative tug. It slides up, but not as quietly as I'd like with the door behind me ajar. At a dead stop, I listen. And listen. Did he hear me?

A rustle and shuffle carry from the other room. I still every muscle, straining to hear Brand above the pounding in my ears. His footsteps grow louder, echoing over the kitchenette linoleum.

I creep backward to hide behind the door. It swings open half a second before I'm ready. I rear back to press myself against the wall, rotating my ankles out to let the door open that much farther. (Who's got no turnout now, Madame Willikers?)

Brand's footsteps pass through the room, and even my blood turns to solid ice. I can't move. Physically. Impossible.

Something drops onto the bed. Another door shuts. I dare to breathe, to peek around the door, still half-hidden in its shadow. The laptop and Samir's menu lie on the ratty bed quilt. The only other door in the room is closed, light leaking around its edges.

My chance. I steal back to the window. He's closer now, though we have a closed door between us. I have to wait for the right minute.

And it comes with the sound of a flush. I yank the window open, practically dive out, and ease it shut.

I focus on regaining my breath and moving my feet down the rungs of the fire escape with as little vibration as possible—not on the words of the email. Not on the facts I confirmed. Not on the blatant lies Brand's feeding up the chain about Samir. Lies that will cost lives.

I already knew he was a traitor. The email only confirmed it. Now I just have to prove it.

And I will. Tonight. Brand should definitely recognize the menu, from Samir's actual restaurant. The signal—a star by the Friday night special, a circle around the 22 in the price—is clear enough for a spy: meeting tonight at 2200. In fact, in hostile territory, that would be flirting with suicide.

269

But the only hostile here is Brand. I can only hope he shows.

Good thing Samir and I already have our plans in motion. I rendezvous with Samir again at my car, and we pass the time rehearsing possible scenarios for the meeting with Brand. We have to convince Brand to act right away on this seriously actionable intelligence, while I record the whole thing so he can't deny this happened when he fails to file a report.

We're as ready as we'll get. The sunlight faded hours ago, and every minute drops the temperature another degree. I tug my jacket tighter around me and check the dash clock again. Samir's already hidden in the alley down the street, waiting.

And Brand's late.

We've tipped him off. I don't know how, but he has to know. Or maybe he doesn't feel like pretending for Samir's sake anymore. Why would he? It's not like he's really running Samir. He's faked the reports and taken the money, so why bother with any of the other motions?

Or maybe, deep down I'm hoping he won't show. Because, yeah, that'll solve everything. And he'll just quit his tidy little side income, pack it in and go home.

I'm definitely not that lucky.

So I'm not sure whether it's good luck or bad coming due when the teal Nissan pulls up and pauses at the curb. Show time.

I should call that in to—oh. I don't have any backup to radio, no one to signal that we've got the RABBIT in our sights and the FOX is on the hunt. Cold needles stab into my stomach, regret and fear fighting for position. I'm taking him on alone.

Brand rolls out. Those ice needles spread to my veins. We're all trained never to pursue a high value target, an armed enemy, a real threat all by ourselves.

But considering how he made me feel those weeks at Langley—vulnerable, cut off, isolated—taking him on, taking

Brand down one-on-one, is fitting. Right. Just.

And even more dangerous.

Brand's out of sight now, and I'm safe enough to start my car. I won't be safe for long.

Normally I can't jog to the corner store without a surveillance detection run. Tonight it's worth the risk. While Samir and Brand make sure nobody's following them (or as much as Brand will fake it, anyway), I'm heading straight to what I hope is their final destination, that run-down warehouse across town. If they change en route, Samir will text the code to abort.

The trip to the warehouse feels too short, and I doubt it's because of my years-long habit of making all those stops and doubling my travel time. I'm parked a safe distance away, barely able to watch the warehouse from my position behind the next building over. Without any idea how long Brand will take getting here, I need to move. I need to get in there. But I can't.

Deadweight fills my lungs, growing heavier every second. If I don't move soon, I'll never make it in the building.

This situation could spin out of control faster than that little Iranian arms deal in the eighties. I've got nobody to back me up, no physical advantages except surprise, nothing.

If I'm honest with myself, I could be at the bottom of the Ottawa River in an hour. Chances are usually lower than this, though every day I confront that danger.

This time there's one thing I can't leave unfinished. I stare at my phone, but not for the clock. Not hoping Samir texts to cancel this op. Not calling in backup.

At least, not yet.

I can't help it. Danny has been there for me, the one constant. The one thing that stayed true when every other part of my life turned sour and off-kilter. And all he's asked . . .

All he's asked is for me to stop being so selfish, though he'd never use those words. To let him in. To let myself trust him.

To let him know all of me. Before I can rethink it, my fingers type the message. *Alive. If I don't check in within an hour, call the police.* I finish with the address of the warehouse and hit send.

My better judgment kicks in right away. Stupid, stupid, stupid. Leaving an electronic trail is bad enough, and worse when it leads straight to Danny, but if the guy has any sense—

The screen hasn't even gone dark when my phone rings. Yep. He's got sense. I shouldn't answer. But I have to. "Hey." Like I didn't basically tell him I'm facing down death.

"Please tell me you're not about to do something stupid. Again."

The pain in his voice stops me short. I still have to play this cool, reassure him, though there's no heart behind my hollow humor. "Not any stupider than normal."

"Talia."

"Danny." I mimic his tone of reproach, but the joke fails. Because I can sense the things he can't say, the hurt he can't share, the concern he can't speak.

"Am I supposed to sit around while you risk your life? Except maybe to call in backup?"

I guess he *can* speak it. "Please, Danny, this is my job. The Top Secret-y stuff."

"I know." He sighs. "Doesn't mean I have to like it."

"No. But you'll have to learn to put up with it if we're getting married."

"I—what is this 'if' stuff? There's an '*if* we're getting married'?"

"No." I let the smile steal onto my lips, though my eyes focus on the warehouse looming in the rearview. That's the *if.*

"I love you," I whisper at last. "And I'll prove it."

"You'd better." He's kidding. Mostly.

I'd like to sit here and flirt with him as if I'm not about to confront a man who shot Elliott, who tormented me. If I don't get in there, I won't be confronting him at all.

We repeat our *I love you*s, and Danny reminds me again to call him. Like I'll forget.

We're done, but I can't end the call. I draw every ounce of strength I can from this connection. Anxiety sinks in my stomach, an uneasy beast ready to strike.

Courage isn't running blindly into danger without fear. It's acting in spite of fear.

Fear? Check. Now to get past inertia and check off the action.

"I love you," I say one last time. "And I'm coming back."

"I love you too." He doesn't add the "you'd better." I try to ignore the foreboding sinking in my heart as I end the call.

Then I remember: I never backed up my USB drive. Stalling? Maybe. But if something happens to me—

I glance at my bag of supplies, though what I need is in the glove box: an adapter cord. A gift from Danny. (If gift = him having an extra and me asking for it.) I hook up my phone and the USB drive. Once the files are encrypted with the one-time key, I send them to Danny. *Hold onto these for me. Until I come back.*

He writes back before I've put the adapter away. *You know that isn't how digital files work, right?*

You're my backup. I type it meaning a literal, digital sense, but as I send that message, the other meanings that will come in handy tonight hit me.

I keep thinking I'm alone. How could I forget? You're not better off alone. And it's about time I put that lesson into action.

I grab my bag and climb out of the car, tossing my phone under the seat. If Danny emails, I'll get it when I get back.

I'm coming back. I'm coming back. No matter what the anxiety in my gut tries to tell me, I. Am. Coming. Back.

I hope.

CHAPTER 30

PICKING THE WAREHOUSE DOOR LOCK is taking longer than it should, even for a secure lock. Not that great with manual picks, especially not with a Maglite in my mouth (never liked the taste of flashlights, and they hurt your teeth), but I'm using what I've got. Even with all my training, picking a lock is still a matter of persistence and luck. And also good lock maintenance. Dirty, crusty locks are sometimes the best defense. And on that front, this one is putting up a good fight.

I reset the tension wrench and once again attack with my favorite pick, but—yeah. Persistence and luck. Time is not on my side, and every minute I sit here scraping tiny little metal filings out of this lock is another minute Samir and Brand get closer.

Finally, the tension wrench moves. Relief sinks in, and I twist the wrench the rest of the way, then try the door.

Locked.

Oh. Great. I just locked the locked door. Again. They taught us a way to supposedly tell if you're unlocking or locking it, but never—Not. Even. Once.—has it worked for me.

I turn the lock back to its vertical, locked position and start over. (*Again.*) But the dirty lock works in my favor: a couple pins must be stuck in place, because I only have to pick half of them before it rotates the other direction.

Once I'm in, I stake out their meeting spot: the empty area between the loading docks and the metal racks. A square of light shines on the cement floor from the only skylight. That makes the metal racks my best vantage point. I hunker down behind a low wire shelf, in the shadows.

Tension turns every little creak into a gunshot, every little animal scurry, an army's march. Something skitters through the shadows. I shudder. Might as well be crawling up my back. But there's no time for pedestrian panic triggers now. Mice, rats, freaking huge bugs—sorry. Tonight there's a lot more to be afraid of.

No. I sit up straighter, grit my teeth, square my shoulders. Tonight's the time for closure. Tonight's the time for justice. Tonight's the time for revenge.

Bring it, Brand.

I sit in the dark and the near-silence for a very long time. My internal clock reads fifteen minutes, but it feels like hours. Plenty of time to completely freak out.

Gotta keep sane. Gotta keep moving. Check my equipment bag. Night vision goggles. Superquiet camera. Classified version of a parabolic mic. Gun. Check, check, check. I tuck my holster in the back of my waistband for better access once they're here.

If they're coming. Is Samir okay? Could Brand suspect *him* of being the mystery texter?

I close my eyes to the dark and run through the reasons I can't trust Brand, why I have to act now. I'm not getting cold feet—I'm not. I'm steeling myself for whatever might come when I call Langley as soon as this meet is over. I'll take some heat until they prove Wasti's working against the UN, Brand's helping him, and Samir told him about it. I have to get this all on tape.

The metallic crack jolts my heart into overdrive. The door. They're here.

Samir emerges from the shadows first, followed by Brand. They're maybe twenty feet away from me, a great distance to see—and be seen.

Once again, not my objective tonight.

I check Brand's hip, his shoulder below the casual blazer (ugh), the back of his waistband. Not obviously printing, but he could still be carrying a gun.

I dig in my bag of tricks and pull out the superquiet camera. Yes, cameras aren't known for being noisy, but when the shutter's click can give me away, I'll opt for the safer route. In the low light, the exposure time could make the pictures blurry, so I've got to steady it on something. I use the nearest wire shelf, still out of sight. Brand sets up a chair for Samir in that square of moonlight. Samir stays on his feet, pacing.

How nervous is he? Could he blow this whole operation?

No. I have to believe in him. Especially when he's having trouble believing in himself. We don't have an actual psychic connection (I'm sure that's next on DS&T's docket), but I've done all I can to show my support for him out loud. Now I'm the one who has to listen to what I've told him all along: believe he can *be* this part.

"Have you told . . . whoever it is?" Samir begins as soon as Brand sits in his own chair. The nerves in his voice actually fit, and I exhale the silent relief.

That letup is short-lived. "Walk me through this again." Brand checks his watch.

Samir carefully details the phone call with Wasti. Brand doesn't ask the right questions, but Samir adds the analysis we need anyway. Why they killed Ali Muhammad. A darn good guess at how. Details of the UN plan. He's got so much intel that he's either talked to his cousin again or got an amazing tactical imagination.

Brand barely plays a token role in the conversation, except to take a break from the weighty stuff with small talk. Samir indulges him for a minute, then directs the conversation back to the intelligence.

My internal clock ticks through the minutes. Ten. Twenty. Thirty. I'm getting anxious about that hour deadline I gave myself to contact Danny. Around forty minutes, Brand stands to stretch. Like he's done.

My back turns cold. If Brand's done, then my part is just beginning.

"But the UN," Samir says. "You must do something. You must tell . . . whoever it is."

I switch to video mode in time to catch Brand's answer. "Yeah, yeah, it's taken care of. You don't need to worry."

It'll be obvious on Monday Brand isn't keeping his word. Samir will know he's lying about stopping Wasti. Which means Brand doesn't care. Maybe he's got nothing left to lose.

Just when I thought he couldn't get any more dangerous. My palms start to sweat.

Brand begins wrapping up the conversation, shutting down Samir's attempts to share more information, to show how important this is, to urge him to act.

That's all I need. I hit the button to stop recording. And then it happens: my grip slips. I scramble to catch the camera, but I'm watching my hands via time-delay satellite feed. I'm too far away and too far behind to make them move in time.

The camera clatters onto the wire racking. Then the cement floor.

I can't breathe; a cold shock of fear socks me in the chest.

Brand flinches, whirls around. He hasn't seen me yet, but still—I'm dead.

Brand recovers from the surprise first. He seizes Samir's arm. "What's going on?"

Sure, *now* he's interested in the guy's intel.

Samir tries to backpedal, metaphorically and literally, but he can't break Brand's grasp. "Please, I know nothing—"

"Right," Brand grinds out. He pulls Samir closer, whips him around to use him as a shield against the mysterious noise. Or use him as a hostage.

Samir twists, and the moonlight reflects off something metal in Brand's hand. A gun.

My stomach plummets. Brand arriving armed to a meeting with someone threatening to expose him? Sure. Me coming here armed? Duh. But Brand showing up armed to a meeting with an asset? That goes beyond preparation. That's backed into a corner. Threatened. Reckless.

He's going to lash out at Samir, or at me.

Samir has done his part. I'll step up to do mine. If I come out aiming at him, though, I'll lose any chance of talking him down. I climb to my feet and slowly march out, my hands aloft. "Go ahead and let him go," I say. "Nobody has to get hurt."

Brand huffs out a half-laugh. "Let's all go skipping home. What are you doing here?"

"I was in the market for some metal racking," I snark. "Take a wild guess."

"You're taking this relationship with Samir to an unhealthy level."

"I gave you more credit than I should've. Thought you'd figure this out by now."

Brand's eyes grow watchful. He still isn't putting it together.

Maybe we *can* all go skipping out of here, and I can make the call and leave Brand to the authorities.

He tugs Samir closer. Samir cowers and tries to pull away. Brand tightens his white-knuckled grip.

"Brand." I lower my hands in a calming gesture. "Let him go. We can work this out. Maybe at the office Monday."

"Monday—when Wasti's supposedly bombing the UN?"

Brand glances at the ceiling. "Checking up on me after every meeting with Samir wasn't enough? Now you're manufacturing intelligence?"

Lying is so automatic to him now, he's even lying to himself. I'll go with it if it means getting out of here.

"That's right." I try to keep my placating tone subtle. Patronizing him would set him off.

"And I passed, huh?"

Whatever. "I guess we'll see come Monday, won't we?"

Brand smiles like he's getting away with murder. Because he is. And despite his rhetoric, he knows it.

He lets Samir go and shoves the gun in his waistband. I edge toward the door, signaling that the whole encounter is over, resolved, safe. Samir silently consults me, then Brand. Brand nods at him, and Samir heads out. When Brand falls in behind him, I can finally do the same. And take a deep breath. We're in the home stretch.

Samir walks through the fire door. Brand pauses at the threshold. "Oh, there's something I've been meaning to ask you about," he says, turning to me. I can just make out his hand, offering an object, though I can't quite see what in the shadows. I squint and lean in.

A key. To his apartment. That I made.

A rushing sound fills my ears. I set it down—when? Working on his computer. On his table. Right before I had to run.

My gaze flies to the fire door behind him. He's there in an instant.

I run after him. Samir dives into action, too. Brand's moving twice as fast as us. He pulls his gun and whacks Samir on the head. Before Samir recovers, Brand pushes him, still moaning, out of the warehouse. I scramble to get at the door, but Brand shoves it shut.

I've got to pick my battles, and the biggest danger here is

that Glock. Brand's focused on the door, so I lunge for his weapon. He jerks it back, but only in time to wrench it free of both our grips and send the gun flying into the shadows.

I grab the door handle. Brand holds it fast and locks it with another key. I clutch at that, too. It plinks to the ground and skitters away.

When I turn to look after the sound, Brand reaches under my jacket to yank my gun free. I spin back to wrest it from him, but as soon as I touch the weapon, he hits the magazine release. The magazine drops and he kicks it into the dark after his own gun.

Still have one in the chamber. I try for the gun again. Brand shoves me off. Before I rush him, he deliberately pulls the slide to clear the last round. The bullet pings over the cement floor, and Brand. Just. Smiles.

I'm trapped.

CHAPTER 31

I SLINK BACK, and Brand stalks me to the square of light. Even with the night vision goggles, I couldn't see a way out of this safely.

At the Farm, I pictured Brand's face on every opponent in hand-to-hand combat. Still, I never expected to battle *him*.

The basis of self-defense is being honest about yourself and your strengths—and your limitations. Much as I hate this fact, my biggest weakness is that I'm a woman. That has nothing to do with the crap Brand put me through. Simple facts of physics and physiology: an average-sized guy (or above average, if you're Brand) has mechanical advantages over an average-sized woman (i.e., me). No training can fully overcome the advantages of limb proportions, bone density and basic weight.

"Think you're clever, don't you?" Brand sticks my gun in his pocket. "'I'll be wearing a blue jacket.' 'If the price is right.'"

I retreat two steps rather than let him get closer. I need to think this through, come up with a believable scenario that doesn't end in my death.

He shakes his head. "True, you know. Everything has a price. And so does everyone."

"So what's yours?"

Brand gives a little laugh, still slowly circling me. "I never went looking for this. It found me. He found me."

"Ali Muhammad."

He pauses. "Quicker than I thought you'd be."

"Not brain-dead. He was in Tajikistan. What happened? Recruitment turn on you?"

Again with that laugh like someone so simple couldn't possibly understand. And no, I couldn't possibly understand, but it's not because I'm stupid.

"Then what?" I ask. "You got in trouble, and Ali Muhammad was the one who got you out?"

Brand scrutinizes me for a second, like he's sizing me up, weighing whether I can handle the truth. Whether I deserve it. "Something like that."

"Ali Muhammad's dead. Not on good terms, either. So why protect his brother?"

"Wow. Are you—are you really this naïve? It's too late. Wasti would roll on me, and I'd spend the rest of my life on the run."

That is *way* too good for the guy. "Better to sacrifice innocent people at the UN?"

"You've been in Canada too long. No such thing as innocent people. Especially not at the UN."

Realization and dread hit rock bottom in my stomach. He's signing a death warrant for hundreds of people, innocent or not, just to cover this up. What won't he do to the one person who can expose him?

And yeah, maybe they'll find my intel and stop him eventually—but there's no way they can before Monday. I didn't tell Danny about that deadline.

So much for my backup.

"Okay, let's be rational," I say.

"I am. I'm being totally rational. All part of the Great Game,

Talia." He stares at me, as if he's mystified that I don't understand him. "What difference does any of it make?"

"It makes a difference to the people who work at the UN, their families. You can still fix this, you still have a choice—"

"Are you kidding? I had to make my choice a long time ago, and I chose the one thing I can depend on. The one person I can trust. Me."

Those words are a little too familiar. And yep, he's desperate, reckless and dangerous.

"I'm not playing to win the Game for someone else. I'm playing for *me*."

Can I get through to him? "And *you* can still be a hero, here. Don't make things worse."

"Doesn't get a whole lot worse than it already is, does it? Or were you not pulling the strings on blue-jacket Josh?" Brand keeps up his pitying/disagreeing laugh. "'Meet me at the mall.' How did it feel to make me jump?"

We're both dropping our pretenses, I guess. Why bother lying? "Good. Felt really good."

Brand stops sauntering and simpering and staring at the floor. He turns to me. "You know, I was almost concerned, seeing you that first day. Bumping into you on an SDR. Thought you knew then. I shouldn't have worried."

"Excuse me?"

He turns his back, like he has so little to worry about from me. "You said it, didn't you? Nobody gets promoted to Canada."

"Canada to Brand: you're assigned here, too. How does that make you better than me?"

"Think about it, Talia. At least they wanted to see me in action. More than once. And obviously I screwed up—but you. Fluent in Russian? Lived in the country? They weren't even interested in seeing what you've got. Not quite bad enough to fire you, so they squirrel you away in the safest, slowest post in the world."

That can't be true. It can't. Getting me into law school here took a year of work. That cannot be true. I fight back indignation and shame and heat rising to my face. "That isn't how it works."

"Isn't it? You've certainly proved them right, haven't you?"

"What do you know?" I scoff.

"The Turkmen scientist? Your fiasco with Fyodor Timofeyev? Slipping on Morozov?"

The words sting, but I jut out my chin. "I only slipped on Morozov because I was busy tracking you. Think I picked the bigger threat."

"Worked out well for you, too, didn't it? You came so close—I had the money on me at Between Friends. You never even knew, and now I get to keep everything while the Agency will hardly miss you."

I set aside the fear flipping in my middle and force myself to chuckle to shore up my bluff. "Don't you see, Brand? It's too late. I've already reported it. Langley has everything they need to bring you in."

He doesn't take the bait. One eyebrow sneaks up to a sarcastic angle, and he glances around. "Then why haven't they?"

"I just barely sent it." But the explanation rings hollow (and lame).

"Ty-pi-cal, blowing the biggest case of your career."

"It's too late for you, Brand," I try again. "You'll be lucky if you make it to a trial."

In a flash, he's in my face, that casual pretense long forgotten. I stumble back a step, out of the light. Brand catches my upper arm and my throat (figuratively). "You didn't."

But that's not insisting he's right. It's begging me to be wrong.

"Of course I did. The biggest case of my career, isn't it?"

"Right. The biggest case of an officer assigned straight to Canada." He drags me an inch closer. "Want to know why you're here?"

"Sure," I say, heavy on the sarcasm. As if the desire to know isn't burning through my brain.

"Then tell me the truth." His growl is more than a threat.

"The truth?" Yeah, right. "You're on borrowed time."

His icy eyes search mine, his jaw set in such determination my lungs frost over. "If I'm on borrowed time, then so are you."

He hauls me in another inch, grabs my other arm. My last tenuous grasp on my composure snaps, but instead of flying into a fear-filled freak-out, I let the anger take charge. I struggle against his hands, edging backward, trying to get away. "Stop it. Let me go—"

"You'll listen like it's the last thing you'll ever do." He tightens his grip. "It might be."

That stills me long enough to meet his gaze. He stares at me with pure hatred.

I have to end this. The person who starts the fight is usually the one who finishes it—and that's got to be me.

"You want to know why you're in Canada?" he keeps monologuing. "You're lucky they didn't fire you. You already owe me big time."

"You mean—" I recover my sarcastic front, and hope he didn't see that real vulnerability in my faltering. "You can't seriously think you had anything to do with my assignment. You're delusional. Again."

His face becomes menacing. "I had everything to do with your assignment. You wouldn't give me what I wanted, so I took what you wanted. Think about it: everyone knows me, trusts me. Loves. Me. You were nobody. That hasn't changed."

Cold flashes through me, and for half a second, every muscle freezes. Brand sees the opportunity and pounces on that, too, jerking my arms to bring me within millimeters of his face. "Now I think it's time for payback. For everything you owe me."

Heat evaporates that freezing fear. I bring my forearms up between his, wheeling them out to break his grip. He drops me; I stagger backward a foot.

The menace in his expression hardens into something more dangerous. I steel myself against the terror and the reality of taking on a guy who's much bigger than me.

He may have nothing left to lose, but I've got everything to protect.

I charge forward, and Brand lunges at me. I sidestep him, then shove an elbow into his kidneys. He grunts, but it isn't nearly enough to stop him.

I backpedal for the shadows until Brand whirls around to attack.

And then we both hear it: the metallic clang of a door closing, deep in the warehouse. In that shaft of moonlight, Brand turns to stone.

I have no idea whether I should be reassured or even more terrified.

"Who's there?" Brand demands. "Samir? Is that you?"

"Guess again, dude."

Oh no. No, no, no. My heart tumbles off a cliff and my stomach follows. Adrenaline pours into my muscles. I stay frozen in the shadows.

Footsteps echo through the warehouse, their pace casual. Brand doesn't move either, scanning the dark surrounding him, like he can get the jump on whoever's closing in.

I should move. I should find the newcomer. I should shout for him to run, run now, run as fast as he can. But I can't move a muscle, not even to yell.

"Who's there?" Brand demands in a shout.

"Come on," rings that too-familiar voice from the dark. "Haven't figured it out yet?"

I have, but every cell in my body wants my brain to be imagining this, to be wrong.

"Sorry." Brand laughs, back into that dismissive mode. "Is all this posturing supposed to scare me? One guy all by himself to bring me in?"

"Bring you in? Better than you deserve."

Brand snorts. "Points for style. Still at zip for substance."

The footsteps finally reach Brand. Time slows as that beam slides higher on the man stepping into the light.

Danny.

CHAPTER 32

TERROR TRAMPLES ALL MY OTHER THOUGHTS. I see Danny there in the light, though in my mind I keep seeing him battling Brand, facing off with Fyodor, bleeding and broken.

Not a pretty picture.

Danny looks my general direction. "You about done, T?"

He doesn't call me that. Nobody does, except for— "Elliott," I breathe.

It's enough; they both wheel on me with apprehension in their eyes. I understand Danny's worry immediately. I told him over and over that Elliott was the only one who could help me, so now he's got to *be* Elliott.

If I let Danny maintain this pretense, Brand will think he's taking on the guy who jumped out of the helicopter after General Aytmatov.

I don't know which is the lesser of these dangers, but if this is the length Danny will go for me, how can I *not* let him?

"What are *you* doing here?" I pour impatience into my tone.

"Who were you expecting?" Danny asks. "The Prime Minister?"

He hasn't spent much time with Elliott, but he's mastered the cavalier attitude down to the you-know-you-love-me smirk. He *is* the part. And I'll do my part to help him keep this up.

"No," I say. "Good ol' What's-His-Name hasn't been returning my calls."

"Rude." Danny tsks. "Shall we go?"

"Oh no," Brand breaks in. "We're just getting started." He stares Danny down. "Elliott, huh? Sorry, guess I was expecting . . . more."

Danny folds his arms. "Same to you, dude."

Brand scrutinizes him. "This is really the great, jumping-out-of-a-helicopter Elliott?"

My breath stutters and dies, though Danny maintains that smirk. "Did you want to see my ID?"

He reaches for his back pocket. Why is he going for this bluff?

Elliott's ID. I had it. Did I leave it with Danny?

Not a good move. They're not exactly twins. But he's already pulling out his wallet.

Brand heaves a sigh and looks away. "You could be the president. Wouldn't make a difference to me."

But it makes all the difference to our situation, and to the balance of power—*if* I can handle this right. I've lost this game too many times already, and unfortunately, it's not something that gets easier with repetition.

Apparently it isn't my turn. It's Danny's. He glances back and forth between us. "I'm sorry, am I interrupting your stand-off?"

"Yeah, and we'd all like to get back to that." Brand rolls his eyes. "Thought you were having problems at home."

Danny looks to me. My heart skips. That's a giveaway. He doesn't know his story. My gaze drops to the cement floor, though I try to give Danny the slightest nod as a signal.

"Can't believe you told him that," Danny mutters. "Yeah,

289

okay, things are rough. So I'd like to get back there and work on it. Now, let's end this: you're guilty. You've got rights."

Not . . . exactly. We're not law enforcement, and we have no obligation to abide by *Miranda*. (And considering I got my law degree in Canada, I only know what I've seen on TV.)

Danny isn't done. "Well, I'm sure you *will* have rights. *If* you're arrested." He grins, and for a minute, I'm not sure he won't take waaay too much pleasure in enhanced interrogation techniques.

(Remind me to *never* cross Danny.)

Brand shoves his hands in his pockets and starts up his circuit—toward me. Danny and I both move as well, a slow motion chase around this little square of light.

"Don't make this difficult." Something like that should sound coaxing, but Danny makes it condescending.

"Here's the thing," Brand begins. He pauses in our rotation. "No thanks."

Brand barrels across the circle and throws his momentum into a swing—at Danny. He ducks, and Brand's fist whooshes through the air.

But Brand already has a backup plan: me. His missed punch transitions into hooking that arm around my waist. My stupid heart leaps into my throat, choking me.

I squirm back, shove at him, try to get out of reach. Danny's there in half a second, grabbing Brand by the shoulders to yank him off me.

Not enough. Brand pulls me tighter. I cram the panic into a corner of my mind so I can act. I stomp on Brand's foot. He barely grunts. I fake a knee to the groin, and he takes the bait, doubling over to protect himself.

Exactly what I'm aiming for. His face is in range. I slam the heel of my hand into his nose. The bones of my wrist connect with his teeth, jarring us both. He shouts in pain, and releases me.

Danny lets go of Brand to catch my elbow and my waist. Brand reels backward, holding his jaw, stumbling into the shadows.

"You all right?" Danny's voice is an undertone as he scans the darkness. I'm not sure whether he's "being" Elliott or Danny for a minute.

This is one time they'd do the same thing. "Fine. We can't let him get away," I whisper, panting from adrenaline and fear.

Danny points in the direction of the door we both came in. I answer with a thumb over my shoulder, indicating the door behind us. "Those the only two doors?" he asks.

I wish. We could guard them and wait him out. "Has to be a way to the front offices."

Somewhere in the warehouse, a dull thud echoes. I glance at Danny. Unless Brand walked into something in the dark (fingers crossed), I don't think that's good for us.

Numbers are our one advantage. Brand's already out there, maybe setting traps, picking his hiding spot, possibly making his escape. We need to act this instant. "Split up," I whisper.

"Bad idea." Danny's inflection plays a tune that matches his words.

I start the direction we last saw Brand go, cautiously creeping until my eyes adjust to the dark. "Pretty sure I can handle myself."

"Have it your way, T."

When I check behind me, there's no Danny-sized shadow. After all the times I've left him in the dark, suddenly I appreciate how much that experience sucks.

I turn my back on the light and the disappointment and worry and terror—I ignore everything. Most people are afraid of the dark. No, they're afraid of what lurks in the dark. When you already know what's out there, you can see the dark for what it is: a great equalizer. Brand is just as blind as we are. We all have the same weakness.

I close my eyes to shut off the in-born reliance on sight. Straining to make out shadow from shadow would distract me from the real clues.

After a couple seconds I hear it: the sound to my left. Reverberating metal. I slink that direction, rolling my feet to keep them silent.

I can only hope he's concentrating so hard on what he's doing and the sounds he's making, that he doesn't hear me coming.

The vibrations get closer. I stop short and open my eyes in time to see the huge metal racks feet in front of me. I reroute to avoid the obstacle. What could Brand be doing to make that noise?

As if on cue, the noise stops. I pause to scan the area. That last sound almost seemed like it was . . . above me.

I raise my gaze, slowly scaling the thirty-foot tower next to me. My visibility ends way before the shelving does. The wire shelves are at least five feet apart. Can he climb up? I rotate to take in the 360° view. The absolute, utter silence and the complete, total blackness steal my breath. I try to swallow. My dry mouth balks.

What was Danny saying about not splitting up? Where is he now? I shut out the ravening black, but the quiet is no more help. Wherever Danny went, he isn't moving now. The only thing I hear is my own heartbeat muffled in my ears.

Until another soft sound echoes from far off. Danny. Giving his position away.

Suddenly the whole room feels like it's spinning in a void. I have to help him. I have to find him before Brand does. I have to save Danny.

I edge away, trying to get my bearings. The back of my heel strikes something hard, and I suck in air, fast and sharp. My thoughts crystallize into ice. Now I've given myself away.

Above me, the metal starts vibrating again. He's going after

Danny. I've got to stop Brand. Without being able to see him—

Sacrifice play.

I whirl and send whatever I hit crashing to the ground. (Wood?) One stride into my escape, I kick another obstacle. I tumble to the ground, slamming onto something hard. The impact knocks the wind out of me. I don't have time to be hurt.

I struggle to my hands and knees, the need for air dulling my senses. Finally I drag in a breath, and my vision clears. In the reflection from the skylight, I can make out the silhouette of something by a low shelf a couple feet in front of me. My camera and equipment from earlier.

I pull myself to standing, but again I only make it one step. This time, it's not my own blindness that stops me.

It's the arm wrapped around my throat.

I try to dip my chin to block him. That only works to prevent the lock. I'm too late.

I still haven't recovered from falling, and instantly, the desperate need for oxygen screams through my veins, filling my hearing and my sight. I can't even squeak.

Danny is out there, risking his life to help me. He could be ten feet away; he could be on lock-down at Langley now, it wouldn't make a difference. Either way, he can't know I need to be rescued.

Heat and pressure are mounting behind my eyes. Sleeper hold. This knocks you out by cutting off blood flow to the brain. Couple seconds too long, and you don't wake up.

I claw the air behind me, but Brand's face isn't there. I shoot elbows at his waist; he sidesteps. I kick at his shins and his feet and his knees. Every movement gets slower, using precious oxygen, killing me faster.

Finally, that training kicks in. I push back a step. Brand isn't ready for my weight, I guess, because we both tumble back. His grip loosens for half a second and I gasp for air, roll away, try to blink away the red crowding my vision.

Not enough. Brand's on my back in a second. I dip my chin. This time he's anticipating the defense. He snatches a handful of my hair and forces my head back. Pain flashes hot through my skull. His arm around my throat strangles my screech before it starts.

Again, I'm swinging an elbow, still finding nothing. Brand's weight across my back is too much, and we both slam onto the cement. The air I managed to grab is trapped between his weight and his arm.

The red tint advances across what little I can see. The edges of my vision grow black.

The last thing I'll ever see in this life: my super-silent camera. Better make this worth it. I brace my toes and push those last couple inches, straining my fingers for the camera. My mouth is working, trying to croak out something, anything to distract Brand from my goal.

"You want to know why?" he whispers, his breath seething against my ear.

I can't see anything, but my fingers find the camera. I hit the button to record a video.

Nothing.

I can't even feel the defeat.

"What?" Brand continues. "You'll die happy if you can figure out how I went wrong?"

I move my head a millimeter, a nod. Then I feel it: the camera's lens zooming.

I turned it on. The hollow triumph boosts my strength to hit the record button again.

"Why else?" Brand whispers. "I did it because I could. Is that what you want to hear?"

It barely registers that my forehead is cold. The camera's getting heavier. I can hardly feel my hand.

No, I have to fight, I have to protect Danny, I—

I have to do this for him. I fight for him. I have to let him fight for me, too. I have to let him *know*.

The camera tumbles away.

Will this be enough? Will they get Brand? Will Danny forgive me?

I'll never know.

A blinding light grows closer, and I let go.

CHAPTER 33

SUDDENLY, I'M ON MY BACK, sucking in air, hacking, coughing, sputtering. It's black again, but if I can just blink, if I can just breathe, if I can just be, I'll be okay.

Did I live?

My eyes recover before my ears. I'm still in the dark warehouse. Brand is gone.

Then my hearing kicks in—no, what I've been hearing all along registers. A yelp followed by a wet thud. And again.

I force myself up, still choking, like my body figured I wouldn't be doing this breathing thing anymore, so it didn't have to remember how. I drag myself toward the yelping—a bright light. A figure kneeling on the ground, hunched over. Hunched over someone on his back.

My burning lungs clamp down on the little air I've caught. I've destroyed everything. I didn't give Danny a chance to fight for me, I set him up to take on Brand alone. Now he's got Danny—he's got Danny—he's got . . . Danny?

The kneeling man: Danny. And on the cement floor: Brand. Danny has a knee and all his weight in Brand's stomach. Danny's phone, in flashlight mode, casts them both in grotesque chiaroscuro.

That bright light approaching me as I passed out.

"Stop, stop," Brand begs. He's got ahold of Danny's arm with one hand; the other arm is twisted beneath him at an angle that makes my stomach quiver. Danny has him by the shoulders. Danny's grip tightens on Brand's jacket, and he yanks him up and slams him down. That wet crack is Brand's head hitting the cement, his rolling arm rolling my stomach right along with it.

He groans. "Please," he whimpers. "Please."

Danny's fingers tighten again.

"Don't!" The voice is so hoarse I don't recognize myself. I throw my hands against Danny's chest, like he couldn't understand me.

"Don't tell me you're coming down with Stockholm syndrome, T."

I shake my head between gasps. "Too good for him," I croak.

Danny shifts his weight to press on Brand's shoulders instead, and Brand dissolves into ragged moans.

If you expect me to have any sympathy for the guy—sorry. Please take it up with my chafed neck, bruised windpipe, scarred lungs, overloaded brain, etc.

On cue, that brain seizes with pain. We need to end this. Pinning Brand down is effective for the moment, but we have to get Brand totally neutralized.

I still can't see much—hope that's from the dark and not permanent brain damage—so I have to work by feel. I slide my hands down Danny's chest until my fingers hit his belt. He jumps back a millimeter. I ignore him to undo the buckle.

"Hel-lo?" A dead-on imitation of the same reaction Elliott would've had. (Okay, just about any guy would react that way.) "We're a little busy."

"Don't flatter yourself." I cough and tug the belt free in two tries. "Roll him over."

Danny scrutinizes the situation for a second until he figures out the best way to do that without letting Brand go (tricky) or ripping his arm off (optional). Once he's maneuvered a still-groaning Brand face down, I give the belt back. "Wrists."

Again, Danny obeys. With Brand securely bound, I can take a full breath. Sort of. Danny keeps one knee in Brand's back and pulls me close. "You okay?"

I bury my face in his chest. Not exactly "okay" yet, but I will be. After about three seconds of comfort and relief, all the freezing fear left in my system converts to fury. I withdraw to backhand Danny's chest. "What were you thinking, coming here?"

"I was thinking, 'Gee, why don't I sit around and let Talia get killed? Yeah, sounds like a good Saturday night.'"

My brain grapples for a witty comeback to his sarcasm, and fails. So I backhand him a second time. "Don't you ever do that again."

Danny pulls me closer again. "Not a promise I'm willing to make."

"Since when do we get to pick and choose our promises?"

"Are you going to let me kiss you or not?"

I manage not to purse my lips so he can do just that.

"Wait—wait—wait a second." Brand shifts beneath our weight with a squeak of pain. "You—what about your fiancé?"

"I think I just changed my mind about introducing you. Meet Danny."

Brand's jaw clenches. "A civilian?" he hisses. "Are you kidding me?"

"Maybe you're slipping." Danny adds an I'm-totally-not-mocking-you-even-though-I-totally-am smirk.

"After all," I continue, "nobody gets promoted to Canada, do they?"

Danny draws me in for another kiss, but stops short. "What

do we do with him?"

We have about 1.7 seconds to consider that conundrum.

The metal doors slam open, light floods the warehouse, and pounding footsteps run in. Men everywhere, swarming over us, dragging me and Danny apart. I try to fight, to pull free—no way can we let Brand escape now.

Until the guy towing me backward changes tacks. He wraps his arms around my waist, locking my arms to my sides. I try to push my weight back into him, but he's onto my strategy. Picking me up and pivoting, my attacker brings me face to face with— "Will?"

He gives me half a grin. "Nice job, Talia."

The guy holding me lets go. I barely land on my feet. The mental jolt of seeing Will leaves me reeling. My not-exactly-attacker slings an arm across my shoulders. I shove him away before I see it's Justin. "But—but you and Brand—" I whirl back to Will. "And Brand said—you were—"

Will raises an eyebrow, and I bite off the rest of my incoherent blubbering. "I'll . . . I'll have to explain in my report. Have you known about this all along?"

"No, *someone* finally tipped us off tonight." He glances at Danny, wrapping up a studious conversation with several more men.

I almost don't dare to ask. "How did—?"

"Not what I intended when I gave him my card, but well played." Will nods to Danny, who's now sliding an arm around my waist.

"Didn't think you were coming," he says to Will.

"Would've been here sooner, but you have to plow through a lot of red tape to bring in an officer." Will shakes Danny's free hand, then moves on to direct the guys hauling Brand out.

"You can thank me any time." Danny shoots me a smirk.

"You can stop being Elliott. Seriously."

He puffs out a breath like that's the biggest relief of the

night. "Thought you'd never ask." He turns me to Will again. "I'm guessing you should go be Top Secret-y."

Samir—the camera—the files. "Will!" I call. "We've got work to do!"

Six hours later, I'm still pacing the embassy hallway. I've done all I can: retrieved the camera, filed it with Will, got Samir to share his intel again. Now we're waiting on cooperation from the FBI.

"Never thought I'd want to be here *less* than during the polygraph," Danny murmurs.

I jump and spin around. He's still in the same chair, waiting like me—but I thought he fell asleep hours ago.

He rubs his eyes and shifts in his chair. "Still nervous?"

"Yeah." I settle in the seat next to him.

"Seems like you've done that a lot lately."

"What, be nervous?"

Danny slides one hand between both of mine. I realize I was twisting my engagement ring around my finger. "Actually, I kind of do it to keep calm. Anchored."

He interlaces our fingers without taking his eyes from mine. "You've given all you can."

You don't have to be a spy to interpret that code. It's enough. I've everything I could. For my country (I hope). For Samir. For Danny.

Will pokes his head out of the room. I have never been so glad—or so stressed—to see those graying temples. "Time."

I'm on my feet and across the hall before I can think about it, still clinging to Danny. But Will doesn't move from the door to the command center. He isn't looking at me.

He's peering at Danny. Danny takes the message faster than I do. He squeezes my hand and releases me. "Tell me how it goes." He steps back from the door. "If you can."

That little act of faith in me speaks volumes, though I only nod. Will sweeps me into the darkened command center. The half dozen men in the room are seated around the conference table, but they're all watching the scene projected on the screen: a quiet Colonial home in a quiet neighborhood, though the green night vision tint does add an air of stress.

"Westchester," Will whispers. Where Wasti told Samir to meet. "Live feed, courtesy of the FBI."

"Playing nice?"

"So far. Three checks at the UN. Looks like they hadn't placed anything yet. Highest alert for the week." Will and I take the last two seats and join the tense silence.

"Perimeter secured," comes a voice from the feed. "Go."

Shapes and shadows converge on the two-story brick house. I grip the edge of the table. Cottony silence descends on us.

"Move the camera," Will says in an undertone. I think he's talking to himself until I see he's on the phone. The guy on the other end gets the message and obeys—sort of. The feed switches to a camera carried by one of those shadows, jumping us to the door.

Our accidental cameraman is holding up one finger, then lowers it. The team explodes into action, bursting through the door and into the house. Hard to make out exactly what's happening in shades of green and black, but five or six men in the living room leap off the floor. Several agents—assuming they're all FBI—jump in to take them down. Camera Guy has a bigger fish. He wends his way past the arrests in progress and up the stairs.

Target spotted: the bedroom guarded by a thug asleep in a chair. Shouts from downstairs finally rouse the thug. Not in time to fend off the two agents who come from behind Camera Guy to slap on the cuffs.

There's no time to breathe for us or Camera Guy. He keeps moving, AR-15 at the ready in this first-person shooter video game that's beyond my control. A battering ram efficiently eliminates the door. Camera Guy sweeps the room with his rifle. Two more agents rush in to tackle the man climbing out the window.

Camera Guy closes in and shines a flashlight on the man. The burst of light blinds us, so I can't ID him, but Camera Guy has no problem. "We got him."

The soft sigh of celebration is all we get. The feed continues through the arrest, but that's enough for me. Will stands too and shakes my hand, then gestures for me to follow him. He leads me out a different door than we came in, and through a series of hallways. Every minute we get farther from Danny, I can't help the worries multiplying in my mind (and my middle). Surprises like this are seldom good in the CIA.

We reach a door and Will opens it without preamble. In the room, an armed guard stands over a bloodied Brand, hand-cuffed to his chair and still reeling. His eyes land on me like fists.

"Well, hello," I say. "Too lazy to get out of those cuffs, or is it not worth it in Canada?"

Brand aims his gaze at the wall.

I consult Will, still standing in the hall. He gives a go-on nod. Sure. We're all in the right frame of mind for interrogation. But if this is our last chance to hit Brand when he's weakest, I'll do it. No need for a hint on what I should ask. The questions have been ringing through my brain for weeks.

I step in and the door swings shut behind me. "So. Long night?"

Glare.

"Yeah, me too. Want to talk about it?"

Glower.

"Oh, I didn't peg you for the strong, silent type. Since

you're not either of those."

"What do you want?" Brand finally breaks.

I dismiss the question with a condescending smile. "What do *you* want?"

He reverts to the silent treatment. I slide into the chair across from him. "Seriously," I continue. "What makes you tick these days? Moved beyond sadistically torturing your exes?"

"One of us has," he mutters.

"Yeah, I'm living in the past. Sure." I sigh. "We both want to be done with this, right? Let's cut the crap. You tell me the real reason you did it, and I'll leave."

"What difference does it make? It's all the same."

I fold my arms, and he takes that as a challenge. He leans forward. "Tell me it isn't all the same. Don't you ever get tired of being a pawn?"

"What are you talking about?"

"The Wastis, the Agency, the UN—we're all part of the Game, aren't we? Does it matter what side people claim to be on?"

I'm on my feet without a thought, heat surging through my muscles. "Seriously? Because manipulating people is fun for you? Playing fast and loose with their lives is all a *game*?"

"The Great Game. That's what we call it. Why not play to win?"

My turn to scowl in silence. "Sure, Brand. It's a game." The heat in my veins grows chill. I bend down, grit my teeth, get in his face. "But if it's just a game, then you're just the loser."

I don't even care how he reacts. I pivot on my heel and march out.

Will's still in the hall. His back to me, he's conferring with someone, blocking my view. I linger there for a minute.

"Yep, I'll take it from here."

I know that voice. I maneuver around Will, and there he is, sling and all: Elliott. He pretends to elbow me with his good

303

arm. "I hear there's an opening at Keeler Tate."

"I dunno, dude. Nobody gets promoted to Canada."

Elliott and Will both snort in derision. "Who told you that?" Will asks.

I don't bother fighting back my answering smile. "Nobody."

Elliott jerks his head toward Brand's door. "You soften 'Nobody' up for me?"

"He's all yours."

Elliott rubs his hands together, careful of jostling his shoulder, then opens the door. "Hello, old friend," he chirps. "Name's Elliott. I think you've heard of me."

The door swings shut, not fast enough to muffle Brand's shriek of indignation.

That feels a little too good. Will pats my shoulder, and I lead the way back to the conference room. "Starting to learn your way around," he says. "Care to join me?"

"Flattered, but no. And if Danny ever wants to work for the Agency, we'll let you know."

"'Don't call us, we'll call you'?"

"Exactly."

Will eyebrow-shrugs, but doesn't press it. We round a corner to find Danny still on his feet, hands in his pockets like I'm interrupting mid-pace. Just seeing him triggers that final release in my ribs: relief. I almost run to him. He wraps me in his arms and kisses the top of my head, clinging to me like we've survived a very long battle, and I'm finally home. We both are.

And then it hits me. It doesn't matter what Brand thinks. It doesn't matter if he did recommend I get sent to this American espionage backwater. (Sorry, Canada.) Serving here is the only way I'd ever have met Danny, and he is definitely worth it. So, hey, thanks a lot, Brand. Nice knowing you.

Danny pulls back to eyeball the conference room door. He doesn't have to ask the question; I give him a double thumbs up. I take his hand, and we find our way out.

We're both too tired for conversation until we reach his car, parked across from the National Gallery. I don't know what they've got going on in there, but the glass towers glow red at night. Danny opens my door and once again draws an envelope from the glove box. I take my seat and the envelope. "You've been carrying this around the whole time?"

"Came today." Danny shuts my door and rounds the car to get in the driver's seat. "Open it."

I tear back the flap and pull out the papers inside. The first page has instructions for . . . what to wear. A wedding dress? I furrow my brow and study Danny.

He takes the stack of papers back and shuffles through them until he finds one that he gives to me. I recognize the letterhead immediately: The Church of Jesus Christ of Latter-day Saints. And in the corner, *Nauvoo Illinois Temple* below an illustration of the iconic building. I cast him one quick glance and try to ignore the hope—elation—filling my chest.

"Figured it was close enough, or far enough, for everyone. But they were booked."

The little rise of hope puffs out faster than flash paper.

And then Danny continues. "Except for a seven PM slot on the twenty-eighth."

"That's a . . ." I mentally review the calendar. "Wednesday. Who gets married on a Wednesday?"

"We do, if we're going to do this at all."

I spear him with a sarcastic expression. "There's an '*if* we're going to do this'? Is a little international conspiracy supposed to keep us from getting married? You'll have to try a lot harder than that."

"*I'll* have to try harder?" He looks heavenward. "You're welcome."

"For what?"

"Let's see." He ticks off the items on his fingers. "Arranging the wedding pretty much singlehandedly, scheduling the honeymoon, and . . . oh yeah, saving your life. Again."

I shoot him an evil look. "Hey, last time, I saved you, thank you very much."

"Let's try to nip that habit in the bud. Starting to get embarrassing."

I lean across the console to lay my head on his shoulder. "So, tell me about these honeymoon plans."

"Nope."

"Fine. I'm sure I'll enjoy Paris just as much, surprise or not."

Danny pulls back to gape at me, truly hurt. What did I—? "You said you wouldn't look."

"Oh—oh—I was kidding." My disappointment rings through in my voice. "I didn't mean to guess."

He purses his lips for a minute. "You're tricky."

"It's a gift."

His eyes turn serious. "Thank you. "

"It's not that kind of gift," I joke.

"No, for calling me—calling anybody tonight."

"Seems like I should be the one thanking you." I'd only be dead if it weren't for him.

"You didn't have to call. And you did."

"You didn't have to come." I offer my hand over the center console, like he did to me last night. He takes it. "And you did."

"Pretty glad I did, too."

In the glow off the National Gallery, he gives me half a smile. I did the right thing texting him, and not just because he saved my life. Because I was letting him in. Because I trusted him.

"Did I ever tell you Finnish is my first language?" I've spoken Finnish in front of Danny, but mixed with Russian, so I doubt he knows this little fact.

He quick-shakes his head in surprise. "No—really?"

"*En valehtelisi.*" I wait a minute before I add the translation, "I wouldn't lie. *Rakastan sinua.*"

He raises an eyebrow.

"It means 'I love you.'"

"Oh, now, that I know." He leans across the center console. Before he kisses me, he whispers again, "That I know."

THANK YOU FOR READING!

If you enjoyed this book,
please tell your friends & review it online.

To sign up for information on upcoming releases, please visit
http://JordanMcCollum.com/newsletter/.

Visit my website & help spread the word about *Spy for a Spy*!
http://JordanMcCollum.com/loved-spy-spy/

MR. NICE SPY

I, Spy prequel novella number one — FREE ebook

Elliott Monteith is a CIA operative in Canada. But that's easy.

Tracking a mole at the US Embassy? Cake.

Choosing between your fellow spy and your fiancée? Uh . . .

SPY NOON

I, Spy prequel novella number two — coming soon

CIA operative Talia Reynolds *is* her job. So when a new co-worker shows up, dredging up too many painful memories and upstaging her, Talia has to figure out how to cope. But first, they need to catch an elusive counter-spy threatening their Iranian double agent. Yeah, all in a day's work.

SPY ANOTHER DAY BOOK THREE

Coming 2014

CIA operative Talia Reynolds is off the clock, off the continent and off on her honeymoon—but when the Agency calls her new husband in for a special mission, there's a lot more at stake than the stolen plans for the spy drone he designed.

ACKNOWLEDGMENTS

SEQUELS ARE ALWAYS CHALLENGING. This one was no different. This book challenged me so much that I seriously considered calling the whole thing off. But I'd made a commitment to my readers, and I had to see it through.

As always, my wonderful husband, Ryan, supported me throughout this tough process with a listening ear and helping hands. My children, Hayden, Rebecca, Rachel and Hazel, endured a long summer of drafting and editing and rewriting.

Once again, my parents, Ben and Diana Franklin, were my first editors. They continue to help make my books all they can be. Along with my sisters Jaime, Brooke and Jasmine, they have believed in and encouraged me.

I would also like to thank Ross and Jane, my in-laws, for being nothing like any of the terrible in-laws in this book, and for all the kind support you've given me and our family.

My critique partners, Julie Coulter Bellon and Emily Gray Clawson, helped me take the raw material that fell so far short of my vision and gave me the encouragement I needed to make it into what I'd always hoped it would be—even though that meant a lot of rewriting, and a lot of rereading for them.

My next readers helped to make sure that work was worth it. Thank you to Becki Clayson, Arline Holbrook, Deanna

Henderson, S. M. Anderson, and, as always, Sarah Anderson and Benjamin Franklin (AKA Dad).

Rustin Lewis, Heidi Kimball and Valérie Williams helped with my Québécois French. Angela Millsap and Dasha Ivanova perfected my Russian and the transliteration. Benjamin Franklin (again) fixed my Finnish.

Jason Hanson of Concealed Carry Academy and formerly of the CIA was kind enough to answer every question I had the courage and wherewithal to ask (which was about two, but good enough). His Spy Escape & Evasion course will have an impact on this book and many more.

My editor, Jenn Wilks, gave me valuable feedback and the encouragement I (still!) needed. She and Diana Franklin (AKA Mom) helped to make sure the manuscript was as free of typos as possible. If there be errors here, they be the mistakes of the printers. Finally, Kierstin Marquet also gave me a boost of confidence I sorely needed.

And of course, you, my reader, for once again making my characters come to life for more than just me.

Thank you!

ABOUT THE AUTHOR

PHOTO BY JAREN WILKEY

AN AWARD-WINNING AUTHOR, JORDAN McCOLLUM can't resist a story where good defeats evil and true love conquers all. In her day job, she coerces people to do things they don't want to, elicits information and generally manipulates the people she loves most—she's a mom.

Jordan holds a degree in American Studies and Linguistics from Brigham Young University. When she catches a spare minute, her hobbies include reading, knitting and music. She lives with her husband and four children in Utah.

www.ingramcontent.com/pod-product-compliance
Lightning Source LLC
Chambersburg PA
CBHW070548260626
47161CB00002B/544